Caryl stepped into the shower and turned up the hot water as hot as she could stand it while she soaped off. She had learned valuable lessons about who she was during her manless ten and a half months and the first of those lessons was a simple one – she had a low tolerance for pain. Another woman might have stayed and turned a blind eye to Alexander's duplicity but doing so would have destroyed her. Lesson number two - the right man could complete her but the wrong one would only bring grief and she wasn't up for that. Lesson number three – being with a man was great but being on her own was fine too. She had loved how Alexander had looked after her and how she felt being the center of his world but it had all been an illusion. Now she was responsible for herself and for keeping it real. Lesson number four – if she could survive Alexander, she could probably survive anything. If Joshua was not Mr. Right, it wouldn't be the end of her world. She just had to keep reminding herself of that and she would be fine.

JUST AN AFFAIR

EUGENIA O'NEAL

Genesis Press Inc.

Indigo Love Stories

An imprint Genesis Press Publishing

Indigo Love Stories
c/o Genesis Press, Inc.
1213 Hwy 45 N, 2nd Floor
Columbus, MS 39705

All rights reserved. Except for use in any review, the reproduction or utilization of this work in whole or in part in any form by any electronic, mechanical, or other means, not known or hereafter invented, including xerography, photocopying and recording, or in any information storage or retrieval system, is forbidden without written permission of the publisher, Genesis Press, Inc. For information write Indigo Love Stories c/o Genesis Press, Inc., 1213 Hwy 45 N, Columbus, MS 39705.

All characters in this book have no existence outside the imagination of the author and have no relation whatsoever to anyone bearing the same name or names. They are not even distantly inspired by any individual known or unknown to the author and all incidents are pure invention

Copyright© 2003 by Eugenia O'Neal
Just an Affair

ISBN: 1-58571-111-X
Manufactured in the United States of America

First Edition

Visit us at www.genesis-press.com
or call at 1-888-Indigo-1

DEDICATION

To Aisha, T'Sha, Linton, Pearlin and Andrea. Everytime I ask, you guys come through. Thanx a mil!

CHAPTER ONE

Scowling fiercely, Caryl Walker strapped on her seatbelt and checked her rearview and side mirrors before pulling slowly out of the airport parking lot and into the road in her ageing Jeep Cherokee. Tortola's mountain roads, narrow, winding, and with precipitous drops on the side to the breathtakingly beautiful sea below were full of good reasons to check your mirrors and drive slow. If it wasn't children darting in front of your car, then it was a pig with sudden urgent business on the other side of the road or a lamb wanting to rejoin its mother.

Usually, Caryl was patient with the livestock and the people who stopped their cars, without warning, to chat with friends walking by. Living on Tortola had taught her to slow down, that life did not have to be lived in a series of New York minutes. But today, well, today she had spent two hours at the island's noisy, airless airport waiting for the man who had chartered her boat for a week and he hadn't shown up. Caryl was not in the mood for livestock on the hoof. When she rounded Paraquita Bay and came face to huge behinds with an ambling herd of well-fed cows walking three and four abreast, she took a deep breath, counted to ten and leaned on her horn. The cows continued on their shambling way, oblivious. Caryl counted to ten again and waited until the road was clear before gunning her engine and overtaking them. The cows didn't even look her way as she passed. Caryl let the speedometer rise to forty and didn't slow down again until, in a record twenty minutes, she pulled into the Nanny Cay parking lot, jumped out and almost ran to the *Elendil*.

Despite her mood, she felt a rush of pride as she stalked up Dock B where the *Elendil* was moored. When its owner, Janus, Inc., a U.S.-based company, made her the captain of the new 70-foot Jordan about ten months ago, she had felt enormously proud and grateful. The sleek, blue and white boat with its fine trim was a real beauty, excellently crafted and powerful. Three double staterooms, each with its own bathroom, as well as crew quarters and a spacious saloon, made it a comfortable and luxurious getaway for as many as six clients.

Noel Richardson, Caryl's first mate, was standing on deck checking the diving equipment when Caryl ran lightly on board. Richardson was a burly, middle-aged, cocoa-colored man who'd practically grown up on the sea around the forty plus islets and cays that made up the British Virgin Islands. When she took up the appointment as captain, there had been some initial tension between them. Richardson wasn't so good at taking orders from a foreigner, a woman at that. The good relationship they had now was due mostly to his wife, Patricia, Patty to friends, who acted as the perfect foil to their quick tempers. Patty was always ready with, as she put it, "a jar of virgin olive oil to pour on troubled waters." Olive oil was all the nut-brown woman used in the galley where she reigned supreme.

"Cheerio, my girl." Richardson greeted her amiably with a phrase he had picked up from their last clients, a group of Britishers.

Caryl gave a most un-amiable snort.

"He wasn't on the flight!" she snapped. She liked Richardson enormously but his bounteous cheer when she was stressed could be a bit trying. Certainly she had no time for it now. First, Joshua Tain had brought forward his charter date, then he hadn't bothered to show up on his scheduled flight. It was enough to make Caryl spit.

"Mr. Tain arrived about a half-hour ago," Richardson answered with a grin.

"He came via St. Thomas, so he just took the ferry to West End and caught a taxi here." As if on cue, the saloon door behind him opened and a man ducked his head under and came out. The Improbably Tall and Handsome One. The sour thought popped into Caryl's head as the man straightened up in front of her. He had to be at least six foot five. A beige shirt, tucked neatly into white pants of soft, Sea Island cotton, set off his dark complexion with its bronze undertones. Anytime Ralph Lauren wanted another black man for his ads, here he was, Caryl thought. Tain, with his dark, aristocratic features, looked as if he would be right at home in a desert tent surrounded by Turkish rugs and overstuffed cushions, a setting favored by the designer.

A winged brow lifted at her.

"Since I've met Mr. Richardson and his wife, you must be Captain Caryl Walker. They didn't tell me you were a woman. I hope I didn't put you out unduly by coming through St. Thomas." He smiled at Caryl and extended his right hand. "I'm Joshua Tain." His charm was palpable but Caryl, still miffed about the time she'd spent at the crowded airport, was determined to resist it.

"Caryl Walker. I hope I've not put you out unduly by being a woman," she responded dryly, taking his hand in a firm grip.

He chuckled and held on to her hand a tad longer than Caryl, who took it away, thought necessary. His touch, warm and hard, somehow disturbed her.

"If women can be astronauts, there's no reason under the moon why they can't be boat captains or anything else for that matter," Joshua said, his eyes twinkling with mischief.

"We can cast off right now, if you like," Caryl said, ignoring the banter.

"I like," he murmured. His eyes bored into hers making the double entendre obvious.

Caryl smiled politely. If he noticed the smile didn't reach her eyes, so much the better, she thought turning to nod to Richardson. She'd had it with men a long time ago and one like Joshua Tain, oozing confidence and come-hithers, wasn't about to make her change her mind, no matter how good looking he was. The sooner he understood that, the better. Caryl turned and climbed up to the pilothouse without another glance at her guest.

Richardson leapt agilely from the deck to the dock as Caryl started the engine and checked various instruments.

"Okay." She waved to her first mate.

Richardson quickly untied the knots, threw the ropes on board, then jumped back on himself.

The *Elendil* moved smoothly away from the pier.

Caryl had obtained her captain's license a week after her graduation from Georgetown University's Law Center. Months of weekend lessons while she was a law student had helped her realize a dream she'd cherished ever since a childhood visit to a Coast Guard facility. Then, for almost two years after acquiring the license, she'd hardly ever gotten a chance to go boating. Through her mother's connections, she'd become a clerk to Geraldine St. James, the first black woman on the Supreme Court. That was a dream job and the experience had stood her in good stead when she applied to Thorne, Mercer and Johnson, one of New York's premier black law firms. It was on one of her too infrequent vacations from TMJ that she'd come to the Virgin Islands and, in one day, fallen in love with their tranquil beauty. A year and a half later, when her reputation lay in the ruins of scandal and gossip among New York's legal community, it was to the Virgin Islands that she'd fled.

This time it was her father who, through his seat on the board of directors for Janus, Inc., got her the job of captain on the *Elendil*. It was what Caryl wanted, to get away from it all, to do something totally different from law, among people who knew nothing about her. Now, as she skillfully maneuvered the cruiser out of the crowded harbor, she took delight in its easy handling, the way the helm responded to her touch with just the right amount of resistance.

Caryl liked to be alone in the pilothouse when just starting a trip and Richardson respected that. Staying down on deck with guests, he pointed out places of interest on land. From the Nanny Cay marina they headed to Virgin Gorda, the third largest of the British Virgin Islands. For much of the trip they sailed fairly close to Tortola's coastline and as they passed them, Richardson pointed out various areas he thought might interest newcomers. Road Town, the capital. Baugher's Bay, home to the territory's only AM radio station. Kingstown, which had been given to freed Africans by King George III. Beef Island, where the airport was, and more.

When they neared Virgin Gorda he explained that the island had been settled in the 1600s by planters from Anguilla and Barbados and their slaves. Caryl, up in the pilothouse, found herself listening for Joshua's interjections and questions. He had a rich, deep voice that was as smooth as honey and just as soothing.

Slowly, the huge boulders for which Virgin Gorda was famous, the spire of the Catholic Church, and the roofs of the Little Dix Bay villas came into sharp focus and Caryl headed to Spring Bay, a wide inlet with a narrow mouth that would be their anchorage for the rest of the day. As Caryl eased the boat into the bay, the prow made gentle waves ripple through the sparkling clear water. On the shore, graceful palms and squat sea grape trees bordered the beach which glittered invitingly in the afternoon sun.

"This is what I've been missing."

The *Elendil's* male guest bounded up the steps. When he moved to stand beside Caryl where she sat at the helm, she became uncomfortably aware of his nearness. The air around him seemed charged with electricity.

"It's really beautiful," he murmured, looking at the view before him.

Caryl nodded.

"Yes, it's lovely, isn't it? Sometimes, if you're lucky, you can see hawksbill and leatherback turtles and schools of fish swimming about."

When Joshua moved away from her to peer hopefully over the boat's side, Caryl felt as if she had been released from some unknown pressure. She smiled with proprietary pride at the man's appreciation of the scenery. These islands she had taken to her heart filled her with a fierce love, and her estimation of him went up.

She dropped anchor about fifty feet from shore.

"Mr. Tain." Caryl paused, not wanting to break into his reverie as he continued to stare down into the waters around the boat.

"Joshua, please," he said without turning around to look at her. Then suddenly, he called out, "there, look, a turtle. Wow! That's a big one."

He leaned over the railing to follow the turtle's progress, then turned triumphantly to her. "I saw one!" he exclaimed. His eyes gleamed in his dark, finely chiseled face.

Caryl grinned. "You'll probably see many more. Perhaps you can take a picture next time."

"Damn, I brought cameras. I should've thought of them before." He looked as if he could kick himself.

"Sometime after we have lunch and you've rested, you can snorkel and take as many pictures as you like. There's a great coral formation right over there." Caryl pointed to the east side of the bay where the seabed was obviously darker.

"I'd enjoy that." Joshua turned around once again to look at her before going to the steps. She followed him down.

The aft deck's drop-leaf table was covered with a white damask tablecloth on which Patty had laid out a spread of crab salad, baked potato, fresh vegetables and fruits and white wine.

"We can be as formal or informal as you like, Mr. Tain. If you wish to dine here by yourself that will be fine, or, if you like, we can accompany you." Caryl smiled at him, hoping he'd choose to be alone. The less contact she had with a man with his magnetism the better for her comfort level. "We would not consider you rude were you to request privacy."

"No, please join me. I'd love to know more about the islands and about yourselves too, if I may." Joshua waved a hand towards the cushioned chairs around the table.

"Thank you." She would just have to make the best of it. She nodded to Patty and Richardson to take their respective places at the table.

"Breakfast depends on when our guests waken but lunch is usually served between twelve and two and dinner at six. We can be quite flexible but scheduled times for lunch and dinner remove uncertainty and let us get on with our other chores in the meantime," Caryl told Joshua as she took her seat between him and Patty.

"No problem. I can go along with the program," he answered, flashing a smile around the table.

Over the leisurely lunch, Richardson took the conversational lead, expounding on every topic from religion to politics. Caryl joined in every now and again, as did Patty, but they left most of the talking to the ebullient Richardson. Listening keenly, Caryl was amused by his not-so-subtle fishing for clues about their guest. It netted him the information that Joshua lived in New York, that he had never been to the British Virgin Islands before, had stayed in Jamaica's Blue Mountains two years ago, and not much else. Joshua was adept at parrying questions and heading the conversation into new, less personal directions. Richardson eventually gave up, rolling his eyes quickly at Caryl and Patty in frustration as his last probe was deflected.

"That Joshua's quite a dish," Patty whispered, under cover of her husband's voice. "And charm to sell. I like him."

Caryl chuckled. Patty had once worked under a Cordon Bleu chef at St. Thomas's only five star resort, the Castle Morant. She'd picked up quite a few things from the master chef, developing a talent for taking classic European recipes and adding her own distinctive Creole touch. If she took a particular liking to a guest, all on board would eat very well.

"These islands are real close to the American Virgin Islands so they're much more obviously Americanized but U.S. culture pervades the whole Caribbean. You can go to the remotest village on an island like St. Vincent or Trinidad and still find people who know exactly who Walker, Texas Ranger, is, or even Sinbad, or any other celebrity you want to name," Richardson was saying as Caryl picked up the thread of the conversation.

"That's true around the world, though. Wherever the American media penetrates, so also does American culture," Joshua countered. "American television creates a demand for Big Macs and then MacDonald's moves in. But that's the thing about free trade." The heaping servings he had given himself had disappeared and Patty again proffered the crab salad.

"Perhaps so, but then who can compete with the moguls of

Hollywood who create a somewhat distorted view of American life and then manage to not only make the rest of the world believe the myths, despite the headlines, but also desperate to live that life too?" Caryl demanded.

"If you all were so interested in free trade, you would make it easier for foreign films to be distributed in America and perhaps even encourage a quota of foreign programming on American television," Richardson added.

"Quotas are not free trade," Joshua pointed out before swallowing the last mouthful on his plate.

"But it would be similar to affirmative action, wouldn't it?" Patty murmured, somewhat distractedly as she too finished eating.

"Exactly!" Caryl beamed with delight, slapping her hand on the table.

Joshua laughed and threw up his hands.

"I'm feeling too sleepy to continue this argument. Can we reconvene this evening? I'd really like to take a rest so I'll be wide-awake to snorkel later. The trip down was tiring and I haven't slept much in the past week." He pushed back his chair, rose and stretched.

"If you like, we can call you at three-thirty. You'll get about three or four sunlit hours in the water today. Picture taking in natural light will still be possible," Caryl said.

"Aye, aye, captain." Joshua sketched a salute and disappeared into the saloon. "Patty, me girl, that man sure looked as if he enjoyed your grub."

Richardson gave his wife an affectionate slap on her bum as she began to clear the table.

"Yes, that he did, but you were well checkmated. You hardly learned anything about him except his views on American foreign trade and such." Patty's lips curved into a teasing smile.

JUST AN AFFAIR

"Yeah, well, he's obviously some kind of undercover agent or he wouldn't have been able to resist me." Richardson lifted his hands, palms up, in a gesture that said the matter was thus beyond him.

"Perhaps he's CIA or DEA and he's here to figure out the extent of charter boat involvement in the drug trade," Caryl suggested, sparking an appreciative chuckle from Richardson.

"Or an industrial spy scouting marine locations for toxic dumps," he hissed to her behind his hand. He winked.

"You two!" Patty shook her head as she walked to the dumbwaiter hidden in a recess at the side of the saloon door and deposited a tray piled high with crockery.

Still chuckling, her husband helped her clear the table.

Caryl wandered distractedly into the saloon. Her long-fingered, capable-looking hands idly running over the plush fake regency chairs she passed, she mulled over the mystery of their guest. Admitting to herself that the Tall and Handsome One was probably neither CIA nor DEA, much less an industrial spy, she gave herself a mental shake. There was no reason why she and her crew should know anything more about the identity of their guest than his name and, besides, this was only the first day. He could just be the type of person who took more time to reveal himself to others.

Stopping in front of the saloon's wide mirror, Caryl circled her head to remove the tension in her neck. Starting with her temples she kneaded her scalp, rubbing each area firmly but gently, her thumbs doing most of the work. Finishing at the base of her neck, she linked the fingers of her hands and slowly pressed her head between her palms.

She looked at the high-cheekboned, caramel-colored face that stared back at her and thought, not for the first time, how irregular her features were. Taken separately each feature was alright but together they made an odd combination, giving her a look that spoke strongly of African, Indian, Spanish and possibly other ancestors. Her mind ran on her maternal grandmother, Pilar, a small but strong-willed Brazilian woman who had died a few years before after suffering a stroke which left her completely paralyzed. Marcianne, Caryl's mother, never tired of telling Caryl that she took after Pilar, in looks as well as disposition. She, herself, didn't think they were anything alike. Pilar had been a free spirit who hadn't worked a day in her life. Caryl, on the other hand, was a career woman, intent on making partner at a prestigious law firm and creating an identity separate from that of her family. Or, at least she had been, until her heart got in the way of all that and landed her in the British Virgin Islands.

Caryl sighed and turned away from the mirror. Maybe she had been deceiving herself all those years. Clearly she hadn't been the focused and driven woman she had thought she was or Alexander Thorne would never have been able to derail her plans so easily. Almost a year had gone by now, eleven months of hiding out in the islands, but she could not do this forever. Caryl rubbed her forehead as she made her way slowly down to her cabin. Cruising the Virgin Islands was lovely but it wasn't what she wanted to do with the rest of her life.

CHAPTER TWO

Caryl was on the aft deck, her head buried in her book, when Joshua Tain reappeared.

"The sun feels wonderful. I hadn't realized we would have air-conditioning aboard," he said, suddenly materializing through the saloon doors in a pair of metallic silver bathing trunks, a towel draped carelessly over his shoulders.

Caryl raised her head to look at him, saw his hard, athletic build, the muscles rippling in his stomach, and felt a glow of appreciation. This man is truly fine, she said to herself, before dragging her gaze to his face. With a shiver she realized he was watching her, a mocking glint in his eyes. Determined not to let him guess how much he unnerved her, she gave him a wide, welcoming smile.

"We have two generators and a chilled water air conditioning system but it's easy to see why the ancients worshipped the sun as the source of life," she answered, keeping her voice neutral.

"Yeah, no worrying about basal cell carcinoma for them, eh? Nowadays, even us dark mortals have to slather up. Will you be joining me, captain?" he asked

"No, I won't," she said. "Guests usually snorkel by themselves but are, of course, accompanied on the dives."

"Hmm, now that *is* a pity." A grin broadened Joshua's face and his eyes twinkled. Caryl's hand fluttered up to pull her earlobe. Why did this blasted man make her so uncomfortable? It wasn't like she wasn't accustomed to flirting. She needed to say something that would put him in his place, let him know right away that she wasn't in the market and was definitely not about to succumb to his charm, however much of it he had. She had just opened her mouth, hoping something witty would come out, when he jumped down to the boat's teak bathing platform and, in one fluid motion, took off the towel, threw it to the side and dived into the water. Seconds later he re-emerged and began swimming strongly in the direction of the coral reef.

"He didn't take a camera," was all Caryl could say as she watched the powerful figure slice through the water.

"Looks like something's happening here, woman. Care to talk about it?" Richardson asked, coming up to stand at Caryl's shoulder. She had forgotten he was around.

"Nothing to talk about, nothing's happening," Caryl answered. She made herself busy tidying up the snorkeling equipment before ducking inside and heading to her cabin.

Flinging herself on her bed, she reviewed the day's events thus far. One thought kept resurfacing. Joshua Tain disturbed her peace of mind. Thumping the pillows in frustration, Caryl wondered why this should be so. He certainly wasn't the best looking man she had ever seen and not the most adept flirt either. There was no reason why she should be getting a funny feeling in the pit of her stomach whenever he smiled. Hadn't she told herself she was off men? *But you aren't a nun and the man is fine*, a little voice argued. Alexander was fine too, she reminded the little voice. *Yeah, but he was married. This brother isn't wearing any ring.* Caryl groaned. *It doesn't matter, shut up already. I'm not looking,* she screamed inside her head. The little voice shut up. Still troubled but exhausted from the preparations for the trip, Caryl fell into a light sleep.

An hour and a half later she woke again and hurried to the aft deck to see if Joshua was back on board. Richardson, who was still

JUST AN AFFAIR

there, informed her that Joshua had not left the water, pointing to the bright orange tip of his breathing tube visible on the far side of the bay. Richardson looked at her curiously but didn't ask the questions obviously burning his tongue, and the two friends made small talk until Joshua rejoined them just as the sun began to sink behind the hills.

"It's beautiful. Really, mad beautiful!" Joshua exclaimed, shaking his head in wonderment as he pulled himself up the swim ladder. Drops of water sparkled on his hair and body like chips of crystal and Caryl again admired his hard, dark body. Clothed, he was deceptively slim. Clad only in swimming trunks, his broad chest, slim hips and long, finely muscled legs were a woman's dream.

Giving herself a mental shake, Caryl resumed the role of captain.

"There are a couple books in the cabinet in the saloon which describe the different kinds of coral, fish and other sea life in these waters."

"I'll look at them later tonight," Joshua responded, turning on the fresh water shower over the bathing platform to rinse off.

"This looks like the ideal spot for jet skiing. Perhaps I could rent one tomorrow, somewhere. Really have some fast fun." Joshua arched his brows in Caryl's direction.

"Sorry, you're out of luck." Richardson's deep bass broke in on them. "Jet skis are illegal in the British Virgin Islands. People think they're too dangerous."

"Give me a break!"

"It's the law." Richardson shrugged.

"Cars are dangerous in the wrong hands, too. Why aren't *they* banned?"

Richardson shrugged again.

"I agree with you that it doesn't make any sense but we could lose our cruising license if we allowed it," Caryl said. "As you may know, Mr. Tain...Joshua, we do have water skis on board. We can take the dinghy out any time you wish. We also have a couple of windsurfers."

"It's not the same thing but I'll think about it. Would it be possible to see something of life on land tomorrow?"

"Yes, sure. We have an arrangement with a rental company in The Valley, Virgin Gorda's capital. We can go over to the marina tomorrow and rent a jeep. I can give you the deluxe tour if you'd like. We also have a moped on board for the use of guests." Joshua slung his towel around his neck.

"No tour if I choose the moped, right? I'll be on my own. I'll go for the jeep. What makes the tour deluxe?"

Caryl tore her eyes from his stomach and raised them to his face. His eyes were twinkling again. Oh hell!

"Oh, it's just...just...," she stammered.

Once again, Richardson's bass startled her with the reminder of his presence.

"Deluxe means you get a historical, environmental and every other kind of tour in one," he said. His voice betrayed only a hint of amusement at his captain's discomfiture.

"Yes, exactly," Caryl agreed and threw him a grateful glance. She grasped the opportunity to back away from Joshua. "Let me go and check on the weather," she said, her cheeks suffused with heat as she left them.

What on earth was coming over her? Mooning over the blasted man like a love struck puppy. *Get a grip*, she told herself sternly as she flicked on the radio, tuning it to Channel Sixteen to get the hourly weather report. Slumping in the pilot's stool, she listened idly to yachties calling in to each other as they too waited to hear the weather. Her thoughts began to wander.

JUST AN AFFAIR

Since she had come to the islands she had behaved like she'd heard the call and entered a convent. A man could ask and get the time of day from her but anything more was completely out of the question. Men were trouble with a capital T. What was the use of meeting them if they were just going to bring pain? Shayna, her best friend back in Virginia, kept insisting she get herself an island man, let a local stud help her forget about Alexander Thorne. But Caryl relied on her busy charter schedule. That, and the fact that she had never heard from Alexander again, meant she had a real chance to get over the man she had loved beyond reason just a year ago.

Of course, none of that explained why she'd responded to the sight of Joshua's gleaming torso minutes ago in a way she had never responded to Alexander's. Caryl bit her lip. There was no way she could give a man like Joshua, sexy and super-confident with it, more than a second look. Besides, he was a client and business was not allowed to mix with pleasure on Janus's boats. Not that she wanted it to, not at all. Inside her, the little voice sighed in disappointment but Caryl ignored it. Life as a nun was just fine.

A male announcer's voice interrupted her thoughts and she listed intently as he relayed the information coming from the meteorological service in Puerto Rico. The weather was basically going to continue fine that day though an upper level trough moving east from Anguilla could mean heavy rains tomorrow. Caryl hoped not. If it rained they would have to scuttle their plans to take a tour. It was no fun driving around from one soggy attraction to another. Caryl switched the radio off, leapt back down to the aft deck and headed to her cabin to write out the *Elendil's* log before rushing to get ready for dinner.

The first dress she pulled from her closet after her shower was a hot strapless number but she discarded it almost immediately. Joshua

Tain was exactly the type of man who would think she was wearing it to impress him. *And wasn't she*, the little voice asked innocently. Caryl did not dignify the question with a response and, instead, dropped a simple shirtwaisted midnight blue dress over her head. She had absolutely no desire to impress anyone. None at all, she repeated to herself. But she did take a little bit more time applying her make-up and she did wear her diamond stud earrings, the ones that appeared to make her eyes sparkle. Just so I don't look too plain, she said to herself.

By the time she arrived on deck, everyone else was already seated. Joshua smiled a welcome and gave her a once-over. *Not bad, but could have been better his expression* seemed to say. He himself wore a cream silk shirt whose simplicity clearly belied its price. She couldn't see his pants from where she sat but, if his past attire was anything to go by, she knew they were of the same designer-level quality.

"Joshua was just asking if we shouldn't go and get you," Patty said, crinkling her forehead at her as if to say what took you so long.

"Sorry, I got caught up with what I was doing and didn't notice the time. Everything looks great, Patty."

Dinner that night consisted of herbed pasta with a vegetable salad followed by dessert crepes with powdered sugar and mango jam laced with a ginger-based seasoning. A jug of sorrel, traditionally considered a Christmas beverage in the Caribbean, was the perfect accompaniment. Preoccupied with keeping thoughts of herself in Joshua Tain's arms at bay, Caryl didn't put herself out to make conversation but let Richardson fill in the gap.

Joshua noticed. "Captain, you're rather quiet tonight and you don't even have the excuse of an exhausting swim," he said.

"I'm mentally plotting our course for the week, actually," she lied. The *Elendil* followed a fairly standard itinerary based on the length of a trip, but he wouldn't know that.

"From Virgin Gorda," she continued crisply, avoiding her crewmates' eyes, "we'll turn around and cruise through the island chain. On the third day, we'll anchor off Salt Island and you can dive down to the shipwreck Richardson probably told you about on the way here. The booking agent said you were certified for basic diving, yes?"

Joshua nodded.

"Good," Caryl said, pleased. The marine environment around the Virgin Islands was varied and beautiful but only a small percentage of visitors to the territory did more than snorkel, missing the richness of life far below the surface.

"Will you be joining me in the water at any time?" Joshua interjected softly, almost as if they were alone.

"As I said before, Mr. Tain, I don't usually join guests in the water unless it's a dive with three or more guests or there are poor swimmers among them."

"Is there nothing I can do to persuade you to change your mind?"

Caryl caught the smirks Patty and her husband exchanged. Great, so now she was providing entertainment for her crew.

"No." She gritted her teeth and smiled. "You enjoyed your swim today, did you?"

"Yes, it was fantastic. Like a tonic." This time he looked around the table including them all. "Everything that's been on my mind lately just melted away in the water. Fantastic."

"Do you get much stress in your line of work?" Richardson asked.

Caryl's lips twitched. It was a skillful line of enquiry.

"It's high pressure but you learn to flow. The thing that's been putting a tick on my ass is I'm trying to fight off a guy who wants to buy my company." His eyes darkened. "The man doesn't know a thing about my business but he wants to buy it and he's got the bank to do it too."

Caryl exchanged a look with Patty.

"Isn't there anything you can do?" she asked sympathetically, surprised he was speaking so freely. The swim must really have loosened him up.

"I'm doing it. Got the lawyers and the accountants working around the clock and I think I've beaten him off, but he didn't get to be the man he is by just accepting defeat. I think we're just going through a lull now. He'll be back and that's why I decided to take a break, recharge the batteries."

"You've come to the right place to do it. This is God's own paradise," Richardson boomed.

"I thought that was the United States Virgin Islands."

"Nah, they're 'America's Paradise.' There's a big difference." Richardson waved his hand in dismissal and almost knocked over his glass.

"I think I know what it is," Joshua responded, and gave Caryl a meaningful look.

"Aren't there any advantages to getting bought out? I read all the time about people selling out for millions and millions," Patty said.

"Not me. I built that company from the ground up and nobody is going to take it from me. Nobody." Joshua's mouth tightened and his nostrils flared. "It's got everything of me in it."

His words hung in the night air and nobody said anything. Caryl admired his refusal to give in and let go of something that obviously meant a lot to him. She was just thinking that maybe she could unbend a bit around him, not be so standoffish since he was obviously going through a difficult time, when he looked over at her and grinned.

"Of course, there's a lot of me still left over," he said. "For other things."

"In the Virgin Islands we don't really take to leftovers," Caryl responded, crisply.

Patty suffered a sudden fit of coughing that her husband considerately tried to relieve by thumping her on her back. Patty pushed his hand away, tears in her eyes.

"It's okay, I'm okay," she said as everybody stared at her.

"I was just trying to help," her husband said, offended.

"I know, sugar apple, I know. Thank you."

"Is there anything else I ought to know about what you do and don't take to in the Virgin Islands?" Joshua asked, giving Caryl an innocent look.

"We'll let you know as it comes up." Caryl smiled. Round two to me, she thought to herself with satisfaction.

As if her comment was their cue, Patty and Richardson excused themselves and rose to begin clearing the dishes. Springing to her feet herself, Caryl began to help them. It was not the captain's function but she never minded doing what had to be done. Tonight she was positively enthusiastic about it and excused herself with pleasure from her guest's company.

"Struck with him she is," said Patty, nudging Richardson as Caryl followed them to the galley to retrieve the dishes they had stacked on the dumbwaiter.

"Didn't I tell you from the first that he looked like her type?" Richardson responded.

"My type! Ha! I have no type and I have no idea what you two are talking about but please don't let that stop you." Caryl rolled her eyes at her crewmates, her tone withering. She helped Richardson put the dishes in the sink as Patty put on her rubber gloves.

"My God, girl, when you said that thing about leftovers I thought

I was going to die laughing."

"Is that what you were doing?" Richardson looked at his wife, shocked.

"Yes, you big lug. He told her he had more of himself left over and she said she didn't want any. I can't believe you didn't get it." Patty gave him a poke in the ribs.

"That man likes you, Caryl," Richardson said.

"Definitely," his wife agreed, as she began to wash the dishes.

Caryl snorted. "Oh, please! You've hardly known him a day, Richardson, and you've managed to figure this out? Maybe I should get Janus to bankroll an 800 number for you and you can set up your own psychic line," she teased. "With the accent and everything people will think you've got the real voodoo lowdown. You'll give Miss Cleo a run for her money."

Richardson chuckled. "Seriously, Caryl, he's been checking you out ever since he met you. The man is lonely, he wants a woman."

"Next you'll be peering into tea leaves and collecting the bones from his plates. He's just playing around. If I showed him the least little bit of interest he'd forget he even knew my name. Anyway, what he wants really isn't any of our business."

"The way you've been looking back at him, I thought it was. Seemed like the attraction was mutual." Shrugging innocently, Patty turned back to what she was doing.

"You're imagining things, Patty. The man doesn't do one thing for me." But Patty was right on the money, at least as far as she was concerned, and everyone in the tiny room knew it.

Upset that the older woman had discerned the feelings she was doing her best to hide, Caryl spun past Richardson, whose massive figure almost blocked the galley exit where he was loading coffee on the dumbwaiter.

JUST AN AFFAIR

On her way back to the deck to make sure Joshua hadn't fallen overboard and drowned himself or gotten into any other kind of trouble, Caryl thought about what her crewmates had said. Joshua *was* having an effect on her. She could hardly look at the man without her heartbeat racing. But she didn't want that right now. And, anyway, when she was ready she was going for a nice, safe, unattractive man, a near-sighted accountant with a Volvo maybe, somebody who would never hurt her. Joshua Tain, she was certain, was the Maserati type: fast cars, fast women, fast life. She would just have to keep backing him off until he understood she was off limits.

Opening the door to the saloon she found Joshua settled on the couch with a book. A pair of wire-rimmed spectacles gave him a scholarly, intellectual look but there was nothing safe about his expression when he turned to watch her walk past. She felt his eyes on her back until she left his field of vision but steeled herself to act nonchalant. Out on deck, she retrieved the coffee things from the dumbwaiter and laid them out on the table.

By the time she passed back through the saloon Richardson was talking to Joshua who had swung his legs off the couch and sat up.

"Richardson and Mr. Tain are deep in conversation," she reported to Patty on re-entering the galley.

"You know, I used to think men didn't bond as well as women but that's not true. They get together and they can kick back and talk about sports, women, whatever. It's women who have it harder."

"Patty, that's not true. Look at us. We became friends quickly."

"Yes, that's true, child, but there's more competition among women. My good-good friends, when I look back on my life, have mostly been men."

"You grew up in a family with five boys and no sisters. That's why you think like that. My best friends have always been women. I don't have to explain as much. A woman gets what I'm saying quicker."

"Probably, but I also think women who have good friendships with men have the best love relationships."

"What?" Caryl was astounded. "What are you talking about?" For one wild minute, Caryl wondered if Patty knew about her past, but she dismissed the notion almost as quickly as it came. That had been a long way away and though the world was getting smaller and smaller it had not yet shrunk so much, of that she was almost willing to bet.

"Think about it. Go over all your friends and think about it. Women who get on like tongue and teeth with men don't see them as being so different. They know men make mistakes, have needs and desires just like them. But women who don't get on so well with them seem to think they're not quite human. They sometimes expect the impossible." She glanced at Caryl. "I can't explain it better but you can put your pot on for that. It's true."

Richardson entered at that moment, putting an effective end to their conversation.

"Mr. Tain says he doesn't drink coffee and wants no alcohol tonight," Richardson explained as he came in. "He said to let you know that at breakfast, he prefers tea."

"With no sugar and a lot of Caryl, I'm sure," Patty chortled.

"Give it up, you all. Please."

"She's right, captain. The man has definitely got, what is it you Americans say, the jones, for you. He asked me how long you've been in the business and if you had a boyfriend."

"He did not."

"He did."

Caryl struggled with herself but she knew if she didn't ask the big man wouldn't tell her.

"What did you say?"

"The truth. You've been here for about a year and you don't have no man"

"Richardson! How could you say that?"

"It's the truth. What did you want me to do, lie?" Richardson looked at his wife. His eyes appealed for support but she grimaced as if to say leave me out.

"Nothing. You didn't have to tell him anything. I can't believe you said that. He's a client, not a Love Connection candidate and my business is my business. Next time keep your trap shut. That's an order."

Whirling around on her heel, Caryl spun out of the galley.

Furious at herself for letting Patty and Richardson upset her, Caryl stalked past Joshua's once-again prone figure in the saloon with barely a glance. Out on deck, she gripped the railing as she looked out over the bay. The half-moon's light gave the water a silvery luminescence that at any other time would have given her a pleasurable thrill. Now Caryl was too angry to even notice. Pulling rank made her feel uncomfortable, especially since Richardson was older than she was. But he had pushed her to it. Joshua Tain was a guest and professionalism required that she keep her distance. Whatever it was she felt for him would have to disappear; there was no room for it on the *Elendil*. Richardson should just have said he didn't know or told him to ask her, himself.

"You know, you don't notice the moon when you live in a city. You hardly look up at the sky. You're too afraid you'll be mugged or worse. And even if you do look up, you'll hardly see anything because there's so much light around. Even from my window, the view isn't all that."

Caryl did not reply. Her heart had leapt at the first sound of his voice and she was concentrating on slowing it back down.

"When I saw you almost run past me, I wondered if you would

keep going into the sea so I came after you. Are you okay?" Joshua asked.

"Yes. Thanks. I just needed some fresh air." Good, she thought, her voice had not wobbled. In fact, she sounded quite calm.

"This place has that and more in abundance. Damn. This is really a breathtaking sight. This bay. The moon. Look, stay here. I'll be right back." He disappeared into the saloon.

Caryl debated staying. It could very well lead to trouble, but if she left, it would look rude. She had just about made up her mind to give her apologies in the morning when he returned with a camera bag and tripod.

"You're really outfitted. Are you a photographer back in New York?" Caryl asked, before she could stop herself.

"No, I'm not, but I've enjoyed taking pictures ever since I was a kid. Back then all I had was one of those one tens. They took good pictures though." He screwed a Canon EOS onto his tripod.

"Yeah, I know. Galen Rowell's first photography book was made up of photos taken with his one ten."

Joshua paused to stare at her. One eyebrow lifted in surprise.

"You know Rowell's work?"

"Yes, why wouldn't I? Because I'm a boat captain?"

Try as she might, Caryl couldn't keep her reply from being tinged with more than a hint of bitterness. Tourists always seemed to think that because she lived on a boat in the Caribbean she wouldn't know about anything else that was going on in the world. Truth was, she had been a photography buff in high school and still had more than a passing interest in the art form.

"That's not what I meant. You can pick ten people at random on any city street and easily win a bet that at least nine won't know Rowell, much less what he took pictures with for his first book."

JUST AN AFFAIR

He smiled at her and Caryl found herself smiling back. There was no hint of the mocking tone that often underlay everything he said, and she found herself warming to his evident good humor.

"But are you from the British Virgin Islands? Sometimes it seems as if you talk like an American with a slight Caribbean accent; other times it seems the reverse."

"I'm actually from Virginia but I consider these islands my home. At least, for right now I do."

Joshua shot her a questioning look but he didn't say anything, and Caryl appreciated his respect for her privacy.

Soon, the only sounds to be heard in the stillness of the Caribbean night were those made by the camera and the lapping of the waves against the boat. Caryl thought that if the scene before them was reproduced on his film, Joshua's photos would be stunning, almost surreal in their beauty.

Just when she thought he'd forgotten her existence, he turned to her. "I've a favor to ask of you. Would you go over by the railing? Turn your back to me like it was when I came outside."

Caryl did as she was told but had to fight hard against the rising tide of self-consciousness that threatened to overtake her.

"Yeah, that's good. Put your arms out along the side and look back at me over your shoulder. Okay. Great. Now turn back to me and put your arms out like before."

Caryl knew men considered her attractive but none had ever been interested in taking shots of her quite like this. The fact that it was Joshua Tain who was doing it, a wildly good-looking man on a lovely moonlit night, filled her with a heady excitement. She felt dreamy, languid, almost as if she were drugged. She closed her eyes and let the night wash over her, hearing only the sound of the camera shutter and the waves. Then the clicking stopped but she only half opened her eyes, not wanting the feeling of floating, being suspended on warm clouds, to vanish.

The pressure on her lips was light as a dream, soft as velvet. Caryl raised her face, hungry for more. Her mouth opened slightly and then she felt his strong arms go around her, cradling her like a child. In her mouth was the taste of sorrel, bittersweet with an almost metallic coolness, and in her nose, the smell of an expensive men's cologne, musky with a hint of cinnamon and sandalwood. Caryl's eyes flew open.

"No," she said, firmly. She pushed past him, almost running. At the saloon door, she paused, turned. She had to tell him, make him understand. She just did not want a man right now but the words dried in her throat as she looked at him.

"I didn't mean to offend you. You are so beautiful." His eyes pleaded with her.

"I can't. This is wrong." Her hand waved between them, at heart level. "I just can't. What do you take me for?"

"I'm sorry. I thought...please..." He made as if to reach out and touch her but she shied away.

"I could lose my job." And that wasn't the half of it. She stepped through the door and left him standing there, his hands hanging at his side.

In her cabin, Caryl flung herself fully clothed into her bed. She was acting as if she didn't have an ounce of the sense she was born with. One minute she was furious with him, the next, like that afternoon, she was going gaga at the sight of his muscled, half-naked body. Clearly, making whatever she felt for him disappear was going to be more of a challenge than she'd originally thought but disappear it must. There was no other way.

CHAPTER THREE

When she woke the next morning Caryl remained in bed, staring up at the ceiling. Above her was the aft deck and above that, the endless sky and somewhere around was Joshua Tain. Caryl sighed and tried not to think of her disturbing client as she rolled out of bed to go for her swim.

Outside, the air was chilly and the sky was a pale gold dome. On the nearby shore she could hear the soft, mournful cooing of zenaidas, the turtledoves for whom it was thought Columbus had named the neighboring island of Tortola. These were the mornings Caryl loved best, when only gentle sounds disturbed the peace and when, because the sun had not yet warmed the winds, the sea was perfectly still. There was no sign of the rain the weatherman had warned about.

The words to Bob Marley's "Sun Is Shining" rose insistently to her mind and she hummed the first few lines as she tossed the towel on a lounge seat, then lowered herself quietly down the swim ladder, mindful of the others who were still sleeping.

Once in, she dived to the sand floor before swimming strongly back up to flip over and down again, ignoring the water's chill. She felt an almost childish pleasure in her strength and swimming ability. Floating to the surface again, she kicked out for the shore. In the shallows she flipped on her back to float, suspended, staring up at the sky.

The more she thought about Joshua, the more memories of Alexander dredged themselves up to disturb her. As she undulated gently with the waves, she remembered her dream of the night before.

She had been walking up a city street looking for her car. She knew she had parked it in front of a particular store before going to work but now it was night and the car was nowhere to be seen and she wanted to go home. As she walked back down the street, growing increasingly frustrated, Alexander had stepped out of the shadows.

"Is this what you're looking for?" He held up an unfamiliar key ring from which her car key dangled.

Caryl had looked down at her empty hands, trying to remember if she'd had her keys in her hand when she came out of her building. She thought she had.

She looked back up at Alexander, astonished to find he no longer wore the business suit she had first seen him in. Now he had on brown linen shorts and a loose shirt of some silky material.

"Give me my key," she demanded.

"No. It's not what you really want."

She lunged at him but he evaded her neatly, stepping to the side like the graceful dancer he was. He laughed.

"Think, Caryl. What do you want? What do you need? Tonight, they are the same." And then he'd vanished and the dream had ended.

Her head bumped against something and Caryl turned to realize that the waves had brought her into the beach. She got to her feet and walked out of the water, alarming a small crab on its way to the water's edge. An opaque, almost pearlescent gray, in color, Caryl almost didn't see it before it scurried back down its hole. She walked on, envying the crab's ability to disappear from view. When her affair with Alexander exploded in her face, that was exactly what she'd done, dropped out of sight. So what did Alexander mean by suddenly reappearing in her dreams like some bad penny she couldn't even give away? And what on earth did the dream itself signify? There wasn't a thing Alexander had that she wanted or needed or would ever want or need again. What he did have was a wife and, Caryl did some quick calculations, a child who must be almost a toddler by now.

"I need neither your wife, nor your child, Alexander," she muttered into the morning air, "you can keep them. It was what you meant to do all along, anyhow, wasn't it?" There was no-one around to hear the bitterness in her voice or to see the angry tear slipping down her face. Almost an hour passed before Caryl felt calm enough to re-enter the sea and return to the *Elendil*. She struck out for the boat, churning the water with her legs and arms, delighting in the fury of her swift, choppy movement through the water, distracting her from all thoughts of infuriating men.

She reached for the swim ladder to pull herself up and suddenly realized Joshua was leaning against the railing watching her. Her heart skipped a beat. She let go of the ladder and dove to the depths to gather herself before she had to speak to him.

By the time she re-surfaced, he was treading water a few feet away.

"You're a fine swimmer," he said.

"Thank you. I hope you slept well." I am the captain of this boat; I am a professional, she repeated to herself and smiled politely at him.

"Do you? Why?"

Caryl sighed. It was really too early for this. Couldn't the man see she was doing her best to treat him with the politeness he deserved as a client and make a reciprocal effort? Remembering the kiss she had practically run from the night before, Caryl's heart lurched.

"I want your vacation to be relaxing," she said. It was true. She was sorry about what was happening with his company and hoped he'd beat off whoever was trying to take it from him. She looked at him, then glanced away. "I do," she repeated as if he were debating the point with her.

"That's nice to hear." His lips twitched. "What *I* would like is to continue what we started last night." His eyes drew hers even against her better judgment. His expression was unreadable.

"I...I can't, it's against Janus's rules and, anyway, I can't just be kissing strange men." Was it the waves or had he purposely moved closer to her? Whatever, Caryl felt it best to put more distance between them.

Joshua threw back his head and laughed. It poured out of him like something forgotten but delicious that he hadn't done in a long time and intended to make the most of.

"I meant taking photos. I think you're very photogenic. Those cheekbones," he said, still chuckling.

Caryl glared at him. The serenity she had felt upon emerging into the dawn of a new day was quickly dissipating.

"I don't think so," she said. "You'll need to find another model."

"But I like this one."

His sudden movement brought them almost face-to-face and he grabbed her by the arms, pulling her to him. His lips met hers and a quiver of heat coursed down her spine. Her nipples hardened with sudden arousal. Shocked and totally unnerved by his touch, Caryl splashed backward but her body forgot to float and she sank. Without thinking she inhaled, then surfaced, coughing and spluttering as the salt stung the back of her throat. When Joshua tried to pat her on her back as Richardson had done to Patty the night before, Caryl dove away from him and towards the swim ladder. Putting space between herself and this man until she could at least pretend he had absolutely no effect on her was the only thought in her head.

Her guest's laughter rang in her ears as she hastily clambered aboard and she wondered how she had ever found anything pleasing in the sound of it. Clearly, she would have to be on full alert around him. Though she had told him she wasn't interested, the man was still trying to roll on her.

Caryl flung open the door to her cabin and burst inside, her chest heaving. It had felt good, no, better than good, his mouth on hers that morning and the night before had felt like something she hadn't known she needed. If she were honest she would admit it took every ounce of willpower she possessed not to fling her arms around the man's neck and fasten her lips to his like a woman dying of sexual hunger. It had to stop. She had sworn off men for the foreseeable future and she had meant it. She had issued no qualifiers. All men. Including Joshua Tain.

Later, at breakfast, Caryl scooped up her servings and took a seat as far she could get from Joshua.

"Captain," Patty started diffidently making Caryl realize her crew was probably still thinking she was upset with them.

"Yes, Patty?" she said. Patty and Richardson were her friends and she didn't want them to feel they were going to have to tiptoe around her for the rest of the trip. It was going to be difficult enough without that.

"Mr. Tain was just telling us he would like to snorkel again, take some pictures and then go over to the marina, probably around midday, as you suggested," Patty continued, smiling her relief at the younger woman.

"Sure, that would be fine. I've already radioed Chris at the rental company to expect us at one." Caryl spoke with cool confidence and felt quietly triumphant about it. It may be an act where you're concerned, Mr. Joshua Trouble Tain, but it's going to be a darned good one she thought with satisfaction. If you think you're going to use me to play some little game, you're going to have to think again. The idea brought a small smile to her face and she stared out to sea, pretending to ignore her handsome guest as he replenished his plate. For his part, Joshua seemed content to act as if nothing untoward had happened between them. If anything, he was more subdued than she had ever seen him. It was very suspicious, but as long as he kept his distance she was happy.

After breakfast they all went their separate ways, and Joshua spent most of the morning off the boat. Caryl saw him take another camera with him, a Nikonos V, often used by professional photographers and her curiosity about him deepened. Joshua, himself, seemed totally disinterested in any further discussion about what he did for a living. She didn't believe he was a photographer because it didn't fit with what he'd said about the takeover but she had a hard time imagining him in a traditional sort of business.

Caryl tried to concentrate on the book she was reading but the pilothouse was an excellent vantage point from which to keep an eye on the *Elendil*'s guest. And, as a professional captain concerned about the well-being of her client, it behooved her to keep track of him. Caryl saw when he snorkeled by the reef and noticed when he appeared to be taking pictures, when he lay on the sand for a while and when he walked down the beach.

Every now and then he shaded his eyes with his hand, looking toward the *Elendil*. When that happened, Caryl bent her head over her book, pretending fascination with what she was reading. At least from that distance he couldn't know her heart raced every time she thought he might catch her watching. Remember, she whispered to herself, you're being a nun. But a little voice murmured back, *All the more reason to admire God's Creation.* Caryl lowered her book for another long, thoughtful look at Joshua. Maybe it was time she left the convent.

By the time Joshua returned to the boat hours later, Patty and Richardson had begun laying out lunch.

As Joshua toweled himself off, Caryl made her excuses.

"I won't be lunching with you, Mr. Tain," Caryl addressed Joshua's lean muscled back as he stared out to sea. She wondered if he noticed she wasn't using his first name anymore. "While you eat I think it would be a good idea for me to take the boat over to the marina. That way we'll be ready as soon as you are for your tour. If your bathing trunks have dried by then you might wish to continue wearing them under some suitable clothing as we'll go to one of the Territory's best beaches afterwards."

"Fine, captain. Whatever you say," he tossed carelessly over his shoulder.

Caryl gritted her teeth. He could at least have been civil enough to face her when he spoke. Her eyes narrowed for a second before she remembered her resolve to act cool, no matter the provocation from the man. Nodding to the Richardsons, she picked out her servings, then remounted the ladder to the pilothouse. After depositing her plate on a ledge above the controls, she lifted anchor and set the cruiser in motion. Sitting back on her stool she began to eat, trying not to feel miffed by Joshua's coolness. Obviously, the man had a mood a minute. Caryl shrugged and actually managed to put him out of her mind for the twenty minutes it took for the boat to arrive at the Virgin Gorda Yacht Harbor.

Putting her plate down, she concentrated on maneuvering the *Elendil* into her usual place at the pier reserved for boats owned and managed by Janus, Inc. It was a job for the skillful because of all the boats in the marina, but she managed it as neatly and smoothly as a seamstress threading a needle.

Richardson appeared below her on the pier and secured the boat to nearby bollards with the mooring ropes. He turned to look at her and gave her the thumbs up. Caryl grinned back, glad he approved. She had come a long way since Janus hired her. On her first attempt at mooring at this marina she had passed a group of people on a beautiful blue sailboat moored in the harbor who started gesticulating and shouting at her as the *Elendil* glided on. She had waved proudly back at them, thinking they were hailing her. It was only when Richardson had come up to the pilothouse and showed it to her that she realized she had ripped the dinghy from their boat without even noticing.

Caryl watched Christopher Francis, the manager of the car rental company the *Elendil* usually booked with, hurry up the walkway. He waved to Caryl, then stopped to talk to Richardson. The two men had a brief conversation after which Chris, with another wave to Caryl, headed back the way he came.

"I told him we'd be ready in about an hour. Would that be okay with you, Joshua?" Richardson was asking as, empty plate in hand, Caryl lowered herself back to the deck.

"Certainly. I'm almost finished with this fantastic meal." Joshua smiled at Patty, who, to her captain's amusement, almost simpered with delight in response.

"I'll go and change shortly," Joshua continued, looking at Caryl.

"I'm glad to hear you enjoyed your meal, Mr. Tain. We're very lucky to have Patty," she said.

"The Caribbean's true treasure is its people," Joshua responded smoothly, his gaze never moving from Caryl. The air seemed to hum with a sudden electrical charge as Caryl stared back at him, unable to drop or shift her gaze. His brown eyes, hard as flint, were doing things to her she had only read about in romances. She was right, he wasn't

JUST AN AFFAIR

like Alexander at all or rather, he was Alexander cubed.

"I'll see you in a few minutes then," Joshua said, breaking their eyelock with a lazy wink.

Caryl looked at his retreating back in bemused confusion. In one minute, he had basically treated her like part of the furniture; in another he'd made her feel as if she were the only woman in the world. It was incomprehensible.

"Still waters run deep with that one," said Patty sagely behind her.

"What do you mean?"

"I just think he's got a lot going on beneath the surface."

"Maybe but, whatever it is, it isn't any of our business," Caryl repeated her newly adopted mantra as she began to gather the dishes.

Nothing more was said on the subject and they made idle chitchat about other things as they cleared the table. Whenever Caryl thought about the upcoming tour, she felt herself tensing. She could pass it off to Richardson but she didn't want to do that. Land tours, unlike deep dives, were the primary responsibility of the captain and if she didn't do it, Richardson and Patty would think she couldn't handle herself professionally. Captains were supposed to deal with whatever came up, from hurricanes to accidents to attractive male guests. Caryl flexed her shoulders and bit the bullet. She offered her crew the afternoon off, packed a cavernous tote bag with snorkel equipment, sun block and towels, then settled herself on a lounge chair on the aft deck to wait for Joshua.

In front of her a couple pelicans worked hard for their lunch. The big sea birds soared up to a great height then hurtled down to scoop up bills of fish. They did this again and again, until, finally sated, one floated among the moored boats while the other came to rest on a bollard on the adjacent pier.

"I'm ready." Joshua's voice startled her.

"Good." She smiled brightly and got to her feet.

He wore jeans and an olive-colored linen shirt unbuttoned to his chest. He smelled clean and fresh like the earth after heavy rains, and he glowed with good health as if he'd trapped the Caribbean sunlight beneath his skin. Caryl felt a stab of desire in the pit of her stomach and lowered her eyes so he wouldn't see it shining there.

She led the way down the pier, completely conscious of him behind her.

"Hey, Caryl, long time no see," a male voice hailed out to her. Its owner, a short, barrel-chested man, leapt out from a nearby boat to stand beside them.

"How are you, Miguel?" Caryl greeted him warmly. The Dominican Republic native was among the first of the other charter yacht captains to accept her as a colleague despite her gender, and she remained grateful to him for his quick friendship.

"Okay, the season is good and Ana and I are expecting our second." A proud grin almost made his eyes disappear and Caryl's smile deepened.

"I'm happy for you, Miguel. Tell her "hello" for me, will you?"

"Sure, sure. I see you later, eh?" With a last look of curiosity at Joshua, he reboarded his boat and disappeared, troll-like, down the hatch.

The car rental office was inside the marina's shopping complex and they had to pass a couple of open-air restaurants before they got there. Caryl waved to a small group of people she knew under one of the huge umbrellas, conscious with every breath of Joshua beside her. It didn't escape her notice that more than one woman let her eyes linger on her companion. Stealing a look at him, she saw he was watching her. His lips twitched but he didn't say anything and Caryl glanced away, mortified that he'd caught her checking him out yet again. She pushed open the door to the car rental office, thankful for the cool of the air condition and the light scent of the potpourri in a bowl atop some brochures.

"How you doing, Captain?" asked the slim, light-skinned young man behind the counter.

"I'm okay, Louis. And you?

"All the better for seeing you."

Caryl shook her head in wry amusement as he handed her the keys. Louis made some variation on that remark every time he saw her.

"It's the red Suzuki right outside the door. I brought it around."

"Thanks. See you later."

As they pulled out of the marina area, Caryl began her monologue, pointing out places of interest en route to Coppermine Point, Virgin Gorda's best-known historical landmark. Worked on by the Dutch in the 1800s, the copper mine for which the bluff was named was in the process of being restored by the BVI National Parks Trust, Caryl informed Joshua as they entered the dirt road that led up to the site. He was quiet during the ride, asking only for clarifications, and she shot him a distrustful glance. She had not known him long she knew, but she instinctively felt that this docility was quite unlike him.

CHAPTER FOUR

Joshua sighed deeply as he took in the spectacular view at Coppermine Point. Before them, the ruined walls of the old mine rose in testimony to the passage of time while beyond, the sea stretched, blue and indomitable, until the horizon seemed to merge with the sky. A couple sailboats, trailed by rippling, foam-laced scars, made their way to other anchorages.

His eyes fixed on the vista spread out before him; Joshua uncoiled himself from the jeep and went to the mountain's edge. Watching him drink in nature's beauty, Caryl warmed to him. A man with such an unabashed appreciation for nature in its wild, unfettered state, who seemed to adore the sea's magnificence, couldn't be too bad. She hung back, unwilling to disturb him.

He turned to look at her and Caryl felt her heart begin a drumbeat in her chest as his face broke into a smile.

"Thanks for bringing me here, captain," he said.

Unslinging his camera, he began to snap away, framing the view from different angles. Caryl wondered what she would do if he asked her to pose again, but all his concentration was on the endless sea.

When he re-slung the camera over his shoulder, Caryl attempted to give him a brief history of the area, pointing out where the early settlers had worked on the different mining operations, but he had little interest. His gaze returned again and again to the sea or wandered over to the distant hills of the island's North Sound.

Caryl gave up.

"You're not really interested, are you?"

"No, actually, I'm not. Humanity's assault on nature is nothing I don't know about. I would really rather we just sat and looked at the sea for a while. I feel like I can see forever from here." He shrugged. "I don't expect you to understand; you've probably lived with this for a long time. Maybe you don't even see it any more, really see it, but in New York, there's nothing like this. What you get of nature is put on display as if to say, 'Look at this, this is nature, conquered.' I hate that, but this, this is the real thing." He spoke with a barely-suppressed passion and Caryl felt an answering thrill.

"I do know what you mean. The zoos and the parks seem almost like prisoners of war, hemmed in by high-rises and developments," she responded eagerly. The environment was a hot topic at get-togethers on Tortola since generations of British Virgin Islanders had depended on either the land or the sea for their livelihood. She didn't mention her own experiences in New York. That might have brought up how she came to be in the islands, a topic best left alone.

Joshua found a stone slab jutting out of the hillside for them to sit on. Testing his weight on it first, he made room for her to sit beside him.

"Nature is under threat here as elsewhere, though," said Caryl. Even in the relatively short time she had been in the islands she could see the damage being wrought.

"Is it?" Joshua turned to look at her.

"Sure." She enumerated the destruction for him. "The mangroves are disappearing, there are fewer birds because their habitats are vanishing, parts of coral reefs have been destroyed. The whole ecological balance, on land and in the sea, has been disrupted by all the development." Caryl had argued the same point many times before in long-distance conversations with her father. He was an ardent supporter of development and two of Tortola's newest hotels were owned by Janus. David Cassavettes felt that if it helped the people improve their standard of living, then any damage done was necessary. At her urging, however, he pressed the corporation to put policies in place requiring environmental and social impact assessments that were even more thorough than those required by the islands' government. Now, future Janus developments in the Caribbean and around the world would be guided by the new policies and rules to minimize adverse effects on surrounding ecosystems and communities.

Joshua looked out to sea, a pensive look on his face. "Do people care?"

"Yes, some do. We have the national parks system and so on, but there are other areas that need attention and we need much more local involvement in the issues as well."

"People get caught up wanting to make more and more money and don't bother too much about other things."

"Yes, there's that, too, but Mother Nature doesn't have a voice so we have to speak for her and for the wild things."

Joshua turned to her and smiled in a way that seemed to reach down into the roots of his soul and made him look like a totally different person from the mocking stranger who'd caressed her cheek that morning.

"Sometimes I think I'm wasting my life. I've had big success, but I want to do more, much more." His voice was low, somber, almost as if he were speaking to himself. He looked away from her, back out to sea.

"What do you mean?" Caryl looked at his profile and wished she could see his expression.

"I really admire the people who give their lives to a cause, like, you know, those people who chain themselves to trees and put themselves

JUST AN AFFAIR

in front of the whale hunters. I read about them and I'm ready to go out to California or the Amazon myself." He grimaced and gave a choked half-laugh. "I suppose you think I'm a nut. I've never actually said that to anybody else before." He glanced at her.

"No, not a nut." In fact, she wasn't quite sure what to think. Joshua Tain! Out in the middle of nowhere and hugging a tree! She coughed into her hand, hiding the insane giggle that threatened to burst out. Bye-bye GQ, hello fig leaves. "Maybe you can retire early and do things like that," she said, quickly, rubbing her nose to stop herself from laughing. "Or you could do it for a couple months each year, sign up with Earthwatch or Greenpeace. I have a couple of friends who do that."

"You do?"

"Yeah, they were in Ecuador last year building a well. They've been all over the place."

"Have you ever thought of going with them?"

"I've thought of it." Caryl smiled ruefully. "But I just end up donating money."

"The easy way."

"Yes."

For a minute they sat in silence, a nearby bee making the only sound.

"Maybe we can do it together one day," Caryl said, wanting to lighten the mood. He turned to face her, his eyes soft.

"I would like that, captain. Captain of my soul," he whispered. Before she could stop him, he leaned over and brushed her lips with his own.

Startled, Caryl leapt forward and up, but her feet gained only uneven purchase on the slope. She teetered, was about to fall. Glancing down the stony hillside, Caryl half-screamed, half-moaned, her arms windmilling. Almost immediately, strong hands gripped her waist and hauled her unceremoniously backwards, not stopping until she was a good five feet from the edge.

"Stupid woman, you could have been killed. Don't you think before you act?" Joshua shouted, spinning her around to look at him, his face contorted in fury.

Still frightened by her near-accident, Caryl glared at him.

"Well, I didn't fall, did I?" she screamed back, determined to give as good as she got from the blasted man.

"Because of me, that's why." Joshua's index finger stabbed his chest.

"Ha, that's rich, my brother. It was because of you I almost fell."

Joshua stared at her, his nostrils flared, then suddenly his mouth opened wide and his shoulders shook in hearty laughter.

"That takes the cake, woman. How was I to know a simple kiss would make you want to go and kill yourself?"

"Oh, you!" Furious at herself for letting him get to her, Caryl stalked back to the jeep.

Still chuckling, Joshua followed her.

Caryl flung the jeep into gear and tore down the hill, taking a perverse pleasure in the fierce jolting the pitted, rocky road gave them.

"Okay, okay. I apologize. I shouldn't have laughed." Joshua threw up his hands.

"Please. Slow down. You'll kill us both." At this last bit, Joshua once again convulsed with laughter. He looked so funny almost bent over in his seat, Caryl joined in, her laughter merging with his.

Their next stop was on a roadside a few miles from the copper mine.

"What are we going to see here?" Joshua asked as she pulled over and began to get out.

"Zebras."

"Zebras! You're kidding me." Joshua jumped out and looked at her over the roof of the jeep.

"No, there's a biology professor who works with the college on Tortola but she lives here."

Caryl waved her arm at the expanse of land in front of them. "This is her farm and she's got a couple zebras, a horse, sheep, well, the sheep are over on the other side, behind that hill."

Caryl shaded her eyes and looked around for the zebras' distinctive black and white markings.

"Look, there's one." It was about one hundred feet away. Caryl put two fingers in her mouth and whistled. The zebra raised its head to look at her but then lowered it again and walked off.

"Okay, that's Piper. He plays hard to get sometimes. If she heard, Tina'll be here in a moment. She likes people."

Joshua leaned against the fence and peered at Piper.

"Do they mate?"

"They haven't yet. But they've only been here a year or so. They're probably still getting accustomed to everything. Oh, here comes Tina. That's the girl." Caryl pointed to where another zebra was emerging from the bushes surrounding a shady neem tree.

Tina cantered up to them and Caryl put out a hand to stroke the zebra's muzzle. Somewhat tentatively, Joshua patted the animal's back.

"Soon we won't be able to do this."

"She's shutting up shop?

"No, they've broken down this wooden fence about three times trying to escape, so she's planning to build a tall, chain link one."

"Hmm." Joshua said, his tone doubtful. "How did she get them?"

"A dealer in the States. They weren't cheap and she did have to show that she had the area to maintain them. Look, Piper's jealous so he's coming over."

It was true. The zebra was walking towards them but he kept his head down as if he were grazing and had no idea that he was drawing close to the people he'd scorned just a few minutes before. When he was almost close enough to touch, Tina gave a small whinny and butted him gently in the flank. Piper raised his head and looked Joshua in the eye.

"Hello." Joshua scratched behind his new friend's ear.

Piper nosed Tina out of the way and planted himself in front of Caryl.

"He likes you." Joshua's eyes sparkled with delight and Caryl's heart turned in her chest. There was something about the man, more than his looks, more even than his charm. She didn't quite know what it was exactly but it should have been declared illegal.

"He's accustomed to me," she said, keeping her eyes on the zebra and doing her best to act as if she were unaffected by Joshua's nearness.

"Do you feed them?"

"No, she doesn't encourage it."

"They're beautiful."

"Grevy's zebras, the largest of the three species. They can live up to thirty years in captivity."

"Not so much in the wild, right?"

"No." He had such an infectious smile. *Keep it together, Caryl, keep it together. He's just a man and you're on time out, remember.* "In the wild they've got to contend with hungry men, I mean lions, well, men, people. They get hungry." Caryl's voice wobbled and she stopped abruptly. She was making an absolute ass of herself. Without looking at him she took a deep breath and continued. "They have predators to deal with, plus they don't get the good medical care they can in captivity nor the guaranteed feeding."

A frown creased Joshua's forehead. "Give me liberty or give me hay, hmm?" If he'd taken note of her confusion, he'd obviously decided not to call her on it.

Caryl shrugged. It was a huge dilemma. Animals were losing their homes all around the planet, dying of disease, being wiped out by human beings and other predators and needed to be saved. If they couldn't stay in their own habitats but could be kept safe someplace that wasn't too different from their home, then places like these were providing a valuable service.

"A lot of kids would never see one in real life if it weren't for Professor Bernstein. Maybe they'll care more about wildlife, here and all over the world, after meeting the zebras up close," she said.

The zebras began to walk away, their heads together as if gossiping about their visitors. Joshua watched them break into a canter and disappear behind some bushes.

"That's the goal, isn't it?" He raked his hand over his hair and Caryl admired the veins cording his arms. "I think in two hundred years or so we'll be lucky if there are any animals in the wild at all."

"And we'll be lucky if there are any humans anywhere!" she quipped.

Joshua chuckled as they got back into the jeep.

It was in a companionable mood that they headed to the next site, The Baths. Parking the car at the top of a low-rising hill, Caryl led the way down the footpath to the beach. It was relatively empty when they got there. A few people, tourists and locals alike, were scattered here and there. Caryl smiled with satisfaction, she hated crowded beaches. Looking around at the other people she realized Joshua was already attracting attention. Two young girls sitting on beach towels near a couple of the huge boulders that made the beach a must-see for tourists were staring at him. Realizing Caryl had caught them, they turned away, giggling and whispering to each other.

"You're being noticed," Caryl told her companion.

"So are you," he said. He inclined his head to his left.

Following his gaze, Caryl saw a young man watching her from under the shade of a coconut tree.

With a cry of pleased recognition, Caryl dropped the tote and ran over to the tall figure.

"Keith, it's good to see you," she said, reaching up to give him a hug. "You're back! How was it?"

"Tough, girl." Keith's full lips split into a smile over perfectly formed teeth. "But the Germans just ate us up and the English want us to come back to London in September for another Caribbean jam." Keith's band, the Virginites, was in demand overseas as well as locally now that one of their songs, *Island Girl in the City*, was climbing the U.K. charts.

"Hmm, so were you a big hit with the girls?"

"You know the bassman is *always* a hit with the ladies. Every time." Keith pantomimed a riff on an air guitar and winked at her.

"If you say so." Keith with his short dreads, high cheekbones and sleepy-sexy eyes would be a hit with or without a musical instrument.

"Seems like you're not doing so bad on your own either, eh?" He jutted his chin in Joshua's direction.

Caryl glanced back. Joshua had walked to the water's edge and was looking intently out to sea as if he'd forgotten all about her.

"Client. Guess I've got to be getting back."

"Hmm, he looks like he could be a match for you. You broke your decision not to give it up to anybody yet?"

Caryl rolled her eyes. Keith was one of her most persistent admirers but that didn't stop him from wishing her other suitors well.

JUST AN AFFAIR

"No. Nobody's ever gonna get it." She laughed as she spun away from him and waved goodbye. Keith mimed wiping away tears, but there was a broad grin on his face that said he didn't believe her.

Joshua had taken up a position sitting on a boulder from which he could survey the whole beach. He jumped back lightly to the sand as she came up to him.

"I suppose you don't think there's any reason why I should know who that was?" he asked dryly as Caryl picked up the tote and led him to what seemed an impenetrable wall of boulders behind where the two teenage girls sat.

"No, I don't," she responded over her shoulder. Let him stew on that for a while, she thought with grim satisfaction. He wasn't the only one capable of drawing admiration.

Ducking, Caryl led him through a narrow passage that quickly opened into a dusky, intimate chamber brightened only by a natural skylight made where the tops of the giant rocks failed to meet. The walls of the chambers soared thirty, forty feet above their heads. As the waves lapped gently at the shore, Joshua turned full circle, his eyes alive with delight.

"It's like some sort of primitive cathedral. Wow. Look at it." Joshua spoke in the hushed tones deemed appropriate for religious sites. "This definitely calls for pictures." He inserted new film and was soon busy clicking away. Caryl waited patiently; glad there were no other visitors to intrude.

"Captain?"

"Yes?"

"Would you mind posing again for me, here?"

What to say? What to say? Caryl cast about desperately for an answer that would be polite but firm. You don't need a man, you're taking time out, remember. Flaunting yourself in front of the man will only lead to trouble, trouble you already know about and definitely do not need, she told herself sternly. And Janus would definitely not approve. But her self-lecture had no impact. She didn't feel she could help herself. Caryl began to take off her tee shirt and shorts, tossing them over a nearby rock. Underneath, she wore a white one-piece that was also cut to suit her wide-hipped figure. The halter-type top drew attention to her smooth, slim shoulders and toned back, showing them off to perfection.

Joshua gestured for her to walk into the sea and Caryl tried to appear nonchalant, as if this modeling business was something that happened to her every day and as if Joshua were just an ordinary man, and an unattractive one at that. She tried to ignore the fact that his kiss had shown her there was nothing ordinary about him or his effect on her. As his lips touched hers, she had felt a stabbing pleasure radiating out from the pit of her stomach like ripples in a lake. Had she not stopped him when she did, she would surely have been unable to regain the composure she was fighting so hard to maintain in his presence.

Joshua was a guest, a guest, she reminded herself as she walked into the sea and ducked below its cool surface. Holding her breath, she opened her eyes. The sunlight beneath the water made her feel as if she were trapped in emerald, caught in the gem's clear green light. She wished she could stay there like that, not have to resurface and face Joshua and all the feelings he stirred in her, but her lungs were bursting. Caryl let herself rise back to the surface and turned around to make her way back to shore.

Joshua was using a towel to pillow his camera on a rock and he began to click away as Caryl rose out of the sea, her short hair beaded with sparkling drops, and walked towards him. Beyond commanding her to walk slower, Joshua said nothing until finally she was standing only a few feet away. He straightened and gave her a long, considering look.

Caryl stepped back.

"Yes? What is it? Is something wrong?"

"Nothing's wrong. Absolutely nothing. Do you know how perfect you are?"

"I don't think I should be hearing this."

"I think you're just the person who should hear. Who else?" In three strides Joshua closed the distance between them to enfold her in his arms. His mouth came down on hers and Caryl felt all her resolve wash away in a flood of passion. Her arms rose to encircle his neck as she returned his kiss with equal fervor, pressing her body into his hard, muscular length.

"I've wanted to do this since I first laid eyes on you," Joshua groaned, pulling his lips from her mouth to rain kisses down her neck, leaving a trail of fire as he went. His hand rose to tug aside her swimsuit and expose a breast to his questing lips. The feel of his tongue on her nipple shocked Caryl into remembering her pledge of abstinence.

"No. No. I can't do this." She tore herself from his embrace and turning, ran for the grotto's entrance, pulling the top of her suit back into place.

Emerging into the bright sunlight, she walked to the opposite side of the beach and threw herself on the bare sand, glad Keith was no longer around. Joshua didn't follow her and she didn't know whether she felt glad or sorry about that. Their embrace just now should never have happened but she'd done nothing to prevent it. If she were honest, she would admit hoping to have just that effect on him. Caryl hid her face in her hands and took a deep shuddering breath. Abstinence wasn't all it was cracked up to be but it was a hell of a lot better than the alternative - heartbreak, humiliation and worse. She just couldn't risk going down that road again, not for any man and not for Joshua. He would have to understand. Caryl let the sun's heat sink into her bones like warm honey pouring from a rock. It took a while but eventually her heart stopped racing and her jangled nerves quieted.

The sun went from being almost directly overhead to hiding behind a mountain by the time Joshua emerged from the grotto. His hair was beaded with water and his towel hung heavily around his neck. Beyond glancing at her, he appeared to take no other note of her presence before setting off back up the hillside path that led to the jeep. Along with his camera, he carried the tote. Caryl followed him in silence. At the top, he handed her the bag and she saw that her clothes were packed neatly inside. She felt so miserable she had forgotten all about them. Her thanks were met with continued silence and he waited in the Suzuki as she pulled on her shorts and buttoned her shirt.

Caryl matched his silence which, this time, was both complete and far from companionable. If he had unbent just a little and talked to her she would have explained. Not everything, not about Alexander. But she would have told him about her vow to abstain from sex and relationships, no matter the temptation, for at least one year. That was the time she had promised herself to get her head and heart together and he had to understand. She didn't want him to think she was just playing some kind of mind game with him. But Joshua kept his head straight and his lips zipped so she didn't say anything. He was obviously in no mood to listen to what she might have to say. By the time, they arrived back at the marina, Caryl felt as if the tension between them had hardened into a glacier no tropical sun could melt. She returned the jeep's keys to the rental car company and slowly followed Joshua's lithe figure down the walkway to the *Elendil*, her shoulders drooping. Richardson was sitting on deck and informed them that his wife was fixing dinner.

Joshua nodded curtly at this news before striding into the saloon. Richardson's brow rose.

"Everything went okay, Caryl?"

"No, but I don't want to talk about it. Not now, anyway." Right now she felt she just needed to clear her head. "I'm going to take a shower and a nap." And Caryl made a beeline for her cabin.

CHAPTER FIVE

The following day, Caryl woke early and hurried up on deck after rousing Richardson to make preparations for departing Virgin Gorda. There was no one around on the dock as Richardson jumped down to undo the ropes and Caryl went up to the pilothouse. In minutes, the *Elendil* was sliding quickly and quietly from its place, threading its way past the other boats in the harbor.

As she sat at the helm, Caryl could tell it was going to be a beautiful day. A bank of clouds on the horizon looked like peach-colored cotton candy and, in the distance, Tortola's hills were bathed in the golden glow of the rising sun.

Caryl waved to a black couple who motored across her path in a small dinghy and they waved enthusiastically back. Below her, she could hear the clatter of cutlery and the murmur of lowered voices as Richardson and Patty laid the table. She wondered if they were talking about her and Joshua, about what may or may not have happened on the tour yesterday. It would certainly have been on her mind if she were them. In fact, getting it out of her mind had taken her way past her bedtime last night. On the one hand she wished she could somehow disappear off the boat and on the other she couldn't wait to see the man again. Did she really have so little self-possession she couldn't keep it together around him? It was as if her relationship with Alexander never taught her anything. Where was the self-control she thought her year of celibacy had strengthened?

Caryl was deep into her ruminations and they were almost at their

JUST AN AFFAIR

next stop when she heard Joshua's deep voice greeting her crew. Caryl's stomach clenched and she counted to ten slowly, willing herself to relax. If he had stopped talking to her, well, so much the better. The challenge he posed to her equilibrium would be reduced.

Caryl headed the *Elendil* into Lee Bay on Salt Island and made use of the moorings system provided by the National Parks Trust. She checked over her equipment, flipped through her logbook, then, finding no other reason to dawdle, descended to the aft deck to join the others. Patty, Richardson, and Joshua were all seated around the table.

Richardson was well into an explanation of the moorings system and barely nodded to Caryl. His hands flew in front of him as he gave a detailed description of what he and Joshua would see on their dive to the HMS *Rhone* later that day.

Caryl sat down, served herself and made an effort to join in, adding that the wreck was by no means the only one in the BVI. Other wrecks were scattered throughout the islands, many of them near Anegada, the northernmost island whose large barrier reef was a challenge for navigators. The *Rhone* was the most picturesque of all, however, which explained why it was chosen as the location for the 1980s movie, *The Deep*, starring Jacqueline Bisset.

"At any rate, it's a good dive site for advanced and beginner divers alike," Caryl said, smiling at the *Elendil's* client. But she might as well not have bothered. Joshua, after training a particularly penetrating glance on her, seemed to forget she existed.

"What is going on with you?" Patty whispered to her later in the galley as she put away the breakfast dishes.

"Nothing, nothing. What do you think could be going on?"

"Listen, missy, you don't fool me. You're looking like something the cat wouldn't drag in and he's suddenly pretending you don't exist. What happened yesterday on the tour?"

"I don't know, Patty. That's the truth. One minute we're having a good time then…but I don't want to talk about it yet. Okay?"

"Sure, okay. Look, Caryl, you know I'm not just being nosy."

Caryl gave the older woman a quick hug. "I know," she said.

A few minutes later, Caryl retreated to the pilothouse, determined to concentrate on something other than the *Elendil's* male guest and the way he made her feel. She was bent over a copy of the latest, best-selling spy thriller when she felt a hard, warm hand cup her bent neck. She jumped up, spinning to face Joshua.

"No falling off down a hill this time, eh?" He grinned at her and her heart lurched crazily.

"What is your problem?"

"I want you. You've cast a spell on me, my captain."

"What? Are you mad? You've been ignoring me. You haven't talked to me since yesterday afternoon." Her complaint burst out of her before she had a chance to stop it.

"What did you expect? Sometimes I feel like I would rather kiss you than speak to you," he murmured. "I want to curse the grapes of joy and drip red wine all over your body." He nuzzled her neck.

"That sounds a bit like a Langston Hughes poem I read in high school," Caryl said, even as her knees turned to water at the touch of his lips on her neck.

"It's his alright." Joshua answered. "I can't remember exactly how the poem goes but I know he had to be thinking of you when he wrote it."

In the next second they were in each other's arms and his lips had gained firm possession of hers in a caress that set Caryl ablaze with desire. In passionate betrayal of her common sense she hugged his hard body to hers, reveling in the feel of him against her.

"Why do you blow hot and cold?" he asked, his mouth against

her throat.

"Me? What about you?"

"Woman, from the time I saw you I've made it clear that I want you. I don't think I've left you in any two minds about it."

"Maybe not. But I am. In two minds, I mean." With a pain she felt almost physically, Caryl squirmed out of his arms and put as much distance as she could between them.

"What do you mean?" Joshua's eyes narrowed.

"I made a pledge to myself. To be celibate for at least a year. I don't want to break it."

"When will this year be up?"

Caryl did some quick calculations.

"In about seven weeks."

"That's alright. That's over in no time. I don't mind. You know, there's a lot we can get going with that won't violate your pledge." He reached for her but she spun out of his way.

"No, you don't understand. I mean I don't want a man."

Joshua drew back. His eyebrows shot into his hairline.

"You're gay?"

"No," Caryl snapped. She drew a hand across her forehead, pressing her thumb into her temples. "I'm just taking a break from relationships, that's all."

Joshua leaned back against the stool she'd been sitting on just a few minutes ago.

"I can't believe it. I meet a knockout woman and she tells me she's on break."

Looking at him, Caryl could well believe he hadn't heard that before.

"So where does that leave us?"

"Without an 'us'," Caryl answered curtly. This was so difficult.

Even as she congratulated herself on her backbone, she itched to jump his crazy-sexy bones.

"Baby, I can't believe you mean that." He took a step towards her, his eyes soft and pleading.

Caryl stood her ground.

"I do." She made her voice as hard and flinty as she could. He must have bought it because he brought up short and something changed in his face.

"As you wish." His voice was hard enough to match hers and for a minute Caryl wanted to shout that she was taking it all back. But an image of Alexander came unbidden to mind and Caryl pressed her lips shut.

Joshua turned and left the pilothouse.

Caryl crossed to her stool and sank weakly into the seat. There was something she had to keep in mind every time she thought about giving in to her desire: The fact that Joshua wanted her didn't mean he was in love with her. In fact, he had never said word one about love. Clearly, he was just seeking a diversion, a hot holiday affair he could boast about to his friends back in New York. Not that Joshua came over like the kiss-and-tell type, just the opposite, but still, one never knew with men.

Below on deck, she heard Joshua and Richardson begin their preparations for their two-tank dive to the *Rhone*. Both Caryl and her first mate had advanced certification in most of the types of diving to be found in island waters, but Richardson was more experienced.

The *Rhone*, a British ship, had split in two and sunk during a hurricane in the 1800s. They would tour her two halves, giving Joshua the opportunity to take pictures of the fish, sponge and other life in residence at the site.

Caryl strained to hear what the two men were saying as the

JUST AN AFFAIR

Elendil rocked gently in place, but Richardson was simply going over the diving procedure. Joshua's PADI certificate obviously hadn't gathered dust; his questions about hand signs showed he knew what was involved. Caryl peeped at them and saw Joshua checking his primary regulator hose. He looked around to say something to Richardson and Caryl jumped back so he wouldn't see her spying on him like some silly adolescent.

Caryl re-opened her book after splashes signaled the divers' departure but it was no use. The words all seemed to run into each other, making no sense. All she could think of was Joshua Tain. Tossing the book aside, she went in search of Patty, making a beeline for the galley where the older woman spent most of her time. As Caryl entered, Patty was using a rolling pin to vigorously flatten a ball of dough. Four other balls arrayed on the kitchen and the strong smell of curry signaled that *rotis* were on the menu for lunch.

"Need help?"

"No, child. Everything is going on fine."

Caryl nodded and leant pensively against the doorjamb.

Patty put down the rolling pin.

"You don't look quite like how you did at lunch. You're looking funny. I don't know how to put it exactly." Patty stared at her, her brow up quizzically. "Cautious, like a cat with a bowl of cream in front of her who's not sure it's really cream and not, say, glue."

Caryl burst out laughing.

"Oh, Patty, you're too much. Cats and I don't have a thing in common."

"Though your lips are tight like a snake swallowing a bush pig I think your expression has more than a little bit to do with our handsome guest."

Caryl sighed.

"Maybe he's getting you to rethink your whole Sister Celibate thing, eh?"

"No, Patty. That's just not up for debate. I made a pledge to myself. I can't just abandon my plans at the first sight of a handsome man."

"One, this isn't your first sight of a handsome man. Remember Samuel Prescod? He liked you too." Samuel was a hotel owner on Tortola who had made his interest in Caryl known almost as soon as she set foot on the island. "He wasn't anything to sneeze at in the looks department and then there was Gilbert Shipmann and Keith, what was his name? You know who I mean, the musician. Caryl, there's been no end of attractive guys after you and you haven't given them a second look. Joshua is the first one who's gotten under your skin."

"Hmm." Caryl thought about it. "You could be right, but why?"

"Who knows? That's how the heart works. But the bigger question is why you just can't go along with it."

"I chose to take time off because I needed it." Caryl stopped. She was on the brink of confiding in Patty about Alexander but she wasn't quite ready to talk about him yet. Almost a year, but the wound still throbbed like her heartbreak was today's news. "I can't give in now."

Patty gave her a shrewd glance. "Can't or won't? Sometimes we hurt ourselves more when we don't take a chance than when we do. I don't know why you've given yourself time off and I don't want to know until you're ready to tell me, but maybe your feelings for Joshua are your body's way of telling you to forget the calendar and go with your heart."

Caryl gave a weak laugh. That was exactly what she'd told herself about Alexander two years ago. *Go with your heart, girl*. Look where that had gotten her. All her dreams of having it all, starting a family while kicking legal ass, had gone up in smoke just because she'd followed her heart and fallen for a married man. That heart crap was just a bill of goods and she didn't plan to fall for it again. Not in this lifetime.

Feeling virtuous but somehow depressed, Caryl left Patty to her galley and headed for her cabin. Curling herself around her feather pillow, she thought about what she'd said to the older woman. Every word of it was true but neither could she deny that every fiber of her being responded to the man, flamed at his touch. Maybe Patty was right and it was time to test the relationship waters, but wanting a man like Joshua Tain was like boating in rough and uncharted seas. Dangerous. Exhilarating. Foolhardy. But at least he wasn't married. There was no way any sister in her right mind would let a husband like Joshua roll out on vacation alone.

Eventually, the soothing motion of the boat on the waves and her own tiredness lulled Caryl to sleep.

Hours passed before she reawaked.

"Had a good nap, eh? I looked in on you but you were out like a light," Patty said when she went back up on deck. "You couldn't have gotten much sleep last night."

"No, I didn't, actually." Caryl watched her warily. All she needed now was to be accused of dereliction of duty.

"The men are back. Joshua loved it."

"Oh, good. I'm glad." And she was. She would have loved to talk to him about it but he might not feel like talking, not to her at any rate.

Caryl followed Patty through the saloon and began to remove the lunch dishes from the dumbwaiter. A few minutes later Joshua and Richardson joined them.

Joshua wore a pair of cotton shorts and an unbuttoned shirt of gauzy white linen that showed off his dark, muscular chest. He looked like some master craftsman's carving, an ebony sculpture come to life before her eyes. Caryl dragged her eyes away from him by a superhuman effort of will. As the others arranged themselves around the table, Caryl took a deep breath and looked out to sea. Joshua had said nothing to her, merely glancing her way as he entered the aft deck. Richardson moved in to fill the void, his voice loud and, to Caryl's ears, over-hearty as he talked about that morning's dive.

The *rotis* were served wrapped around curried chicken, with mango chutney and stir-fried vegetables on the side. Joshua decided to forego the cutlery and was soon licking enthusiastically at the curry gravy running down his fingers. Throughout the meal Caryl shot quick glances at him but he kept his eyes turned toward Richardson. It was her own fault. Hadn't she told the man she wasn't interested? He'd have to be a glutton for punishment to still seek her out. Caryl felt miserable. If only he would look at her, smile, say something, but he seemed to have come to a decision of his own and ignored her. Caryl began to think maybe she had made a mistake. No man had ever stirred her senses the way Joshua Tain did. Maybe they should get it on and she could get him out of her system. So what if any relationship might be temporary? She could settle for just one or two nights with this sexy man who inflamed all her senses, couldn't she?

Embarrassed at the turn her thoughts were taking, Caryl glanced quickly around the table.

Patty was staring at her with an indecipherable expression on her face but Joshua and Richardson were chatting amiably about their

JUST AN AFFAIR

dive and about the *Chikuzen,* a recent wreck north of Virgin Gorda. Richardson whipped a book out of his pocket on the marine life in the islands and began teaching Joshua the names of the various fish and other marine life they had seen.

Caryl put a forkful of *roti* in her mouth and smiled with what she hoped was innocent friendliness at Patty.

Caryl maneuvered the *Elendil* into the harbor and up to a vacant slip at the Peter Island Resort and Marina around mid-afternoon. Peter Island had once been owned by a local family before being bought by the Amway Corporation. It remained largely undeveloped and was a favorite destination for the rich and famous, which explained the crowded harbor. Caryl watched Richardson secure the boat to the jetty, then joined him on deck below.

"Want to go for a drink? Patty's reading and Joshua's gone to his stateroom." Richardson winked at her. If he had his suspicions about what was going on between her and Joshua, he was clearly keeping them to himself.

"I'd love to." She could do with a drink and some company that didn't include Joshua Tain, plus it would give her something to do. If they left now she need not see their guest again until dinner.

The resort was just a stone's throw away from the dock but it was enough of a walk for Caryl to feel soothed by the trade winds blowing like a balm over her face. By the time she and Richardson arrived at the bar, she had almost forgotten her worries about Joshua Tain and was looking forward to a good time. A group of noisy charter people was gathered to one side of the bar and Caryl knew she'd made the right decision to take a break. Chartering in the islands was about being in a club of loud-talking, hard-drinking, sometimes contentious but always there-for-you-in-a-storm men and women. Caryl had not understood that at first and they had been wary of her too. New people had to prove themselves; they had to show they were responsible yachties who were ready to lend a helping hand in an emergency and always took care not to damage the environment. Then and only then were newcomers accepted into the club.

Now that Caryl belonged, she and Richardson were greeted with wide smiles, claps on the back, and proffered drinks. Caryl refused a beer and ordered a fruit punch without the rum while Richardson accepted a Red Stripe, his favorite beer. The shadows around the pool beyond the bar lengthened as the group got louder and bigger with new arrivals, some of whom included yacht clients who were repeat visitors and known to many in the group. Caryl was laughing at a joke one of them had made about a mix-up with Immigration the day before when, out of the corner of her eye, she saw a tall figure enter the bar area. She almost spilled the drink in her hand as she jumped up and craned her neck to see if it was Joshua. It was. Caryl dropped back down. She had not even missed or thought about him in the last, she glanced at her watch, three hours. Goodness, she should have returned to the *Elendil* by now. No wonder the man was looking for her.

"Hey, Caryl, you're not listening." The man waved his hand in front her face.

"I'm sorry, Eddie. I've got to go." She shot a look in Joshua's direction wondering if he had seen her yet. He had. He was standing looking at her, his hands in his pockets, waiting. Like he knew she would notice him without his having to call to her or signal for her attention in any way. Caryl grimaced and put down her drink.

JUST AN AFFAIR

"You're coming back?" Eddie asked. He was captain of the *Saracen*, a sailboat also owned by Janus.

"I don't think so."

"I guess I know why." He glanced at Joshua and smirked.

Caryl rolled her eyes but made no answer as she began to push through the small crowd. The closer she got to Joshua, the tenser she began to feel. By the time she reached him, her chest was as tight as a street boxer's fist.

"Good evening, Mr...," she started.

He didn't give her a chance to finish.

"Patty said I would find you here," he bit out, frowning. Caryl's brows soared. The man was insufferable. Did he really think she was just going to sit, forlorn, in her cabin waiting for him to notice her again?

Collecting herself, she pasted on what she hoped was a gracious smile. Insufferable or not, he *was* her client.

"Yes," she answered. "Everybody seemed occupied so Richardson and I came here. Would you care to join us?" She gestured toward the others and realized that the group's decibel level had dropped and curious glances were being thrown their way. Caryl sighed to herself. Another thing about yachties was their insatiable curiosity. That had taken a big city girl like herself a lot of getting used to.

"No. Actually, I think I'll just go for a walk. I'll see you later." He turned and left. Caryl stared after him. Brother-man had a mood for every hour. Heck, every nanosecond. She had said nothing for him to get snippy about, so what was his problem? She wasn't supposed to enjoy herself without him around or something? She half-hoped he would get lost. For good. It would take some doing on the seven square mile island but could be accomplished with effort. Or help.

"Was that one of your clients, Caryl?" A woman detached herself to come and stand next to Caryl, her eyes on Joshua's retreating back. "Are you keeping him for yourself? Why didn't you introduce me?"

Caryl could not believe it, though she should have known. Maisie was a red-haired white woman who had been chartering in the islands for as long as anyone could remember. Flaunting every rule in her employer's book, she made sure she bedded as many of her clients as she could in the short time a charter took. Married or single, it was all the same to her. And, if she wasn't on charter, then other people's clients were fair game.

"Give me a break, Maisie."

"Oh, come on, Caryl. He's too fine not to be shared. Richardson," Maisie called out, her voice rising above the din, waving to get his attention.

"Yeah, Maisie. What's up, girl? Ready for me to stand in as one of your studs? I keep telling you, you're letting this big body fool you. The race is not to the lean but to those who endure." Richardson was hugely amused by Maisie and never lost an opportunity to josh her, as he put it. Everyone knew he was devoted to Patty so he was perfectly safe.

Maisie grinned at him.

"Your turn soon come, big man. Soon come."

"Never mind that," Caryl broke in before Richardson could make a response. "I'm going back to the *Elendil*." Caryl had had enough. She edged towards the door.

"Whoa, hold on, cap. You want I should come too?"

Maisie watched the exchange with a smile on her face. Caryl knew the woman couldn't wait to get Richardson alone to interrogate him about Joshua but Richardson was having a good time and it really didn't matter what he told her about their client. From what she'd seen, Joshua would be more than a match for any day-tripper like Maisie.

JUST AN AFFAIR

Caryl grinned at her intentional pun on the Beatles song. For yachties, day-trippers were people who only wanted to go out for a few hours, preferring the land to be under their beds at night.

"No, Richardson, stay. Don't let them keep you up all night, though. Remember we've an early start tomorrow."

"Aye, captain." Richardson barely had a chance to raise his beer bottle and smile at her before Maisie took his arm and with an ironic little wave to Caryl, led him off.

Caryl trudged back to the boat, unseeing and uncaring that the stars shone brightly above her and that the moon had transformed the harbor into a silvery dream. She was beginning to think Joshua was living proof that abstinence had a lot more going for it than even the Surgeon General knew.

Patty was reading in the saloon when Caryl came aboard.

"Oh, you're back already?"

"Sure. I didn't plan to overnight." Caryl instantly regretted her sarcasm and let a sheepish look cross her face so Patty would know. She glanced at the older woman.

"I know, it's just…I thought…Oh well, did you see Mr. Tain? He said he'd be dining at the restaurant."

"Yes." Caryl grimaced. "He went for a walk. I left Richardson at the bar. Look," she said impulsively. "Why don't you join him?"

Patty shrugged and smiled. "I don't know…I suppose I could."

"Go then. It's okay. I'll hold down the fort," Caryl encouraged. She recovered the thriller she was reading earlier and settled on the couch, thinking she would read until the others returned. Five chapters later none of the three were back and after making her brief log entries, Caryl called it a night.

CHAPTER SIX

Waking before dawn the next morning, Caryl emerged on the aft deck to find Richardson there waiting for her. Greeting each other quietly, they cast off and headed to Norman Island. A discovery of pirate treasure there in the early 1900s had inspired Robert Louis Stevenson to write his famous *Treasure Island* and this, along with its coastal caves, made the islet a favorite with tourists.

From their first stop at Treasure Bay, they would cruise over to The Bight where the *Elendil*'s guests could hike to the top of Pear Point. Local legend had it that the pirates who sailed the islands in past centuries hid their ships in The Bight and posted lookouts on Pear Point, so-called because of its rounded tip. When a likely looking vessel hove into view, the pirates sailed out to rob it of its treasures. Pots of stolen gold and precious jewels were said to be buried all over the island, but if any had been discovered in the last five or six decades, the finders were keeping it a well-guarded secret.

Few boats were at the popular anchorage and Caryl was again able to make use of the

National Parks Trust's mooring system. The trip there from Peter Island had taken a half hour and none of the others were up yet by the time she rejoined Richardson on the aft-deck.

"We had a really nice dinner last night. You should have stayed," Richardson told her. His voice sounded hoarse but Caryl attributed this to his socializing. "Joshua joined us, to Maisie's great delight."

JUST AN AFFAIR

Caryl tried to subdue the stab of jealousy turning like a splinter in her chest.

"Oh," she said, her voice studiously casual.

"Yeah." Richardson began to laugh at the memory. "Joshua didn't take her on none at all. He just flicked her away like a mosquito."

"Oh." Caryl perked up. This was good to hear. So he was not a complete skirt chaser after all.

"No, man. He wasn't interested in her. It was you the man was looking for last night."

"Well, that's why he came up to us at the bar, wasn't it?" Caryl stared at a newcomer to the anchorage, a sleek red sailboat she had seen here and there about the islands. The crew was attempting to moor her but was clearly having some difficulty.

"No, I mean, he came looking for you to join him for dinner."

"Whaat?" Caryl's heart lurched. "What?" she demanded again, turning to give Richardson her full attention. "How do you know? He said so?"

"That's what he told Patty when he left the *Elendil* last night, that he intended to join the captain for dinner. I don't think he knows any other captains around here, do you?" Richardson grinned, enjoying the effect his news was having on her.

Caryl gave him a look she hoped was cutting.

"But why didn't he say so then?"

"Him, Mars. You, Venus." Richardson gave a hearty chuckle.

Caryl glared at him. Try, just try, to get a straight answer from the man when he was in a good mood. It was like putting up a sail in a hurricane.

"Just how many Red Stripes did you say you had last night?" she snapped, running her hand over her short hair.

"Ooh, pussy cat."

Caryl took a threatening step toward him and Richardson threw his hands up in mock fear.

"Okay, okay. I'll be good." The big man sobered up. "I don't know why he didn't say anything. You can't expect other people to say and do things the way you would or when you would or anything at all like that. My guess is he got scared when he saw all the other people around you." Caryl sniffed at the idea of Joshua Tain being scared of anything but didn't argue the point. "He didn't know how you would react, didn't want to put himself out there with an audience. Something like that maybe." Richardson's tone showed he wasn't too convinced himself. "You'd have to ask him that one."

"I can't do that. I can't even let him know you told me. Or can I? Should I?"

Richardson hunched his shoulders and dropped them. "That's up to you, me girl. But I'll tell you, it's been my experience that a man shouldn't let a woman know everything he knows and I think that goes vice versa, eh?" Richardson sneezed loudly, then gave a couple of dry coughs.

"You're right but…" Caryl was going to ask if Joshua had said anything indicating interest in her but she let it drop. That he had asked or rather told someone he wanted her to go to dinner with him was good enough for now. Patty's reaction to her appearance back on the *Elendil* was no longer a mystery. But why hadn't she said something? If she had, Caryl knew she would have gone right back out to look for him.

"I was thinking…" Richardson interrupted her thoughts. "He seems very knowledgeable about a lot of things. I'm wondering if he's on Wall Street or something. He looks like a stockbroker."

Caryl sighed. Where did Richardson get his ideas?

"Please," she said, holding up a hand as if to ward off his miscon-

JUST AN AFFAIR

ceptions. "All people on Wall Street know about is money and how to make more of it." She thought about her own Merrill Lynch broker who had the personality of a limpet but was brilliant at picking bargain stocks. "I guess that means you still don't know what he does for a living. It's day four. You must be losing your touch," she teased.

"Yeah, yeah. Don't I know it!" Richardson made that sucking sound with his teeth that came so natural to West Indians but which she had yet to master. "Captain, I'm not feeling so good. It feels almost like a cold coming on. You mind if you take him to the Caves instead of me?"

Now that she thought about it, he did look a bit peaky and he had been sneezing and coughing.

"Sure. No problem." She would have preferred to stay as far away from Joshua as she could but colds were things best nipped in the bud. If she didn't want Richardson to feel even worse he should look after himself now.

Joshua and Patty soon joined them on deck. Joshua threw a smoldering glance in her direction but confined himself to conversing with her crew.

After breakfast, Caryl informed Joshua that, at his convenience, she would offer him a tour of the nearby caves.

One eyebrow rose.

"Is that the only thing you can offer me?" He stared straight at her. The double entendre was obvious and Caryl dropped her eyes to her plate in confusion.

"Yes," she managed to reply.

She was saved from having to make a further response by loud throat-clearing from Patty, who rose to begin taking the dishes off the table. Everyone dispersed and it was not until mid-morning that Patty knocked on Caryl's cabin door to tell her Joshua was ready for their excursion. Wearing a modestly trimmed racing tank with full bottom coverage Caryl met him on the aft deck in minutes. Joshua wore white trunks, his magnificent physique bringing reluctant appreciation from Caryl, who lowered her eyes so he couldn't read her expression.

She bent over the storage bin containing the snorkeling and diving equipment and handed him a mask, tube and flippers.

"Will this be a long swim?"

"No, about an hour and a half or so."

"Any chance of finding us a few chests of buried treasure?"

"As much chance as finding Jimmy Hoffa," Caryl said wryly, making herself busy arranging her own goggles and flippers so he wouldn't notice the effect his smile had on her. She stepped off the swimming platform into the warm, clear, water. Joshua followed her in and they started their exploration of the caves and their fishy inhabitants.

Schools of yellowtail and sergeant majors flashed past them while giant fans and purple tube sponges reached up from the sandy floor, as if in greeting. Caryl had forgotten to warn him about fire coral which stung any unwise enough to touch it, but she saw from the careful way he maneuvered around a giant outcrop that he was aware of the danger. A pity. A touch of the coral's burn would have done him a world of good, she thought, sighing internally.

The first cave she led him to was actually quite shallow and Caryl heaved herself up on a rock to wait for Joshua, who was diverted by a school of playful butterfly fish.

"Can we walk in from here?" he asked, finally rising from the water like some pagan sea god.

"Yes, but it doesn't go in very far. We can snorkel over to the other caves, they're a bit deeper." She led the way, determined to keep her eyes off him so she could still the wild beating of her heart at his nearness. As they swam she was careful to keep a sedate distance from him, leading him far into the northernmost cave for a look at the golden cup corals on the walls then back out again. For his part, Joshua was entranced by the fish and the corals and, eventually, Caryl relaxed enough to enjoy the swim herself.

"I just realized…" Caryl said when they got back to the *Elendil*. "You forgot to take your camera."

"No, I didn't. I just realized that sometimes you see less, not more, when you're looking through a lens so I thought I'd give it a rest."

"Mmm." Caryl darted a suspicious look at him, wondering what he meant, but he had turned his back to her. He pushed off his mask and dropped it into the bin.

"I really enjoyed that. In fact," he faced her, "I've really enjoyed everything so far."

"Everything?" Caryl let a little flirtatious note color her voice.

"Everything," he repeated, his voice raspy. "Some more, much more than others, of course." Caryl stared at him, unable to look away, to move.

"Joshua." Richardson burst out on the aft deck. "There's a call for…" The big man's voice faded as he realized he had interrupted something. "I'm sorry." His eyes shifted from one to the other but Joshua's never left Caryl's face.

"Who is it?"

"Your grandmother."

Joshua broke eye contact with Caryl and his face relaxed with pleasure.

"Oh, good. I missed her earlier. Wait for me." He squeezed Caryl's arm. "I'll be back." He strode past Richardson into the saloon.

"Girl, I'm sorry. You okay? You look like you just seen the inside of Davy Jones's locker."

"Me? No, I'm fine." Caryl didn't know whether to be glad or sorry for the interruption. One more minute and all her resolve to stay out of the man's arms would have been thrown to the winds like a New Year's resolution. "I'm going to change. See you later." Caryl gave Richardson a tight smile and walked past him. There was just no way she was going to sit about on the aft deck waiting for Joshua to return. That would be as foolish as going out in a category five hurricane with an umbrella.

In her cabin, Caryl stepped out of her swimsuit and looked at herself in the mirror. Her nipples were taut and it wasn't because of the air conditioning. Picking up a towel and wrapping herself in it, she dropped down on the bed and closed her eyes to block out the image of Joshua standing in the sea like some African water god. She didn't know how to make what she was feeling for the man go away.

Caryl twisted around on her belly and pondered the pillow in front of her. Maybe if she gave in to temptation, then he would lose his effect on her. Maybe it was like eating chocolate cake. Hold out and you practically went mad wanting it. Give in, and after a couple mouthfuls you were wondering what the fuss was about and calculating how much exercise you'd have to do to make sure it didn't sit on your hips forever. Maybe, after all, she *should* let him kiss her, play with her navel, suck on her nipples. A jolt of lightning zipped up to Caryl's chest from her groin and she rolled over, jumped up and ran to the shower. She turned on the cold water full power and stepped in. If it worked for men, it could work for her.

Caryl lifted her face and let the water stream over her forehead, down her neck. A year without sex and she had been doing good, real good. Had hardly missed the bump and grind at all, but now Joshua Tain, Tall Dark and All That, was making her feel as hot and horny as a bitch in heat. It wasn't fair. It had to stop. One way or another.

That afternoon, Caryl guided the boat to its next anchorage on Norman Island and tried not to dwell on thoughts of Joshua. The *Elendil* plowed into oncoming waves and Caryl focused on the feel of the sea beneath the boat, on the coolness of the helm beneath her hands. She concentrated on the heat of the sun bathing the roof of the pilothouse and on the wind that caressed her face like an old friend, bringing to her nose the sharp scent of salt and sea. Joshua receded from her mind and Caryl began to feel more relaxed than she had in days.

"Will you be taking me on the hike?"

Caryl jumped as if bitten, turning around on her stool to stare at Joshua. Her pulse thundered in her ears and she realized she was only fooling herself. She was wildly attracted to this man. Feeling nothing for him was not an option, not if he was anywhere within sight, smell and sound.

"Umm. No. I don't know…Richardson…," she stuttered. She had forgotten about the blasted hike.

"Captain, captain. Why so flustered?" he asked her softly, his brown eyes warm.

"Nothing. I'm not flustered, I mean," she hissed, disturbed by the stirrings in her pelvis, a region that, lately, had been making her more and more aware of its existence.

Reaching out, Joshua grabbed her left hand. Instinctively, she tried to snatch it back but his grip was firm.

"Why don't you wear a ring?" he asked, turning her hand over to look at it.

"Because I'm not married. Isn't that the usual reason why?" She managed to twist her hand out of his grasp.

"You could be one of those people who don't wear their rings, hiding the fact that they're taken or something. I'm not sure I'm buying the celibacy thing."

"Good, because I'm not selling and I don't lie. If I were married to the man of my dreams, I'd be proud to wear his ring."

"And who is he, this dream man?" Joshua's lips twitched in amusement.

"I haven't met him yet," Caryl snapped. *And if it's you, you'll be the last to know.*

"Yes, but what will he be like? You must have some idea. Otherwise, how will you recognize him?"

"Why do you want to know? It isn't any of your business."

"It could be."

Caryl decided to ignore that. "I have no idea what he'll look like or how he'll be but my heart will know him." The one thing she was sure of was that he would be completely single, no wife, no girlfriend, no nothing lurking in the background.

Joshua was silent, his eyes unreadable.

"You still haven't answered me," he prompted her. "The hike?"

"I don't know," she said, summoning all her cool. "I'll have to see if Richardson is up to it." But she was already preparing herself for the prospect of taking Joshua out alone. With an indifference she didn't feel, she returned her gaze to the sea in front of them.

Despite the fact that every cell in her body was alert to Joshua's nearness, she studiously ignored him, keeping her eyes fixed on the view in front of her. He stood beside her for a couple of tense seconds, seemed about to say something, then made for the ladder instead. When she was sure he'd really gone, Caryl released the breath she'd been holding and relaxed, allowing her shoulders to drop.

CHAPTER SEVEN

"How high is it?" Joshua asked. He was on his best behavior now that they had begun their hike to Pear Point. Richardson hadn't appeared for lunch and Patty reported he was lying down. Caryl was disappointed but knew her first mate would recover faster if he rested. A strenuous, uphill walk in the sun was probably not what the doctor would order but that left her with what she was sure would be a tension-filled excursion on the small island. She need not have worried. Joshua was being a model guest. After she secured the dinghy to the small jetty, they had set off to explore the uninhabited island.

"Pear Point, at seven hundred feet, is the island's highest hill. That's where we're going. The view is magnificent," she answered, noting he had brought his Canon.

Joshua nodded and they settled into an easy quiet. The only sounds were those they made as they pushed their way between and around bushes.

"The silence is awesome," he said, breaking it.

"Yes. You don't really get this if you come with a group. Everybody's chattering but it's really special."

"I'm glad we're alone." He shot her a sideways glance but Caryl made no response to what was clearly an opening salvo.

"What do you do?" she changed the subject, wondering if the direct approach would be more successful than Richardson's oblique probing.

"I'm president of Tain Music and Entertainment, at least I was the last time I looked," he said, surprising her with his ready answer. "I started out being a promoter when I was in high school but now I also have my own record company."

Caryl frowned at the arrogance she always perceived in people, mostly men, who named their companies after themselves. Lawyers like Alexander did it all the time.

"I love it but it's not easy. You get hundreds of demo tapes a week from all over the country and only one or two might show any real talent. Their voices or their lyrics. Sometimes, but very rarely, both. You sign them on, finesse their act, get them shows, they get some airplay then, wham, they want to sign with a bigger, badder company."

"Is it dangerous?" Caryl asked, remembering something she'd read in a magazine about a feud between rival rap record companies that escalated into open warfare. She waved her hand to shoo away a curious bee.

"It didn't used to be. That kind of thing was restricted to a small circle but it's spilling over as the big companies get involved with some of these small but rich fry, sharks I should say. But it's mostly good. You know, when one of these kids you nurtured makes it big, when you see them come into their own as artists and individuals, you get a great feeling. Of course, the money doesn't hurt either." He grinned and Caryl found herself responding to the warmth in his voice. She wondered which artists he worked with.

"Dawn Bradford is on my label," Joshua said, as if reading her mind. He was breathing a little harder now as they climbed.

"I know her. She did that remake of a Nina Simone song, 'To Be Young, Gifted and Black'."

"Yes, that's her. She's only twenty but she's got some lung power."

"Another Whitney, the critics say."

"Uh-huh." Joshua nodded. He reeled off the names of some other

JUST AN AFFAIR

big name stars on his label.

"You remember that guy I was talking with at The Baths? Tall with dreads?"

"You mean the one who couldn't stop staring at you? Is he your boyfriend or something?"

"No, of course not." *Was he jealous?* "I brought him up because he and his band have a song, 'Island Girl in the City,' that's on the British charts and the rest of their CD is pretty hot, too."

"Which label are they on?"

"Not sure. I think Virgin but I could be wrong. Anyway, I know they really want to break into the American market."

"I'll listen to their CD but I can't promise anything. What sells in Europe doesn't always sell at home."

"That's alright. I know you'll like them and when they hit it big I'll call and tell them they owe it all to me."

"Looking for a commission, eh?"

"Of course, but don't worry, I'll only bill them for about twenty percent of their first ten million."

She winked at him and Joshua laughed.

"Tell me..." Caryl began, suddenly remembering. "Why did you say at least the last time you looked? When you were talking about being president of the company."

"Oh, well, like I told you, there's a shark trying to take over the company. Just before I left I bought up all our available shares but he's been going to my major shareholders directly, offering them a better price than they would get on the market. If they go for it, I lose. I can't match his price."

Caryl was sympathetic. "That just doesn't seem fair, does it? After all the hard work you've done."

"And the thing is, the man doesn't know the first thing about music. He's got old money and most of it came from construction, industrial projects and real estate for God's sake. He wouldn't know Ice-T from lemonade!"

Caryl giggled.

"Anyway, I came here to get away from all that madness for a while and I chose the right place to do it. This trip has reminded me there's more to life. *You've* reminded me."

A thrill of pleasure shot up Caryl's spine. "Look, that's a soapberry tree," she said to distract him and pointed to a tree laden with small, yellow fruit. "If you pound a few and mix the pulp with water it makes a soap-like lather, which was what the locals used for clothes, their hair, everything, before they found out about Ivory and Pears and such."

Her tactic worked. "And those over there?" Joshua gestured to upright green spires sprouting from what looked like gigantic aloe plants. Many of the spires were small, just formed, but others soared twelve, fourteen feet into the air, abloom with thick-petalled yellow flowers obviously popular with the large black bees buzzing around them.

"Those are century plants or at least that's what they're called here. They bloom only once and then they die."

"They're awesome." Joshua craned his head to look around at the hillsides around them.

"Yes. On Tortola and some of the other islands, the islanders cut them down when they've bloomed and keep them dry. Then they spray paint them, usually silver, and use them for Christmas trees in December."

"Recycling. I love it." Joshua smiled wide.

The *Elendil*'s guests were not always interested in knowing about the flora and fauna of the Virgin Islands or in knowing their uses.

JUST AN AFFAIR

Caryl was pleased Joshua was different.

"Now what about you?"

"Huh?" They were walking single file now and Caryl turned to glance at him.

"You've quizzed me about myself and you've told me a hell of a lot about the plant life but I hardly know anything about you."

"Oh." Joshua's question was innocent enough but Caryl's mouth dried. "Not much to tell, really." She stalled, thinking. Her inner voice was impatient. *What's wrong with you, girl? He's not asking you to run away to a pleasure dome in Xanadu with him.* "What do you want to know?" she asked, just barely stopping her voice from catching. "I'm simply a captain on a rather gussied-up boat. Life begins and ends with the sea." That hadn't always been true but there was no need to tell him that.

"I've a feeling there's more. I may be wrong but I don't think there are many women captains in the Caribbean from Virginia, even fewer those who are as interested in political and environmental issues as you, and fewer still who know more than a little about photography. Did you always want to be a boat captain?" Joshua's voice behind her was gentle.

Caryl evaded the question. "Always is a big world. I wanted to be everything when I was young, a historian, a fire-woman, a biologist, a lawyer." She had enjoyed her legal career too. Enjoyed the hunt for precedence, the in and out-of-court duels, matching wits with the best and brightest. The firm had just offered her a junior partnership when her affair with Alexander blew up in her face. She was still amazed by how suddenly everything she'd worked so carefully to build fell down around her. Her father had suggested she move back to Virginia and, with her parents' connections and her own education and experience, get a job there after joining the state bar. But she was certain the rumors would follow her. The black legal community was a tight-knit one. Gossip, particularly if it was about sexual misconduct, spread like a brushfire in high wind.

"Actually," Caryl said. "I have a law degree from Georgetown and I practiced in New York before coming down here."

"Aha!" Joshua's tone was triumphant. "I get you now. You're one of those buppies fleeing the fast-paced hustle. You dropped out of the rat race."

"Something like that." Caryl saw no need to disabuse him of the notion. A lot of people she knew were doing that. Quitting and heading out to places like Arizona and Vermont to take up something entirely new, like ostrich farming or pottery. It was the modern equivalent to the search for self that occupied so many people in the sixties. The difference was that the people who were doing it now drove Volvos, had shares in Linux and while they might have given up their Palm Pilots, they were not about to let anything come between them and their ThinkPads. Of course, *they* were doing it voluntarily while she hadn't seen any other choice. But Joshua didn't need to know that either.

"Captain, what's the bird?" he asked behind her, interrupting her thoughts.

He pointed to his right where a dark brown bird was perched on the top bloom of a century plant. The bird's head was inclined to the side as he watched them with a look of avian hauteur.

"It's a sparrow hawk. Locally, it's called the killy-killy because of the cries it makes." Caryl spoke quietly so as not to frighten off the bird, but with a shrill call, it launched itself into the air, veering higher and higher before disappearing around the mountain.

"Blast!" Joshua said, re-slinging his camera over his shoulder.

They were near the top of Pear Point now. The trees and bushes

JUST AN AFFAIR

around them opened into a field of wind-bent grass through which Caryl led Joshua to the mountain's pinnacle. South, the sea stretched blue and unbroken into the horizon. But to the north, east and west, the hills of the neighboring islands rose, presenting themselves to view like the humps of shy, gargantuan sea creatures.

Caryl glanced at Joshua's face, which beamed his appreciation for the scene spread before him like a sumptuous banquet. He began to shoot away with the Canon, a look of concentrated delight on his face. Leaving him to it, Caryl strolled over to the shade of a nearby tamarind tree, laden with fruit, and stretched up to pull the brown pods to her. Breaking them open she sucked on the tart pulp inside, spitting out the seeds as she wandered around to the other side of the massive tree. Not for the first time she wondered how old it was. It would take about three people standing around it, their hands outstretched, to encircle its rough circumference.

She was so engrossed in picking tamarinds for Joshua that she didn't hear him come up behind her. His hands pressed into her shoulders, his fingers on her skin light but firm. She dropped the fruit she was holding and willed herself to relax as Joshua's thumbs kneaded the tense knot at the nape of her neck, the knot his touch had instantly caused. A slow fire spread upward from between her legs as she felt Joshua's body heat behind her. Her nipples hardened, aching to be touched. She groaned softly, her eyes closed. Joshua's hands went up and down her arms, pressing them to her side. Caryl groaned again. She longed for him to open her blouse and stroke her breasts' smooth, dark nakedness.

"No. Oh, my God. Stop." Caryl's eyes flew open and she scrambled to get away from him but he held her tight.

"What is it? What's wrong with you? I know you want me," he grated as she struggled against him.

"Yes, I do," she admitted wretchedly. "But I don't know anything about you. Are you single? Do you sleep around? Is there a woman waiting for you back in New York? Women?"

"No, nothing like that. I don't sleep around and I don't cheat on my woman."

Caryl wished she had a portable lie detector, something no bigger than a Star Tac, but Silicon Valley was obviously busy with other things.

"So why aren't you involved? Are you telling me you can't find somebody in a place like New York?"

"I had a woman but we broke up about five months ago. I've been single ever since. I'm way too busy, got too much going on, to spend time on the dating routine."

"What caused your break up?" Caryl asked, managing to squirm around in his arms so she could face him.

"It was just a lot of problems. I couldn't do enough to reassure her. My business involves a lot of socializing. It's all flash, little substance, but you gotta let yourself be seen. She didn't understand that." He grimaced at the recollection. "She was just really insecure anytime I couldn't be with her, started treating me like she was my own personal warden. I had to let her know what I was doing, who I was with almost every minute of the day," said Joshua, continuing. "I tried to get her interested in the business so she could be a partner to me. Tain Music funds a foundation to help inner-city youths. It's no longer confined to the Bronx, but moving into New Jersey, Pennsylvania, D.C. Laura's public relations and organizational expertise would have come in handy but she told me the whole thing was a waste of time, just a drop in the bucket." Joshua shrugged. "It took me a while, but I finally realized she was really quite shallow. All she cared about was Laura, and I got tired of having to answer for my time. I want a woman who's about something other than herself, and me, of course." He grinned at her and Caryl's resolve weakened.

"Why have you been so cold to me in the last day?"

"I was angry at myself. I knew I wanted you but I wondered if I was wrong for you. You're right. We've only known each other a couple of days but that's how I am. I don't like to waste time. If I see something I want, I go for it. But I realized I might be scaring you away instead, so I was trying to back off."

Caryl could not fault him for that. It was the same with her, wanting him one minute, wishing she didn't have to see him again the next.

"Are you more sure about things now?"

"I want you and I really don't give much of a damn about anything else. Not even your vow of celibacy. I just want to hold you and have you hold me. That's what I've wanted from the first time I saw you, and now that I've gotten to know you a little bit better, I want you a thousand times more." The naked hunger she read in his eyes and heard in his voice broke down the last of Caryl's resolve. With a moan, she threw herself against his chest.

As Joshua's lips fastened on hers, shivers of ecstasy ran down her spine. Caryl arched her body against him, loving the feel of his arms around her, inhaling his musky scent. They were alone on the mountaintop, probably alone on the island and she didn't stop him as he pushed up the bottom of her tee shirt, tugging aside her brassiere to expose her breasts to his mouth. Desire flooded Caryl's body, making her feel weak and boneless as Joshua's teasing tongue flicked the hard knobs her nipples had become. Whimpering with long-suppressed need, she pressed his head to her chest, encouraging him to suckle her like a baby. His hands cupped her buttocks and squeezed them urgently to him. His lips left burning imprints on the skin of her throat as they moved upward to claim hers. Caryl twined her arms around his neck and pressed her hips against his arousal. Joshua's breathing grew ragged and he pulled back from her, his eyes glazed by passion.

"There is one thing I want to know, though. What was that about not being my concubine?"

"What?"

"At The Baths. You said you didn't want to be my concubine. Do you remember?"

Caryl drew away from him, her cheeks warm with embarrassment, amazed that he hadn't forgotten. "Yes, I remember. Have you ever been to the Philadelphia Museum of Art?"

"What?" It was Joshua's turn to be puzzled.

"There's a painting there of a Moorish chief. You look like you could be his younger brother. All hawkish and proud. Very handsome, too," she admitted, shooting him a wary look from under her lashes. His shoulders began to shake, and gales of laughter gusted around her. Caryl glared at him, miffed.

"I'll offer you a deal." Joshua's eyes were merry. "You don't have to be my concubine if you'll accept the post of wine maiden. My very own wine maiden, Caryl," he whispered, suddenly serious, his voice husky.

"Done. I'm yours." Caryl was through caring about whether or not it made sense to get involved with him. She had stuck to her vow as long as she could and she need have no regrets about giving it up now. No one had ever made her feel like this. Her every pore, her every cell, yearned for his touch. Every kiss, every caress, electrified her. She knew in a split second that having a one-night stand with Joshua was better than having nothing at all. She would submit to their passion. There was nothing else she could do. Joshua stared at her. Her tee shirt was still up and her nipples stood at attention like

JUST AN AFFAIR

twin Hershey's kisses tempting his mouth with chocolate sweetness. With a half-muttered groan he reached down to flick them with his tongue before rearranging her brassiere and pulling down her shirt.

"Not now. Not here. We don't even have towels for you to lie on."

Caryl pouted but had to admit the wisdom of delay. The ground beneath their feet was hard and stony.

"So much for being swept away," she said, not hiding her disappointment.

Joshua chuckled, delighted by her impatience.

"Soon," he whispered. "I want you so bad you'd better believe it'll be soon."

And with that she had to be content.

CHAPTER EIGHT

Later, back on the *Elendil*, Caryl and Joshua went to their respective cabins to get ready for dinner. Now that things between them were clear or at least clearer and she could ease up on her self-imposed demure dress code, Caryl chose a strappy black slip dress that enhanced her toned shoulders and showed her long legs to advantage. Slipping it over her head, she delighted in the dress's silky feel and thought mischievously of the effect it would have on Joshua. Her dark berry lipstick color brought out her eyes, enhancing her whole face so that she had little need of other makeup. Little shivers of expectation rippled down her spine. She could hardly wait to see Joshua again or to feel his lips on hers. It might not be love, not yet, but Joshua aroused feelings in her she'd thought dead.

She wouldn't make any demands on him. If he wanted her beyond the end of his cruise, that would be wonderful but, if not, she had to be ready to face his rejection with equanimity.

Pushing her anxieties aside, Caryl twirled out of the room in black sandals she had not worn since her New York days. She would live for the moment and, with Joshua at her side, what a moment it would be. Caryl's lips curved in a smile of anticipation.

He was there before her. So were Patty and Richardson, but she hardly noticed them. Joshua was standing with his back to the saloon door, his hands on the railing as he looked out across The Bight. The full moon cast a magical, silvery radiance over the sea rippling against the *Elendil*. In the distance, the lights of a passing boat bobbed like a dancing firefly.

As if called, Joshua turned to look at her. A smile brightened his face and desire snaked through Caryl's body. Joshua took a step toward her, his eyes trained on hers. Caryl stood stock-still. Under his smoldering glare, she felt as if her will had turned to water, her muscles to jelly.

Richardson's cough broke the spell.

"Er, captain," the burly man said, his voice low. "Dinner is served."

"Thank you, Richardson."

"Captain, you look fantastic." Joshua's voice was a soft murmur but Caryl knew her crew had heard by the glances they gave each other. Was she imagining it or did Patty's back stiffen? Her friend had encouraged their involvement all along. Was she having second thoughts now it seemed things were heating up? It was too late for that, much too late. Caryl was beyond caring what anyone thought. She was a grown woman and as long as they were discreet about it, why shouldn't she and Joshua live their passion?

"Thank you," she said to him.

Joshua pulled out her chair for her, then went around to take the seat opposite. The dinner itself smelled delicious. On the menu was Patty's special ginger chicken, long grain rice and roasted vegetables. Bottles of white wine cider accompanied the meal.

At first, nobody spoke as they served themselves. Even the scrape of serving spoons, the wash of the waves and, on shore, the cries of birds settling down for the night seemed hushed, muted. There was a dreamy quality to the peace and beauty of the moonlit sea but the people gathered around the table were too nervous with unreleased tension to notice. Caryl thought that if the silence went on long enough they would all explode. Patty and Richardson's silence was difficult to figure out but she thought it arose out of their concern for her. Maybe they were thinking she would get hurt or fired or worse if she got involved with Joshua.

She resolved to take charge of the situation.

"Are you fully recovered, Richardson?" she asked, realizing she hadn't seen him since her return from the hike.

"I don't know about 'fully.'" The big man grinned at her, his voice full of relief that someone else had taken the initiative and broken the silence. "I laid down for most of the afternoon," he continued, "and I drank gallons of orange juice. Patty gave me a couple of zinc tablets. You know she swears by them." He winked at Caryl. "They really seem to have helped, though. Take more than a cold to keep this seadog down, eh?"

"A lot more," she agreed.

"How was your hike?" Patty asked, looking at Joshua. A quick, involuntary grimace showed Caryl Patty had spoken without thinking and regretted bringing up the topic. Obviously, something had occurred between their handsome male guest and the captain but the less said about it, the better.

Caryl gripped her fork. Her breathing slowed as she waited for Joshua's answer.

"The hike was one of the most wonderful experiences of my life," he said, looking at Patty. He smiled and transferred his gaze to Caryl who quivered at the possessiveness she read in his eyes. "What time do we sail tomorrow, captain?" he asked.

"Actually, we go over to Jost Van Dyke tonight so we can get an early start over there, then come back to Tortola in the evening."

"Is Jost Van Dyke as nice as all the others?"

"You'll see for yourself. It's not very highly populated but they've got a stunner of a beach over there."

JUST AN AFFAIR

"It's actually the party island of the Virgins," Richardson interjected. He explained that the island was known internationally for Foxy's Annual Wooden Boat Regatta which took place every August. People came from around the world to race their boats and to party hearty. Foxy, a native businessman and restaurateur, also hosted a New Year's party that was billed as the second-best place to be after Times Square. Hundreds of people converged on the tiny island to ring out the old year and ring in the new with the few locals who lived there. "Next year" was how everyone said "goodbye."

The tension around the table gradually relaxed as they talked and by the end of the meal, everyone was laughing over Joshua's anecdotes about his recording stars. Caryl particularly liked the one about the rapper Joshua took to lunch at Maxim's to celebrate his signing with Tain Music. Confronted with the chichi menu, the diamond-toothed, Hilfiger-clad rapper requested a bacon cheeseburger with fries for his entrée and M&Ms for dessert. In impeccable French. It turned out that the rapper's family was from the black upper class and he had attended the elite Phillips Exeter school where he'd learned not only French but Spanish and German too. His background was a secret to his legions of hard-core inner city fans.

To cool down the palate after the spicy meal, Patty presented an ice cream dessert laced with Worcestershire sauce, giving it an elusive, tangy flavor. The ice cream itself was made from the soursop, a large fruit with a green spiny skin. It was a favorite of Caryl's and she took a hilly bowlful, then excused herself from the table.

As she walked away, Caryl felt Joshua's eyes on her. Warm flickers of desire swept through her but she refused to turn around and look at him. She might not be able to continue walking away if she did. In the pilothouse, she lifted anchor and set the *Elendil* in motion for her next anchorage. Jost Van Dyke lay northwest of Tortola. It might be a party island in August and December but, for the rest of the time, Jost Van Dyke was, arguably, the quietest of the populated Virgin Islands. She was definitely looking forward to showing it to Joshua.

The *Elendil* had barely rounded Tortola's West End on the way to Jost Van Dyke when Caryl felt rather than heard Joshua join her. They did not speak as his hands ran over her afro, down her neck and across her shoulders. Caryl sighed deeply at his touch; she felt as if she had been longing and waiting for this all her life without knowing it.

"I love your hair. It really suits your face and the work you do," he murmured.

"Thanks. Low maintenance is a priority," Caryl said, luxuriating in the feel of his fingers on her scalp.

"You look gorgeous tonight. This dress is the bomb. If you had worn it on the first night I would have snapped you up long ago." He caressed her shoulders, kneading them lightly with his thumbs. Caryl moaned as he brushed aside the feather-light straps of her dress and pushed it down so that it fell around her ankles in a whisper of silk. The moonlight revealed the smoothness of Caryl's bare breasts. Her nipples were taut, aching for Joshua's touch. He did not disappoint them. His hands moved lightly, brushing the little pebbles of flesh, kneading and pulling gently on them. Caryl groaned as Joshua's tongue flicked in and out of her ear. With her last ounce of self-possession she set her course for Great Harbor on Jost Van Dyke and put the *Elendil* on autopilot.

That done she rose and threw herself into Joshua's waiting arms, offering her mouth to his with the eagerness of a drowning woman grabbing a life raft. Joshua moaned as he crushed her to him. His lips descended to claim hers in a firm kiss that threatened to rob Caryl of her senses. Naked except for her underwear, Caryl pressed herself against Joshua in an urgent demand for his full possession. His hands caressed her back, moved to the waistband of her satin panties and beyond, felt the sweet moistness of her desire. Joshua took a shuddering breath as his fingers delved into her, and Caryl slid her hand between their bodies to return his caresses with her own. His sex strained for release against the soft material of his pants while she fumbled to free its hard length.

"Woman, you are driving me crazy!" Joshua moaned against her neck as she ran her hand up and down his throbbing manhood.

"I need you," Caryl whispered in response, certain that being with Joshua was the most right thing in the world. She pushed his pants and boxers to the ground.

Their mouths opened to each other again, and Joshua's tongue licked at hers as he picked her up and sat her on the stool.

"I can't wait anymore. I wanted to but I can't," he groaned. The flame burning in Caryl's belly flared at the need she saw in his eyes.

"I've already told you I'm yours," she murmured. *And celibacy be damned.*

Joshua reached into his pocket and drew out a familiar foil square.

"You don't mind, do you?" He looked at her anxiously.

"No, baby. It's all good." She was actually kicking herself for not having thought of it first.

He tore the square open and unrolled the condom over himself. Caryl's heart flooded with tenderness. She ached to have him inside her.

Joshua gently spread her legs to receive him. Caryl leaned back in the stool and groaned as his hard manhood touched her pleasure button. He rubbed himself against her and was rewarded when she lifted her hips in an unspoken invitation. Unable to restrain himself any longer, he plunged his hardness into her, gathering her hips in his hands to drive himself against her in an ecstasy of need.

Caryl threw her head back oblivious to anything but the feelings churning in her body. Delirious with pleasure, she would have screamed if Joshua had not claimed her mouth in a hard kiss. Caryl moaned deep within her throat as she rocked her body against his. Tight at first, she could feel herself opening up as her juices gushed to welcome him. Their passion drew itself around them. Caryl felt the quickening in her womb and Joshua's breathing grew labored as sweat beaded his forehead. His face tightened, his eyes becoming fixed and focused as they bored into hers, and she knew he was reaching the peak of his pleasure. Clutching him to her, she nodded, a small smile on her lips. She was ready. Joshua moaned. He was coming and she was coming too and it was all good, so good. His arms cradled her as their bodies shook in an ancient tango.

Spent, they held each other tightly as their chests heaved. Sweat beaded their foreheads and ran in rivulets down their stomachs.

"I wanted to wait until tomorrow when we were off the boat," Joshua said. His eyes searched her face and she realized he was looking for signs of regret.

"Why?"

"I thought it would be better."

"Because of Janus's rule about consorting with guests? It doesn't matter. I'm prepared for any consequences."

He pressed a kiss to her forehead.

Over his head, Caryl saw the lights of Jost Van Dyke. She pushed him gently away and picked up her dress and panties, moving with unconscious ease despite her nakedness. As she shrugged her clothes back on, Joshua removed the condom and put it back in its packaging before throwing it in the wastebasket. He pulled his pants back on and buttoned his shirt as Caryl guided the yacht into Great Harbor, the small island's only port of entry.

Joshua leaned against the control panel to watch the island's lights, one hand resting possessively on Caryl's knee.

"I wish I'd booked for longer," he said pensively as she dropped anchor. "Everything about these islands is so beautiful I can understand why you love them so much. At home everything is rush, rush, rush. Everyone wants to reach the top and they don't care who they step on to do it." He moved into her open arms as he spoke, finding there a refuge from thoughts of his return to New York.

"Are you thinking of the guy trying to take your company over?"

"Yes." Joshua's clipped answer told her how worried he was about it.

"Everything will be okay. You'll see." But she saw that worry continued to lurk in the depths of his eyes. "When was the last time you took a vacation?" she asked, inhaling the spicy scent of his hair.

"Five years ago, when I worked for Atlantic. Since I started Tain Music I haven't been able to take time off till now. Every trip I've taken, even the one to the Blue Mountains, involved business." Joshua sounded bone weary.

"Perhaps if you got away more often, even just for weekends, it might help to defuse the stress," Caryl suggested, her hand rising to stroke the back of his head.

Joshua pressed his lips against her temple. His kisses wandered down her cheek before his mouth sought hers. They kissed, their arms tight around each other.

"I feel as if I could stay here, like this, forever," Joshua said, drawing away from her to stare into her eyes.

"So could I," she whispered and pulled him back into her embrace.

It was bittersweet pain for Caryl to finally pull away from him. Only a few lights enlivened the darkness on shore, and Caryl knew it was very late.

Their fingers interlaced, they descended to the deck and walked to Caryl's cabin just beyond the galley. At the door, he kissed her once, hard, then turned and strode away. It was the right thing to do. Sleeping together in one bed aboard the *Elendil* would be madness. Patty and Richardson would feel caught between their affection for Caryl and Janus policy. Still, Caryl hated to see him go.

That night she dreamt that she and Joshua were marooned on a small island and all they had to eat were the chocolate fruits growing everywhere on big-leaved vines. When a big cruise ship showed up to rescue them, they hid.

As the morning light seeped into her room, Caryl buried her face in her pillows, reluctant to leave her dream behind. But her skin tingled and her eyes flashed open as she remembered the night before. Joshua had been so tender, so sexy. Breaking her period of abstinence for him was more than worth it and the reality of their day ahead would probably be better than any dream, however arousing.

Caryl swung her legs out of bed, stretched and rose. Today was for her and Joshua, and she didn't want to waste a minute more lying in bed thinking about him when she could be up and about. Activity would make the time go quicker until she saw him again. She washed her face, donned her swimsuit and hurried up on deck to take her morning swim. The sun was just beginning to turn the sky a magnificent coral pink that was threaded with pale violet clouds that looked like silk, tie-dyed scarves streaming in the wind. The sea was so still the *Elendil* looked as if it had glided onto a shiny, silvered mirror.

JUST AN AFFAIR

Tossing her towel on a deck chair, Caryl jumped down to the swimming platform and slid into the quiet waters, striking out for shore.

Along the Great Harbor waterfront, a half-dozen restaurants, bars and guesthouses, doors closed, windows shuttered, waited for the sun's warmth and the cheer of bustling bodies. As Caryl walked on the beach she thought how different the place looked like this, empty and expectant. On New Year's Eve and during the Wooden Boat Regatta in August one could scarcely see the island for all the people and the harbor was clotted with boats. Now, though here and there a dog barked and a rooster crowed, the island was, for the most part, still.

Caryl looked out to the *Elendil* and wondered if Joshua was up yet. The sun was higher in a sky that had changed from the pink, gold and violet pastels of minutes before to a uniform wash of pale blue. The new day was sharpening, bringing the world into focus. Houses, trees, boats were regaining the definition they lost at night. Soon she saw male figures emerge on the *Elendil*'s aft deck. By the time she swam back, Richardson and Joshua were in conversation.

"Good morning, captain," they said, almost in unison.

"Good morning," she responded, her cheeks warming as Joshua's gaze swept over her in slow admiration.

"I'm…er…I'm going in to change." Caryl spun away from them into the saloon. On the way to her cabin she berated herself for behaving like a schoolgirl in love for the first time. Yet, she admitted to herself, that was exactly how she felt. As if all her other relationships, even the one with Alexander, had only been pale and insubstantial dreams of love. What she was experiencing with Joshua was a passion that raged through her in a way nothing had before.

When Caryl returned to the aft deck, Joshua, Richardson and Patty were digging into Creole omelets made from eggs, cheese, sweet potatoes, green peppers, onions and Patty's special mixture of spices.

A jug of orange juice was almost empty.

"What's on the agenda today, captain?" Joshua asked from where he lounged on a deck chair. Caryl smiled at him. The white jeans shorts he wore with a navy and white striped shirt open to his navel suited him to perfection.

"Jost Van Dyke," she said, waving her arm to indicate the island. "It's where William Thornton, the man who designed the Capitol in Washington, D.C. was born."

"Really? I never knew that. Actually, I didn't even know who designed it." He grinned sheepishly at her.

"You won't be able to see it because time and people have done their work but his family had a sugar plantation here. Jost was also the birthplace of Thornton's friend, John Coakley Lettsome, the man who founded the London Medical Society."

Caryl's eyes shone. The tiny unspoiled island was her favorite and she loved telling its history. As she talked, however, she noticed that both Patty and Richardson were unusually quiet. Caryl wondered if their silence signaled disapproval of her behavior with Joshua and made a mental note to bring it up with them later. For now, she pushed it to the back of her mind.

"There's a little doggerel about John Coakley. It goes like this." Caryl cleared her throat.

"I, John Lettsome blisters, bleeds and sweats 'em.

If, after that, they please to die, I, John Lettsome.

Of course, that was when they used to use leeches."

Joshua threw back his head in a full-throated laugh.

"Now, like Richardson said last night, Jost Van Dyke is a party island," she said as his laughter faded. She described the island's various celebrations and Foxy's shindigs.

"Most people live in Great Harbor, which is where we're anchored now. There's still some farming going on but most people are into tourism. They either own restaurants and or hotels or they work for the people who do. We'll have lunch at The Hungry Man." Caryl glanced at Joshua who nodded. "It's one of the more popular places and it serves a buttered grouper that will knock your flip flops off."

"I'm all for that. Viva the shoeless!" Joshua raised his hand as if making a toast.

"And maybe they'll have a fungi band," Caryl continued, grinning. "You'll be in for a treat if they do."

"Fungi band. What's that?" Joshua turned to Patty. "Didn't we have something you called fungi for lunch a couple days ago?"

Patty grinned. "Yes, we did. But this is a musical band. Tell him about them, honey." Patty nodded to her husband.

"It's great, man. Fungi music is the traditional music of the Virgin Islands."

"He should know. Richardson's father is 72 years old and still playing with the Pepperpot Men," Caryl broke in, laughing as she gave Richardson a friendly slap on the shoulder. "What do the women say? The pepperpot man is boss?"

Richardson grinned and shook his head. "Laugh all you want. They know what they're talking about."

"What?" Joshua held up his hands. "You all are losing me. What's this about pepper and women?"

Patty's eyes twinkled. She drew her fingers across her lips as if zip locking them and Richardson pointed to Caryl. "Let her tell you."

"Me?" Caryl protested. "It's *your* culture."

"What? What?" Joshua smiled, looking from one to the other.

"Okay, alright, I'll tell him." Caryl shook her head at her crew. "Really, it's nothing. Just here, instead of talking about libido or sex, they'll talk about pepper." Joshua's puzzled look deepened. She needed to be more explicit. "Okay, for instance, if a man says his wife gave him plenty pepper last night, he means that there was a lot of love-making."

"Oh." Joshua's eyebrows rose and he smirked, giving her a meaningful look.

Caryl dropped her eyes and hoped neither Patty nor Richardson had noticed.

"May I go on about fungi bands now?" Richardson's voice was dry.

"Go on. Go on. Who's stopping you?" Caryl enquired, her eyes wide as she smiled in what she hoped was complete innocence at her first mate.

Richardson gave her a wry look. "As I was saying, fungi music originated in the 1800s when the slaves got together to play homemade instruments like a piece of tin strung up like a banjo, and a dried calabash against which they scraped a stick or a spoon, that kind of thing. Mostly they played for themselves, on Sundays and at Christmas when they didn't have to work in the fields. Sometimes, the master would ask them to play for guests." Richardson made a face as if this part of the history was distasteful to him. "Nowadays," he hurried on, "we have eleven or so bands in the Virgin Islands and the music has gotten really popular. My father's band plays at birthday parties, weddings, government events, that kind of thing. The Tourist Board even sent them to New York to play at the opening of their new office."

"Do they still use the same instruments?"

"Not really," Caryl answered. "The instruments they use now are more sophisticated, the ukulele, the guitar, the tambourine and so on. Some bands still use things that have other purposes, like galvanized washtubs and PVC pipes, but that's mostly for entertainment. If you want to shake your groove thing in tropical style, fungi bands will get you going." Caryl shook her shoulders to demonstrate drawing an appreciative smile from Joshua.

"I'm psyched! What are the chances we'll hear a band today?" he asked, leaning forward in his chair.

"Good, actually. There are a lot of boats in; a lot of people will be about soon. At least one of the restaurants should be putting on a band." Caryl looked around the harbor. The *Elendil* was the only yacht of its kind around; the other eleven were graceful sailboats.

"I'm really looking forward to this then. What time will we go ashore?"

Caryl glanced at her watch. "It's almost nine now. What about in an hour's time?"

"Sounds good to me. I'll meet you later." Joshua jumped up. "See you guys."

"Have a good time in case I don't see you later," Patty called after him.

"Thanks. I know I will." Joshua disappeared inside the saloon.

CHAPTER NINE

Caryl was waiting on the aft deck when Joshua re-emerged around ten in jeans and a simple sky-blue cotton shirt. His eyes twinkling, he bent down to brush her lips with his own and, unable to stop herself, Caryl's mouth opened to draw him into a deep, lingering kiss. Minutes later, when they drew away from each other, his eyes were alert with arousal.

"Perhaps we should stay on board after all. It might be more interesting," he said, raising an eyebrow.

Caryl pulled away from him, suddenly remembering Patty and Richardson who had gone inside earlier but could return at any moment. Her pleasure in Joshua would have to wait for the discretion of night. She did not want to embarrass her crew.

"I think we should get going," she said. Averting her eyes from Joshua's, she headed for the dinghy.

"Are you regretting what happened between us last night?" Joshua asked, settling himself in the small boat so he could dip a hand in the water.

Caryl stared at him. She couldn't believe he doubted her appreciation for what she had already chalked up as one of the best experiences of her life. Joshua glanced at her, then looked away again, his lips pursed. With a start Caryl realized he did very much doubt it.

"I enjoyed our lovemaking more than I've ever enjoyed anything," she said, reaching out to squeeze his arm, her eyes soft as they looked into his. The worry lines disappeared from his forehead and his face relaxed.

"I'm glad to hear that," he said, his face somber. "I don't ever want to cause you any regret."

Caryl looked at him. He had said it like he meant it. He looked so serious. He *did* mean it. She wanted to fly into his arms but she couldn't and still keep control of the dinghy.

"That's the sweetest thing anyone's ever told me. Thank you."

"I should be giving you thanks. Caryl, you've made me very happy. You know, I don't think you realize what you've done for me."

"Aw shucks, it's the islands." Caryl grinned teasingly. "They had that effect on me too when I first got here."

"They're very picturesque, I won't deny that. The kind of thing you might see on a postcard," Joshua said, craning his head to look at the island before turning back to her. "But I think you can take the lion's share of responsibility for how great I feel, how great I'm feeling right at this moment looking at you."

"Let's just say it's half and half, then. I'll share equal credit with the beaches and the sea."

"We'll agree to disagree then. I'm giving you eighty percent of the credit." His eyes twinkled at her and Caryl grinned back.

They arrived at the dock, secured the dinghy to a bollard and set off along Great Harbor's sandy main road, the sea on their left and a line of bars and restaurants on their right.

"This island isn't very developed, is it?" Joshua asked, looking around.

"No, that's what makes it so postcard pretty."

"Do I detect a note of facetiousness? I thought you weren't a great fan of development."

"I'm not but at the same time, I don't know. You look at the people here…" Caryl raised her hand to return the greeting of a small knot of middle-aged men sitting on an upturned rowboat underneath a coconut tree. "They don't do much more than sit around. It's their life and that's all some of them want. I don't know. I guess it's just me being American. I want to see more..." She groped for the word.

"Ambition?" Joshua suggested.

"Yes, that's part of it. I mean more seizing life. More grabbing it and shaking loose a contribution to humanity. Do you know what I mean?"

They sidestepped the fallen trunk of a sea grape tree and caught the enticing smell of baking bread from a nearby house.

"I do." Joshua grabbed her hand.

Caryl noticed the curious glances they attracted from the people they passed. She knew some of them, and they hailed her with the easy friendliness that marked Caribbean people.

"You think they should achieve, go out there, slay dragons, find the Grail."

Caryl laughed. "Or at least start up a dot.com and make a killing on the market."

Joshua grinned. "Yeah, that too. Yahoo could do with some competition."

"Morning, Caryl. Looking good." A teenaged girl in curlers waved from the window of a small, concrete house, its yellow paint faded almost to white. A blue lace curtain flapped around in the breeze, threatening to obscure her.

"Hi, Necie. How you doing?"

"Good, good."

But when Joshua waved to her, the girl ducked shyly behind the curtain, disappearing from view.

"Hey, how do you know all these people?"

"It's different here from the States. If you live here or even if you're just passing through, people make it their business to know you." Caryl's hand was warm and comfortable in Joshua's. This is what it must feel like to be on honeymoon, she thought. Everything was perfect. The sun shone brighter than it ever had and the island looked clean and fresh, as if just emerged from a passing shower.

"All the attention can get a bit annoying at times because there's never any anonymity. You can't lose yourself like in a bigger country. But people who know you will look out for you too. Get sick and there's a neighbor on your step with soup. That kind of thing."

"It used to be like that, still is, in some African-American neighborhoods. We're losing it quickly though. Where are the plantations you mentioned before?" he asked abruptly, glancing about him as if expecting emerald fields of sugar cane to suddenly reveal themselves.

"These islands haven't produced sugar in more than a century. The plantations were in the hills, away from the coastline. The ruins aren't much more than piles of rubble. Almost as soon as the British ended slavery in 1834, blacks turned to producing their own vegetable crops, fishing, smuggling and so on."

Further up the road, a squawking hen fluttered across the road in front of them, an amorous rooster with lowered white-spotted wings not far behind, in hot pursuit.

"Ha!" Joshua exclaimed, delighted. "Do you know," he swung Caryl's arm up and down in a happy, child-like gesture. "I've never been that close to chickens that weren't actually ready to eat on a plate in front of me. Do people keep them?"

Caryl shrugged. "If you don't see them in a coop, they're wild. And if you had a rooster living next to you and waking you up every morning at four like I did when I first got here, you wouldn't be so charmed."

"You're right but I'm not living next to them now. You know,"

Joshua's face turned sober, "it's hard to imagine something as ugly and monstrous as slavery happening in such a beautiful environment."

They were now walking out of the village, heading for the low-rising hill before them. Here and there, a colorful house interrupted the lush vegetation around them, but the hum of village life was left behind. A herd of cows munched leisurely on grass in a pasture near the top of a nearby hill, oblivious to Joshua and Caryl's passing.

"Jost Van Dyke had at least two sugar plantations and one cotton plantation. The island is very close to St. Thomas, which belonged to Denmark until 1917 so when abolition was imminent, some planters here sold their slaves to planters there. It was illegal but they did it anyway. The Danes didn't free their slaves until more than a decade later."

"St. Thomas was Danish?" Joshua quirked an eyebrow at her.

"Yes. A lot of people don't know it but the United States Virgin Islands were Danish colonies until 1917 when the U.S. bought them. Then they became known as the U.S. Virgin Islands. Of course, trafficking in slaves wasn't the only illegal activity people engaged in. Smuggling is a time-honored tradition around here."

"You're kidding!"

"No. During Prohibition in America, Tortolian traders bought rum from the southern French islands, then smuggled their product into St. Thomas. From there it made its way up to the mainland."

Joshua shook his head. "One man's Prohibition is another man's profit."

"Now greedy men smuggle boatloads of cocaine and marijuana." Caryl grimaced. A young man who had worked for Janus repairing the boats had sunk into the hell of drug abuse just a couple months after her arrival. He'd begun to show up hours late for work, if he came at all. The manager had let him go after finding him in a bathroom, a

JUST AN AFFAIR

vial of crack in his hand, about to light up. Months later, Caryl had seen him outside Shopper's Way, one of the supermarkets. His shirt hung ragged and dirty from his thin shoulders and his cut-off jeans exposed bony, blistered knees. He had run right out of his sandals in his eagerness to get to her and ask for a loan of five dollars to buy lunch. Instead, she had gone into the deli and come back out with a sandwich, a cup of soup and a small bottle of apple juice. He had taken them with a rueful smile and disappeared into the parking lot. A couple of days later someone told her that when people gave him food, he sold it for drugs.

Joshua's gentle pressure on her hand brought Caryl back to the present.

"What is it?"

"Nothing." Caryl attempted a smile. "I don't want to spoil a perfect day." But even with effort, it took a few minutes of silent walking before her mood began to lighten again. They were nearing the crest of the hill and Caryl smiled at Joshua, anticipating his first sight of White Bay. Of all the Virgin Islands' many beaches, it was probably the most alluring.

Joshua's reaction did not disappoint her when they rounded the final bend and the beach appeared before them.

"My God." He came to a stop and gave a long, low wolf whistle. "God exists and I'm in heaven," he murmured to himself. White Bay glittered below them. Far from shore, the water was an emerald and azure kaleidoscope which faded to a light blue as it approached the beach and kissed the sparkling white sand curving into the horizon. Tall palm trees fringed the beach like watchful sentinels, their fronds waving gently in the tropical breeze. Snow-white clouds drifted slowly overhead, as if reluctant to leave.

"This is gorgeous, my captain." He had not yet taken his eyes off the beach.

"Yes, it is."

"For somebody accustomed to beaches that have five people per square foot and water that looks like what you might find in the tub if you work in mud and haven't washed in a month, this looks like pure heaven."

"You go to the beach a lot in the States?"

"I grew up with my grandmother in New Jersey and she used to take me to Jersey Beach every chance she got. She loved the beach. She's eighty now but I've got to bring her down here. She's gotta see this."

Caryl grew warm. So Joshua was definitely thinking of coming back. It was a hint, a small one, but she would take what she could get.

"Bring everyone." She realized he had never spoken about his family before. "Your mom, sisters, everybody. Maybe I'll get a commission from the tourism people."

"Don't count on it. My mom's dead, I never knew my father and I'm an only child. At least on my mom's side." The timbre of his voice suggested to Caryl that family was something of a sore point for him, a topic he didn't discuss easily.

"Oh." She pulled a face. "I won't get much of a commission with just your granny but maybe you all can figure something out, wear disguises or something. I'm willing to give you a cut, you know."

Joshua chuckled. "Oh, yeah? And what do you think would make it worth my while?"

"Who mentioned making it worth anybody's while but mine? I'm thinking five percent should be more than sufficient."

"Ha!" Joshua grabbed her up and swung her around. "That won't even keep my gran in fried catfish for a month!" He let her slip down through his arms until her feet were again on solid ground. Caryl's arms rose around his neck and she gave herself up to the comfort of their embrace. Loving the feel of his physical response to her, Caryl pressed harder against him. Joshua's lips brushed her cheeks, stopped to nuzzle her neck then moved back and across to nibble at her ear. One hand moved down her back to cup and caress her behind and she squirmed as little shocks of desire swept through her.

When they pulled apart minutes later, Caryl felt as if she'd just gone through some sort of electrical storm. If Joshua had wanted to take her right then and there in the middle of the unpaved road, she could not have stopped him. Peeping at him from under her lashes, she wondered if he knew just how strong her reaction to him was.

There was an expression of equal parts desire, curiosity and annoyance on his face as he looked at her.

"Yes?" Caryl felt a turning in her stomach. Maybe he thought she was too brazen.

"Do you know you're like some strong wine that'll send a man to his knees with just one swallow?"

"You mean like Night Train?"

"Night Train is the last wine I would liken you to, my wine maiden." Joshua threw his head back, laughing with the delicious abandon she had witnessed before. "More like some expensive *pinot grigio*."

"Light with a nutty yet peppery aroma best left to age for a couple years?"

They were on their way again and Joshua swung her hand.

"Most certainly not. Full-bodied, rich in color with a charming chocolate aroma. Also a subtle hint of fruitiness. To be uncorked immediately."

"Fruity, eh?" Caryl poked him in the side.

"Yes." Joshua sniffed the air above her head. "Raspberry, I think."

He fended off another poke.

Five minutes later they were at the beach. Caryl kicked off her sandals and stepped onto the sand. She'd only taken a few steps when her feet sent an urgent message to her brain. "Ouch, ouch. Oh, hot, hot." Her face contorted in pain, Caryl ran to the water's edge. Sinking her heels in the cool, slushy, water-soaked sand, she let the water run up to her ankles, soothing her feet. A strange snuffling sound reminded her that she'd left Joshua behind and she looked around. Her companion was shaking, almost doubled over in laughter, his mouth behind his hand. Seeing he was caught, he dropped his hand and his laughter roared out around him.

"Woman, you looked so funny. Like a cat on a hot tin roof."

"Yeah, yeah. Laugh. But that is what people do at the beach." She started to walk away from him, staying within the water line and away from the hot sand as she looked for a shady area in which to set down their things.

"Yell ouch and leap around like demented dancers?"

"Funny." Caryl gave him a withering look. "I mean take off their shoes instead of flicking up sand with every step they take in their flip flops. As you're doing. The only thing to be said for you is that at least you don't have on socks too."

"Hey, I read *Vogue* and *Essence*. I know better than that." His amusement subsided but there was still a chuckle in his voice. "Plus, I wouldn't want to embarrass the most beautiful woman on the beach...she does that well enough on her own." He burst into another gale of laughter.

"Alright. Keep on. Have your fun. We like tourists to have fun." She waved to the bartender at a small, thatched bar they were passing. He was doing good business; almost all of his stools were taken up with a good mix of both tourists and locals.

Spotting the perfect area to settle, Caryl made a beeline for the group of shady, coconut trees. Since she started across with wet feet, the sand did not feel quite as hot as it had at first, and she was able to walk over to the trees quite normally. In any case, she would have preferred eating the sand to giving Joshua another laugh at her expense.

"I can hardly believe the blues and greens of the sea," he said, staring out to sea.

"A guest on the *Elendil* once joked that before she got here she just thought the islanders got up every morning and poured dye into the water."

"Do you ever see yourself leaving these islands, moving back to the States, for instance?" Joshua's back was to her as he looked into the horizon and Caryl wondered what to say. If he meant, would she leave the islands right now to take up a life with him, the answer would be an unreserved "yes". She would miss everything here but she had never seriously thought she would live in the islands for the rest of her life. It wasn't what he'd asked, though. She must not read what she wanted into what Joshua actually said.

"This has been more in the nature of a working vacation for me." She was trying to answer him honestly while not revealing too much. "I love these islands a whole lot but five years ago I didn't imagine myself living here. I didn't even know these islands existed."

"You don't really look like a rolling stone to me." Joshua laid out a bamboo beach mat for her and then one for himself. He sat down cross-legged and looked up at her.

"I'm not. Leaving this place won't be easy." She did not add that, after having known Joshua for only a few days, she would definitely consider a premature departure if it meant they would be together.

Caryl gave herself a mental shake. Here she was, planning a life with a man who had not given her the slightest inkling he had the same thing in mind. Determined to ignore her misgivings, Caryl stripped down to a navy-blue swimsuit. Without a backward look, she ran past Joshua and into the waves.

CHAPTER TEN

At White Bay, a person could wade out almost fifty feet before the water reached their waist. Trying to get away from Joshua and the feelings he aroused in her, Caryl practically ran the distance, churning the water in her path to foam. Finally, she was in the deep and she dove in head first, kicking away from land.

As the warm water closed over her head, Caryl twisted and turned to dive down and touch the sandy bottom before floating to the surface again. But Joshua was still on her mind. Trying to shake him loose, she struck out, legs kicking powerfully, her arms wheeling quickly overhead, plunging toward the horizon. Near to shore the sea was calm, it's spirit broken by a reef that ran parallel to the beach, but, as Caryl passed an opening between the coral, the waves deepened and she strained to make headway. Eventually tired, she stopped and turned on her back to stare up at the sky, her arms and legs relaxed so that she felt like a piece of drifting seaweed.

"Ahhh!" A painful cramp seized her left leg with the suddenness of lightning and she cried out. Struggling to remain afloat, she reached down to stroke her leg with her hands. She pressed down lightly with the tips of her fingers, drawing them upward from her ankle to her thigh. This was basic training stuff but it did not help. The cramp felt like it was in her bone and worsening by the second. Her heart pounded. The shore was far away. She would have to backstroke in, taking care to put as little pressure on her leg as possible. She twisted on her back and struck out strongly. For five minutes she swam. It was slow going but she felt sure she was making progress. When Caryl calculated that she should be in far enough to wade the rest of the way, she turned over to look to shore.

"Ancestors." She sent up a wordless prayer. She was no closer to the shore than when the cramp had taken hold. And now Caryl realized why. She was caught in a current, not a very strong one, but one that in her present condition she was not up to fighting. Once more she flipped onto her back, the pain in her leg now a secondary concern as she tried to swim her way to safety. But she was tired and it told against her. The current pulled her out to sea despite her efforts.

"Stay calm. Don't fight it," a terse voice ordered. Joshua was treading water less than ten feet away from her.

"Help me," she called out to him. Her hands clawed at the water as she tried to leap to him. Instead, she sank, surfacing again more by instinct than design, her legs scissoring beneath her.

"Float, Caryl. I can't take hold of you until you calm down. Float. Do as I say."

He was right, of course. Caryl closed her eyes and tried to concentrate. But it was hard with the current under her making her feel as if the sea had plans for her that she was in no position to do anything about. A tendril of fear uncurled inside Caryl's chest. Where was Joshua? Her eyes flew open and she saw he was beside her. Tears of relief leaked from Caryl's eyes as she felt his arm go around her chest. She forced herself to be still. His labored breathing as he began to slowly pull her out of the current's grip let her know that this was no picnic for him.

"Need some help, man?"

Caryl turned her head. Two men had swum out to meet them. She supposed they were from among the crowd she'd seen earlier at the bar.

JUST AN AFFAIR

"Thanks. We're okay. It's not far now."

"No problem, man." It was the dreadlocked one who spoke. His companion was clean-shaven but big gold hoops in his ears made him look like a pirate. "We'll just swim in with you to make sure, if that's alright. These currents can be tricky."

"Sure. Thanks." Joshua was restricting himself to a minimal conversational effort as he continued to pull Caryl who smiled her own gratitude at the men.

Minutes later, they reached the shallows.

"Thanks for coming out, guys."

Joshua was panting slightly, as he put out his hand to shake that of the two men.

"No problem, man," Dreadlocks said. "You did it all, anyway. Your woman is lucky you got to her so quick. Later." With smiles at Caryl, the men swam off.

Shaken and exhausted, Caryl allowed Joshua to help her straighten up. The sound of clapping drew their attention up the beach to where the crowd from the bar was standing, waving at them. Thankful for Joshua's strong grip around her waist, Caryl waved back and Joshua gave them the thumbs up sign.

"You know that if you had drowned, it would've been your own fault." Joshua breathed heavily but his voice still managed to be brisk and impersonal. His face had hardened into the grim mask of a stranger as he looked down at her.

Caryl was struck by the injustice of it all. All she wanted to do was reach her beach mat and sink down on it.

"It would not. How can you say that?" Overwhelmed by her first simultaneous experience of both a cramp and a current, she shivered and pulled away from him.

"You had no business going out so far by yourself. You should've waited for me," Joshua grated. He gripped her arm and forced her to turn around and look at him.

"By the time I got into the water, I could hardly see you," he snapped, obviously unmoved by her tears.

Cary's resentment grew. She had almost lost her life and he was treating her like some spoiled child in need of correction. She certainly wasn't going to tell him she'd fled into the water to get away from him.

"I could have handled it," she hissed. Her brown eyes flashed in matching anger.

"Woman, please! This is the second time I've saved your life. And this time I risked my own. The current could have gotten us both."

"Oh, is that it? Well, I'm sorry I inconvenienced you, Mr. Tain. Next time you can let me drown."

A glint of humor lightened his dark eyes.

"I thought you said you could have handled it?"

"Any day of the week." Caryl's tone was frosty.

"Ha!" With a delighted cry, Joshua pulled her close to him. "You're a hardheaded woman. You know that?" He bent his lips to her ear. "Promise me you'll never do that again. When I saw you being pulled out to sea, you frightened me like I've never been frightened in my entire life." His hands caressed the small of her back.

"Thanks for coming to save me," she murmured against his chest, mollified.

"Any day of the week." His voice was husky. They stopped talking as Joshua's lips roamed over her face. Caryl molded herself against him, her arms tight around his waist. She felt as if she were drowning all over again in a current of passion sweeping her far away from everything she had ever known and held dear. As Joshua's mouth left hers to explore her neck and his hand rose to caress her nipples through her swimsuit, Caryl felt as if she were bursting to tell him all she was feeling, her joy at his caress, her sadness at his imminent departure, her hope that he would return. And her preparedness if he didn't. Keeping all that secret required a thousand times more effort than it had taken to obey him when she was drowning moments before.

Joshua loosened his hold on her and stepped back. "If we don't stop now, I won't be able to," he said.

"It's okay. I don't want you to." Caryl smiled and allowed her hands to wander over his flat, hard stomach, to play with the waistband of his trunks.

"What? No obscenity laws in the British Virgin Islands?" He caught her hands and held them. He was making an effort to be lighthearted but Caryl could see it was costing him. His arousal was plain and he was eyeing her like a wolf spotting prey in winter. If she provoked him even a little bit more, he might throw caution to the winds and take her right there on the sand in full view of the people at the bar. She drew away from him and Joshua heaved a sigh of relief.

"I need a drink. Do you want anything?" he asked, stooping to remove his wallet from his shorts.

"Isn't it a bit early to be drinking?"

The look he flashed her spoke volumes of his desire.

"Darling, I need a drink. You hear what I'm saying?" His voice morphed into a Southern accent. "This man needs something to calm himself down." He pretended to fan himself with his hand. Caryl laughed.

"Alright. Get me a passion fruit juice then."

She watched him walk away, his feet making large, clearly defined imprints in the sand. So...thoughts of her disturbed him. She hugged the pleasure of that discovery to herself and lay back on the mat, worn out from her narrow escape moments before.

She was woken from her light doze some time later by what felt like an insect crawling over her face. Waving her hands in front her face to frighten it away, Caryl sprang to a sitting position and realized Joshua had returned. He was leaning against the tree, almost doubled up in silent laughter. Caryl raised an eyebrow at him and he opened his palm to reveal the handful of sand he had been drizzling onto her face.

"Oh, very funny, smart guy." Caryl rolled her eyes.

"It is, it is."

Caryl dusted the sand off.

"You were gone a long time."

"Yes, I got you this." He handed over a thin tube of cream.

"They're making passion fruit in strange ways now." Caryl held it up for examination.

"I got it for your scrape." Grasping her left leg by the ankle, he held it up for her to see.

There was a long, shallow wound, crusty with sand running down her shin.

"Wow. I never even felt that."

"The salt water should help it to heal but I brought this anyway. It's antibacterial." Gently, he poured some water he had in a plastic cup over the cut to remove the sand and dabbed it dry with a clean towel. Taking back the cream, he opened it, squeezed a little bit on his index finger and rubbed it lightly on her wound.

"How's that feel?"

"Good. Thanks." She was touched by his thoughtfulness.

"No problem." He gently set her foot back down, then handed her the plastic cup of passion fruit he had put down in the sand behind him.

They sat side by side under the coconut tree sipping their drinks.

JUST AN AFFAIR

"Why did you run out to sea like that? We were getting along just fine and then suddenly you were running away from me like I was the monster in some B movie."

Caryl felt a knot gather in her throat. She almost gagged on her drink.

"There wasn't really a reason, *per se*."

"I think there was." Joshua's voice was soft, but firm. Setting his beer down in the sand, he turned to face her. He crooked one long, muscled leg around her, then slipped the other under her knees, cradling her.

Caryl took a long sip of the passion fruit to give herself time to think.

"I just felt like going in and I did. Why must there be more to it than that?"

"I've a feeling so, that's why." He raised his hand to trail a finger down her arm and a shiver crawled up Caryl's spine.

"Okay, alright. If you insist." Caryl sighed. "I was just thinking how much I'm enjoying you and I wondered what I'd do with myself when you left."

"Caryl, sweet, look at me." Joshua took her chin in his hand and gently pulled her face around to his. Their eyes locked.

"What we have won't end here. I'll go home tomorrow but I'll be back before you even realize I've gone and then we'll take it from there. It's too early to know exactly where we'll end up, but I know I want you in my life." He nuzzled her cheek with his nose. "Ah, sweet captain of my soul, if you only knew the spell you've cast on me, you would never think I could forget you."

Their lips met in a tender kiss and Caryl allowed herself to get lost in the sweetness of the moment. She didn't think Joshua would lie to her. If he said he was coming back, she knew he meant it. Then again, people said all kinds of things in the heat of the moment. She had to remember that and be ready for disappointment if she never heard from him again. If what was between them was just an affair, it could end tomorrow, evaporating like rain falling on a hot city street.

Joshua rose to his feet and reached down to pull her up beside him.

"Feel like going back in?"

"Not really. I'd much rather stay here and admire your perfection," Caryl teased.

"Oh, yeah? Well, I think you can do that very well in the sea with me. Not scared, are you?"

"Of course not!"

"Great! Then you won't mind this." Joshua swung her into his arms in one fluid motion, picking her up like a baby. With her in his arms, he half-ran, half-stumbled to meet the clear waters of the Caribbean Sea.

"Put me down. Put me down," Caryl said, laughing and trying to twist free.

"Are you sure that's what you want?"

"Yes. Yes."

They reached the water's edge and Joshua plunged right in.

"Sweet, I'm gonna put you down now." He began to loosen his hold on her.

"No. No. Not now." Her arms flew up around his neck but...

"Too late." Joshua half-turned and swung her gently into an incoming wave.

"Ugh, you...you." Caryl rose to her feet in the thigh-high water, spluttering. Joshua's shoulders shook with laughter.

Indignant, Caryl drove the heel of her palm against the sea's surface, sending a glittering rainbow-hued spray in his direction.

JUST AN AFFAIR

"That means war, woman." He dived at her.

Affecting fright, Caryl tried to swim away, but when she felt his hands grip her ankles to pull her back to him, she let herself relax and float into his arms.

For more than three hours they splashed and played in the shallows, venturing out only once or twice for quick forays into the deep water. When they were finally ready to leave White Bay, they were exhausted and hungry.

"Lunch had better be good. I could eat a sea-full of fish," Joshua groaned, trying to lean on Caryl, who giggled and danced away from him.

"So what else is new? The way you devour Patty's food should make headlines."

"A man's got to eat, woman. Especially if he's going to keep up with you."

CHAPTER ELEVEN

When Caryl and Joshua arrived at The Hungry Man Bar and Restaurant around two o'clock, the lunch crush, or what lunch crush there could be on an island of 465 people, had tapered off. People Caryl knew from a catamaran in the harbor were sitting near the door to the kitchen and she waved to them from the table for two she chose in the front.

"I like to see what's going on around me," she explained, taking the seat facing the island's only road.

Joshua took the seat opposite.

"I like to see you," he responded. A hot shiver ran up Caryl's back. Embarrassed by the way her body reacted to him, she dropped her eyes.

"You do the same to me," Joshua bent forward to murmur to her. Caryl glanced quickly at him.

"What?"

"I know what you feel because I feel it too. That's never happened with any other woman. I feel like I truly know you. Every beat of your heart sends thunder through me; every look you give me feels like a scanner over my soul. I feel naked before you." Joshua's hand reached across the table to grab hers.

"Hurrrumph, ummph, umph." Someone loudly cleared their throat beside them. Caryl's lips twitched at the surprised look on Joshua's face as he, once again, became aware of his surroundings. He grimaced in annoyance at the slim, petite woman standing by their table. There was an order pad in her hand and a knowing grin on her face.

"Hello, Stacia. How are you? How's Basil?" Caryl smiled at the woman. Stacia and Basil Chinnery, a husband and wife team, had first opened The Hungry Man in the early 1970s when Jost Van Dyke was far off the beaten tourist track. Pictures over the bar showed that it had been little more than an assortment of thatch and galvanized sheeting back then. Now it was a spacious two-story concern with seating for up to thirty people on the ground floor and a dance area cum community lounge on top. Basil's superb culinary skills and Stacia's friendly service complemented each other, ensuring their success.

"I'm fine, Caryl. Basil's in the back. As soon as I tell him you here, you know he going come hail you." Stacia had the careless yet gracious politeness of so many islanders. She would maintain her distance but Caryl could tell by the strained way she avoided looking at Joshua that she was burning to know who he was. Stacia had more than once stressed to Caryl the importance of finding a man and settling down. "Life on the sea for man, not woman," she would say, her arms akimbo. The alleged plight of aging, single women was a running joke between them.

"No fungi band today?" Caryl asked.

"Nah, two of the men had to go Tortola to look about some court business. Maybe tonight you hear them."

"Too bad." Caryl was disappointed for Joshua. "We're not overnighting here. Got to get back to Tortola ourselves."

"Oh, that's a shame! Michael just wrote a new song for them and it sounding good. Well, maybe next time you see them, eh?" She glanced down at the pad in her hand. "You take a look at the menu yet or you want more time?"

"It's okay. We can order now."

"I'll put myself in your hands," Joshua said to Caryl. His suggestive look told her she could take that any way she wanted. Caryl struggled to suppress the bubble of laughter that threatened to surface at the effect his comment had on Stacia. The woman's eyes opened wide and they heard her quick intake of breath before she recovered enough to close her mouth and pretend she'd heard nothing out of the ordinary.

"Stacia, I'll have the buttered grouper with fungi on the side. My guest will have the grilled lobster. Only one other place makes it as good, the Big Bamboo in Anegada," Caryl said, as an aside to Joshua.

"And to drink?" Stacia permitted herself a glance at Joshua.

"A pitcher of maubi will do, thanks." Maubi was a slightly tart local drink made from the bark of the tree of the same name.

Caryl decided to put Stacia out of her misery.

"Stacia, this is Joshua Tain, the *Elendil*'s guest. Joshua, this is Stacia Chinnery, the proprietor."

Joshua half rose from his chair in an old-fashioned gesture that made Stacia's lips twitch as they shook hands.

"Pleased to meet you. You from the States?"

"From New York." Joshua leaned back in his chair to look up at her.

"Oh, I love New York. It's the best city in the world." Stacia became effusive. "My daughter, she studying engineering at Columbia University." She rolled the name out as if on a red carpet. "One more year to go and she finish. She is a bright girl, been bright-bright since she was knee-high to grasshopper."

"She must be to have gotten into Columbia." Joshua smiled.

Stacia nodded vigorously.

"Yes, man. I tell her stay up there and look for work when she graduate but she say she coming home. It don't make sense. All kinda Gulf Oil and Texaco want her come work for them because her grades good-good but she say she want to come back here." Stacia looked around the restaurant and out into the street as if searching for what could be making her daughter want to return. She shook her head, her expression grim. "Children don't listen to them parents no more," she concluded.

"Money isn't everything. It's good she knows that at her age." Joshua looked thoughtful.

"Yeah, but she could set up herself and come back anytime. Anyway, please excuse me. I going be right back with your drinks, eh." Stacia hurried away.

"She's very nice," Joshua said when he thought she was out of hearing distance.

"The whole family. In fact, most people on these islands. Something about the beauty around them must work some kind of magic. It's not the same for us expatriates. It's harder for us to slow down, enjoy life and other people."

As she spoke, two little boys ran past in the street, chasing a bright red ball. There were only three cars on Jost Van Dyke and one hadn't worked in months so they were perfectly safe.

"So why doesn't she want her daughter to come home?"

"Elise is a really smart girl. On the dean's list every semester, and Texaco and Gulf Oil are just a couple of the companies courting her. Basil showed me an article about her in the campus newspaper and it's clear their daughter has a lot going for her. She's the first to go to college in their family, you know. But there isn't much scope for chemical engineers in the islands. Whatever work she found here wouldn't challenge her."

"Yes, I can see how it wouldn't, but maybe there are other compensations."

"I don't know. If she really does come back, she'll stay a couple years, realize she made a mistake, sign up for grad school and then go on to work for a multinational. It's what a couple of other young women I know here plan to do. In the Virgin Islands, Elise will be a woman in a field dominated by two or three men. The first female engineer of any kind. Abroad, she'd be walking on ground already broken, more lucrative and easier to travel."

Stacia's return with their maubi, Basil at her heels, interrupted Caryl.

"Yo, Caryl. Good to see you." Basil bent down to give her a hug. "And who this?" He looked at Joshua in frank curiosity.

"Basil, meet Joshua Tain. Joshua, Basil Chinnery, Stacia's husband."

The men shook hands.

"So man, this your first time to the place?" Basil drew up a chair and sat down while Stacia left to refresh the drinks of the catamaran group.

"Yes, and I'm having a great time." Joshua glanced at Caryl, whose cheeks warmed at the meaning she read in his eyes.

"Good, good. I'm glad to hear that. That's the best boat on the sea out there, the *Elendil,* and this is a good captain, a good woman." He looked shrewdly at Joshua. "She only been here about a year but she come like one of us now and we look after our own." It was his turn to trade a meaningful look with Joshua.

"That's cool, man." Joshua held up his hands, palms up. "But you'll have to stand in line because I'm looking after her now."

The men stared at each other in a non-verbal duel of the eyes until finally Basil broke the contest. "You the man." He laughed. "You got the right constitution for our Caryl." He clapped the other man on the shoulder.

"Now that we've gotten the macho stuff out of the way…," Caryl said dryly.

"Don't feel no way, Caryl. You know you don't got no family here. Is we so who have to make sure and look out for you." Basil's voice was full of affection.

"Thanks, Basil, but I'm a grown woman, you know."

"That don't say. Anyway, he pass the test and I have some fish to fry. I going see you around again, eh sah?" He looked at Joshua.

"I hope so." Joshua grinned.

"I like him," he said when Basil left.

"He's good people. I'm glad he liked you too."

"But do they always think you're dating the guy they see you with?"

"This isn't the first time I've been here with a man but it's the first time Basil's acted like that. Some kind of island intuition or something."

"Whatever it is, I'm glad I'm the first he's tested and I plan to be the last."

"Oh, you do, do you?"

"Yes."

A thrill of pleasure curled in Caryl's stomach at the possessiveness in his voice but she strove to keep her face neutral and raised her glass to her lips with studied nonchalance.

"Here we are, Caryl, your grouper just the way you like it." Stacia deposited a full plate in front of her and turned to Joshua. "And here's your lobster, sir. Enjoy."

"It smells great. I bet I will."

"How is it?" Caryl asked after his first mouthful.

"Umm." Joshua opened his eyes wide in appreciation. "It's got a slight smoky taste but it's so moist and meaty."

"Yes." Caryl eyed his lobster with vague envy. Her grouper was spicy but the lobster looked even better.

"Would you like a bite?" Joshua held out a forkful to her.

"Thanks." Caryl leaned forward. "Ummm." It was as good as it looked.

"Are the lobsters always this big?"

"No. You've lucked out. Sometimes they're quite small but the Conservation and Fisheries Department has a program to encourage fishermen to let them reach a certain size or age. Looks like it's working." She returned her attention to the grouper.

"You know, I haven't felt so relaxed in years. New York feels like it's a million miles away."

"Probably not so many."

Joshua made a face.

"I'm really sorry you're going to miss out on the fungi band but there's a gift shop at the hotel you'll be staying in tonight and they should have CDs."

"You think they'll be open?"

"Should be."

"I was looking forward to taking you out on the dance floor. Are you a good dancer?"

Caryl grinned, remembering the nights she, Shayna and other friends would spend rocking in clubs when they were at university. It was a wonder she'd gotten any work done. But she'd buckled down after graduation and then, of course, she'd met Alexander, who wasn't big on shaking his groove thing.

"I'm good, but you know you don't have to do too much moving to Caribbean music of any kind."

"That's not true. I've seen Patra."

JUST AN AFFAIR

"She's a singer but you can get away with just standing in one place as long as you're moving your hips."

"Come to think of it, you're right. I've been to the West Indian clubs. It looks like making love standing up."

Caryl took a sip of her maubi.

"It's really sexy."

"I know. I'm getting hot under the collar just thinking of, what do they call it, wining, with you."

Caryl laughed. "That's just because the fan overhead isn't working."

Joshua glanced up. It was true. There were five fans placed strategically around the ceiling and all were spinning except the one above them .

"Say what you like, I think the heat has a lot more to do with my imagining you wining against me than any fan." He scraped up the last of his potato salad and put it in his mouth.

Caryl watched his jaws move and thought she wouldn't have minded testing her dance skills against him.

"Maybe when you come back."

"If I can't get away for some time, will you come up to see me?"

"I'll try. Do you think it'll be hard getting away again?"

Joshua spread his hands on the table and leaned back in his chair. Worry tightened the corners of his eyes.

"If everything's fine and if I can beat off that wolf at my door I'll be back before you've noticed I've gone but…" He grimaced and let his sentence taper off.

"Don't worry, the wolf will huff and puff and he'll find you've built your house of stone. He'll deflate quicker than a Macy's Thanksgiving Day Parade balloon and you and I will be dancing at Quito's before the month is out."

"I hope so, my captain, I really hope so." He reached across the table and took her hand in his.

"You'll see." Caryl turned her hand over and tickled his palm until he smiled and his eyes lightened.

"Do you want dessert?"

"No, I feel full already."

Stacia came to pick up their plates and brought them another pitcher of maubi.

"On the house, Basil say," she informed them, smiling.

When she left, Joshua moved his chair to sit next to Caryl.

"This is life," he said, raising his arm to drape it around the back of her chair.

"Ha. Only if you're independently wealthy."

"Do you wish you were?"

"Yes, sometimes, but then I think I would get bored. I could fill my time with philanthropy but I would still want a real job, something where I could feel I wasn't just being a consumer but was producing too."

"I don't know what I'd do without Tain Music. It's my life." Joshua's tone was soft, his voice low. "I love it. I love seeing the name on the wall. I love my office. I love hearing the magic in the studios. And the singers are just great, egos out to the horizon but they can be really big-hearted. Working with them gives me a natural high." He paused, a smile on his lips, as if thinking about it. "Is it like that for you with the *Elendil*?"

"No, not quite." More elaboration was needed. "I really love it but I don't think I get quite the level of excitement from it I can hear in your voice when you talk about your company." That was actually how she'd felt about the law but she didn't want to go into that with him yet. Later, if they got serious, really serious, then she would tell him. It didn't make sense to do it now when they still weren't sure how things were going to work out between them.

After they finished their maubi they chatted with Stacia and Basil for a few more minutes before strolling back to the jetty where a ferry was getting ready to make a run to Tortola. Caryl and Joshua stood and watched. Five of the passengers were tourists who had taken a day-trip to the island. A few were government workers who staffed the police station and the tiny administration building where the islanders could pay their income tax or apply for a liquor license.

"I guess everybody who lives on these islands takes the sea for granted," said Joshua, his arm around Caryl's waist.

"In a way, I suppose we do. There is no place you can go and be more than five minutes away from it."

In front of them, the ferry pulled slowly away from the jetty. As it passed a red and blue yacht anchored near the harbor's entrance, it began to pick up speed and, in a few more minutes, was out of sight around a bend in the coastline.

Joshua and Caryl untied the *Elendil*'s dinghy from the pier and headed back to the yacht, crossing the ferry's wake.

"I've had a fantastic day," Joshua said, his face glowing. "I feel like I don't want it to end."

"Life is full of endings," Caryl sighed. Perhaps she was just fooling herself with this idyll. "Life itself ends."

"Don't be so gloomy, woman." Joshua dipped his hand in the sea and scooped up some water to splash on her. "I promise you, what we have won't end." He leaned forward, threatening the stability of the dinghy, to kiss her. Caryl returned his kiss with fervor and gave him a bright smile when he sat back down, but in her gut a knot of anxiety twisted itself. A promise was comfort to a fool. That was how the song went, wasn't it?

Back on the *Elendil,* the deck was empty and Caryl imagined that her crew was in their cabin since it was not yet time for Patty to begin preparing for dinner.

"Heading back to your stateroom?" Caryl asked Joshua as she busied herself unpacking their snorkeling equipment.

"Baby, I'm heading wherever you are." Joshua grinned broadly.

"I'm going to take a nap. By myself," she added, seeing Joshua's grin deepen. His face dropped.

"What is it, Caryl? Your mood's changed on me."

"No, it's not that. You know it's against Janus's rules and I really don't want to embarrass Patty and Richardson. Not any more than we already have, anyway."

"Janus needs to rewrite their rules. We're consenting adults. At least, I'm definitely consenting." His eyes twinkled.

Caryl grinned. "I'd consent too, you know that, anywhere but here. But I've been getting some funny vibes from Patty and Richardson. I don't know what they're thinking so let's not push it, okay? Please?"

"Damn, woman. I've been looking forward all day to getting with you but, okay, it's your job. I can't fault you for trying to follow your company's rules." Joshua's tone was dejected.

"Thanks. I knew you would understand. I'll see you later, huh?" She reached up and gave him a chaste kiss on the cheek before striding past, into the saloon. If he touched her, if he tried to hold her back, she knew she would surrender to him but what she needed right now was to put some distance between them. Rules were rules and she had flouted them enough for one trip.

Caryl opened the door to her cabin and flung herself onto her bed. Living for the moment with no thought for rules was what she and Alexander had done. It was wrong then and it would be wrong now. Caryl

JUST AN AFFAIR

would never forget the day Barbara, Alexander's wife, had shown up at the office, her belly high and swollen with new life. She had burst past the secretaries, into Caryl's office and paralyzed the younger woman with shame and misery. Alexander had sworn that whatever there was between him and his wife had died years ago, that they were in the process of getting a divorce. Barbara never came to the firm's social functions, the New Year's Eve party, the Founder's Day Dinner, so Caryl had had no way of knowing the truth until that day. The pregnancy was proof she had been living a lie. The older woman's face had been contorted in anger, a love note from Caryl to Alexander clutched in her fist. Even now, more than a year later, Caryl could hardly bring herself to remember what Barbara had said, shouted really, for the whole office to hear. Caryl's shame and embarrassment had mingled with her awareness of Alexander's deceit and betrayal. Everything he had told her was a sham.

"I'm sorry. I'm sorry," she had whispered to Barbara, stunned. Seconds later, Alexander had rushed in. Caryl never knew who had called him. Barbara had lunged at him and he'd tried to restrain her, to hold her by her wrists, but she'd kicked and flailed at him like a madwoman. Tears had run down her cheeks in rivulets of mascara as she shouted that he was a dirty dog, a bastard and worse.

Alexander hadn't looked Caryl's way once as he struggled with his wife, all his attention focused on her. In a weird way, it had been as if she, Caryl, wasn't even in the room. Even when he had finally pushed Barbara out of her office and was leaving with her, he still hadn't looked back. And that was what had hurt Caryl the most. If only, he'd said something, anything, she could have tried to forgive him, to understand why he'd hurt her so but he had walked out of her office without a word, without even a glance of apology.

As soon as they were gone and the shock had worn off, Caryl had stuffed the pictures on her desk into her handbag, grabbed her laptop and run out of the office. She'd called her parents to let them know she was on her way and caught the next available flight to Virginia, her mind reeling, the image of Barbara going round and round in her brain like a bullet ricocheting off walls in an empty room. Her beautiful, worried mother had met her at the airport and taken her home, her manner brisk, cool but also solicitous.

For the first few days Caryl had mostly hung out in her room or on the garden bench beneath the apple tree, not talking much. Though her parents had kept their distance, her mother took time off from her publishing company to make sure their Grenadian housekeeper cooked Caryl's favorite things just the way she liked them. Often, when David and Marcianne thought she wasn't looking, their concerned glances flew around her head.

It was about a week before Caryl broke her silence. She told them everything, about the way Alexander had made her feel, about the concerts they'd attended, about the trip they'd taken to New Mexico, about the plans they'd had, and finally about Barbara and what had happened at the office. David flew into a rage. He wanted to call Alexander up right away to tell him what a good-for-nothing he was, but Caryl begged him not to. Marcianne simply walked over to her side of the table and gave her a long, tight hug.

"What will you do?" her mother asked.

"I don't know, Mumsie. I know I can't go back there."

"You've done nothing wrong," her father snapped. "He's the lying, cheating son of a…alright!" He waved Marcianne's raised hand aside. "Point is, you've done nothing you can't hold your head up about."

"I'm not going back there, Daddy."

Her father looked at her and realized it wasn't up for debate.

"Ready to come work with your father then?" It was his dream but she wasn't ready to make it a reality.

JUST AN AFFAIR

"Not yet. I still want to know I can make it on my own first."

"Darling, you've been making it ever since you left university. You don't have anything left to prove." Her mother stroked the hair away from Caryl's face, her voice gentle.

"I'm not ready yet for Henry Enterprises." And there the matter rested.

Later, after she had finished watching Larry King and was on her way up to her room, she heard her parents arguing in theirs.

"I still believe she should know that he called. She has that right," her mother said in her cool, dispassionate way.

"I'm not talking about rights!" Her father snapped. "She doesn't need him in her life. He lied to her. Abused her trust. What kind of man is he? It should have been me who answered the phone. I would have told him to go to hell."

Caryl drew closer to the slightly open door, her blood pounding so loudly in her ears she could hardly hear what was being said. Alexander had called? When? Then she realized her parents had known what had happened before she told them.

"He sounds very determined to speak to her so I'm sure he'll call back. You can tell him then. He also said he would like to come here, to speak to us. He wants to explain himself."

"Explain himself! What is there to explain? The man was running around on Caryl."

"David! Caryl's the other woman here, not the wife."

"Yes, yes. Whatever. The point is that the man doesn't have a trustworthy bone in his body

Caryl warred with herself. One part of her argued that eavesdropping was wrong. The other admitted it but wanted to stay to hear just a little bit more.

"Love comes in many shapes and forms, none of them perfect.

Alexander may well love his wife but I spoke to him and I could hear his sincerity. He's truly sorry for his deception and he wishes to talk to Caryl. I think he owes at least that to her but I also think he wants to start again with her. He feels she knows everything now and that there will be no lies between them."

"No lies! There's his wife's pregnancy between them. Is he saying he would just pick up and leave his wife? Now? I didn't think much of him before but if that's what he's proposing to do, I think even less."

"Well, when he comes on Tuesday they can thrash it out."

On Tuesday? Caryl started in shock. Today was Saturday. Tuesday was only a few days away. Caryl drew back from her parents' bedroom and walked slowly to her room, her legs feelings as if they would buckle under her with every step. She wasn't ready to see Alexander. She had to get away. That was the one clear thought in her head. Flight. But to where? Then images of clear waters, white sand and friendly Caribbean faces came to mind.

Caryl stayed up the whole night packing and planning for her trip. The next morning, at breakfast, she announced she had booked her passage to Tortola over the Internet. She would leave on a ten o'clock flight out of Reagan National. Her parents were alarmed but she was firm, careful not to betray any hint that she'd overheard their conversation of the night before. No, she did not want company. Yes, she had enough money. She didn't know what she would do but she would find a job. Yes, she understood that American-trained lawyers needed extra training to work in the British colony. She would do something else. Maybe be a boat captain; don't forget she had the license from the Coast Guard. They were not to tell anyone, and she meant anyone at all, she had said looking fiercely at Marcianne.

Hours later, she was on her flight, winging her way to the tropical paradise that was the British Virgin Islands.

CHAPTER TWELVE

Caryl stepped into the shower and turned up the hot water as hot as she could stand it while she soaped off. She had learned valuable lessons about who she was during her manless ten and a half months and the first of those lessons was a simple one – she had a low tolerance for pain. Another woman might have stayed and turned a blind eye to Alexander's duplicity but doing so would have destroyed her. Lesson number two - the right man could complete her but the wrong one would only bring grief and she wasn't up for that. Lesson number three – being with a man was great but being on her own was fine too. She had loved how Alexander had looked after her and how she felt being the center of his world but it had all been an illusion. Now she was responsible for herself and for keeping it real. Lesson number four – if she could survive Alexander, she could probably survive anything. If Joshua was not Mr. Right, it wouldn't be the end of her world. She just had to keep reminding herself of that and she would be fine.

And finally, Lesson Number Five – whether she was looking for a fling or for marriage, no married or otherwise taken men need apply. She wasn't ever going to go for another love that had to be kept on the down low.

Pushing memories of Alexander and the pain she'd felt at their break-up firmly to the back of her mind, Caryl turned the shower off and grabbed her towel. Minutes later, dressed comfortably in jeans and a lacy blouse, she went looking for Patty who was in the galley peering into the open fridge when she came in.

"I was thinking gazpacho, then salsa shrimp, then finishing with brownie ice cream melts. What do you think?" Patty asked, glancing across at Caryl.

"And good evening to you too. Thank you, yes. I had a lovely day."

Patty shook her head as she closed the fridge door and leaned over the counter to retrieve two papayas from her fresh fruit basket. She laid them beside the jalapeno peppers, cilantro and scallions already on the galley's counter.

"I'm sorry, Caryl." Patty grinned. "I forgot I haven't seen you since this morning. How was Jost? More importantly, how was Joshua?" Patty's left eye closed in a wink as her hands flew above the cutting board, dicing the salsa ingredients with quick strokes of her knife.

"Not too bad. Nothing to write home about." Caryl waved her hand airily as she moved over to the sink and began to remove the shells from the large shrimp Patty had put in there.

"Child, please! When I mentioned Joshua you lit up like the lights in our festival village so I know you had a good time. Spill those beans rattling your gourd. Your secrets are safe with me." Patty's tone changed, became serious. "Richardson and I talked about it, you know. We..." She paused, searched for words. "We like you a lot. We wouldn't do anything to cause you problems. Do you understand?"

"Yes, I do. Thank you." Caryl reached over and gave Patty an impulsive hug. She had hoped they would feel that way but actually she hadn't been at all sure they would support her. If they had decided to tell Janus, she could have been out of a job and that was one headache she couldn't handle right now.

"So you think it's going to go anywhere?"

"I don't know, Patty. I really like him and I would love it if it did but it's a holiday thing, you know. I don't know what the stats say but

JUST AN AFFAIR

I don't think that's the best beginning for a long-term relationship."

"Hmm, I don't know about that. My cousin Annie met her husband in Antigua when she went there to see a cricket match between England and the West Indies. They got married six months later." Patty reached into the fridge for a few more tomatoes.

"Yeah, but will it last?"

"They've been married ten years now, longer than a lot of couples who met through friends or through work."

"I like that story."

"Yes, I thought you might."

The sun was setting by the time the two women emerged from their labors to find that Richardson had already set up the drop leaf table. Caryl helped her crew lay out the dishes and the cutlery and she smiled and nodded at the appropriate spaces in their conversation, but she was really thinking about Joshua, willing him to hurry and come up on deck, wondering what he would wear tonight, longing to see his smile. He was clearly taking his time, however, and the minutes were like hours. At loose ends after the table was ready, Caryl drifted over to the railing to look at the lights of Jost Van Dyke glimmering across the water. On another night, another charter, the scene would have calmed her, soothed any jangled nerves, but tonight Joshua was on her mind and there was nothing soothing about her thoughts.

Caryl folded her arms under her breasts, hugging herself. She was about to turn back to the table when, behind her, she heard Patty and Richardson greet their guest. Caryl froze. He was here. She turned slowly around. Joshua was looking straight at her. Staring back, she felt as if they were alone in the world. Nothing and nobody else existed or mattered.

"Er...Joshua." She stopped, cleared her throat. "Patty went to extra lengths to prepare a memorable last dinner for you. I hope you'll enjoy it."

"She forgets to say she helped," Patty broke in, beaming at her captain.

"Reveal my hand, why don't you?" Caryl quipped. She felt happier than she had any right to be, her doubts seeming absurd in Joshua's presence.

"Well, now I know it'll probably be the most memorable dinner, not just of the trip, but of the year so far."

"Hear, hear," Richardson said. "Now let's eat."

They scraped out their chairs and sat while Patty ladled out the soup.

"This gazpacho is fantastic, Patty." Joshua shot the cook a thoughtful glance. "You know, a friend of mine is opening a restaurant in Greenwich Village."

"What?" Caryl howled in outrage. "Not from right under my nose. I know you're not trying to steal Patty from right under my nose."

"It's an idea but what I was going to say was that if you ever wanted to offer a course in Creole cooking, I'd try to get his people signed up."

"Oh." Caryl subsided. "But where would she hold it, in New York?"

"No, not necessarily. I was thinking Janus might want to offer a culinary cruise. You know, sign up a few people and Patty could teach them as they cruise the islands."

Patty nodded slowly. "That does sound like a good idea. But..." Her head bobbed in a sudden attack of modesty, "do you really think I'm good enough?"

"Patty, of course," Caryl cried. "You're the best." And she should know, Caryl thought. Alexander was a foodie who thought nothing of driving for miles to check out a new restaurant or an up and coming chef.

"You're excellent! The meals I've had on this cruise outstrip any I've had in most of the major capitals of the world." Joshua smiled. "Let Caryl suggest it to Janus. It could be a new marketing strategy for them."

"I will. It's a great idea, Joshua." Caryl beamed at Patty. If Janus went for it, it would mean more pay for the older woman.

Patty's next course, the spicy salsa with grilled shrimp, white rice and a green salad, was also a hit.

"I'll remember this meal for a very long time." Joshua raised his wineglass to toast Patty who smiled bashfully, looking like a shy schoolgirl who suddenly found herself the center of attention.

"So how did you like Jost?" Richardson asked.

"It's an interesting little place. Quiet-seeming but with a lot going on beneath the surface. Caryl was telling me about the drug-smuggling."

"Uh-huh. It's tough for the police to get a grip on that and it's getting worse." Richardson shook his head. "A lot of the kids are growing up seeing their daddy and sometimes their mommy in the business and they just think it's normal."

"It's so bad kids feel they just have to pick up and leave the island altogether if they don't want to find themselves mixed up in it," said Patty. "Jost is isolated and it's small, there aren't many job options."

"Government needs to pay more attention to the place, to all the sister islands, actually." Caryl had argued this point before with Patty and Richardson. "The politicians can't just throw up their hands and say, well, what choices are there? They've got to bring choices to the people. Organize eco-friendly developments. Inspire more entrepreneurship. Just because the people live on Jost doesn't mean that the things they produce have to be sold there."

"Yes, there is a global market out there." Joshua nodded soberly in support.

"For what?" Richardson challenged.

"All kinds of things. Art. Music. Crafts. Exotic produce."

"Ganga," Patty chimed in.

"Yeah, there's a huge market for that. You're right." Richardson smirked.

Caryl shook her fist at them in mock anger before excusing herself to begin preparations for the last leg of their trip. Around the *Elendil*, the lights of the other yachts and the lights on land were comforting, relieving the darkness of the now moonless night. Every now and then, voices and the sounds of music reached them, crossing the inky sea like gifts, but Caryl had work to do. In the pilothouse, she checked her equipment, lifted the anchor, then put the *Elendil* smoothly in motion. From Jost Van Dyke to Cane Garden Bay was a half-hour trip. Caryl glanced at her watch, it was just after eight so they would arrive in good time for the nine o'clock check-in she had arranged with the hotel's receptionist.

The lights of Cane Garden Bay shone in front of her, clear and welcoming, as the *Elendil* plowed through the waves. Caryl was disappointed Joshua didn't join her, but she reminded herself it would be wrong to expect him. After all, hadn't she made it clear that she wanted to be alone? If she desired his company, she would have to search him out.

A half-hour later, she dropped anchor and descended to the deck. Now she knew why Joshua had not come up to her. Richardson was moving his bags off the diving platform and into the sturdy dinghy.

Caryl leaned over the railing to watch him. Catching sight of her, he grinned.

JUST AN AFFAIR

"I think somebody is glum that their captain is giving them the cold shoulder."

"But I'm not. Not really."

"Uh-huh."

"Captain, will you be coming with me?" Joshua's deep voice at her back startled her. She swung around to look at him.

"No…no, Richardson will take you."

"Why not you?" He stepped closer to her, his magnetism intensifying with his nearness.

"Richardson will be more help with the luggage. There's no need for me to come." Pressing her back against the railing, she slid away from him.

Joshua's hand reached out and gripped her shoulder. His hold was not painful but neither did it allow escape.

"There is every need," he said, his voice low. "Can't you tell? Don't you want to spend our last night together?"

"Yes, I do." Caryl felt as if her limbs were turning to water.

"Then I'll come back to the boat after we check in. You won't leave, will you? Promise me you'll wait."

"Where would I go?" she asked, trying to make him smile. "You'll have the dinghy and it's too late for a water taxi operator to be around."

"Good." Joshua's features relaxed into a relieved smile.

"Maybe you shouldn't go at all. We book people into the hotel so they can get a last minute taste of nightlife on the island."

"You're the only thing I want a taste of tonight."

Warmth flared in Caryl's stomach and her breasts tightened as if he'd actually touched them.

"Tell Richardson we're having a change of plans, and I'll let the hotel know you won't be coming."

"It won't be a problem?

"No, the hotel's owned by Janus."

"Great." He turned away. "Richardson," he called out.

Caryl smiled as she went back up the pilothouse ladder to make her call. Joshua had looked like a little boy who got just what he wanted for Christmas.

Neither he nor Richardson was around after she finished her call but the dinghy was once again in its position.

Caryl hurried to her cabin. If he thought he'd had the dinner of the year that night, well, she would make sure he also got the loving of his life. A sumthin-sumthin he wouldn't forget in a hurry, whatever his plans. Caryl put on a Luther Vandross CD, shed her clothes and stepped into her shower. When she stepped out, still wet because she liked letting herself air-dry sometimes, she rummaged around in the bottom of her bureau drawer. She hadn't used her Fred Hayman 273 since she'd arrived in the islands, but it was the perfect scent for what she was planning. Caryl slathered on the lotion and then layered it with the perfume. She sniffed at the crook of her arm. Umm, she smelled good.

Caryl rummaged some more and fished out a red nightgown with lacy cups that felt buttery smooth in her hands. She shrugged herself into it, her eyes gleaming as she thought of Joshua's reaction to the effort she was making for him. Last but not least, she dipped her finger into a pat of shimmery powder and dusted it on her shoulders.

A minute later, a soft knock made her heart race. She checked herself in the mirror. Her skin glowed, her lips were moist. *Girl, even if I say so myself, you look sweet enough to eat.* Caryl blew her reflection a kiss before turning to face the door. "Come in," she whispered. Then louder, "Come in."

Joshua pushed the door open and walked in. A wide, appreciative smile split his face at the sight of her.

"You like?" she asked, twirling, so glad to see the tenderness in his eyes, to see him.

"Yes. I like very much."

"You are kind." Caryl batted her lashes.

"I'm besotted, that's what I am," Joshua murmured, crossing the room to encircle her with his arms. He pressed hot, quick kisses against her throat, her face, her shoulders and Caryl felt weak with desire. Her arms encircled his neck as his teeth nibbled her ear and his tongue began a teasing exploration of its delicate contours. She could feel his manhood stirring against her stomach and she pressed herself against him, doing a little bump and grind to Luther's beat.

Joshua moaned, his breath hot against her neck. He pushed the nightie's thin straps aside and took a step back to look at her as the gown dropped away and Caryl stood nude and proud before him, the nipples of her small, perfect breasts jutting out. His fingers working quickly, Joshua tore off his shirt and pulled her to him, crushing his bare chest against her. His lips sought the softness of her mouth, nuzzled at her neck. Holding her to him, he drew her to the bed and lowered her to it.

"You never asked but there's something I want to tell you. The condoms." He took the pack out and put it on her nightstand.

"Yes?"

"I just don't want you to think I travel with them like I'm always ready for sex with whoever. A friend gave them to me as a good-bye present at the airport. Just pressed them into my hand. I thought of throwing them away, but then I said, what the hell, so I kept them. Anyway, my point is, I'm not a sex maniac. I don't want you to worry about me when I'm gone."

"I didn't even think about them," Caryl lied. She *had* wondered.

After all, everybody knew men who took condoms with them on solo trips were men looking for action, men to stay away from.

"Richard knows I've been single for a while. I guess he was hoping I'd let loose on vacation."

Caryl kneaded his shoulders. "I think you're less tense than when you got here. You don't look so tightly-wound."

"I don't feel so, either. You've worked a miracle, woman, and I love you."

It was what Caryl longed to hear.

"I love you too, Joshua Tain," she murmured, as she undid his belt and opened his pants. She allowed her hand to wander over the front of his blue silk boxers as Joshua again took possession of her lips with a kiss. He was an expert kisser and it was hard for her to pull away but she had a lot more in mind for tonight.

"Wha...baby?" Joshua's face reflected his confusion.

Caryl put a finger to her lips. "Shhh."

She pushed him up the bed so only his feet dangled over the edge and grabbed up the massage oil she had put on the nightstand earlier.

"Sweetheart, it's time for the massage of your life," she purred. "Are you ready?" She poured some of the almond scented oil into the palm of her hand and gave him the sexiest look she knew, her mouth slightly open as she showed him the tip of her tongue.

Joshua's face was open, eager. "Woman, I'm completely in your care."

Caryl rubbed her palms together and placed them at the pit of his stomach. Slowly, firmly she began to move her hands in wide, fanning circles, moving them up to his shoulders and down again. Joshua moaned softly and Caryl bent forward to brush his lips with hers. He tried to push himself up to prolong the kiss but she pulled back and poured some more oil in her hands. She began gently kneading the

JUST AN AFFAIR

sides of his stomach, again moving upward until she reached his chest. Joshua closed his eyes as his face softened into bliss.

Caryl followed the kneading with long, light feathery strokes using only the tips of her fingers. This last obviously had an effect on him. His sex stirred against her but maybe that was only because she had shifted herself so he was firmly between her legs and every now and then she gave a slight, teasing squeeze so he wouldn't forget what was coming up on the menu later.

Joshua groaned.

"Woman, please, please..."

He reached for her but she drew back.

"Come now, turn on your stomach."

"Ohhh. I can think of something that would relax me even more."

"You mean you don't like my massage?" Caryl injected a hurt tone into her voice.

"Woman! Didn't your momma ever tell you not to tease the nice man?"

"No, she never did. Now turn on your stomach." Caryl slapped him lightly on his thigh.

Still groaning, Joshua did as he was told.

Caryl used the same moves on his back as she had on his front but she took more time kneading all his muscles, paying particular attention to his firm, well-made bottom.

"Caryl, your fingers have magic in them. That feels damn good." Joshua waggled his head as if amazed by how relaxed his neck and shoulder muscles were.

"Okay, now my turn." Caryl wiped her hands on the towel she had put on her pillow and threw herself back on the bed, her nipples hard because she had been waiting for this part all along.

Joshua grinned as he reached for the bottle. When his fingers first touched her stomach, Caryl closed her eyes to revel in the wave of pleasure crashing up from her groin. But when he began to massage her breasts with firm circular strokes, Caryl reached down and surprised him with a massage of her own.

"If you keep doing that, I won't be able to continue what I'm doing," Joshua whispered hoarsely into her ear.

"Who says you have to?" She pulled him down on top of her, too filled with desire to pretend she could wait any longer.

The next day, the morning's rosy light was already streaming into the cabin when Caryl awoke. They had thrown the sheets aside and Joshua was pressed against her side, his arm across her chest, one heavy leg over hers. Caryl pointed her toes and raised her arms behind her head in a sinuous stretch. Joshua's arm tightened around her and she turned on her side to look at him. One eye was open, staring at her; the other was hidden by his pillow.

"Good morning, my captain." Joshua smiled and her heart turned over.

"Good morning." Suddenly shy for no good reason at all, Caryl sat up and pulled the sheet up under her chin.

"I will be back. I *will*." It was as if Joshua sensed her secret fear.

"You always seem to know the right thing to say," she said, watching the fine lines radiating from the corner of his eyes. Her hand drifted over to smooth them and Joshua leaned forward, pressed a kiss on her forehead, on each cheek, on her nose and, finally, on her lips. He drew aside the sheet that covered her nakedness and pushed her gen-

JUST AN AFFAIR

tly on her back.

"You are so beautiful," he murmured. He knelt on the bed at her feet, his eyes greedy for the sight of her body. With a quick movement that took her by surprise he lifted her foot and began to plant kisses on her toes, lightly sucking each before moving on to the next one. Caryl shivered with pleasure. Her nipples puckered with desire as Joshua pushed himself up to dot the shins of both her legs with kisses and nibbled her knees. His hands began to knead her thighs, his lips following the path they made. He pressed a firm kiss between her legs, then pushed himself up to plant one on her mouth. Pulsing with desire, Caryl arched her back, pressing herself against him even as he sank down into her arms.

In contrast to the night before, their lovemaking that morning was slow and intensely tender. They didn't leave Caryl's cabin until the sun was almost high in the sky, washing the room with golden light. By the time they made it up on deck where Patty and Richardson were relaxing over their breakfast, it was after seven thirty.

"Good morning, Joshua, Caryl," they chorused. Richardson ducked behind a newspaper but not before Caryl caught the smirk trembling on his mouth. She exchanged a rueful glance with Joshua. When you lived on a boat with other people, your business was theirs and vice versa.

"How're you all doing?" Joshua asked as he and Caryl began to help themselves to the pancakes, bacon, eggs and fresh fruit on the table.

"Good, good." Patty answered for Richardson, who lowered his paper to look at them.

"Maybe not as good as you, though, eh?" he chortled, the paper rising again.

Caryl shook her head and rolled her eyes.

"Maybe," said Joshua and smiled broadly as Richardson re-emerged to look at him.

On shore, the bustle of island living had begun. They could hear car horns tooting and a stereo blasting "So Many Rivers to Cross," an old Jimmy Cliff hit.

Caryl looked around, admiring the view of the island from the boat. Heavy February rains made the hills that rose above Cane Garden Bay lush and inviting, almost obscuring the higher hillside houses, and every now and then, a car appeared on the ribbon of mountain road that looked almost carelessly draped over Zion Hill. Hill House, the Janus-owned hotel where Joshua had had a reservation for the previous night was plainly visible, its whitewashed walls rising from a low cliff which jutted into the sea.

Closer to the *Elendil*, there were at least twenty to thirty boats of varying shapes and sizes anchored in the large harbor. A small cruiser sporting the distinctive star and stripes of the Puerto Rican flag was anchored nearby, its adult occupants sunning themselves on deck, clearly deaf to the shrieks of their children playing in the water around the boat. The clatter of dishes as Patty rose and gathered her and Richardson's plates together brought Caryl back to the *Elendil*.

"We're just going in now. Call us when Joshua's ready, okay?"

"Thanks, Patty. See you later." Joshua's plane left at 10:00am. They had very little time left.

"Are you coming to the airport with me?" Joshua asked as he brought a mouthful of dripping pancakes to his mouth. He was booked on an Air BVI flight to Puerto Rico, connecting there to Kennedy.

"No, I don't think that would be a good idea." Caryl reached over and wiped a drop of syrup from the corner of his mouth with her finger. Looking at him from under her lashes, she ran her finger over her

JUST AN AFFAIR

lips then slowly licked them with the tip of her tongue.

"Ah, woman, you're giving me a good reason to stay on this boat. You know that, right?"

Caryl laughed. "Sorry. I was just fixing you up so when you got on the plane everybody will know you have a woman who takes care of you, doesn't let you walk around with glop on your mouth."

"If you come to see me off, then they'll know what the woman who takes care of me looks like." He snapped off a bite of crispy bacon.

"Ha. That's okay."

"Afraid you wouldn't be able to resist following me, eh?"

Caryl's smile widened into a grin. "How did you guess?" The more boring reason was that she had to take the *Elendil* back to its slip before she could go off on her own. That was a Janus rule and she didn't want to break too many of them.

"Maybe I shouldn't have left so soon after staving off that takeover bid, but I really needed the break." He stretched his arms overhead. "I have to see how everything is before I can know how soon I can leave again, though. And then there are the Black Music Awards coming up in June." Joshua's brow furrowed as he talked and Caryl realized that, however promising he thought his employees, he was apprehensive about what he might find when he got back.

"I'm sure everything will be okay. If something had gone seriously wrong, they would have moved heaven and earth to reach you."

Joshua smiled. "Yeah, you're probably right. A week shouldn't make a big difference."

"Are you going to miss me?"

"By the time I get to Puerto Rico I'll probably be missing you so bad I'll have to catch a return flight and come right back."

"You know, I never believed…" Caryl's voice trailed away. She was going to say she never thought she'd find love again but it wasn't time for true confessions.

"I never believed I could be so happy," she amended, smiling at him. It was true, watching his handsome face, the way his eyes twinkled when he smiled, made her feel good all over.

"Caryl, believe me when I say I was beginning to doubt it myself."

"How could you? Don't you know you're what every healthy black woman is praying for? You're not kicking it with men; you're not in prison. My God, you own your own company." If they did make it down the aisle anytime in the future, she would be the envy of all the single sisters she knew.

"Maybe. I've had my share of come-ons." Caryl could bet he had. "But I get the impression women aren't always checking me for who I am. More for how I look or what I have. And those things aren't important. They aren't the real me."

"The real you is ambitious and driven. What you have is a result of that and I don't think you can blame women for noticing it and finding it attractive." She certainly had.

"Yeah, I suppose, but a lot of women don't want it to go any deeper than that. They just want to relate on that level. It's all about the bling-bling, like my man Dread Eye says."

Dread Eye was a rapper with two songs currently on the BET Rap City chart.

"Is he on your label?"

"Yes. Signed him when he was just twelve."

"Hmm, I think you've got to cut the sisters some slack. They see a fine-looking guy like you roll up wherever in your Bee Em wearing your Versace, they're going to do more than just flash the green light. But don't worry." Caryl grinned. "Soon as they know I'm the Sister with the Mister, they'll back off."

"Oh, yeah?" Joshua grinned back at her. "You're going to be packing heat or something?"

"If I have to."

She glanced at her watch.

"Shoot, Joshua. It's after eight. You've got to go now if you want to catch your flight."

"Maybe I don't." He grabbed her hand and held it tight.

"Yes, you do." It would be great if he could stay a day, even an hour more, but she wouldn't hold him back. He needed to know she wasn't a clingy woman. There was no way she would try and come between him and his love for his company. She took her hand back and rose to her feet.

"I'll go call the Richardsons."

A few minutes later, Caryl's eyes blurred as the dinghy, with Richardson astern, pulled away from the *Elendil* with Joshua. Caryl flicked the wetness away, determined not to cry, not now anyway when Patty, who stood at her side, would see. Their goodbyes had been quick, almost formal. A brief kiss and a longer hug. Joshua held her hand until the last possible minute. Now she watched as he stepped up onto the hotel's small jetty, turned in her direction and waved both arms to her in a semaphore of love. She waved furiously back, time suspended as they stared at each other across the expanse of water. *Come back, don't go*, she wanted to shout. Joshua backed away down the jetty, still waving; then, as he reached the hotel steps he stopped, turned, disappeared.

"That was quite a charter, hmm?" Patty teased as she began to pick up the rest of the breakfast dishes still on the table.

"It was. It certainly was." But Caryl refused to be drawn out any farther. The *Elendil*'s next charter was in two days. Forty-eight hours of time stretched in front of her, and she wondered if she should have gone to the airport. Surely, it would have done no harm. One more hour or so with him before all the hours without him. But no, she had done the right thing. Letting him go now was hard, but it would have been much harder to see his plane disappear into the clouds.

CHAPTER THIRTEEN

Two anxious days passed before Caryl heard anything from Joshua. Then, just a few minutes after their new clients came aboard, Caryl was passing through the saloon when the boat phone rang. It was a bad connection and, for a minute, all Caryl could hear was static.

"Hello," she yelled. "Hello."

She was just about to give up when she heard his voice.

"Caryl," Joshua shouted.

"Yes. Yes. It's me." She was absurdly happy.

"Caryl…business…coming down…see…" He was breaking up. She couldn't understand what he was saying.

"What? Joshua, I can't hear you."

"I'll be…couple weeks…give…" It was impossible to make out what he was saying. She could have screamed.

"Are you coming in the next couple of weeks?" she yelled. "Just say yes or no." She gripped the phone to her ear but all she got in return was a blast of static.

"I miss you," she yelled on the off chance he could hear. Pressing her finger on the phone disconnect, she hung up and then dialed Joshua's direct line at the office. He had to be there, it was mid-morning.

"Good morning. Tain Music, may I help you?"

Caryl, slowly, put the phone back in its rest without speaking. If his secretary was answering his line, that meant he was unavailable, on his phone, in a meeting or out on the road. But, hey, what did it matter? He had called and he was coming back. She was sure that was what his garbled words meant.

That night, Caryl was in her cabin preparing for bed when Patty knocked on her door.

"You have a call, Caryl."

"I do? Who?"

"It's not Joshua," Patty said, shrugging as she followed Caryl up to the saloon. "The voice is unfamiliar. Not your Dad's, either."

Puzzled, Caryl picked up the phone.

"Hello. This is Caryl Walker."

"Caryl, thank God, I've found you."

Caryl almost dropped the phone. Her knees dissolved and she sank down on the couch next to the table on which the phone was kept. She suddenly felt like an old, tired rag doll who'd lost her stuffing.

"Alexander?"

"Yes, it's me. I've had a devil of a time finding you. Nobody would help me. Your family and friends wouldn't even give me the time of day. How are you, baby?"

Caryl was speechless. What did he expect her to say? Her fingers felt cold. She touched them to her cheek.

"Caryl. Caryl, are you there?"

Why, oh why, was he coming through loud and clear when Joshua, the man she really wanted to hear from, had been unintelligible?

"What do you want, Alexander?"

"Baby, baby. Please. I want to come see you. There is so much I want to tell you. Please, baby. Everything's been sorted out now. I'm booked on..." But Caryl didn't let him finish. She hung up the phone

JUST AN AFFAIR

and then sat staring warily at it as if she expected it to come to life and bite her. Her hands trembled.

What did this mean? Alexander calling her months, no, almost a year after their crisis. She rubbed her head with both hands, kneading her scalp even as a headache began to make itself felt at her temples.

But how had he found her and what did he mean he was booked? On a flight to the Virgin Islands? Oh no, he had to be crazy. She shouldn't have hung up when she did. He had to be stopped. Suppose he arrived when Joshua did. They might travel on the same flight, even, by some hellish coincidence, in adjoining seats. If they met, her secrets would come tumbling out. Hell, they would be sitting right there beside Joshua in blood and bone. Alexander had to be headed off. Her stomach churned at the thought of talking to him again. Alexander was her past, why was he trying to make himself a part of her present? She would have to call him, tell him in no circumstances was he to come to the islands. She didn't want to see him, had nothing she needed to say to him and he couldn't possibly have anything to say to her that she wanted to hear. Caryl jumped up from her couch and ran to her cabin to look for her address book. Minutes later, she was on the phone again, the book open to Shayna's new number.

"Shayna, I need your help."

"And hello to you too, girlfriend," her friend's sleepy voice answered. "Why, I'm doing just fine, thanks for asking."

"Shayna, Shayna. Please listen. Alexander just called."

"Alexander? Shoot! I told that dog not to bother sniffing 'round you no more."

"You told him…? When did you talk to him? Why didn't you tell me he was calling around?"

"Shoot, girl! He's been calling me every couple weeks for the past three or four months, trying to get me to tell him where you are. I didn't tell you about it because I figured he'd give up and get lost. Guess I was wrong."

Caryl raked her fingers over her hair. This made no sense.

"Why, Shayna? What does he want?"

"Honey, I can only tell you what he told me. He said he's got everything together now and he wants you back in his life. Said he's been like a madman ever since you left. According to him, you're the love of his life." Shayna sucked her teeth as if to say she hadn't believed a word.

"So it's been, lessee, a'most a year since it all went down and he suddenly can't get me off his mind?"

"Weeeell…" Shayna dragged out the word as if she were trying to delay what she had to say next. "It seems like he's been looking for you ever since. I met Tula in Sassafras," Caryl remembered the coffee bar where they all used to hang out, "when I was in the city last. Back in November, I think. Anyway, she said Alexander had called her at her workplace, even come around. He was looking for you."

"Shay. You should have told me. Why didn't you tell me?"

"Honey, like I said, I thought I was doing what you wanted. Anyway, what good would it have done? She told him she didn't know where you were and that was the truth. You'd been down there in the islands for months before you let on where you were to any of us. Me included."

Caryl sighed. She knew her secrecy then had hurt her best friend and she had tried to make up for it, but keeping her whereabouts from Alexander had been the most important thing to her at the time.

"But you could still have told me he was looking for me, Shay." Not, she remembered, that her parents had done any better. Caryl could still recollect every word of the conversation she'd overheard between her parents.

JUST AN AFFAIR

"So now you know, sugar," Shayna said, bringing her back to the present. "Grapevine confirms he got a divorce and his ex-wife's checked herself into some kind of rest home for money-dripping nutcases. I didn't ask him about none of that because I didn't want him to think I was any interested. Or that you would be."

A brief silence followed as Caryl tried to collect her thoughts. Alexander, free and looking for her, that was news indeed, but he still didn't stand a chance. Not after the way he'd treated her. And not with Joshua in her life. Remembering Joshua reminded Caryl of the reason for her call.

"Shayna, do you have his number?"

"Alexander's? I thought you wanted to stay far from that guy."

"I do and I need the phone number to tell him. I just panicked and hung up on him when he called. I've got to phone him back and tell him to stay the hell away."

"Geez, girlfriend, I'm sorry but I never wrote it down. Didn't think I would ever need it."

"That's alright." But Caryl couldn't keep the disappointment from her voice. "Hey, you think Tula would have it?"

"I could call her and ask but I doubt it. I wish I had it but all I remember is that it was a California number. That's where he's living now."

"He's working there?"

"Guess so. I don't know if he's got his own firm or what."

"Okay, alright. Thanks anyway, Shay."

"No prob, honey. Stay sweet."

"Yeah, you too."

Caryl flipped idly through her address book as she tried to come up with some way of contacting her ex-lover. He had never had his phone listed before and she didn't know where in California he lived.

He might not even be there anymore. Caryl gave up her vague search and pitched the book across the room, where it fell harmlessly into an armchair. Nibbling her top lip, she rose to pick it up before walking slowly back to her cabin. Maybe she didn't need to call. Maybe things would just sort themselves out. After all, there were several possibilities. One, Alexander was bluffing and would not show up on her doorstep, a possibility heightened by the fact that she was out to sea. But this was just a three-day cruise; she would be back at Nanny Cay in next to no time. Caryl's thoughts hurried on. Possibility Two, Alexander turned up but she sent him packing long before Joshua could get even a whiff of his presence. That was definitely likely. Three, but she didn't want to think about three. Three was really just plain impossible. She would never get caught up in Alexander's lies again. She'd shoot herself first. Four, Alexander arrived after Joshua, saw them together, and immediately crawled back under whatever rock a snake like him lived.

Think, she admonished herself. The possibilities were really endless. Anything could happen. Alexander's plane could even be hijacked, but no, she wouldn't really wish that on anyone, not even him. She must just try not to worry. She would cross whatever bridge she had to, when she had to.

The next day dawned rainy, disappointing the *Elendil's* Chilean guests, but Caryl reassured them that by mid-morning, when they were scheduled to arrive at Peter Island, the skies would be clear. It was what the weatherman had said the night before and he was usually more right than wrong. But heavy, gray rain clouds still hung in the sky and there was a light drizzle when the yacht drew up at the Peter Island Resort and Marina jetty. Looking panicked, like cats threatened with a dousing, the Chileans retreated to their cabins, promising to re-emerge for lunch at the resort.

JUST AN AFFAIR

"I'm getting cabin fever. Why don't we go take a look at the shops?" Patty suggested. "They were closed last week when we were here."

"Good idea," Caryl answered. "We can leave Richardson in charge."

Richardson didn't object when they presented him with the plan and, after promising to be back in a couple hours, the two women ran through the rain to the resort.

The first shop they went into had an extensive lingerie collection. "I bet Joshua would like to see you in this." Patty held up a long, strappy, black nightgown.

"He might." Caryl fingered the cool, silky fabric. She held the hanger up against her. "It looks like my size too." She inspected the tag. It *was* her size.

"Why don't you get it?"

Caryl held the nightie up again. If she bought it, then that would be like saying definitely, yes, she and Joshua had a future. He'd said he was coming back, but suppose he didn't? She would feel so foolish every time she saw the nightie in her drawer, reminding her of another romantic hope gone wrong.

"Nah." She thrust it back on the rack. "But what about you, Patty? Why don't you give Richardson something to think about? Take a look at this." She fished out a long, satin number in cream with wide straps and sheer bra cups. Sexy but not overly so. "This looks like you."

"It might but that man only has one thing on his mind when he comes to bed and that's sleep. I could have on a thong and nipple rings and he wouldn't notice."

"Patty, you're kidding me! Is that true? Don't you mind?"

"Child, to tell you the truth, I don't. When we first got married it was two and three times a night but after the children started coming, it got difficult to work up the energy and, now they're almost grown, it just doesn't seem important."

They left the store empty-handed and headed for a gift-shop.

"But you must miss it? Come on, Patty!"

"Not really. I mean, don't get me wrong, we do get up to mischief but it's like once a month or so now and believe me, that's fine with me. I know he's not straying, so why should I worry?"

"Hmm, I can't imagine it. You have a man and you all don't do the nookie every night?" Caryl picked up a dolphin carved in glass and turned it around to catch the light.

"Child, you're living proof it ain't that important. Look at you. You were without it how long before Joshua came along?"

"Yeah, but Patty, that's different. I didn't have a man at all. If I had one and wasn't getting it we'd be in therapy quicker than you can say 'life-size dildo,' that's for sure."

A white salesclerk who had been hurrying over to them made a quick about turn, her ears red.

Patty burst into laughter.

"You going get that dolphin or you going get us locked up for indecency?"

"I'm getting it." It would make a lovely present for Shayna.

"Captain Walker?"

A young man in the uniform of a bellhop called to her from the reception area as the women emerged from the gift shop.

"Yes?"

"These are for you, ma'am. They just arrived this morning." He turned behind him and picked up a huge bunch of white Easter lilies prettily wrapped in green florists' paper. Beaming, he hurried over and held it out to her. Caryl stared at him. When he saw she was too

JUST AN AFFAIR

shocked to crook her arm to receive them, he helpfully did it for her, depositing the flowers in one smooth gesture. Smiling, he turned away to help an arriving guest with her luggage.

"Oh, my goodness, Caryl. They're lovely. He must have put a lot of thought and effort into getting them here to you."

"Umm. What?" Caryl looked at the flowers in her arms. She was trying to think. Had she ever told Joshua Easter lilies were her favorite? When would the subject have come up? Flowers like these didn't grow in the Virgin Islands. They couldn't have seen them on one of their walks.

"There's a card. Aren't you going to open it?" Patty's excited voice at her shoulder recalled Caryl to the present.

"Yes," she said. "Of course." But it was with a sinking feeling that she extracted the card from the holder and, still gripping the bouquet, struggled to tear it open with her fingernail.

"Here, let me help you," Patty volunteered, taking the card from Caryl's nerveless fingers.

"What does it say?" She held it up to Caryl's face.

Caryl stared. Her arms dropped to her sides and the flowers would have fallen to the ground if Patty hadn't grabbed them. "I'm sorry for everything. You are the only woman for me. Alexander." The writing swam before Caryl's eyes sending shock waves through her. Suddenly very cold, she walked over to the lobby's seating area and dropped into one of the oversized chairs. Patty followed her, concern and puzzlement creasing her brow, the flowers cradled in her arms.

"Child, what is it? Isn't it Joshua?" Considerate to the core, Patty had tucked the card in among the flowers without even glancing at it.

"Read it, Patty. It's okay. I don't mind." Caryl's thoughts were a jumble. The flowers meant he knew her itinerary, so if he wasn't already here, she jerked her head up to look around suspiciously, he would certainly be waiting for her when she landed back on Tortola.

"Who's Alexander?"

Caryl groaned. She would have preferred to never mention his name again to anybody but Patty was like a surrogate mother to her. Anyway, it was silly to keep this from her if Alexander planned to show up in the next couple days.

"He's the reason I came to the Virgin Islands," Caryl said, beginning her story. She left out certain parts, not to make her actions seem any purer or more innocent than they had been, but because she thought they were unnecessary details. She had willingly gotten caught up in a married man's lies. Like a child willing to believe that a fat man in a red suit could lug a bagful of gifts to everybody's house in one night, she had wanted to believe everything he told her about his marriage. That he was separating from his wife, that she'd moved out, had never understood him and that they hadn't shared the same bed for years before the split. Caryl tried not to let her bitterness show. She spoke in a flat, unemotional voice, like somebody reading aloud another person's bad news.

"Wow!" Patty pushed herself back in her seat as Caryl finished with a short account of her discovery of Alexander's wife's pregnancy. "Wow! We always wondered why you left law and came to the back of beyond. That must have been a terrible experience."

"The back of beyond was exactly what I needed."

"I can see why. Goodness!" Patty's voice was full of sympathy.

"And now he's turning up again like some kind of bad penny." Caryl nibbled the inside of her bottom lip.

"Child, there's no use going to pieces about it. He comes, you just got to deal with it. Tell him he can't catch the same bird twice." Patty's tone was firm, un-judgmental.

"Yes, but I don't even want to see him. And suppose he's here

JUST AN AFFAIR

when Joshua gets back?"

"You didn't tell Joshua about him?"

"No, Patty, how could I? I wouldn't even have told you if it wasn't for these flowers. I don't know what you must be thinking of me now." Caryl rocked forward on her seat then threw herself back. "I just want to forget about the whole thing."

"Child, that is your life. My mother always used to say, you can't take milk from coffee. It's true. What's done is done. You just have to learn from your mistakes and move on. And I can tell you, it would be a mistake to hide this from Joshua. Whether Alexander is on the island or wherever, the next time you see Mr. Tain, sit him down and tell him."

"Patty, he'll hate me. I was so stupid. I hurt Barbara so much."

"Honey, I'm not going to say you didn't do wrong. You did." Patty leaned forward and took one of Caryl's hands in hers. "But you were naïve and Alexander played on that. Most married men don't leave their wives; they just want a little piece on the side every now and then so they make up a story about how miserable they are. A man could be married to a saint but he'll find things to complain about and a woman hoping for her own wedding bells will only hear what she wants to hear. That's the way that wind blows." She squeezed Caryl's hand. "Alexander sounds like real bad news to me. You deserve better."

"But suppose I've made another mistake and Joshua's like that too."

"I don't think so. You can tell a lot about a man by the way he treats his mother or whoever raised him, and Joshua called his gran almost every day during the cruise. Plus, he was always sweet to you and, most important, he's not married."

"God, I hope you're right, Patty."

"I am, trust me. Oh, look." Patty sat up in her chair. "Here come the clients."

Caryl twisted around. It was true. The Chileans were heading into the restaurant for lunch. Seeing Patty and Caryl, they waved.

"Let's go," Caryl said, rising to her feet. The knot Alexander's call had tied in her stomach the night before was gone. Talking to Patty had improved her mood no end.

"We're leaving the flowers?" Patty dropped her face into the bouquet, her eyes closed. "Heaven must smell like this."

"You can have them if you want," Caryl replied over her shoulder as she joined the Chileans. But a couple hours later as they all trooped back out of the restaurant, she noticed their magnificent beauty overflowed from a tall glass vase on the reception counter.

The next two days were uneventful from Caryl's point of view. The Chileans swam, snorkeled and dived, Patty and Richardson did what they did and she, herself, breathed deep and long and tried not to think about what she might have to deal with when she got back to Tortola. So what if Alexander showed up when they put in to Nanny Cay? She would deal with it just as Patty had said. When you have no options, no choice in a matter, then you just do what you have to do. She refused to entertain any doubt about her ability to send Alexander away when the time came.

So when Tuesday came and went without any sign of her former lover, Caryl felt almost letdown. The *Elendil* had docked at about ten in the morning so the Chileans could catch their one o'clock flight. Caryl had surreptitiously scanned the harbor for any sign that Alexander was there waiting for her. There hadn't been any. Catching Patty watching her, Caryl gave a thumbs up for the all-clear. She didn't let on that she was wishing with all her heart that the booking agents would call with an unexpected charter beginning the next day or, even better, that same afternoon. But the phone didn't ring and their next scheduled departure wasn't until Thursday, for another three-day cruise. There was no help for it; the *Elendil* would spend the next couple of days accessibly docked at the marina. Caryl contemplated taking the boat out to sea, maybe putting in at Ginger Island, arguably the least hospitable of the island chain. No FTD florist, much less a house in sight. But going back out was out of the question. Running away, she was learning, never solved anything, even if it did make a body temporarily feel a whole lot better.

The next morning, Wednesday, Caryl was on the aft deck, curled up in a lounge chair reading the latest installment in Maya Angelou's biography series when she heard her name being called. She sat up and looked around.

"Phone for you." A young man from the marina office waved to her from the head of the pier.

"Who…" Then she thought better of asking. If it was Alexander and she refused to answer that would just provide the marina office people with fodder for gossip and speculation. Grudgingly, and with all her fingers and toes mentally crossed, Caryl stalked off the boat, her brows lowered in annoyance, ready to give the blasted man a piece of her mind.

"Hello." She tried not to sound gruff and failed.

"Caryl?"

"Joshua! It's so good to hear your voice." And not Alexander's. But that was best left unsaid.

"Thanks, sexy lady. Okay, I've got a confirmed flight for Saturday. Can you wait that long to see me?"

"Hmm, I don't know." Euphoria raced through her and she didn't try to keep it from coloring her voice. "The moon's waxing and you know how us wine maidens get when that silvery, swollen thing is hanging way up there above us."

Joshua chuckled. "I've got something else doing some swelling every time I think of you. Fact is, it's swelling right now."

"Ooh, honey." Caryl dropped her voice to a throaty purr, turning away from the curious stares of the other people in the office. "I wish I could be there to look after it for you. I think I know what to do to take it down and make you feel real good about it."

"Yeah?" Joshua's breathing quickened. "Want to tell me what that is?"

"I'd lick it like an ice cream cone on a hot day in the middle of July and…"

"Woman, stop. Lord, if you could only see what you're doing to me. Whew! This kinda distance from you isn't good for my stress levels at all. I swear my heart is racing."

Caryl burst out laughing. "You started it," she pointed out.

"Yeah, but have mercy!" His voice got serious. "I can't wait to see you, Caryl. I'll be in a meeting and I remember your smile or the way you seem to dance in the sea and I just want to have you beside me."

"How did the takeover business go?"

"I thought we'd fought the guy off but he's making moves again."

"Damn, he just won't let go, huh?"

"I've got a strategy I think is working. Nobody is going to buy this company out from under me. He'll soon know he made a mistake when he set his sights on Tain Music."

"Are you working out a deal with him or something?"

"Better, but I can't really talk about it now. Listen, honey, I can stay for about three days when I come but then I've really got to buckle down. I'm gonna try get this man out my face before you see me but I've got a lot on my plate this month. Playing hooky isn't going to win me fans among either my clients or my shareholders. I've got to get back down to the work of growing this company. Fun and games can't last forever."

"I know that. I'm an adult." Caryl's heart lurched. What was he leading up to? In her world, fun and games lasted maybe about six to eight months, then you got engaged, and then you got married. That was what she had expected with Alexander, and though she had given him longer than eight months seeing as how he was married, things hadn't turned out the way she planned. Was Joshua now trying to tell her things weren't going to work out with him too? That he was just in it for fun and games and then he was gone?

"Caryl," Joshua's tone was urgent. "You know you're the woman for me."

"And you're the man for me." But she was distracted by his comment about fun and games. Men usually meant a whole lot more than they actually said. The trick was in accurately deciphering the code.

"I'd better be but listen, my captain, I've got to go. I've got a meeting soon. I wish I could call more often but I'm on the move all the time. I'm signing up sponsors for a tour, getting the Internet site off the ground, getting pay per view concerts organized and interviews going, working out copyright agreements. On top of all that there are the strategy meetings about the takeover bid. Sometimes I'm up till four and five o'clock in the studio or in meetings. It's just 24-7."

"It's okay. I understand, Joshua." She'd never done entertainment work at the law firm but two of her good friends had and she knew it wasn't all star-studded parties and hit songs. The industry was worth billions and it was vicious. "So I'll pick you up at the airport?"

"Yes. I'm on the Air BVI flight that gets in at two. I'll be on it, I promise."

"Yeah, tell it to the West End immigration people."

Joshua laughed. "Bye, love."

"Bye." She hung up.

"You're saying good-bye, but I'm saying hello, hello, hello."

Caryl spun around.

"Hey, baby. I'm here." Alexander stood in the office behind her. "How you doing?" He watched her closely as if unsure how she would react to him and she wondered how much of her conversation he'd heard. It was just like him to show up when she'd forgotten all about him. He held out his arms, then let them drop to his sides as she continued to stare at him. She'd often wondered how she'd react if she ever saw him again but now that he was standing in front of her she was in shock, unable to formulate a clear thought or impulse.

He looked almost the same, just a little thinner and a little grayer than she remembered, but he was still the handsome, distinguished-looking son-of-a-bitch who had captured her heart another life ago.

"What…what are you doing here?" Caryl kept her voice low but she was furious.

"I came to see you. We need to talk. Did you get my flowers?"

Caryl rolled her eyes. She couldn't believe he'd had the nerve to show up. It just proved what Patty said all the time. If you run away from trouble of the two-legged variety, it just picks itself up and runs right after you. And the ancestors knew she was no Jackie Joyner Kersee.

"Yes, I got them. I gave them away."

"Baby, you didn't have to do that. I thought you loved Easter lilies." His voice betrayed his hurt.

"I do. It's you I don't love." She glared at him, wanting to hurt him as he'd hurt her. "And I don't want any blasted flowers from you." Her voice rose. "In fact, I don't want anything at all from you."

Somebody coughed, reminding Caryl that she and Alexander were not alone. If she wanted to keep her business out of the island's rumor mill, she was going about it in entirely the wrong way.

"Thanks for calling me, Bertie," she said to the young man studiously leafing through a book on a desk to her right. He looked up and nodded. Curiosity warred with good manners on his face as he tried to pretend he hadn't been paying attention to her conversation.

Caryl marched out of the office without another word and led Alexander to a grassy area next to the parking lot. It was usually deserted when the marina wasn't hosting a fashion show or party so she knew they wouldn't be overheard or disturbed.

"What the hell are you doing here?" Caryl rounded on him as soon as they left the parking lot and passed through the border of pink oleanders around the empty lot.

"Asking for a chance. One chance. Please, Caryl."

"One chance? You had one chance. You blew it."

"Caryl, a lot has changed since last year. I'm not a married man anymore." He flipped his left hand up and around for her to see.

Despite herself, Caryl looked. The tan line that usually replaced his ring when he didn't wear it had disappeared.

It meant nothing.

"So?"

"So, Caryl, I haven't stopped thinking of you since you ran out on me. I love you. Everything we talked about, getting married, having babies, we can do it now. I'm a free man."

"You were a free man before, Alexander. Marriage doesn't make a slave out of you. You had choices."

"Baby, being married takes away *some* choices. I never wanted to hurt anybody. I was weak and I ended up hurting you. I am so sorry." He took a step towards her but she backed away from him.

"What? Am I talking another language or something? I don't care about any of this. I want you to leave me alone. Just…just leave me alone."

Alexander took a deep breath and closed his eyes. When he opened them again, Caryl could still see the hurt in them.

"The time for regret is long past, Alexander," she said firmly. "I've moved on with my life. I've got a new man. You have to move on, too."

"I can't. Baby, I won't."

"Now, with this, you don't have a choice." Caryl turned and strode away from him.

"Caryl," he called out to her. She didn't look back. "I'm going to stay as long as it takes. I love you, baby." But he didn't follow her as she headed to her Jeep Cherokee and got in. Not knowing where exactly she was going but knowing she had to get away from the marina and from Alexander, she retrieved the key from under the mat in the front and turned the ignition. Thanking the ancestors that he hadn't followed her, hadn't tried to stop her by puling some melodramatic shit, she exited the marina and turned west.

As the road snaked itself along the coastline, Caryl thought about New York and her affair with Alexander Thorne. How she had loved that man. Fifteen years older than she, he was everything she had ever dreamed of in a man, successful, witty, sophisticated, intelligent. Able to take her from the soulful blues café, Enigma, to the elegant detachment of the Frick Museum and everything in between. He was her personal tour guide to New York's dizzying array of galleries, museums, restaurants and hotspots. A new off-Broadway play? He and the playwright were on a first name basis or he was an investor. A new jazz band? He already had their CD. She had looked up to him as if he were some honey-colored prototype of the ideal man. But Barbara's pregnancy had revealed his flaws.

The memory hurt and Caryl's eyes teared as she rounded the sharp curve by Pockwood Pond. She wiped her cheeks and the steering wheel slipped out of her control bringing the jeep a hands-breadth from the retaining wall separating Drake's Highway from the Caribbean Sea just a few feet away. Caryl pulled the wheel sharply to the right. Behind her, a car horn screamed and a yellow sports car overtook her with just a few inches to spare, disappearing on its way in a cloud of outraged dust. Caryl took a deep, shuddering breath and brought the jeep to a gentle stop off the road. Damn, she had to keep it together. She couldn't go to pieces now. *Joshua is coming on Saturday and Alexander will be gone by then. He will. He'd better.* She started the jeep back up again.

Patty was right, though, she would have to tell Joshua about this aspect of her past. She just had to make sure it really was in the past before she said anything. Then again, if she was just fun and games for him, she didn't have to say anything at all. Just send both men packing and commit herself to being manless for another long stretch. It wasn't like the clock was ticking. She was only twenty-eight, for Pete's sake.

Without planning it, Caryl found herself on the rocky, unpaved road leading to Smuggler's Cove, an isolated beach on the island's western tip. She parked the car under the shade of a listing coconut tree and made her way through sea grape trees, stepping over the lavender blossoms of the seaside morning glory, to the beach. She found a shady spot and sat down cross-legged on the sand to stare at the water, its hypnotic rhythm soothing her. For a few sweet minutes, her thoughts cleared and she lost herself in the tranquility of the sea. Lowering herself on her back to stare up at the clear blue sky, she could almost forget she had troubles.

But it wasn't so easy to pretend nothing was wrong. Alexander was back and he apparently was not prepared to take "no" for an answer. She remembered that his tenacity had been one of her least favorite things about him. Once at an antique store in Manhattan, he had seen the chandelier he had been waiting for since he'd bought and renovated his home on the Upper East Side six years earlier. But it wasn't for sale; it had already been promised to somebody else, a longstanding customer currently out of the country, the owner said. It took Alexander three weeks of daily, if not hourly, phone calls but he finally managed to coax the man into selling it to him instead. That was the man she'd loved and that was the man who'd broken her heart. Caryl closed her eyes and tried to will him out of her mind.

CHAPTER FOURTEEN

"Caryl, where have you been? Your dad called." Patty met her on the aft deck, her brows knit with concern. "You've been gone for hours and look at you, there's sand all in your hair."

"It's okay, Patty. I went to Smuggler's Cove and fell asleep on the beach, like a baby." Caryl shook her head; she still couldn't believe she had slept for almost three hours. Just when she needed to be awake and in full possession of her senses she had instead dozed the day away like a woman without a care in the world.

"What did dad want?"

"He said he and your mother are coming down next week to spend a couple days. He's already spoken to Barry and they have a replacement captain flying in to substitute for you."

"What? He's got to be kidding!" But the message sounded just like her imperious father.

"Nope." Patty shook her head. "Those were his exact words and he's never struck me as much of a kidder."

"And suppose I'm not ready for a vacation?" Caryl inquired. And why the hell was everybody descending on her all at once, anyway? Was there a special on now at Travelocity? Had CheapTickets.com declared June "Visit Caryl Month" without informing her?

Patty shrugged.

"And what about Joshua? He's supposed to be coming down on Saturday. I'm not ready for him to meet them yet." Her mind raced. If she could get Alexander off the island by Friday then it would just be Joshua and her parents she had to worry about and that would be easy by comparison.

"Oh, and Caryl, there's a surprise for you in the saloon."

Oh?" Caryl looked at her warily. "What kind of surprise?"

"Go in and see for yourself."

"It had better not be Alexander, Patty. I warned you not to let him on board." Caryl strode to the saloon door and yanked it open. "I would never…" Whatever else she was going to say died on her lips as she looked around the room. Huge bouquets of red roses sat on top of every available surface, their perfume heavy in the cold, re-circulated air.

"Wow." Alexander had really outdone himself. How on earth had he arranged it with the island's only florist shop, a tiny place that couldn't possibly accommodate so many arrangements? Caryl brought the nearest bouquet to her nose and breathed deep before hastily putting it back down again. They were from Alexander, the man whose betrayal had torn her life apart but who now obviously believed a hundred or so magnificent botanical specimens could erase bad memories and bring them back together. "It ain't happening, Humpty Dumpty," she murmured to herself.

"Er, I think you should read the card."

"No, there's no need. I don't want to see any more." The flowers could not have gotten on the boat without Patty's help and permission. Caryl frowned at her friend as she turned and picked up a card that was propped up against a chair beside her.

"Read it," Patty said, thrusting it at her.

"I said I don't need to."

"Yes, Caryl, you do." And Patty thrust it at her again.

Furious now, Caryl grabbed the envelope and tore it open. The cover was a simple red heart.

JUST AN AFFAIR

"Open it."

"Oh, for crying out loud!" But Caryl did as she was told.

"Enjoy the flowers. I love and miss you," was written across the inside in a bold, heavy script. Underneath was Joshua's signature.

"Patty, you knew!" she shouted and grabbed the older woman up in a hug.

"He called a couple of nights ago and told Richardson what he was planning. He wanted to make sure the *Elendil* was on schedule and would be at the marina. You weren't supposed to know a thing about it so it was good you actually disappeared when you did. I'd been racking my brains all night trying to think what to do with you so you wouldn't be here when they came."

"There are so many! How did he manage it?"

"Child, the man chartered a plane to come here direct from Miami with them. You're one very lucky lady, missy."

"Patty, I know. I've got to call him and tell him how lovely they are."

"My bet is he's waiting to hear from you."

Caryl grabbed the boat phone.

"I'm sorry, ma'am, he's in a meeting."

Great, no static but no Joshua either. Caryl gritted her teeth.

"Er, is this Miss Walker?"

"Yes."

"Oh, hold on please." The secretary's tone got decidedly warmer. "Mr. Tain said I was to interrupt him whenever you called. I'll put you through."

He picked up the phone almost immediately.

"My heart."

"Joshua, the flowers. They're fantastic. Thank you, sweet man. Thank you. They made my day."

"You really liked them? I wasn't sure if you liked roses but according to Richardson, 'what woman doesn't'."

"I love them and the fragrance is wonderful, like a mixture of vanilla and allspice. I can't wait for you to get here so I can thank you in person."

"Grrr," Joshua growled. "I'm coming, woman, I'm coming. You'll get your chance."

"One thing though," she said, suddenly remembering. "My parents will be here. They're coming for a bit of R and R."

"You mean I'll have to share you?"

"Yes, I'm really sorry. They won't be here long but they'll probably be around for part of your visit. My dad never takes long vacations. Feels Henry Enterprises would collapse if he did."

"Henry Enterprises? Who's your dad? David Cassavettes?"

"Yes," Caryl sighed. For a man who liked his privacy, her father was very well-known. There was silence on the other line. "Hey, you there?"

"But your last name is Walker."

"Actually, it's really Cassavettes but I've been using Walker since I got here because my dad is friends with the chief minister and some other influential people. I don't want any special favors just because I'm his daughter, so I try to avoid the connection. Walker is my mother's maiden name. Sorry. It never came up or I would have told you." Her explanation was greeted with more silence. "Joshua, are you hearing me?"

"Yes." His tone had changed, become clipped. "It's David Cassavettes who's been trying to buy my company out from under me for the last six months. I had no idea you were his daughter. Damn!"

Caryl's eyes widened and she got a sick feeling in the pit of her stomach. Her father was the corporate raider trying to take Joshua's company from him?

"Are you sure?" she asked, then could have kicked herself. What a stupid question! Of course, he would know the name of the man trying to take his company away. "I…I don't know much about the business, Joshua," she said, hurrying on. "I never knew about any takeover plans. I'm sorry, really, really sorry." More silence. How could she make this right? "I'll speak to him when he comes. Tell him to lay off. I know how you feel about Tain Music, Joshua. I wouldn't want anyone to take it from you."

"He won't, Caryl, believe me, he won't. Listen, I've got to go now. I was in the middle of a meeting. I'd appreciate your not saying anything to him. I can fight my own battles."

"Okay, if that's what you want, but… I know he'd listen to me."

"Promise me, Caryl. I don't want you interfering."

"I promise," she said, her voice catching in her throat. He sounded like a stranger. "I'm so sorry about it. I…" But the sudden strident sound of the dial tone told her he'd ended their connection. Caryl slowly replaced the receiver.

A casual look at the annual report, that was about as much interest as Caryl took in Henry Enterprises. She and her father had come to an agreement while she was still in high school. She could make a name for herself in whatever career she chose but one day, when her father was ready to retire, she would take over the reins of the family business. Her father was a relatively young man, though, years, decades, away from retiring and Caryl paid the business no mind. Beyond its history and the information in the annual reports, she knew very little. What she did know filled her with pride at the family gumption. Her great-grandfather had begun the business with a sawmill on the outskirts of Henry, Virginia, braving racism and the Ku Klux Klan to serve the black community in the area and even further afield. Then her grandfather had expanded into construction, trucking and shipping. When his eldest son, her father, took over Henry Enterprises about fifteen years earlier, he immediately expanded the company's horizons domestically while looking to the international market for other business opportunities. The last report even mentioned an oilfield somewhere in Mexico. But why would her father want to go into the recording industry? Listening to Louis Armstrong and Ella Fitzgerald on the odd occasion when he wasn't in a meeting, poring over reports or talking shop with one or another of his VPs hardly qualified him to run a record company.

Caryl's shoulders drooped. A business rivalry between her father and her new love raised the definite possibility of rain drenching her parade. For a minute, she toyed with the idea of calling her father but then dismissed it. He would want to know why she was suddenly interested. And then, of course, there was her promise of non-interference. Joshua wanted her to stay out of it and she should honor his wish.

A soft growl from her stomach reminded her that she hadn't eaten since breakfast.

"Looking for something to eat?" Patty asked when she opened the door to the galley a few seconds later.

"Yes, I'm starved." Caryl's mouth watered at the sight of the thick ham and cheese sandwich that Patty had obviously just finished making.

"Good." Patty held the plate out to her.

"This for me?"

"Of course, child, an empty bag cannot stand. I was pretty sure you hadn't eaten since morning so..." Patty shrugged.

"Thanks." Touched by the other woman's solicitousness, Caryl gave her a quick hug. "So, Alexander's here," she said, through a

JUST AN AFFAIR

mouthful of sandwich.

"I figured that might be why you're looking like Atlas shifted the weight of the world to your shoulders. Was that why you went to Smuggler's?"

"Yes, I just wanted to get away. And now, as if that weren't enough, Joshua's just told me he and Dad don't actually see eye to eye about who Tain Music should really belong to." Caryl opened the fridge to get herself some orange juice.

"They know each other?"

"More than that. Dad's the guy who's been trying to buy out his company."

"Uh-oh. Caryl, you serious?"

"Like a heart attack. He never once actually called the guy's name and, of course, Dad doesn't send me bulletins. I had no idea."

"Noel's never going believe this. What a coincidence!"

"It never occurred to me. I mean, what does my father know about music? I can't imagine how he got this idea into his head. I told Joshua I would try to straighten things out, you know, talk to Dad, but he said he'd take care of it himself."

"Men. They've got to do it their way or no way."

"Patty, Tain Music is like his baby, his child. I know how I'd feel if somebody tried to take something that important away from me. I'd absolutely hate them." Caryl shivered. "Joshua's voice sounded so cold. Suppose his heart turns against me? He talked so much about this takeover but I never dreamed it was Dad."

"Child, it doesn't have a thing to do with you or who you are." Patty's face turned grim but her eyes were soft with affection as she looked at Caryl. "I don't know too much about it, but the newspapers are always full of this business taking over that business. Sometimes everything's hunky dory and the company's glad to be taken over, sometimes things aren't so lovey-dovey. If Joshua's going to let that come between you, then he wasn't worth your time to begin with. But I don't think he will," she added quickly, seeing Caryl's face fall.

"Hmm, I hope you're right, but I don't know."

"Aren't I always right?"

"Oh, I don't know about that. Wasn't it you who said Hillary would leave Bill?"

"That was my alter ego."

"Uh huh." Caryl drained the last of her orange juice. "Where's Richardson?"

"Went to see family, run errands, that kind of thing. What are you going to do about Alexander?"

"I don't know. I told him to leave me alone but he doesn't give up easy. I feel like everything's coming down on me at once. Why did he have to show up now?" *And how could she make things up to Joshua? That was the most important item on her agenda right now. Alexander was just a distraction.*

Patty looked at her. "Would you have preferred it if he'd followed you down right after you came here?"

"No, that's not what I meant. If he'd only turned up last month or the month before when I hadn't met Joshua, then I wouldn't be worrying if they're going to meet. Joshua's already got one big surprise about me this week. One more might be too many."

"What will be will be. The old people say if you worry about a thing, you will draw it to you. Put it out of your mind, child. Try don't think about it."

Caryl tried but by the end of the day her nerves were a wreck, and she was glad when Richardson and Patty invited her to play a game of cards. The game would help relax her, distract her from her troubles.

"Fish or Jack?" Richardson asked.

JUST AN AFFAIR

"Fish, of course," Caryl and Patty chorused.

"Can't you women ever ask for anything else?" Richardson groused as he began to deal out a hand.

"No," Caryl and Patty chorused again, giggling.

They were well into their second round and Caryl was enjoying herself when she heard the familiar voice behind her on the pier.

"Good evening. Caryl, may I speak to you?"

Richardson and Patty glanced at her, waiting for their cues.

"Caryl, please. Don't make me beg." Alexander sounded miserable but she wasn't having it. All the frustration of her day bubbled over.

"Why don't you just leave me the hell alone? I've asked you and asked you to leave me alone. What, specifically, don't you understand about that simple request?" Caryl turned to glare at him across the *Elendil's* railing. In the dim light of a lamp some twenty feet away, Alexander looked haggard, the lines on his face deep.

"I just want to talk you, Caryl, that's all. I know you're putting back out tomorrow and I can't let you go without telling you what I have to say."

"If the lady wants you to leave, then maybe you should, my brother." Richardson rose to stand beside her.

"Please. Stay out of this." Alexander's voice was pleasant but firm. "Caryl can tell me to leave, not anybody else."

"Oh, yeah?" Richardson stepped forward. "She can *tell* you but maybe I can *make* you."

"Alright, alright." Caryl had no desire to see the men come to fisticuffs. "Five minutes is all you've got. Patty, Richardson, I'll be right back."

"We'll be waiting," Richardson promised with a scowl at Alexander.

Caryl stepped down to the pier, strode past Alexander and up the walkway. He matched his steps to hers. "Alexander, you've got to go back to the States."

"Caryl, baby, listen." He grabbed her hand. She shook it free and turned to face him, her arms crossed.

"I'm listening."

"Baby, I know I hurt you. I know. I think I hurt myself even worse because I know I was the one in the wrong. Some of the things I told you were true but some were lies. It was true Barbara and I had stopped sleeping together." Caryl sucked her teeth. "It's true," he insisted. "But one night, months before she showed up at the office, she went out somewhere, I don't know, with her friends, I guess. When she came in, it was around midnight. She came into my room and said we had to talk. Caryl, I could smell the alcohol on her from the door. I'm not talking Chateaubriand or anything like that, she smelled of whisky. She was crying. She said she would give me the divorce I'd asked her for the night before." Caryl started, he had never told her Barbara had consented to the divorce. "I know," he said, noticing her surprise. "I was so ashamed of what happened next that I couldn't even begin to tell you about that night. She told me she loved me, only wanted me to be happy and then she said we should make love one last time. Just once for the road, she said and then the next day she would see her lawyer about coming to a settlement with me." The misery in his voice deepened. "I was so happy. I don't know. I made the biggest mistake of my life. I felt sorry for her and let my guard down, Caryl. She was the mother of my children, the woman I had once thought I'd grow old with. Try to understand."

"Are you trying to say you had sex with her because you pitied her?"

"Yes, Caryl, yes. Hear me out. There was no way I could tell you

JUST AN AFFAIR

but I thought she and I had sealed a bargain, that everything would be alright. We'd be civilized about things, the divorce would go through and I could put this whole episode behind me and be the man you thought I was."

"So what happened?"

"She changed her mind. She'd gone to see her lawyer, I knew that much. She even moved out, went to stay with her sister. Remember, I did tell you about that. Everything was rolling along but then two months later my lawyer told me she'd refused to sign, that she was going to contest the divorce. I guess by then she knew she was pregnant. Caryl, I was so shocked. One day I came home from the office and she'd moved back in."

Caryl rolled her eyes. So that was why he'd never taken her to his house. Whenever she'd hinted at a visit he'd either ignored her or given her one excuse after another.

"'I'm pregnant' she announced when I asked her what the hell she was doing. I didn't even ask if it was mine. I knew then it had all been a trick. That was her purpose all along, to get pregnant. She never meant to give me a divorce."

"Do you really expect me to believe all this?"

"It's the truth. Caryl, I know I never told you she'd moved back in. How could I? I would have had to tell you about the pregnancy too and I just couldn't do it. To see the pain in your face and know I'd caused it. So I said nothing."

"What did you think, that the pregnancy would go away by itself if you didn't acknowledge it?"

"I wasn't thinking straight. My children were giving me so much grief, telling me they hated me, couldn't stand the sight of me. My daughter even threatened to drop off her surname, my name. They said they didn't want anything to do with me if I left her. She had filled their heads with lies about me and I didn't know how to begin putting things right with them or with you."

Caryl frowned. He *sounded* genuine but that had been the problem, hadn't it? How could she tell he was speaking the truth? "One night? You only had sex with her once while you were seeing me?"

"Just that once. I never expected...I was stupid. There is no excuse for what I did. I should have known better."

"So you knocked her up with one go. That's pretty potent stuff you got there. You should bottle it and have an auction for the fertility clinics."

"Caryl, don't be like that. God, you've got to believe me. No one was more surprised than I when she told me. I felt like she'd ripped my guts out."

"Join the club."

"Caryl, please, I'm so sorry."

"Why didn't you at least use protection?"

"The condoms were over at your apartment, remember? I didn't have any in the house and anyway, she was my wife..." He stopped, realizing how that sounded. "Look, I just wasn't thinking properly. I know I should have known better."

"Yes, you should have." Caryl chewed her bottom lip. She'd heard worse accounts about the things men got up to in relationships; he could be telling the truth. But how would she ever know? "Why didn't you tell me all this before?"

"Baby girl, I'd just about made up my mind to tell you when she pulled that stunt, coming to the office. After that, you disappeared on me and not one of your people would tell me where you were."

"You could have written, sent it to my parents. I would've gotten it."

"Yes, but would you have read it?"

He had a point.

"This was something I needed to see you face to face to tell you. Caryl, I still love you. Nights, I can't get your face out of my mind. I miss the feel of your body under my hand. I ache to touch you again." Before she could stop him, he reached out to pull her into his arms. Kisses fell on her face, her neck, and despite herself, she felt some kind of response.

"No." She found the will and the strength to push him off. "I don't love you and I certainly could never trust you again. You knew how bad I felt being the other woman but you wouldn't let me end it. You kept promising me marriage, kids, the works. You were so perfect, Alexander, so perfect then the wife you told me had no relationship with turned up pregnant. It doesn't really matter all that much how it happened. It's too late for us, much too late."

"I don't think it is, Caryl. I was wrong for what I did. And you're right, from the minute I saw you at the office I knew you were a very special woman and I pursued you. But you responded." Caryl shook her head, angry at the reminder. "It might have taken a while but you gave in to me because you felt what I was feeling, too. Caryl, I know you. I know your body. You can't tell me you don't want me, baby, I can still feel it right here." He brought his fist to his chest.

Caryl looked away from him and backed off a few more inches. He was too damn close to her. For a wham-bam, one-minute man, he could still turn on the heat something fierce.

"That's just sex, Alexander. Love is about much more than that. It's about trust, knowing you can count on your partner to be straight with you. Oh, but I forget." She called on reserves of sarcasm to see her through this test. "You don't know anything about that, now do you?"

"I deserve whatever you want to throw at me, I know I do. But

Caryl, I will spend my life making it up to you, if you'll let me." His eyes, his face, his voice; everything about him was full of entreaty. "Baby…"

"Stop calling me that."

"Okay, whatever you want. Caryl, please say you'll give me a chance. I know things can't happen all at once. Let's start getting to know each other all over again. Let me take you out to lunch when you get back. Can we pretend we're new people, meeting for the first time?" He held out his hand to her but let it drop when she didn't take it and his words hung in the air between them. Joshua's iciness earlier came unbidden to Caryl's mind and she took a deep breath. She didn't know what to say. Alexander stood waiting quietly in front of her as if afraid any movement or sound might just tip the balance against him. Caryl felt a twinge of pity. There was a time when he would rather have died than let anyone see him looking so vulnerable, so needy.

"I'm waiting, Caryl," he prompted.

Caryl opened her mouth to say something, then closed it again unable to clear her thoughts. Joshua had shown her such tenderness during their week together but that was all it had been, just a week. If he could get all cold and distant just because she was David Cassavettes' daughter, then maybe she didn't know him as well as she thought she did. She had known Alexander longer but not better, obviously, or things wouldn't have gone down the way they had. But now here he was, all but on his knees, begging. They had more history together but it was a history of lies and deceit. She couldn't give him what he wanted; she couldn't even give him an answer to his question. Caryl searched for a way to put what she was feeling into words.

"I…," she started and stopped. She had been going to say she was sorry but he was the one who should apologize, he was the one whose

JUST AN AFFAIR

lies had dive-bombed her legal career, her love life, everything. So what if he too had suffered? "I ha…," she started again, but no, that wasn't quite true either, she did not hate him. They said indifference, not hate, was the opposite of love but she didn't think she felt any of those things.

"Alexander, you came here just expecting things to be alright, no, let me finish." She held up her hand when he tried to interrupt. "Pretending we don't have any baggage or history won't work, we're not children." Misery darkened his eyes. "Alexander," she took a step towards him, lifted her hand to touch his arm but then withdrew it, not wanting him to misunderstand the gesture. "It's too late."

"Caryl, just give me a few days then. Let me see you between your cruises. If you still want me to leave after a couple of weeks, I'll go." The lines on his face deepened, his voice fell. "You'll never have to see me again if you don't want to."

She could see in his face what the words cost him.

"Caryl, you okay?" Richardson had come to look for her and was standing a few feet away. Neither of them had heard his approach.

"Yes, thanks." She gave her crewmate a wan smile. It was a lie. She felt as if she were experiencing an emotional hurricane off the Saffir-Simpson scale. "I'll be right there." Richardson retreated a short distance and tilted his head up, pretending to admire the starry sky.

"I have a man," she said.

"Him?" Alexander flicked his thumb in Richardson's direction.

"No." Caryl chuckled. Richardson as a love object for anyone other than Patty was unthinkable.

"I'm not too late, Caryl. I would only be too late if you were married to this man, whoever he is, and you're not. I don't see a ring. Just a couple of weeks, that's all I'm asking."

"You never give up, do you?"

"Not when it's important."

She heaved a sigh. "Okay." She would probably hate herself for this later but if she gave in to him now, it would be easier to finally dismiss him later. He wouldn't be able to claim that she hadn't at least given him a chance. "But don't expect anything, Alexander."

"Thank you, thank you." He beamed. "You've made me a very happy man."

"Alright, I've got to go. Where are you staying?"

"At Long Bay," he said. It was a sprawling resort on the other side of the island.

"You've got a long way to drive."

"It's okay. I rented an SUV."

Caryl felt a strange reluctance to go.

"How did you find me?" she asked.

"I'll tell you when next I see you. It was an adventure, I promise you." His eyes twinkled and he smiled. For a minute, Caryl remembered how he used to make her laugh with funny stories about the people he knew.

"I've got to go."

"Yes. I know. You have a cruise tomorrow."

They looked at each other, each feeling the pull of memories, but Caryl steeled herself.

"Bye then." She turned on her heel and walked away.

"Have a good cruise."

"Thanks. Have a good drive," she called over her shoulder, nodding to her first mate who pushed himself off the wall to walk at her side.

"Are you okay?" Patty asked when Caryl and Richardson got back to the boat.

"Yes, I'm fine." She smiled to show she meant it.

JUST AN AFFAIR

"Want to play Gin Rummy?" Patty asked, shrewdly guessing that Caryl didn't want to talk about Alexander.

"Yeah, sure. Patty," she said, suddenly remembering, "do something about the flowers inside, please. Maybe a few in other rooms, that kind of thing. We don't want the guests to feel they've wandered into a florist's." And she didn't want such a strong reminder of Joshua either, not if he was going to let his feud with her father affect his feelings toward her.

"No problem. They are a bit overwhelming, aren't they?"

As overwhelming as the man who sent them but the least said about him until she knew where she stood, the better. Caryl shoved thoughts of Joshua to the back of her mind and concentrated on the cards before her.

CHAPTER FIFTEEN

Alexander was waiting on the pier when the *Elendil* returned to Nanny Cay four days later. He stood to one side as the guests' luggage was unloaded and Caryl and her crew said their goodbyes to the two couples.

"Hey," Caryl said, walking over. She wasn't altogether unhappy to see him there.

"Hey, yourself. How did the cruise go?"

"It was fun. They were very nice."

"Would you like to get a drink or something?"

"Sure, I could do with some of the marina restaurant's onion rings."

They fell in step and Caryl thought how natural it felt, just like old times.

"How've you been?"

"Good. Spent most of my time on the phone and faxing."

"Business, eh?"

"Yeah."

There was a brief lull in the conversation and Caryl glanced at him. He was looking intently at her.

"Did you think about me?" he asked.

"I tried not to."

"Ouch, that hurt."

"Yeah, well. It was either not think about you and what had happened or go crazy wondering what I did to deserve your lies."

JUST AN AFFAIR

"I'm sorry, Caryl. I really am. I just want to make things up to you now."

"Let's just drop the subject. I really don't want to go over all this again."

"Fine."

They entered the restaurant in silence and took a table by the wide picture windows.

"You would have liked the guests," Caryl said, because she couldn't think of anything else. Suddenly, it didn't feel so natural being with him, it felt awkward. "They were all professors at Temple University, physics, math, and chemistry. The fourth, the short woman, teaches philosophy."

"Hmm, I'm impressed."

"Yes, we get pretty high-falutin' company here."

"You should at those prices." Alexander shook his head. "Two thousand per night per person. That's expensive."

Caryl's eyebrows shot up. There was a time when twice that wouldn't have fazed him.

"Yes, but look at what you're getting. You're eating good food, you're on a luxury yacht, and it goes where you want. I think it's worth it."

He didn't answer and Caryl glanced at him. He had changed so much. Always before, he had stridden around as if he were a charter member of the Masters of the Universe club.

Now he looked as if his membership were being challenged and his supporters had deserted him.

"Alexander, how are things going?" Caryl blurted it out before she could think of a more tactful way to ask. She would bet a year's salary that Barbara had wanted her pound of flesh and a good bit of bone as well.

"You mean financially?"

Caryl nodded. If Alexander couldn't afford the *Elendil*, his ex must have cleaned up.

"I was wondering when you would get around to asking."

She frowned. He was lucky she was even talking to him, so he had better not be getting cocky about it.

"Barbara demanded the brownstone plus the summer house in the Hamptons and almost all the furnishings in them, the Jaguar and most of my art collection."

A waitress materialized just then and they placed their orders.

"I only just managed to keep my wines out of her clutches," Alexander continued when the waitress left. "But her goal was really to leave me with nothing. I didn't fight her. By that point I just wanted out, so I gave in to most of her demands and sold my interest in the firm to cover my losses." Alexander dragged his hand across his forehead and, despite herself, Caryl grimaced in sympathy. He *had* changed. The Alexander she knew would have put up the fight of his life. "I got myself admitted to the bar in California and now I practice in Los Angeles. I have a couple of consultancies with the state legislature. It was hard at first but I had contacts I could rely on and things are steaming along. I employ one lawyer and have three other people on staff."

"Oh." Caryl tried to sound non-committal. It was a far cry from Thorne, Mercer and Johnson which was bursting at the seams with dozens of lawyers and hundreds of other employees.

"You think I've come down in the world."

"No. No, of course not. But," she hunched her shoulders, "you've got to admit there's a big difference between that and TMJ."

"There is, but I did a lot of thinking after, well, after…you know. I wanted to get away from New York, think about life and what I was doing for a bit."

"And you can do that in L.A.?"

"As well as you can on Tortola."

"Touché."

"Yo, Caryl. I thought that was you over there." A short, round-faced man had come up to their table.

"Hey, Gilbert. How are you doing?"

"Good. Good." He clapped her on the shoulder.

"Alexander, Gilbert is the bartender here and a good friend."

"Hey, how you doing?"

The men shook hands.

"I've been saving your papers for you. You want them now or when you're leaving?"

"Now's fine. Thanks."

He hurried off and returned a minute later with a stack of American newspapers.

"Haven't changed old habits, I see," said Alexander as she began to flick through *USA Today*.

Caryl grinned, remembering leisurely Sunday mornings at her apartment, her bed covered with newspapers she was determined to get through, Alexander beside her, sleeping. According to him, he and his wife were living separate lives by then and Barbara never asked or seemed to care about the nights he spent away from home. Obviously, she had cared a whole lot more than she let on.

"No, being in the islands cures you of the need to know. Geraldo ought to try it. But now and then I do get a craving to see what's happening in the real world."

Alexander was silent, sipping his beer.

"Look at this. The Palestinians and the Israelis are at it again. I can't believe this is still going on."

"Since David," Alexander said dryly. "Why should it stop now just because there's CNN and AP to take the news to the world?"

"And they've caught that serial killer who was preying on old people in Texas. Guess they'll ask for the death penalty. He's young, though, only twenty-six." Caryl held up the paper so Alexander could take a look at the clean-cut, blonde young man.

"Still opposed to capital punishment?"

"Of course, and you?" This had been a long-standing bone of contention between them, making for heated arguments every time the subject came up. Alexander believed the death penalty was an effective deterrent to crime but to her, rising crime statistics in those states that still had capital punishment proved just the opposite. His answer to the statistics was that too many people were having their sentences commuted.

"I haven't changed my mind. More states should bring back the death penalty, especially for serial killers. They can't be rehabilitated. It's a waste of taxpayers money to keep them alive."

"Alexander, you know that with court costs for appeals and everything, it's more expensive to pump a man full of lethal poison than to keep him locked up for life."

"Yeah, but what if he escapes? A life for a life." It was only on this subject that Alexander ever got biblical.

Caryl shook her head and flicked the pages over in disgust. It was impossible to argue with the man. Obviously, they would never see eye to eye on the issue.

She turned to the entertainment section. Preoccupied with thinking how wrong Alexander was about the death penalty, she almost missed the picture of Joshua among a spread of shots on the inside page. He grinned confidently at the camera like somebody who had the world in the palm of his hand. Maybe he did because one arm was draped around the shoulders of a dark-skinned girl who, despite the navel-baring, cleavage-revealing, skin-tight dress she wore, didn't look as if she should be out of the fifth grade. Caryl stared at the picture, open-mouthed.

"Caryl, are you alright? What is it?" Alexander leaned forward in concern but Caryl barely registered his presence.

Slowly, as if in a dream, she read the caption. Rap diva, Kenya, and Joshua Tain, the embattled CEO of Tain Music, let it all hang out during their night on the town. Caryl gave a strangled laugh. Whoever wrote that caption sure got that right. Insiders say the lovely Kenya is helping Tain forget his business worries and that the hot couple may soon make their whirlwind romance official. Caryl threw the paper down, her chest heaving. No, it couldn't be true, what did this mean?

"Caryl, what…"

She didn't let him finish. "I have to go, Alexander. Sorry."

Walking so fast she almost broke into a run, Caryl left the restaurant, her hands balled into fists and her fingernails digging into the palms of her hands. Reporters made mistakes, she knew they did, but that was a picture. Joshua had his arm around that underage, underdressed girl. Was he really seeing her? Were they an item? And was the part about "business worries" an allusion to her father's takeover attempt, or was there something else happening she didn't know about?

Neither Patty nor Richardson was around when Caryl hurried up to the *Elendil* and she went straight to her cabin, grateful she didn't have to see anyone. Closing her cabin door, she crossed the room to slump down into the only chair.

Her first impulse was to call Joshua and ask what the hell the picture and its caption meant, but she resisted the urge. No, she needed to calm down and think first. Contacting him while she was in this state would not do. She would call when she was very sure that she could be detached, unemotional, cool, or at least give a darned good impersonation of someone who was all those things. And what explanation could he have anyway? He'd never mentioned this Kenya to her, and why would he need to be escorting her around the town unless there was something going on? Damn! Caryl pounded the cushioned arms of the chair. Who the hell did he think she was? Little Miss Isolated Behind God's Back? So that she wouldn't hear about him and his goings on? She had news for him.

Caryl sank down further in her chair. Damn! She was tired of men thinking they could get over on her like she was born just yesterday. Alexander had tried that and look where it got him; on his belly doing the *please-baby-take-me-back-please* crawl. Caryl smiled grimly. So Joshua thought he could do the same thing? Fine then, if that's how Mr. Handsome Is As Handsome Does wanted to play it, that's how it would be played. She'd show him what she was made of and then, when he joined Alexander in the *sorry-baby* line, she would tell him where he could take himself. But still, how could he? She had thought him a better man than Alexander but she'd been wrong. His feet were made of the same clay.

At least she would have no time to think about his betrayal. The fax that had come in while she was having breakfast said six VIPs, three major shareholder clients and their spouses, were coming in for a three-day cruise in a few hours. She would have no time to think about the damned man. Sure, Caryl admitted to herself, sure, she was hurt and disappointed but she wasn't the first woman to be taken in by a hard chest and a sexy smile. Okay, it was a sexy everything, but the point was, other women got taken in by the same things all the time and survived their betrayals just as she had survived Alexander's.

Caryl straightened up in her chair. The clients were expected at

JUST AN AFFAIR

one o'clock and it was eleven now. Two hours and then she would be at sea. Three days and then Kenneth and Marcianne would be here and, the ancestors knew, her parents would give her no time to wallow. With any luck, after they were gone, she would barely remember Joshua's name.

A knock on her door interrupted her thoughts.

"Caryl, Alexander's outside. He says he wants to see you."

Caryl opened the door and Patty gave her the once-over.

"You look fine to me," she said, her tone exasperated. "He said he thought you were upset. You just left him and ran out of the bar."

"Oh, I felt a little nauseous that's all. I'm fine now." Caryl smiled. If Patty and Richardson found out about Joshua and his half-clad songbird, they would cluck over her like mother hens. Worse than that, she was embarrassed that she had flouted company rules for what had apparently was little more than a two-night stand. Like lightning out of a clear blue sky, it suddenly struck her that she had been fooling herself. She had never wanted just a fling with Joshua. When she'd told him she loved him, she had meant it.

A fresh wave of hurt almost physical in its intensity washed over her. Fooling herself that she could be content with a temporary affair, a vacation romance Terry McMillan could have scripted, was a trick her heart had played on her mind. Deep down she had been thinking long term. Visions of them married with a split duplex, one perfect child and twin titanium silver M Coupe Beamers were not dancing loudly in her head; they were hidden below layers and layers of self-denial. A half-dressed woman-child thousands of miles away had helped her see the truth. About herself and about the man! Joshua Tain was no different from Alexander and she, herself, she was twice the fool.

"We didn't let him on the boat. He's still on the pier," Patty said, breaking in on her thoughts.

"Yes, okay." A smile faltered on Caryl's lips. Luckily, Patty had already turned away and didn't see it. Caryl felt as if her heart had melted and was now swooshing around at the bottom of her stomach. How could she have deceived herself that way? But she knew the answer. She needed to tell herself she could be content with a fling. It was just a fancy way of giving herself permission to get busy with Joshua.

Just before emerging on the aft deck she steeled herself to look normal but smiling took more effort than she could readily summon. Wordlessly, she walked down to where Alexander waited.

"Are you okay? What happened in there?" He took her arm, his eyes running searchingly over her face.

"Nothing, I didn't have any breakfast and I guess the smell of greasy food cooking made me feel a bit sick."

"I don't believe you. There was hardly any smell in there." He frowned and gave her a little shake. "Don't lie to a lawyer, baby. Oops, sorry, I know you don't want me calling you 'baby.'"

"No, I don't." Caryl extracted herself from his hold. "Look, I'm fine and I need to get back on board and start getting ready for our next cruise."

"You're going out again today?"

"Yes, they faxed the instruction in this morning. Some last minute thing but they're major Janus shareholders, so what're we going to do?"

"I don't think you're well enough to go out again," he challenged. "Look at you. Your skin got gray back there and it still hasn't regained its color. You look like you've just heard a client being sentenced to execution when you were expecting eight months probation."

"I'm fine, Alexander," she snapped. "And what gives you the right to think you can just jump in my life and carry on as though you cared?"

"*Caro.*" She winced at the pet name he had been the only one to use. "I do care. That's what I'm going to spend the rest of my life proving to you."

"You can prove it to the President for all I care. I'm outta here." She turned to go.

"Wait, look. It was something about this paper, wasn't it?"

Caryl whirled back around. Alexander was holding up the offending evidence.

"Is it this guy, Joshua Tain? Do you know him, Caryl?"

"No, I don't. I told you, I just felt sick." She deliberately kept her voice even; injecting what she felt was just the right amount of withering scorn to throw him off the track.

"I wonder if your crew would feel sick too if I showed it to them." He watched her closely.

Caryl shrugged. "Suit yourself," she said, as if tired of the whole business. "Shall I call Patty so you can speak to her?" she asked over her shoulder as she walked away.

"No. Don't bother." Defeat and confusion thickened his voice.

"Bye, then." Caryl tried to suppress the lilt in her voice. Her bluff had worked.

An hour and a half later, she and Patty were back on deck watching Richardson herd the clients to the *Elendil*, their luggage hauled by a dockworker.

"Allow me to introduce you to the captain, the best there is this side of the Atlantic." With a flourish Richardson ushered the people forward.

Grinning, Caryl shook their hands one by one. Joy and Henry Reyes, a short, slim, bespectacled couple, Elaine and Matthew Silvers, dark and athletic, and Louisa and Linton Rattray, an interracial couple.

"You're David Cassavettes' daughter, aren't you?" asked Henry Reyes. "How are you liking this change of pace? Your dad said you're actually a lawyer."

"Yes, I am." Caryl smiled, but inwardly she groaned. She hoped that was all her dad had said. "And I'm liking, no, loving this change of pace. I hope you will too."

"I'm sure we will," his petite wife piped up. Her pert features reminded Caryl of Halle Berry, but her curly hair had vivid red streaks and was longer than the actress's. "We want to do a lot of diving. We've all got our PADI certificates and we've heard the diving's great around here."

"Louisa and I vacationed in the Caymans a few months ago and it was awesome," Linton Rattray chimed in.

"None of the Virgin Islands have the steep, deep walls of the Caymans but we do have some fantastic coral formations, some great wrecks. I think we'll compare favorably."

"More than favorably." Richardson backed her up with a nudge in the ribs.

"You didn't lunch on the plane, did you?" Caryl asked.

"No."

"Good, then Richardson will see you to your staterooms and we'll be ready to serve lunch in half an hour."

"Wonderful."

They began re-appearing almost exactly a half-hour later and Caryl introduced them to Patty.

"Ah, so you're the wonderful chef we've heard so much about," Matthew Silvers said, pumping her hand.

"I heard some guy, a very satisfied customer, sent in a letter praising your cooking and suggesting we offer a culinary cruise," Linton Rattray said. "Don's planning to look into it," he added, peering at her as if her cooking secrets might be written in code on her forehead. Don Jefferson was the Janus Vice President in charge of its cruise operations. If the idea got his support it was as good as implemented.

Caryl's eyebrows flew into her hairline and she exchanged glances with Patty. So Joshua had followed through on his observation. That was nice of him.

Patty grinned bashfully. "That must have been Mr. Tain. He was very appreciative," she said.

"Yeah, that name sounds familiar. Some music muckety-muck, eh?" He turned to Caryl. "He and your dad are in a war of wills at the moment. What a shock he must have gotten, coming to the Caribbean on vacation and finding the daughter of his nemesis. Must have been a bit tense between the two of you, huh?"

"Linton," his wife broke in before Caryl could answer. "The Captain uses her mother's name so he probably didn't even know who she was." Louisa Rattray smiled brightly at Caryl. "Now, let's have no more business talk."

"That's right," Elaine Silvers agreed. "Let's just eat. I'm starved!"

After the salad, Patty produced the lobster linguine main course, and as they ate, Caryl outlined the itinerary for the short trip. She suggested they start with a visit to Virgin Gorda for on-land sightseeing that afternoon and snorkel at The Baths the next morning. By Sunday midday, they could begin to work their way back down the island chain, stopping at the wreck of the *Rhone* so she could gauge their diving expertise. Sunday afternoon they could relax on one of Peter Island's excellent beaches. On Monday morning, if they proved to be the excellent divers they said they were, they could continue to Norman Island, where she would lead them on a deep dive to where the continental shelf dropped off.

"What might we see there?" Matthew Silvers interrupted to ask.

"Sharks, turtles, marlins and other creatures you wouldn't see in more shallow water," Caryl answered, gratified to see delight and anticipation spread over their faces. "There's also a deep seamount where schools of all kinds of fish like hanging out. It's a challenging dive, though." She'd have to be completely convinced they were good divers.

Their voices competed to promise her that they were even better. Caryl grinned. The more adventurous her clients, the better she liked them.

"And if," she looked around at them, "*if* we do dive that morning, then we'll move on to Soper's Hole Marina at West End in the afternoon. They have excellent restaurants. And that night, I'll take you over to Jost Van Dyke so you can spend much of the morning there before we head back to Nanny Cay."

"If we don't?" Louisa Rattray asked.

"Then you'll have more time to spend at Soper's Hole. It has excellent shopping as well," she said encouragingly, seeing the other woman's face drop.

"Don't worry, Lou." Her husband patted her knee. "We'll show her we could have dived with Cousteau."

"Ha! Cousteau wouldn't have been able to keep up," Henry Reyes quipped.

Caryl grinned. "We'll see," she said, non-committally. She remembered the last time she had taken a guest at his word and waived Richardson's objections that the man had not produced proof of his certification as was required. During the dive to the *Comair* the man panicked when a gentle northerly swell enveloped them. Seeing his distress, Caryl made her way to him but he kicked off, heading desperately for the surface. Every time Caryl tried to stop him he waved her off and ascended too quickly. Caryl thought it a miracle he hadn't been affected by the bends.

"It sounds alright to me, folks," said Matthew Silvers. "How long will it take us to get to Virgin Gorda?"

"Not long, about an hour," Caryl replied.

"Is there anything we can do to help?"

"No, all that we ask is that you enjoy yourselves. We take care of the rest. In fact, we'll set off now, unless there are any objections."

The group responded enthusiastically to the idea of leaving, and with a nod to Richardson, Caryl climbed up to the pilothouse. Within minutes, the *Elendil* was gliding smoothly out of the narrow harbor.

Six guests *did* make it difficult for Caryl to think about Joshua, at least in the daylight hours but that night, alone in the anonymous darkness of her cabin, she found it hard to resist memories of herself in his arms, their kisses, the bone-melting sweetness of their lovemaking. She tossed and turned, unable to sleep. It told on her the next day. After the afternoon dive to the *Rhone*, she realized she was bone-tired.

"So do we get to do the Drop Off?" Louisa Rattray asked, almost as soon as they broke the surface.

"Yes." Caryl smiled. "You do." They had aced the dive, looking out for one another, ascending slowly, following signaled instructions and generally performing like textbook examples of what to do on a dive.

"Alright!" Amidst a round of high fives and excited hugs, Caryl slowly swam over to the *Elendil*'s swimming platform. Richardson gave her a helping hand up. "You okay, cap?" he asked, helping to unhook her tanks.

"Yeah, sure. Just a bit tired." Caryl waved him off as she began to slip out of her wetsuit.

She had trouble getting to sleep that night too, but she finally dropped off around one. The next morning she rose early, feeling much better. When she went on deck, the rising sun had drenched the bands of clouds across the lower half of the sky in a pinkish gold light. Lifting the anchor, she set the *Elendil* in motion.

"Captain, good morning. We're so looking forward to this dive," Joy Reyes said when Caryl went down to the deck a couple of hours later.

"Good morning. I hope everyone slept well. It looks like a perfect day for a dive. Visibility will be excellent." Caryl smiled around at them all.

"How are you? You looked a bit peaky yesterday," Elaine Silvers said. Her lovely hazel eyes were full of concern.

"I'm fine, just fine. I could eat a horse." Caryl looked at Patty, who was serving mango and orange fruit crêpes.

Patty grinned. "Sorry, captain, that's not on the menu today," she retorted before continuing more soberly. "Noel's not too well. His ulcer is giving him problems and he was in pain all last night. Will you be able to take the dive by yourself?"

The clients turned to look anxiously at her.

"Of course. Poor Richardson." She smiled around the table and relief flooded her guests' faces.

"Whew, that's great because we're sure looking forward to going down." Linton Rattray rubbed his hands in anticipation.

"Will Richardson be okay?" Caryl asked.

"He's taken his medicine." Patty shrugged. "All he has to do is take it easy and he should be fine by tonight."

"Ulcers are awful. I have a cousin who's had three operations because of them," Elaine Silvers chimed in. As the conversation turned to a discussion of ulcers, Caryl only half-listened. Idly, she

JUST AN AFFAIR

wondered what Joshua was doing at that moment. Probably pawing a writhing Kenya in a darkened studio or tying the knot with the well-developed child. Damn him! She wasn't going to call and chew him out. No sirreee! He would only conclude she was a jealous shrew who didn't know how to play the game. Well, player, I've got your number now and you're history. Caryl gave a disgusted sniff and then could have shrunk with embarrassment when everyone at the table turned to stare at her.

She rubbed her nose. "A piece of mango almost went the wrong way, folks," she said, grimacing.

They gave her curious looks but the moment passed.

"I can see what Mr. Tain meant, Patty," Henry Reyes said. "Everything you've served so far has been delicious. The steak last night was what my teenage son would call 'dope.' And these crêpes! Mmm. Umm."

"We're going to tell Don not to wait a moment more. I think a culinary cruise would be a big hit and I'd be the first to sign up." Louisa Rattray smiled at Patty, who glowed.

"Thanks. You're all very kind."

"No, truthful. Matthew, pass those crêpes over here, please. I want more."

They delayed so long over the meal that it was almost eleven before they were ready for the dive. Patty dropped the weighted shot line over the side as Caryl and the clients suited up. They would follow the line to where the continental shelf dropped off into the indigo stillness of the deep sea. It was the most difficult dive of any on the *Elendil*'s itineraries.

Caryl went over the hand signals with the six. Then she and Patty checked everyone's gear to make sure there were no problems. Finally, Patty checked Caryl's suit and gear and then gave her the thumbs up sign. They were ready to hit the depths. Caryl stepped off the diving platform and, one by one, her guests followed her into the water.

Visibility was good so it would be a good dive for the visitors. As they slowly worked their way down, a school of sunshine damselfish enveloped them and then disappeared, preferring to remain in shallow waters. Caryl pointed to a trumpet fish standing sentry duty a few feet away from Louisa Rattray as it waited for its next meal. Down, down they went, through a school of yellowtail snapper and past a hawksbill turtle. When they were at about sixty feet, a young kingfish flashed up and away past them. A few minutes later a four-foot barracuda swam up to take a look. Lazily, it circled the group twice before swimming away again, evidently concluding that a better meal was to be had elsewhere. They continued their descent. Eighty feet, then one hundred feet, and finally Caryl checked her depth gauge. Two hundred feet. They would go no deeper. Below them, the continental shelf dropped off into blue depths.

Caryl gave the turn back sign. She had done well by her guests: they had seen a small group of black jacks, two blue marlins, and, most special of all, a tiger shark which had swum up from the depths around the seamount to inspect them at close quarters. It was an adult shark about eleven feet long with the distinctive tiger-like stripes on its dark back. As it swam over and past them, it displayed wounds possibly caused by another shark on its off-white belly. Caryl was pleased when it chose Joy Reyes to be the most curious about, swimming up to her and then whipping away to come back again before disappearing altogether beneath them.

After that, the rest of the dive was pretty anti-climactic. Caryl signaled to the others that they should pass her as they had arranged. She would be the last on the line, remaining in the back to make sure no surprises came out at them from the deep. Shark attacks were rare in places where no fish had been killed or wounded but divers never took chances.

Caryl was at ninety feet when she saw the tiger shark again, below and slightly to the left of her. Cursing silently, she gave a quick pull on the line for momentum, kicking her feet as much as she dared, concentrating on not attracting the shark's attention. She tried not to think about the newspaper article she had read months ago about a tiger shark attack at one of Hawaii's beaches. But why had the damn thing come back? She couldn't see it any longer. It had disappeared below her. Relieved, she continued her ascent.

Caryl's heart rate had just slowed almost to normal when the shark suddenly reappeared to her left. It approached until it was almost within ten feet, seeming almost to leer one-eyed at her. Holding grimly on to the line, Caryl watched warily as it swam off to her right. When it banked to return her way, she waved her free arm to frighten it. She was trying to remember what she knew about tiger sharks and shark attacks in general, but all that came to mind was that tiger sharks were known to attack humans. *Please, please,* she pleaded silently, *go away*. It seemed as if the shark heard her because it turned and disappeared again. Caryl felt the tension go out of her but she didn't wait around. It could come back. Giving her depth gauge a cursory glance, Caryl kicked off. Ascent rate be damned, she wasn't going to be caught napping. If she went up faster than thirty feet per minute, well, she had good reason. Better the bends than losing a limb or worse.

Whuumpf! She hadn't seen it coming. Instinct alone kept Caryl's grip tight on the shot line when the shark's snout rammed her from behind. She whirled in the water to face her attacker. The shark retreated but it had clearly decided she was lunch. Glancing up into the sunny waters above her, Caryl was glad Matthew Silver's flippered legs were barely visible. The shark was just interested in her, not the *Elendil*'s guests. Determined to be ready the next time it launched itself at her, Caryl stayed still. Quelling her fear and the urge to get the hell out of there, she hovered suspended in the water. She retrieved the small knife strapped to her weight belt and looked around but there was nothing to see. This in itself was a sign. Fish and other wildlife knew better than to stick around near a shark in full attack mode. Then she saw it. It was coming straight at her. Caryl gripped the knife tightly and faced the oncoming predator, determined to go down fighting. The shark reared up to her, its mouth open, rows of inch-long sharp teeth like a chainsaw on a collision course with her life. Caryl's heart pounded, but as the shark neared, she brought her arm back and with unerring aim landed the punch of her life square on the creature's snout. She threw herself to the side and the shark dived past her. Caryl brought her arm up, then down and across, scoring the shark's back. Blood billowed up from the injury and the shark plunged into the depths below. Knowing it was now or never, Caryl turned and kicked off for the light-filled waters above her. Never had she been so glad to break the surface.

"Caryl. Caryl." Patty waved at her from the *Elendil* about thirty feet away. The guests were ranged along the railing, their anxious faces relaxing into relief when they caught sight of her.

"Oy." Caryl waved her hands, a wide grin splitting her face. She had made it.

She was halfway to the boat when the pain exploded in her chest. Pressing one hand to the agonizing hurt as if that could stop it, she raised her other arm to signal that she needed help. Her sight blurred and she could no longer see the boat. Her arm felt heavy, so heavy. She let it drop.

"Help! Help!" But even through her panic, she realized she was

JUST AN AFFAIR

barely opening her mouth. She felt weak, so weak and the pain… She had no strength in her arms, her legs. Caryl spluttered as she began to sink back into the water. A second later, the sun went out and her world turned dark.

CHAPTER SIXTEEN

Caryl groaned and tried to raise a hand to her aching head but gave up when she realized she could barely lift a finger, much less her arm. Her eyes opened to white walls and a glass window through which harsh daylight entered the room. Puzzled, she tried to turn her head but that set off new alarms pounding along her forehead. Caryl closed her eyes.

"Caryl. Thank God." Caryl's eyes flew open. A woman she didn't recognize bent over her. The smile on her face did not mask the worry in her eyes. "I've got to go call the doctor. He said he wanted to know as soon as you revived." Impulsively, the woman pressed a kiss to her cheek before she straightened and hurried off.

Caryl was still trying to sort out the puzzle of the woman's identity when she returned with a stocky, middle-aged Indian man whose stethoscope dangled from the chest pocket of his white coat.

"Good morning, miss. And how are we today?" The doctor peered at her.

Caryl meant to say "fine" but what actually issued from her mouth sounded more like a gargled snuffle.

"That's alright, that's alright. Don't speak if it's too much for you. You've had a terrible experience. You are lucky to be alive, really."

Caryl frowned. "Lucky to be alive?" But before she could ask him what he meant she drifted back to sleep. When she woke again, the light in the room was softer and the air cooler. Her head no longer ached quite as much and the heaviness in her chest had also lessened.

JUST AN AFFAIR

"Caryl, how are you doing?" The same unknown woman from before leaned over the bed and smiled at her.

"Good, good," Caryl lied. She had no idea who the woman was and her accent was different, from the islands. Caryl was willing to bet the middle-aged woman was no New Yorker, not even American probably, but obviously she expected to be known so Caryl attempted a weak smile.

"Lord have mercy, we thought…well, I don't know what we thought when we took you to the emergency room. Child, I was more frightened than a cockroach in a fowl dance."

"I'm fine now," Caryl said.

"You've been dead to the world for almost a week. You were unconscious for about three days and after that they kept you sedated to give your body time to heal." The woman smiled encouragingly. "You only began to come to yourself yesterday. Don't you remember? You squeezed my hand when I called your name. You had acute decompression illness and you've had three hyperbaric treatments. You also had a burst lung."

"Me?"

"Yes, they said you must have come up too fast or stopped breathing or something."

"Oh." Caryl tried to look as if she knew exactly what the woman was talking about but the truth was, she didn't have a clue. A burst lung. That would probably explain why her chest felt as if a sumo wrestler was sitting on it. Caryl raised her hand to feel the area, her fingers exploring gingerly. Yes, there was a bandage wrapped around her chest alright.

"You're okay now. They put in a chest drain and they said everything's fine. All these scientific terms." The woman rolled her eyes. "But the upshot is, the air that leaked into your chest was drained and you're going to be fine."

Caryl closed her eyes. If the woman was right, then she could have died. A wave of tiredness washed over her and she barely managed to open her eyes to look at the woman again.

"I don't think I can stay awake much longer," she whispered.

"It's okay. The doctor said you'd be as weak as a newborn baby for a few days. I'll take my leave now but I'll be back tomorrow and I'll bring Noel with me."

"Good. Thank you." Best to keep things formal until she had a better idea of who the woman was and what their relationship to each other was based on.

"Child, for God in heaven's sake, you don't have to thank me. You're like my own daughter." The woman leaned forward again and planted another kiss on Caryl's cheek. "I'll see you tomorrow. That red button there is for you to call the nurse if you need her. Goodnight, Caryl."

After the woman left, Caryl looked around at the blank walls. She couldn't get what the woman had said out of her mind. The hospital, if that was where she was, smelled faintly of roses left in water too long. Caryl's nose wrinkled in distaste and she thought how ironic it was that she could identify a smell but had no idea who the woman she had been talking to was. In fact, and the thought hit her like the slap of a wet towel, she had no idea who she herself was. Caryl, the woman had called her *Caryl* so that was one clue. But who was Caryl and how had she come to have decompression illness?

Somehow she knew she had taken advanced courses in diving. She was certified by the Professional Association of Diving Instructors for wreck, cave and deep diving as well as diving instruction. Remembering this, she felt rather proud of herself and tried to sit up. The crushing pain in her chest reminded her that, whatever her certifications, she had still ended up in a hospital. She sank back on her pillows. Caryl, Caryl, she repeated the name to herself, trying to dredge up more revealing facts, but her mind was like a murky swamp. Every time she thought a memory was surfacing and she focused on it, it would sink back down to the depths, leaving her feeling like a failed treasure hunter. Eventually she gave up. Tomorrow was another day and maybe her memory would be clearer then. She closed her eyes and was asleep almost immediately.

"Miss Walker, wake up. Miss Walker."

Caryl opened her eyes. A smiling young woman in the white uniform of a nurse smiled at her.

"I'm sorry to wake you up but it's about seven-thirty and the doctor is coming to see you at eight. He wants you to take some tests first thing this morning to check how you're doing." She held out a small paper cup and a bigger, plastic one of water.

"What are these?"

"The two pink ones are painkillers and the white one is an antibiotic."

Leaning on one elbow, Caryl took the paper cup, tipped her head back and let the tablets spill onto her tongue. The nurse handed her the water and Caryl swallowed, grimacing as the pills rasped against the back of her throat.

"Good. I'll be right back to help you with your bath, and then you'll be set to face the day." With another bright smile, the nurse turned and left.

Caryl was gleeful; she had obtained another vital piece of information. Her last name was Walker. If she was asked anything else about herself, she would just have to fake it. She didn't want doctors poking about one inch more than they had to. Everybody would treat her like…like… An image came to mind of an old woman, her long, wiry gray hair in disarray, her eyes vacant, sitting on a couch in front of a television. Caryl felt she should know the woman's name but try as she might, she couldn't remember who the woman was. It wasn't her fault. Amnesia. The word came to her easily. That was what she had. But how come she could recall her PADI courses and yet draw a blank on almost everything else?

The people she had spoken to so far had an accent, a Caribbean accent. Did this mean she was on vacation, had maybe gone diving, and suffered an accident? That was likely. She remembered going to a place called, she waited for the name and it came, the Virgin Islands, and she had certainly gone diving. Perhaps she had come back for a return visit or maybe this was the same trip and she had never left. She murmured a curse; the more she tried to remember, the less came to mind.

It was noon by the time Caryl was finished with her tests that day – CAT scans to look at her brain, an eye exam to see if she was seeing properly and x-rays of her chest.

"Tomorrow we continue with more tests," the doctor said when they were getting ready to wheel her back to her room.

"What kind?"

"Oh." The doctor waved his hand. "Hearing tests, blood work, hand and eye coordination tests, that sort of thing. No problem. You seem to be recovering well, all things considered."

Caryl almost dozed off on her way back to her room, but the huge arrangement of almost every kind of tropical flower she saw sitting on her nightstand startled her into wakefulness.

JUST AN AFFAIR

"Who...?"

"Here's the card." The nurse plucked a small square white envelope off its stand and handed it to Caryl. "I think the guy was here but he left."

At first, Caryl fumbled the envelope, but she managed to open it just as the nurse, Nurse Kimberley Gittens, according to her badge, reached over to help.

"Hoping for your speedy recovery with all my heart, Alexander Thorne," the card read.

Alexander. Of course. Caryl's face flushed warm. Alexander was here?

"Are you sure he left?" she demanded.

"I think so. But he's been here almost every day since you were brought in. He read to you from the newspaper. Said he knew you wouldn't want to miss any news. Do you remember hearing him?"

"No." Caryl shook her head, regretfully. Alexander knew how much she liked to keep up with what happened in the world. What was it he called her? A news junkie, that was it.

"Comfortable?"

"Yes, thanks." They had returned her to the bed and arranged the hospital robe so that even if she decided to throw over the light cotton sheet they had covered her with, she would still be decent.

"I think Mr. and Mrs. Richardson are in the waiting area so I'll send them on in, okay?"

Caryl nodded. Who were Mr. and Mrs. Richardson? She would have preferred some time to think over the fact that, as soon as the nurse mentioned Alexander, she had known who he was and his connection to her. How could that be? One by one she ticked off the major things she knew about him on her fingers. One, Alexander was a partner at the firm where she worked and, two, under pressure of late hours and constant contact, they'd fallen in love. Three, he was in a loveless marriage but was separated from his wife and in the process of getting a divorce. She wondered if his ability to be here with her now meant he was finally free. Her heart raced at the possibility.

There was a loud knock at the door of her private room.

"Come in," she called.

"Caryl, sweetheart, it's good to see you. How you doing?" A burly middle-aged man rushed up to stand over her. He looked as if he would have liked to hug her but felt he might hurt her instead. The woman from yesterday was right behind him.

"Hello, child. You're looking much better today."

"Am I?" Caryl said warmly. She might have no idea who they were but it was obvious they cared a lot for her. Something about them, the woman in particular, made her feel safe and looked after.

"Yes, your face doesn't look quite as gray and you're much more alert. Doesn't she look good to you, Noel?" she asked the man. "He hasn't seen you since Friday when you were still unconscious."

"She looks good. She looks great."

And when Caryl gave him a "yeah right" look, he shrugged and held up his hands. "By comparison, I mean," he explained.

"My goodness, is this from Alexander?" the woman asked, looking at the bouquet.

"Yes," Caryl answered, beaming. "But I haven't seen him yet. Did he tell you when he was coming back?" They seemed to know him too, but how?

"No." The couple exchanged looks. "He didn't."

"Oh." Caryl subsided into her pillows and heaved a sigh.

"I'll say one thing for him. He's been vigilant." Mrs. Richardson sounded surprised.

"Yes, the nurse said he read to me." If he couldn't be here, at least

JUST AN AFFAIR

she could talk about him.

"Almost 24-7," the man agreed, nodding. "Damn near wore out his voice. It was him got in touch with your parents and arranged for them to get an earlier flight out. He also got you moved here." Mr. Richardson looked around. "This room's almost half the size of the ward where she was, isn't it, Patty?"

His wife nodded as Caryl registered her name.

"So when are my parents coming?" And with that question it all came flooding back to her. She knew exactly who she was, who her parents were, where she had gone to school, the names of her friends, everything. Caryl relaxed in relief. She was, more or less, back to herself. Now she just had to fill in a few details, like her connection with the two people in front of her. At least she knew their surnames as well as the woman's first name.

"They should get here this afternoon. I'm not sure the exact time." Patty glanced at her husband to see if he knew more.

He shrugged. "Maybe that's where Alexander's gone," he suggested. "To pick them up."

Caryl absorbed this in silence. Her parents, her father in particular, didn't approve of Alexander and they had never met. Caryl remembered when David and Marcianne had come to visit her in New York a couple of months earlier. Alexander had asked to meet them and offered to host a small dinner at the hot new Ethiopian restaurant in Grand Central Station. "Maybe when's he's divorced," they'd firmly responded, dismissing the idea quicker than the rapping of a judge's gavel.

"I told him Noel or I should go," the woman hunched her shoulders, "but he wouldn't listen. I hope it'll be okay."

Caryl eyed Patty warily. The woman sounded as if she knew about David and Marcianne's hostility to even the idea of Alexander. Caryl wondered what else she knew, but her tiredness was making itself felt. Her eyelids were getting heavier and heavier.

"I'm so sleepy. Would you mind if I just close my eyes for a second?"

"Sure, dear, no problem. We'll be right here when you wake up." The couple smiled at her and Caryl smiled back. They were nice people, caring.

"Wake me as soon as Alexander comes, and my parents, of course," she added, seeing the puzzled looks they again threw each other.

"Alright," Patty said and started to say something else before her husband shushed her.

"Let Caryl get some rest, honey. She needs it."

Caryl smiled again, grateful for the big man's consideration.

When she woke again, her mother was standing over her.

"Caryl, darling, you're awake!"

"Mumsie."

Caryl's mother leaned over the bed to gingerly hold her in a long embrace.

"It's good to see you, Mumsie." Caryl's eyes teared. Maybe now she could start making sense of this whole experience.

"Do move aside, Marcianne, and give other people a chance."

"Daddy!" Caryl opened her arms wide. "Oh, Daddy." Her father emerged from behind her mother to lean over and hug her in his turn. Caryl inhaled the smell of his familiar cologne and burst into tears.

"Hush, precious, hush. Everything's going to be fine." He stroked her hair, murmuring the words into her ear. But he didn't know the half of it. Caryl almost let it all out, how when she first woke up she hadn't known who she was and now she did but she didn't know *where* she was or who the couple standing off to the side were or what had

JUST AN AFFAIR

happened to place her in this hospital.

"There, there, darling." Marcianne stroked her arm. "Your father's quite right. We're here now and everything's going to be just fine. We've already talked to the doctor and we can take you to our hotel with us after you've done your tests tomorrow."

"Marcianne!" Her father frowned at his wife. "You know he didn't say any such thing. In fact, he said quite the opposite."

"No, darling, he didn't." Marcianne's smile was triumphant. "His exact words were that he wouldn't be responsible for the consequences if we removed her. That she would have to sign a form releasing him and the hospital from liability."

"So that means he doesn't think it's a great idea and neither do I. She's been unconscious for days. I don't want to do anything that would retard her recovery."

"Having her in a hotel suite with us and being looked after by a specially trained nurse - I've already spoken to Lito about it - will hardly 'retard her recovery.'"

Caryl looked from one to the other. Lito was one of Marcianne's first cousins and chief of staff at Atlantic Hospital in Miami.

"Er, what nurse, Mumsie?"

"Lito knows about some agency that hires out highly qualified nurses. He's promised to recruit one for me and send her down on the next available flight or, failing that," she glanced at her husband, " we'll use the company jet."

"I think she should stay in the hospital." A new voice broke in on the discussion.

Alexander. Caryl struggled up from her father's embrace, a wide, ecstatic smile lighting her face. She had not seen him standing by the closet behind Marcianne.

"Hey," she said, suddenly shy in front her parents and the

Richardsons who were watching the proceedings with interest. She held out her hands to him.

"Hey, woman." He took her hands and brought them to his lips for fervent kisses. "God, am I glad to see you up and talking."

Marcianne gave an audible sniff.

"Haven't been able to get much of a word in edgewise, though," Caryl quipped, determined they would all get along.

The woman, Patty, let out a nervous laugh that was more like a cough. "Alright then," she said, looking at her husband, "I guess we'll go. We'll be back to see you tomorrow, wherever you are. It was a pleasure seeing you again, Mr. and Mrs. Cassavettes." Then with a glance at Alexander that Caryl couldn't quite fathom and a little wave to her, they were gone.

"You were saying, Mr. Thorne?" At Marcianne's question, the temperature in the room dropped by at least thirty degrees.

"Just that I don't believe we should go against the doctor's wishes. This is one of the leading dive destinations in the world. The hospital here has wide experience in treating people with decompression illness. An arterial gas embolism, Marcianne, is not something to sneeze at."

Caryl admired how Alexander stood his ground under a glare from Marcianne that she was sure would have made a shark run for cover. A shark. Something niggled at her memory but when it refused to do more than that, Caryl let it go. It was probably nothing anyway, and if it was something important, then it would return.

"Mr. Thorne, I don't recall asking for your opinion and quite frankly, as far as I'm concerned, you don't have a thing to do with it." Marcianne was obviously furious but trying to control her temper. No stress, no excitement, the doctor had warned when they arrived, reminding them that Caryl was still very weak. "She's *my* daughter!"

Marcianne turned away from Alexander as if that clinched the argument in her favor.

"Yes, but I love her too."

"You...you..." Marcianne's voice rose. "How dare you say that, you..." Caryl's father put a hand on his wife's arm. She clasped it and closed her eyes, trying to regain her composure.

"Mumsie, please." It was a small protest but Caryl feared saying anything that would really set her mother off. Marcianne Cassavettes was not known for verbal restraint and if she was trying to contain herself, then everyone around should be grateful and walk as if on eggshells.

"I think you should leave while my wife and I discuss this with our daughter." David's tone was no less icy than his wife's had been, but where Marcianne had glared daggers at Alexander, David wore a look of detached distaste. Caryl rolled her eyes.

"Daddy, I want him to stay."

Caryl couldn't tell which of the three people in the room looked most shocked, but she had no time to figure that small mystery out.

"You do? Why?"

She could have answered her father's question with a simple response, "because he's my lover," but she knew that would offend her parents' sensibilities and sense of propriety. "Because maybe he can help," she said. It was a bit lame but it would have to do. Her mother stared at her as if she had lost her mind.

"When we have come to an agreement we will convey it to Mr. Thorne." Caryl rolled her eyes again at all this formality. "And then," her father continued, ignoring her, "if there's a role for him to play, he will play it."

"Yes," her mother said, nodding firmly in appreciation of her husband's diplomacy.

"I have no objection to that. It's okay, Caryl," Alexander said when she groaned in protest. "I'll be back tomorrow morning."

"But I want to see you alone," she said, not caring too much about the proprieties now she had lost the battle to keep him there while she talked with her parents.

"Really?" Again there was that shocked look.

"Of course, why wouldn't I?" *What was wrong with him?* Her parents she could understand, but Alexander was acting downright strange.

"Nothing, nothing. I'm happy to hear it, that's all. I'll be back first thing tomorrow then." He leaned over the bed and, under the disapproving glare of her parents, gave her a chaste kiss on the cheek. Caryl would have liked to turn her head and change the kiss into something with a bit more heat in it, but she understood his discretion in the presence of David and Marcianne and loved him all the more for it.

"Really, Caryl, I don't understand you," her mother said as the door shut behind Alexander.

"Please, Marcianne, leave it alone. Remember what the doctor said." David Cassavettes frowned at his wife.

"I have to ask, she…"

Marcianne's protest was interrupted by Caryl. "What did the doctor say?"

"That you weren't to be excited or stressed. He also said that you don't seem to know what happened in the accident and we shouldn't question you too closely about it. You should remember in your own time but also you may never remember, which would be okay too. He said you appear well on the road to good health in other respects, so we shouldn't worry if you can't remember the few minutes before your accident." Her father smiled reassuringly at her.

"Ah." Caryl was relieved. Despite his careful questions and all the tests, Doctor Akbar had not been able to guess that her memory lapse went a bit further than a few minutes. How much further she would like to know, but it would be almost impossible to find out without attracting suspicion.

"So, darling, wouldn't you prefer to be out of this hospital and in our suite at Hill House?" Her mother pursued her original line of questioning. "You'll have your very own nurse and the view is so much better. It will lift your spirits and speed your recovery. I know it!"

Caryl thought about it. Hill House was the four star Janus hotel she had stayed in on her previous visit or maybe she had just never left. It was hard to tell how much time might have passed. Certainly her parents looked no different from when she remembered seeing them last. She would love to leave the hospital because clues as to what happened might be easier to come by at the hotel, but she still felt very weak.

"Mumsie, I think I should stay just a few more days here." Disappointment veiled her mother's face. "I'm sorry, but I still don't feel all that well and then there are the other tests. Please understand."

"Darling, they said your last tests would be tomorrow. Anything else would just be a checkup to see how you're progressing."

Caryl glanced at her father but David Cassavettes was silent.

"In case anything happens, Mumsie, I think it would be wiser for me to stay here. Just for a few more days and then I'll come with you. Okay?"

"Alright, darling," Marcianne conceded with grace, leaning forward to kiss her daughter's forehead.

"I think you made the right decision, Caryl," her father finally said now that it was all settled. "She didn't have a scrape, you know, dearest."

"Yes. Yes, I know. It's just that hospitals are so dreary and this place isn't the Mayo Clinic, is it?" Marcianne shrugged.

"I'll call Lito tonight and tell him to hold off on the nurse then. Unless," she brightened, "she comes and looks after you here."

"You are incorrigible, Marcianne. What hospital would allow that?" David Cassavettes shook his head. "She wouldn't be part of their system and even if they allowed it, I daresay they'd be rather resentful of her and of us. They would see it as a vote of no confidence. There might even be liability issues."

"Oh, alright then. It was just a thought." Marcianne waved her hand to end the argument and Caryl began to snicker. If she could, she would have laughed outright but the pain in her chest would remind her of its presence very sharply if she indulged herself that way.

"What are you grinning at?" Marcianne growled at her but a smile played around the corners of her generous mouth.

"You two are like Oscar and Felix, Ernie and Bert…," Caryl answered, searching her memory for the names of more contentious couples.

"Thank you very much. Just because I'm trying to look out for your best interests," her mother protested.

"And I took your side. I'll know better next time," her father said in mock offense.

"Ha, I wish."

Her parents spent the rest of the afternoon and early evening with her, leaving hours after visiting time was officially over. After they were gone, Caryl ate a few more of the crackers her father had brought for her and pressed the remote to flick on the television but she could barely keep her eyes open and was asleep in minutes.

CHAPTER SEVENTEEN

The next morning Caryl was having a breakfast of oatmeal porridge and canned pears when Nurse Gittens ushered Alexander into her room, a smile on her face and a finger to her lips.

"It's way before visiting time, Caryl," she said, "but you have to go down for tests in another couple hours or so, so I'll allow it." With a wink at her patient, she was gone.

"Alexander." Caryl held out her arms to him.

"Hey, baby girl." Alexander crossed the room in a couple of steps and bent over to hug her. He would have kissed her on the cheek as before, but, this time, Caryl turned her head, opening her mouth under his for a long, sexy kiss. Now that her parents weren't around there was no need for restraint.

"See! *That* was a kiss," she declared, smiling, when finally they broke apart.

"It sure was. Er, are you feeling alright?" Alexander's level brows knit as he stared at her.

"Of course I am. Except for some pain in my chest. Is it a problem if I want a real kiss from you instead of the pecks you've been giving me?" Caryl happily patted the bed, indicating where he should sit.

"Umm, no, not really." Still looking puzzled, Alexander sat.

Ignoring him, it was his business if he wanted to act strange; she decided to see if carefully worded questions could help her begin to unravel the mystery of her memory lapse.

"Alexander."

"Yes?"

"This must be my longest vacation ever. We've been here how long now?"

"Here? You mean, here in the British Virgin Islands?"

"Of course, here on Tortola."

"Don't you know?"

Caryl plucked at the sheet around her.

"You know," she said, deliberately keeping her voice casual, "what with being unconscious and all, I've lost track of time."

"Oh. But what do you mean *we*? You and I?"

Caryl lost her patience.

"Of course, you and me! Who else would I mean? I know my parents just got here but I don't know how long you and I have been here. It must have been a while because of all the people I know." She had been going to say because of her friendship with Patty and Noel but that would really be letting the cat out of the bag.

"About a month."

So that would explain it or at least help to. She wondered about asking something more, but a glance at Alexander's face told her he was already suspicious. Was he divorced yet? That was the burning question she would love answered but how could she bring it up? He had to be divorced, though. There was no way he could have been in the Virgin Islands with her for a whole month otherwise.

"We've been having a wonderful time, yachting and hiking and so on and we've been to almost all the islands. Virgin Gorda was your favorite. Do you remember what a good time we had there?" There was a strange expression on his face.

"Yes," she lied, looking him straight in the eyes so he'd believe she was telling the truth.

"We made love at the Baths one night with a full moon above us and no sound around but the lapping of the waves and that noise you make deep down in your throat when you're coming." He paused, peering at her. "Baby, I can't get that night out of my mind."

Caryl grinned. "Now that definitely does sound like me." She wondered if she would ever be able to come straight with him and tell him she was just faking it to make him feel good. Probably never. It would hurt him too much. A thought suddenly struck her. Things back at the firm would be crazy with both her and Alexander gone for so long.

"Does the firm know I had an accident?"

"Er, yes, I told them." He still had that strange expression she couldn't figure out. Did he suspect that she had a more serious case of amnesia than she was letting on? "They wanted to send flowers but in the end they decided to do something for you when you're back in New York."

"So they're coping, okay?" Caryl was a bit miffed that her long absence wasn't having greater consequences. "Maybe I should call and see how my cases are going. The Mottley case was on appeal." She thought hard. "Oh yes, I helped Duran with his Supreme Court brief on that fire brigade discrimination case. I'd like to know how that went."

"The Appeals Court was overruled and the judgment was returned to the lower court for reinstatement."

"Alright." Caryl pumped the air. "That was rather quick, though. I thought they wouldn't hear it for months."

Alexander shrugged. "You never know, sometimes it takes years, other times, like in Duran's case, just months. Anyway, I don't think you should be worrying about the office, okay? You've got to concentrate on getting well. The firm can more than look after itself."

"Okay, masterful one, you're right. I will." She grinned at him, ducking as he reached out to pinch her ear.

"Caryl, the doctor said you don't really remember the accident. Do you remember getting into the water or any part of the dive at all?" His face had sobered.

Caryl shook her head.

"Not really. Getting up, having breakfast, sailing out, suiting up. That's about it," she faked. She doubted her day could have gone much different if she was on vacation.

"Umm."

"What does that mean? 'Umm'?"

"Nothing. I'm just trying to figure out, you know, what happened."

"So I guess you weren't sticking by my side when it went down. Left me to my lonesome, huh?" She tickled him in the ribs, wanting to make him laugh and erase the worry lines that had appeared around his eyes.

"Caryl, sorry, you didn't hear my knock." Nurse Gittens opened the door and poked her head into the room.

"No problem. Come in, come in." Caryl waved to her.

"I've come to help you with your bath. I'm afraid Mr. Thorne will have to leave, though."

"Why? He's seen me naked. Maybe he can help you." Caryl's lips twitched, mischievously.

"Against rules for non-family members."

"Oh, rules schmules. You'll be right outside, Alexander?"

"Sorry, Caryl, but after that then it's time for those tests." The nurse looked apologetic.

"Uggh." Caryl pulled a face. "I guess I won't see you for hours then, honey."

"That's okay. I've got some things to see about and then I'll be

JUST AN AFFAIR

back. Maybe by mid-day?" He shot a questioning look at the nurse.

"She should be long finished by then."

"Okay, baby, see you later." This time when Alexander leaned down to kiss her, it was her mouth he aimed for.

"Hmm, that man is fine even if he is old."

"Kimberley, please." Nurse Gittens had become a favorite of hers. The others exuded a sort of grim briskness but Kimberley always had a cheery word for everybody.

"Alright, alright. He's not old. He's mature."

Caryl took a swipe at her but missed.

"Hey, hey, hold on. You'll fall right out of your bed like that." The bath passed without mishap and it was a fresh-faced Caryl who was waiting for an orderly to come and wheel her to the lab when Patty and her husband came in.

"Hello, dear, you're looking better and better," Patty said as they entered.

"Thank you. I'm *feeling* better and better." Caryl wished for the hundredth time that she didn't draw a blank whenever she tried to figure out who these people were to her. And Alexander had been no use at all.

"Joshua's coming this afternoon. He's been trying to get a flight out since last

Wednesday." The burly man beamed at her, clearly expecting her to be happy at the news but Caryl's heart sank. *Who the hell was Joshua?*

"Oh, good," she said, then seeing the couple's exchange of puzzled looks, "excellent. I'm really looking forward to seeing him." She glanced at them covertly to see if this got a better response. "I've been wondering when he would get here," she threw in for good measure and was rewarded by Patty's nod of approval. Richardson's brow smoothed.

"He's been calling for days he said and leaving messages everywhere, even with the booking agency in New York, but we never knew. I guess with all the craziness here trying to make sure you were okay and arranging for coverage on the *Elendil,* people just forgot to pass on the messages." Richardson spread his hands in front of him.

"Yes." Patty chimed in. "The guy who was supposed to cover for you during your days off is still here and they brought in a substitute crew because we said we wanted to take some time to make sure you were alright."

"Ah." Caryl tried to look wise, as if she understood every word that had been said but the truth was she had become more and more frightened the more the Richardsons talked. Booking agency. The *Elendil.* Joshua. It seemed like the little black hole in her memory wasn't quite so little after all. Despite her best effort, something of the panic she was feeling must have revealed itself in her eyes because Patty leaned forward, clucking with concern.

"Don't worry, dearest. Everything's fine, really. The *Elendil*'s out on a cruise right now but you'll be back on her in no time at all. You'll see." She squeezed Caryl's hand.

Caryl smiled wanly back. She sure hoped everything was fine but *fine* seemed like a far more distant shore than she'd first thought. How long it would take her to reach it, and if she would reach it at all were questions to which she had no answers.

"Ready to go, miss?" It was the orderly, arriving in time to save her from more revelations and from well-meaning but doubtful assurances.

"Yes. Yes."

"We'll be back this evening, Caryl. Good luck."

Caryl, preoccupied with her worries, waved a hand behind her as

231

JUST AN AFFAIR

she was wheeled out.

Down in the doctor's office after the tests were over, she quickly made up her mind to ask the questions bothering her. She didn't think she had any real choice.

"Doctor." He was writing on her file. "What are some of the effects of decompression illness?"

"Let's see, other than what you had, there's paralysis, shortness of breath, blurred vision, cardiac arrest. It's a long list. Why do you ask?" He looked up from the file.

"No particular reason. I just want to understand what happened to me."

"But didn't you learn all this in your advanced diving course?"

He was watching her closely; she had to tread carefully. "Of course, but I wanted to know if there were other symptoms."

"Like?"

"Umm, stroke, amnesia, things that might be rare, things to do with the brain."

The doctor tapped his pen against his front teeth.

"Anything's possible, really. The symptoms you were taught about are the classic ones, the ones most common, but there's a lot of debate about the terminology and about defining decompression illness. What is known, however, is that once a patient is admitted to a hyperbaric chamber in time and begins treatment, the symptoms dissipate. You've had," he flicked some pages, "three treatments."

Caryl sighed inwardly. He hadn't really answered her question, not directly anyway.

"Are you withholding something about your health?" the doctor demanded, staring at her over his glasses.

"No, no." She shrugged and smiled in what she hoped was a disarming way. "Nothing at all."

"I hope not." He snapped her file shut. "Alright, Miss Walker, it's Tuesday now. We'll keep you for observation until Thursday. I hope that will suit your mother." His tone said it had better and Caryl suppressed a grin. Marcianne had clearly met her match in Dr. Akbar.

"You'll let me know what the results are tomorrow?"

"Yes. As soon as I have them I will come to see you."

Dr. Akbar rose to open the door and summon the orderly to wheel her back to her room.

Her parents were already there waiting to see her.

"Hello, darling." Her mother greeted her with a wide smile as she was wheeled in.

"And how is our precious today?" her father asked, inspecting every inch of her face.

Caryl grimaced.

"Bobbing and weaving," she said. It was a boxing analogy he often used.

"That's how it's going to be, I guess, until you're on your feet." Caryl closed her eyes as her father lightly stroked her cheek. For a second, she felt like crying. She was Caryl Walker, well, Cassavettes really, and these were her parents and she'd had a wonderful childhood and worked at a premier law firm. But now she'd had an accident about which she remembered nothing and there were names and people to go along with those names, that she knew nothing about.

"It's okay, honey, if you want to cry. We're here for you." Her father leaned down to murmur the words against her ear.

"I'm fine, Daddy, I'm fine."

"You've had a terrible experience. It's okay if you want to let go."

Over by the window, her mother nodded her agreement.

"No, I'm fine, really. I'm just so happy you're both here."

"Where else would we be, darling?" her mother asked, but her nose was now almost pressed to the glass and her attention was clearly caught by something outside.

"Darling." Her mother was looking out the window. "The florists are unloading a huge delivery of red roses. Goodness! It's just vase after vase."

Caryl had not realized her window overlooked the hospital entrance.

David went to stand beside his wife. "I wonder who they're for. They can't all be for one person. What outrageous excess!"

There were two loud knocks on the door and David didn't have to wonder any longer. Two men trooped into the room, their arms full, and the Cassavettes all watched in bemusement as vases of long-stemmed roses began to fill the room. Their sweet, spicy fragrance scented the air and something stirred in Caryl's memory like a shadow flitting past a cloudy old mirror.

Marcianne was the first to recover from her surprise.

"Who sent these?" she asked the deliveryman as he put down the last vase.

"Joshua Tain, ma'am. They're for Miss Walker." He winked at Caryl and withdrew from the room.

A stunned silence settled among the family. Who the hell *was* this Joshua Tain? Caryl rifled feverishly through her damaged mental Rolodex. She supposed this must be the same Joshua that Richardson had told her was on his way, there could hardly be so many Joshuas running about, but why this over-the-top gesture? Caryl was so distracted by this fresh mystery that seconds went by before she noticed her father's expression.

"Daddy, what's the matter?"

"That, that, blasted man!" Her father exploded. "How dare he intrude on a private family matter? I'll have them sent back. What does he think he's doing?"

"Calm down, David. No need to get so worked up."

"No need? No need? This man stole my people from right under my nose and now he's sending flowers to my daughter! There is every need." A nerve worked furiously in her father's jaw.

"Yes, but don't forget you were the one who started it, trying to take his business away from him."

"A takeover bid, that was all, Marcianne. He could have remained as managing director. You know that. He's the one who turned things dirty."

"Maybe they ran out of olive branches at the florists so he's making do with roses. They do smell heavenly, don't they, darling?" This last question was directed at Caryl.

"Um, yes." Caryl watched her parents in utter amazement. "Look here, I don't understand. What are you two talking about?"

"Darling, your father tried to buy out Tain Music, owned by the man who's sent you these." Marcianne gestured at the flowers. "It didn't go too well. A couple of the consultants David hired to advise him crossed over to Tain and everything fell through. It got quite ugly for a little while. Now I think he's trying to make amends." Her father snorted in derision but Caryl was intrigued. Could her mother be right? Could this Joshua Tain have sent the flowers as a conciliatory gesture to her father? That would mean they didn't really have anything to do with her. But if so, why was he actually coming all the way from the States to see her? She wondered if she should say anything about that but decided against it. Her father looked apoplectic enough without her giving him a reason to launch himself into the cosmos. Then again, when he and Joshua met, as they inevitably would if the man was really on his way, he would self-launch anyway.

"Daddy, I think he may be coming here."

"Who, precious?"

"The same man. Joshua Tain." Her father took a sharp breath. "Look, I'm not sure," she tried to lessen the impact of what she was saying, "but Richardson mentioned a Joshua and stands to reason it's the same guy."

"Tain? But why?" David looked at his wife as if she might have the answer.

Marcianne shrugged elegantly, tucking a loose strand of hair back into the chignon at the nape of her neck.

"Perhaps you are mistaken, darling."

"I'm pretty sure he said Joshua and there aren't that many of those outside the Old Testament."

"The key then must be this Richardson. I've got to go find him."

"Sweetheart, where would you look? The man could be anywhere, including on his way back here." Marcianne obviously didn't like the idea of her husband haring off on a wild goose chase.

"Caryl, don't you know where the Richardsons live?"

"Yes," and she was surprised to find that she did, "in a pink and blue house off the main road in Port Purcell, just a little past Bobby's new mini-supermarket." She smiled triumphantly winning a small battle with her memory loss. But her joy was short-lived. Oh sure, she knew where they lived, but that still didn't answer the question of *how* she knew them.

"Caryl."

"I'm sorry, Daddy." Absorbed in her thoughts, she hadn't heard what her father said.

"I asked you if I should take the Blackbourne Highway or if there was another road."

And she knew the answer to that, too. "The highway goes straight past there," she said, firmly.

"Alright." With a kiss for each of the Cassavettes women, David strode out looking very much like his namesake must have when he went out to meet Goliath.

"So Daddy is taking this thing with Tain pretty hard, huh?"

Marcianne raised her eyes to the ceiling.

"Darling, it's business. Your father thought he was orchestrating a takeover but Tain pulled the rug out from under him. The entertainment industry doesn't work like any other and your father simply didn't have the right contacts and the right information, thanks to those quisling consultants of his." Marcianne's tone indicated her contempt.

"So the takeover failed?"

"It was a serious blow."

"For Henry Enterprises?"

"Not really, mostly just to your father's ego. The business has a firm foundation in construction and that kind of thing, you know. I think it was just some kind of delayed middle-aged crisis that made him want to add the glamour and glitz of the music business to the list."

Caryl digested this in silence.

"So now Tain's name is anathema," her mother continued. "This is an interesting twist." She caressed the petals of the roses next to her. "Very interesting. Is there some chance that you actually know this man, darling?"

Caryl frowned. Not very likely. She didn't move in that kind of glittery, fast-paced circle. Entertainment people only mixed with lawyers when they had a civil suit or a criminal charge hanging over them and, to the best of her recollection, she'd never handled a case like that. Her forte was civil rights law. Then again, her powers of recollection weren't exactly at their height right now.

"I really couldn't say," she answered cautiously. "Was my firm

JUST AN AFFAIR

involved?"

"Your firm?"

"Thorne, Mercer and Johnson." What other firm could she have meant?

"Oh, well." Her mother seemed taken aback. "Not as far as I know. No, I'm sure not. Your father would have mentioned it."

Caryl was prevented from pondering the mystery further by Alexander's re-appearance.

"Wow! Who bought out the florist? You, Marcianne?"

"No." Marcianne's frosty tone indicated that she had not had a miraculous overnight change of heart regarding him and his relationship to her daughter. She stepped back over to the window, finding an intense interest in the view it afforded of the harbor.

"They're from a business acquaintance of Daddy's," Caryl informed him, grimacing her apology for her mother's disdain.

"If that's how his business acquaintances behave, I can hardly wait to see what his friends have planned. How did your tests go?"

"Great! Dr. Akbar says I'm doing great and my chest is healing nicely."

"So when will they release you?"

"Thursday."

"Caryl." Nurse Gittens poked her head around the door. "Lunch's up in a minute."

The tension in the room thawed as Caryl ate. Alexander went out of his way to be charming and there were few who could resist him when he made the effort. By the time Caryl swallowed the last of her ice cream he had even managed to make Marcianne laugh at his description of the perils he'd faced from stray livestock while driving on the island. The way he told it every cow, sheep and goat on Tortola was hell-bent on running him off the road.

It puzzled Caryl that he didn't mention her in any of his anecdotes until she realized he was probably trying not to ruffle Marcianne's feathers by rubbing her nose in the fact of their affair. That was good thinking, but Marcianne was just going to have to get used to the idea of her and Alexander. If he was finally divorced, then she and he would soon make things legal. Caryl's face suffused with warmth at the thought of being Mrs. Alexander Thorne.

"I didn't find him," her father announced, walking into the room. "He and his wife went out just before I got there, one of their neighbors said." The heat of the midday sun told in the light sheen of perspiration covering his face. He dropped into the nearest chair.

"That traffic is hell," he said and looked around puzzled when everyone began to laugh. "What's so funny?"

"Alexander was just telling us horror stories about his experiences on the roads here," Caryl explained.

"Oh." David cast an unfriendly look at Alexander before leaning back to close his eyes. He dug into his pocket and fished out a handkerchief to wipe his face. Caryl's lips twitched. Her mother may have unbent enough to enjoy Alexander's conversation, but her father clearly wasn't in any mood to do the same after his wasted trip to look for Noel Richardson.

"Tain's here." Marcianne's excited voice brought David to his feet. He joined her at the window in three strides.

"It can't be...it *is* him. What the hell is he doing here? I can't believe the man's effrontery." David rushed out of the room.

Alexander raised a questioning eyebrow at Caryl but she shook her head and shrugged. She was beginning to feel a little tired from all the excitement. Raised voices could be heard in the corridor getting nearer and nearer, her father's mingling with that of another man's deep, controlled tones.

JUST AN AFFAIR

"…through a traumatic experience. I don't want her stressed," Caryl heard just before the door opened and it seemed to her that her room was invaded.

A tall, dark-skinned man with chiseled features and eyebrows like wings over piercing eyes strode into the room with an enraged David Cassavettes hard on his heels. The man crossed the floor to swoop down and gingerly gather her into his arms.

"Caryl." Kisses showered her on her face and Caryl realized she was relishing the feel of the man's strong arms around her, the clean smell of his hair, the pressure of his lips. Catching the look on Alexander's face and scandalized by the emotions coursing through her, Caryl struggled to regain her equilibrium. She tried to push the stranger away but he wasn't having any of it and pulled her closer.

"I'm so sorry I wasn't here. I got caught up in my business affairs and I forgot what's really important. Caryl, I'll never leave you again. I promise."

The only people who didn't look as if a breeze could have knocked them over at this speech were Patty and her husband who had trooped into the room a heartbeat behind David. Marcianne was open-mouthed, David looked as if he thought Joshua certifiable, and shock, anger, misery, and something else Caryl couldn't quite define, warred for supremacy on Alexander's face.

"Caryl, who is this man?" Her father loomed over her, glaring at the stranger.

"Joshua Tain," Caryl answered meekly, hoping against hope that that would be the extent of any interrogation.

"I know that, Caryl." Her father gritted his teeth and gave her a look that said he would brook no monkeying around. "What…is…his…relationship…to…you?"

Caryl sighed, as far as she could see her options were closing fast, either she confessed her memory loss or they would discover it themselves. There was no way she could continue to bluff. She had no idea why Joshua Tain would greet her as if she were the lost love of his life. It could be he was playing some elaborate joke on her father but to do that he would have to have known she was having a memory problem, and no one knew that, no one could have guessed. She glanced suspiciously at Patty and Noel Richardson. Beside Joshua Tain, they were the only other strangers in the room. Could they possibly have ferreted out what she had been so desperate to hide?

She tried one more gambit. "Daddy, he's a very good friend. I'm sorry. I didn't know about his business dealings with you. Now, please," she said, firmly, "I'm beginning to feel really tired." She covertly surveyed the faces arrayed before her from under her lashes. Concern replaced rage on her parents' faces, Alexander looked inscrutable and Patty and Richardson looked downright anxious. She didn't check Joshua Tain; he was an unknown quantity. "I really feel I should rest now, if you all don't mind," Caryl continued, pressing her advantage.

Patty and Richardson nodded and began to back out. "We'll see you later," Patty said and gave a small wave.

"We'll go but we'll be back later this evening." Marcianne bent down and gave her a quick kiss.

Her father smiled, "Sorry, precious, I got a bit carried away," he whispered as he too bent over to give her a kiss.

"Do you want me to leave?" The man they called Joshua Tain sounded as if he couldn't believe she would want him to go.

"Yes, you too. Only Alexander stays." She caught the glare David shot Alexander's way as he left but decided to ignore it. Later she would make her father understand about her and Alexander; now was not the time for that particular battle.

"Caryl, why me? Are you angry I wasn't here before?" Joshua Tain sounded genuinely wounded.

"No, of course not." *How could she be?* "Sorry, but there are things I need to discuss with Alexander." *And why are you here, anyway?*

"Alright, if that's what you want." His expression bleak, Joshua Tain left the room looking like a different man than the one who had swept in earlier, sure of his reception.

"Alexander." Caryl patted the bed, wanting him close to her.

"Yes, baby?"

"I'm going to be frank with you. I have no idea who that guy was."

He frowned, his eyes like worried darts.

"Really, Caryl? None at all?"

"No, Alexander, I swear." He had to believe her. Her reaction to the stranger's kisses was just some kind of weird aberration.

"I'm not sure but..." He hesitated, as if unsure what to say next, then took a deep breath. "I think you met him here. Remember, shortly after I, we, arrived, I had to return to New York for a couple days, something came up with the Thomas case."

No, Caryl didn't remember but she nodded anyway.

"That weekend was the full moon party at Bomba's Shack, that place on the south coast. You went without me and I think you met him there. You said you'd met a pushy guy there and that he said he was the owner of a record company in New York but you didn't believe him. Do you remember now?"

"Umm, it's coming back to me," Caryl said. She was uncomfortable with all this lying, but it was either that or admit to having a real problem. The image of the old woman with her lost-looking eyes came fleetingly to mind.

"It must have been him. You said he called you the next day to invite you out and he would hardly take no for an answer. That's why you changed hotels. You must remember now, Caryl. It's got to be the same guy. You have to stay away from him. He's obviously thinking he can get to you now that you're unwell. Look what he did to your father. He's probably one of those obsessive psychopaths you see on America's *Most Wanted*."

Caryl hadn't gotten that feeling. No, Joshua Tain seemed very sane to her, but what did she know? She was hardly in a position to judge, seeing as how people, or at least certain people, were making allusions to things they seemed to think she should know about but which were complete mysteries to her.

"When exactly did we meet the Richardsons?" she asked, trying to make the question sound casual.

"Don't you remember? Caryl, why are you asking these questions? Are you having a memory problem?"

"Me? No, some things are just a bit cloudy. I mean, I couldn't remember exactly when we met them. If it was at the time we took the cruise or before." She smiled. "The *Elendil*'s a beautiful boat, isn't she?" It was a shot in, if not the complete dark, at least dim light. Since Patty and Richardson had both mentioned the boat, it stood to reason that was the one she had taken the cruise on. Something about what the couple had said continued to puzzle her, however. The part about getting coverage, as if she had actually been working and not vacationing at all. But that was crazy. Caryl rubbed her head. She had told the truth earlier; she *was* tired and now she was getting a headache. All this business of trying to piece together her recent past while keeping her amnesia secret was wearing her out.

"Baby, I should let you get some rest now." Alexander was instantly solicitous.

"Yes." Caryl yawned. "I think that might be a good idea. You'll be here later?"

"A horde of personal injury lawyers couldn't keep me away."

Caryl grinned and twisted her arms around his neck, returning his kiss with fervor.

"See you later," she murmured, snuggling her face into her pillow. She was almost asleep when she remembered he still hadn't answered her question about the Richardsons. It would have to wait until she saw him again.

CHAPTER EIGHTEEN

The next day Caryl woke bright and early just as the morning light was beginning to wash the room in the pastel colors of dawn. She yawned and stretched, glad that the pain in her chest had lessened so that she felt it only when she twisted her upper body to the side or took a deep breath. Yesterday evening, the physical therapist had come to give her a massage and take her for a short walk down the hospital corridor. Caryl was glad to see her because, by the time she reawakened, visiting hours were long past and she was alone in the room. At first, Caryl was a bit unsteady, needing every ounce of support the therapist gave her, but she had made it back to her room on her own.

"I'm up to taking a long shower," Caryl said when Nurse Gittens brought her breakfast.

"You're doing great. Must be all the attention from your men." The nurse arched an eyebrow at her.

"Men! There's only one man in my life. Alexander."

"Maybe so but I wouldn't be ruling out Mr. Tain. I think he'll give your grey panther a run for his money."

"Kimberley! Really." But Caryl was surprised that she wasn't really annoyed.

"It's true, but anyway listen, Nurse Crawford said you had some bad dream last night. You were tossing and turning and you called out somebody's name. Joshua, I think she said. That's Mr. Tain's first name, isn't it? She couldn't wake you and eventually you calmed down."

JUST AN AFFAIR

"Really?" Caryl frowned. She didn't remember any of that. She thought harder. Wait a minute, yes, she did remember. She had dreamt she was sitting at a small wooden table in a vineyard, acres and acres of grapevines as far as she could see on every side, and the man Tain sat beside her. They were drinking wine, merlot, she was sure of it, and jazz was playing in the background. There was nobody else around and then without warning she was in the sea, diving in deep water when a shark attacked her. She broke the wine bottle in her hand over the shark's head and it swam away as the sea around her grew red with its blood. Then she was back in the vineyard and the blood was actually the wine in her glass and Tain was sitting and talking across the table from her as if nothing had happened.

"Want to talk about it?"

"No, thanks, it was nothing."

"You don't look like it was nothing."

"It's strange. I think I dreamt I was attacked by a shark but I fought it off."

"Wow. Sounds more like a nightmare." Nurse Gittens looked thoughtful. "Maybe you should talk to the Richardsons about it. They told me that when they brought you into the boat you were clutching a small knife in your hand. You wouldn't let go of it."

"You know them, the Richardsons?"

"Yeah, sure. Noel is the grandson of my great aunt's godmother."

"Ah." Family relations in the islands stretched far back. Caryl knew some islanders were convinced that if one made a thorough check of bloodlines, every Tortolian would find out he or she was related to every other islander, either by blood or marriage.

"They were so worried when they brought you in. Noel's blood pressure was up and we treated him for that. Patty was just as upset."

Later, long minutes after the nurse had left and she'd showered,

Caryl meditated on what she'd said. So the Richardsons cared a lot for her. But why should this be so if she had been just another client on their yacht? Maybe the Richardsons' anxiety meant they thought she might hold them responsible for whatever had happened to her. That made sense, they knew she was a lawyer, and the world and his wife knew Americans loved to sue. They must be afraid she would bring a lawsuit against them. But since she couldn't remember a thing about the accident, she didn't have a case. Anyway, Caryl much preferred presenting cases rather than being party to them herself, but the Richardsons wouldn't know that. She would put their fears to rest the next time she saw them. She'd ask about the knife too. Could her dream about the shark have been more than that, a memory maybe? But no, that was impossible. She had no scratches, no wounds. There was nothing to indicate a shark had attacked her.

"Good morning, Caryl."

Joshua Tain. Caryl looked up from the magazine she was holding. She knew his voice instantly. He was standing in the doorway looking suddenly unsure of himself.

"What do you want?"

"Caryl, please. I'm so sorry I wasn't here for you. Is that why you're mad at me?" He stepped into the room, his eyes dark with entreaty.

"I'm not mad at you. I...I just don't know why you're here."

"My God, Caryl, to see you and be with you, of course. Why else?"

Caryl sat up. Lying down while having this kind of discussion put her at a distinct disadvantage. She was glad she had already showered and combed her hair. Her mother, bless her, had also left a new make-up bag stuffed with designer cosmetics in the bathroom as a surprise gift. She knew the bronze colored Iman lip-gloss that she'd put on just moments before brightened her whole face.

"I don't know, but I want to tell you I'm not some Bomba Shack floozy you can pick up there like a worn out bra." The Shack was liberally decorated with the used underwear of its female customers, but despite this and despite looking as if it had been put together by a lunatic carpenter, it was one of the most popular hangouts in the Virgin Islands.

"Caryl, I would never think you're a floozy! And why are you talking about that place? What's gotten into you?"

"Look, I don't know what you're thinking." Caryl decided to soften her attack; after all she was only going on what Alexander had said she'd said. Joshua and the guy at Bomba's could be two different people. Watching him standing there in his soft chinos and chocolate-colored linen shirt, she couldn't deny she felt an attraction to him. If he really was the guy she'd met at Bomba's, her guilt about her own attraction to him might have caused her to bad-talk him to Alexander.

"I want to thank you for the flowers," she continued, "but I don't understand any of this. Why you sent them, why you're here, or even what went down between you and my father."

"Caryl, that was purely business," Joshua said with some heat. "He tried to take my business out from under me and I turned the tables on him. That happens all the time and, like I told you, I never knew you were his daughter."

"So now you do, so what?"

"What are you doing here?" Alexander's voice behind Joshua spun him around. Neither he nor Caryl had heard the other man open the door.

"I asked you a question," Alexander repeated, his hand still on the doorknob as if he was ready to escort Joshua out, by force if necessary.

"Who are you? I don't have to answer your questions. I don't even know you." Joshua's nostrils flared.

"I'm her man, that's who." Alexander advanced into the room. "And I don't want you bothering my lady."

"Your lady!" Joshua turned to face Caryl. "Is that true? Are you his woman?" he demanded.

"Yes. No, I mean…" Caryl looked at Alexander. "Am I really?"

"Yes, baby. You and only you. Nobody else."

And Caryl should have felt joy at his response but instead, to her surprise, a sudden queasy feeling disturbed her stomach.

"Excuse me." She got out of the bed, waving away the men's help, and almost ran to the bathroom. The feeling subsided as she splashed her face with cold water. She'd been right about the eggs that morning; they were way too runny. She stared into the mirror, delaying her return to the drama outside.

"Baby, are you okay?" Alexander rapped on the door.

"Yes, I'm coming. Give me a minute."

"You caused this. You're making her sick," Alexander accused Joshua when she came back into the room.

"Are you sure it's me and not you?" Joshua jeered dryly.

"Look, stop it, both of you. Yes, Mr. Tain, Alexander is my man." Damn, she pressed a hand to her stomach. There was that queasy feeling again. Alexander smirked. He crossed the room to stand at her bedside as if to emphasize his property rights.

"I appreciate your visiting but there's really nothing for you here." And if she said that a tad regretfully, she was sure neither man noticed. She had to send him away, of course. He was causing just a bit too much disruption. But there was something about him. Remembering her dream of the night before, Caryl felt a liquid fire rise quickly from the pit of her stomach to her heart. "You have to leave," she said firmly, quenching it as was her duty. How could she be feeling anything

JUST AN AFFAIR

for this man with Alexander, the man who was the sun in her life, standing next to her declaring his love publicly? Well, at least, to someone other than her. Could whatever had happened to her memory be affecting her in other ways, turning her into a shameless hussy who could lust for another man in the presence of her own lover?

"Is that what you really want, Caryl?" Joshua kept his voice low, his eyes never moving from her face.

Caryl could hardly breathe under the pressure of his look.

"Yes," she finally managed.

The blood seemed to go out of Joshua's face, but he only stared at her wordlessly and she at him before he turned and left the room.

"Damned straight, he had to leave. Baby, you did the right thing. You saw how he was acting, as if he owned you and getting belligerent."

Caryl sighed. The only one she had seen acting as if he owned her and being belligerent was Alexander, but she supposed he had some right to his feelings. No man liked seeing another trying to step to his woman.

"How are you and the parents getting along?" she asked to change the subject.

"No better than before. Marcianne's gone Arctic again and your father looks as if he'd like to re-open Alcatraz just for me."

Caryl laughed. "It's not so bad, is it?"

"Worse." Alexander grimaced.

"Don't worry. They'll warm up to you. Marcianne won't let her chance to arrange her only daughter's wedding slip by her."

"And just when do you think that wedding will be? I'm ready now." His mood improved visibly.

"Soon." Now that they were finally talking about it, Caryl felt a strange reluctance to set a date.

250

"Baby, we've waited so long. I don't think we should put it off one day longer than necessary. We can even do it here in the islands. They do tourist weddings all the time. I read about it in one of the guidebooks in my hotel room."

"Hold your horses there, pardner." Caryl smiled to take the sting out of her words. "I don't want to rush into things. We've got to do it right. I don't want you to be one of those men who jumps straight from divorce court into the marriage license office."

"But, baby, I've been…"

"Yes," Caryl prompted when he stopped.

"Nothing, never mind. I was just going to say, I've been looking into it. We could get married here in a small ceremony nobody need know about, then wait a few months and get married again in the States. Say our vows twice."

Caryl pondered this for a second. She was pretty sure this was not what he had been going to say but she didn't feel like interrogating him about it.

"No, I prefer to wait. Doing it that way, it would make me feel funny not telling my parents and friends." And the ancestors knew she was uncomfortable enough with all the lying she was doing now. Her amnesia had better resolve itself quickly and fully because she couldn't keep up the charade much longer.

"Ms. Walker." A tall, stern-looking nurse walked in. "Oh, I'm sorry. I didn't realize you had a visitor since it's not yet visiting time," she said pointedly. "I have a sheaf of get well cards for you that people have been dropping off."

"Oh, but why didn't you just let them come in to see me?"

The nurse looked irritated by the question. "Mr. Thorne here," she gestured at him, "said you didn't want any visitors other than family."

"I never said that. Why did you do that, Alexander?" She made a mental note to be sure that his tendency to appoint himself her personal manager was cured before she said any 'I do.'"

"I wanted you to get your strength back up. You've made a lot of friends here." He glanced at the nurse. "I know how just a few people tire you out. Come on, baby, I was thinking of you."

"I would like to see my visitors." Caryl rifled through her cards as the nurse turned and left. There were seven of them but Caryl didn't recognize any of the names. Stacia and Basil Chinnery. Miguel Herrera. Keith. Alexander watched her as she opened them one by one. Caryl's anxiety grew. She didn't recognize any of the names but the messages of affection seemed genuine enough. How could all these people have slipped so completely from her consciousness?

"You must have done a lot of socializing while I was away."

Something about the studied casualness with which Alexander said it caught her notice.

"Yes, I guess I did. They're friends."

"I see. I was just wondering if you had any secret admirers."

Caryl smiled thinly. She didn't know what it was but something about Alexander was beginning to irritate her. She wondered if they were spending too much time together. Instantly, a stab of guilt that she could have such a thought about the man with whom she was planning to spend a lifetime went through her. He had given up so much, they both had. Surely she couldn't possibly be having second thoughts about the man now that he was finally free of his marriage.

"So," she said, trying for a light tone, "how is the firm doing? Have you been in touch?"

"No, not since we last spoke about it."

"I wish they'd hurry up and resolve who's going to be the managing partner now that Kathy is on maternity leave."

Alexander hunched his shoulders but said nothing.

"I really think Ivor would be a good choice. He's so organized he's almost martial."

This too was met with silence and Caryl gave up. Conversation was a two-way game and if he wasn't interested then she could do something else. She picked up the magazine she'd been holding when Joshua came in and began to flip through it.

"Caryl."

"Yes."

She was surprised by how despondent he suddenly looked.

"There's something I should tell you."

"What?"

"It's hard," he said, his voice bleak.

"You're not divorced." She said it flatly, unable to name the emotion that began to curdle her stomach.

"No." He turned to face her and took her hand in his. "That's not it. I *am* divorced."

And Caryl was surprised that she felt no relief, no happiness, none of the things she should be feeling now she knew his marriage wasn't between them anymore.

"Then what?"

"I…" This time it was Marcianne and David's entry into the room that stopped him. As they hugged and kissed her, he retreated to the back of the room. "I'll tell you later," he mouthed to her when she looked at him. Caryl shrugged.

"We went touring yesterday after lunch," Marcianne announced.

"You did?"

"Yes, darling. Don't sound so surprised. It's a lovely little island. Why wouldn't I want to see more of it? I've just never really had the chance before."

JUST AN AFFAIR

Caryl smiled wryly and exchanged a look with her father. "I just never thought you could relax long enough for something as undemanding as a tour."

"I'll have you know I had a fine time. We went to Sage Mountain and saw the rain forest remnant. There was a lizard the size of my arm, Caryl, it was like a mini-dinosaur."

"Yes," David interjected, "and your mother promptly reacted like an extra from Jurassic Park 2."

"I merely made way for him," Marcianne said, waving a hand in airy dismissal of any accusation that she might have been anything other than her usual composed self. Caryl chuckled.

"Baby." Alexander had been shifting from foot to foot and glancing at his watch for the last several minutes, so Caryl had some idea of what he was going to say next. "I've got some calls to make so I've got to go. It's after ten now but I'll be back soon. Want me to bring anything back for you? Chocolates, cookies, anything?"

"No, I'm alright. Thanks." This time when he leaned in to kiss her she turned her face slightly so that he caught only the corners of her lips.

"Darling," her mother started after Alexander left the room then stopped at the warning glance her husband threw her way. "I've got to ask, David. For heaven's sake, I've a right to know."

"It's on your head. I don't think she's well enough for a stressful discussion."

"I'm only going to ask her one question, one..."

"Hey, hey!" Caryl interrupted. "What's going on here? I'm quite well enough to be asked anything, Daddy. Mumsie, what is it?"

"What are your plans?"

"What do you mean? With Alexander?"

"Yes, darling, of course with Alexander, who else?"

An image of Joshua Tain appeared in Caryl's mind but she pushed it firmly away.

"I would have preferred to tell you in my own time, but since you've asked… We're going to get married. He's got his divorce and I love him and he loves me so we're going to the chapel." Try as she might, she could not keep a tone of childish defiance from creeping into her voice. "We love each other," she repeated and then wondered who she was really trying to convince, her parents or herself.

Her father said nothing, keeping his own counsel.

"But I just don't understand this, Caryl. After all he put you through, why would you want to go back to him?" her mother said.

Caryl frowned. Go back? As far as she knew, she'd never left. She tried to remember any argument between herself and Alexander that she might have recounted to her mother but drew a blank.

"So that means you'll be leaving the *Elendil* then?" her father asked.

Caryl's first instinct was to say of course she would, she had only vacationed on the blasted boat, not set up house, but she stopped herself. Something was going on here. Both her father and the Richardsons talked about her and the boat as if the time she'd spent on it was more than just a vacation, but she had to tread carefully here. Any misstep and her parents would jump on it.

"Yes, Daddy," she answered, playing along with his assumption.

"I can't believe what I'm hearing." Marcianne's hands were on her hips. "Are you saying to me that you are going to follow this aging Casanova, no, let me finish," she snapped when David held up his hand to stop her, "this good for nothing, to California? To do what, fry your brain and bake your body? You'll be wasting your life and your education."

"Mother, I love him and the age difference is no more than

between your friend Doris and that guy she picked up in Barbados. How come I don't hear you saying anything about that? She's almost old enough to be his grandmother!" Caryl's voice rose to match Marcianne's. Her mother's allusion to Alexander's age infuriated her so much that it took several seconds for the mention of California to sink in. What on earth could Marcianne mean by it? Why would the question of following him to California, of all places, come up? Alexander didn't live in California.

"Marcianne, dearest, calm down. It's much too hot for all of this."

"David, when my daughter tells me she's planning to ruin her life I am going to have something to say and, believe me, it's not going to depend on the temperature."

"Okay, dearest." David rose to his feet and planted a kiss on his wife's forehead. "Let me say something, though." Holding Marcianne's hand, he turned back around to Caryl. "Precious, we love you. We want what's best for you. When you ran down here, we supported you. You said you wanted to do something entirely different from what you were doing before and we got you work on the *Elendil*. Now you're telling us you want to get back with the man who caused you all that pain, and you must know we would have reservations about that. Strong reservations."

Caryl listened to him closely. Nothing in what he was saying suggested she and Alexander had come to the Virgin Islands together. If they hadn't, it would explain why he hadn't been with her or at least in the vicinity during her accident. But then that could mean everything he had told her about all the things they'd done together was a lie. Caryl struggled to focus on her father's voice and not become lost in her thoughts.

"You know you'll be taking over Henry Enterprises one day," her father said. He squeezed his wife's hand. "I was hoping that day would come sooner rather than later. I've been thinking about retiring more and more."

"Daddy, you're not even sixty yet," Caryl protested. Did this development have something to do with his failed takeover of Tain Music and that wretched Joshua Tain? If she ever saw that man again, he would have some explaining to do.

"Yes, precious, but Henry Ent. has been my life since I was a boy. I want to take a breather, look around, see what else is out there. Your mother and I have always wanted to travel more, haven't we, sweets?" He gave his wife a hug and a meaningful kiss.

"But I'm not ready," Caryl said, plaintively.

"We could always break it up and sell off the parts. There are several corporations that have made offers over the years."

He was bluffing, he had to be. Sell a company that had been in the family for generations?

"Never."

"So you'll come back to start learning the ropes then?" Her father's voice was bright with eagerness.

"I suppose I'll have to if your mind is set on doing nothing with the rest of your life," Caryl grumbled. Any wedding would definitely have to be postponed now. To her surprise she felt no regret at this thought.

"There's a peach of a girl. I knew you'd see it my way." David Cassavettes grabbed her face in his hands and planted a firm kiss on each cheek.

"Good, now that's settled, dearest, can we go look for lunch? I'm starving here." Marcianne's face glowed with happiness as she looked at the two people she loved most.

"So we'll just tell Janus that you won't be returning, right, precious?" her father asked.

JUST AN AFFAIR

"Sure, sure." Who the hell was Janus now? Another boat?

After they'd left, Caryl lay on her bed, her eyes on the whirring fan above her head as she tried to figure out a way to unravel the mystery behind so much that she'd heard in the last few days. The *Elendil* was a boat and she worked on it, that much she could gather from what her father had said and from the Richardsons' concern over coverage. They had been trying to tell her not to worry, that whatever she did on the boat somebody else had been found to take over. Was this some kind of job she had gotten while here on vacation but why? She might not be in the big leagues with lawyers like Alan Dershowitz and Johnnie Cochran, but she wasn't making chump change either, so there was no reason for her to moonlight. What sane woman moonlighted on vacation with her man, anyway? No, she could be pretty sure that whatever she was doing in the Virgin Islands, it was not vacationing. So, did that mean Alexander was lying? To what purpose?

Suddenly inspired, Caryl shoved her feet into the blue brocade slippers her mother had brought her and walked out to the nurses' station.

"Hi," she greeted the gray-haired nurse there.

"Hello. Your lunch will be coming in a few minutes."

"Oh, thanks. That's not why I'm here though. I was wondering if I could have a phone in my room?"

"Isn't there one there now?" The nurse looked surprised. She reached for a file in the drawer behind her. "Hmm, I see your fiancé, Mr. Thorne, had it taken out. He said it would disturb you." The nurse regarded Caryl over her glasses. "You were getting a lot of calls from your friends here and in the States. It was a regular hotline but you were still unconscious. He told us to just take the messages down and give them to him."

"Ah." This was all news to Caryl. How dare Alexander make these types of decisions for her and why was he telling people they were engaged? And where were her messages?

The nurse looked at her as if unsure Caryl could countermand Alexander's order.

"Nurse, I want a phone put in, please. I need to make some calls and I need a local phone book as well. Can you please arrange it?"

The nurse caved. "Alright. It's no problem. I'll call the facilities people now and get somebody to bring one in for you. And you can have this one; it's an extra. It probably came from your room." She held out the phone book for that year.

"Thank you."

Once back in her room, Caryl thumbed through the pages. When she'd found the entry she was looking for, she marked the page and waited for the arrival of the phone. It came within minutes. Caryl waited impatiently for the maintenance man to hook it up, almost grabbing it from him when he was finished.

Opening the phone book to the page she'd marked and balancing it on her crossed legs, Caryl dialed the number.

"Janus, Incorporated. Good morning and how may I help you today?" a cheery voice asked on the other line.

"Very well, thank you, sugar." Caryl lowered her voice and assumed a Southern accent. "I'm trying to get in touch with one of your captains, Captain Casavettes from the *Elendil*. My husband and I had such a good time on our vacation we just wanted to thank her again for her wonderful hospitality."

"We don't have a Captain Cassavettes. Oh, do you mean Captain Walker? She's the only female captain we have but she's on leave right now. She won't be back for a little while."

Walker. Her mother's maiden name. She must have been using it instead of Casavettes, but why? "Is she alright? I hope nothing's hap-

JUST AN AFFAIR

pened to her." Caryl kept her fingers crossed hoping for a revelation and it came.

"Well, ma'am, she did have a little accident but she's recovering well and we hope to have her back as good as new in no time at all."

"Tsk, tsk. I'm glad to hear it wasn't serious. She's such an experienced captain I'm surprised to hear that she had a problem. Been captain for a while, hasn't she?"

"Yes, ma'am. Ma'am, I'm sorry I didn't catch your name. What were your booking dates?" The young woman's voice had turned slightly suspicious.

"Sometime earlier this year, sugar. I can hardly keep appointments in mind, much less dates. I want to thank you so much for talking to me. I guess we'll just have to try to contact Captain Walker again in a week or so."

"Yes, ma'am."

Bewildered, Caryl hung up. She and Alexander weren't on vacation; she worked here in the Virgin Islands. For some reason she had picked herself up and moved from New York, from law, her first love, to the Caribbean. But the idea was preposterous. She couldn't have given up everything she loved to captain a boat off one of the smallest of the Caribbean islands. It was insane; she would *have* to be mad to do such a thing. And yet, what other explanation was there? For a little while, she didn't know exactly how long yet, she had been captain of a boat called the *Elendil*, a charter boat. Caryl reached over and rifled through the magazines on her nightstand for a tourist publication she was sure she'd seen there the night before. She rifled through it, looking for something, a mention of the *Elendil*, anything. She did even better. There on page 13 was a full-page advertisement, the *Elendil* plowing through waves in the big picture and an inset of herself, Patty and Richardson. The boat was beautiful. Caryl tried hard to remember something about her life on it but came up empty. The ad copy, basically a listing of the amenities offered on board, along with a couple overblown quotes from past clients, was useless from her point of view. She concentrated on the picture, but the more she looked at it, the more she felt she was merely looking at an image from someone else's life. The woman standing smiling between the Richardsons was someone else, a twin she'd never met. Frustrated, Caryl tossed the magazine across the room.

CHAPTER NINETEEN

"Hi, Caryl," Patty said as she walked in shortly after lunch.

"Hi," Caryl answered warmly. Her suspicions about the woman and her husband were wrong. Thank goodness she had never given voice to them. "Where's Richardson?" she asked.

"Getting our gear together. We're going out on the next tour. They're sending the replacement crew back to their boat but keeping the captain. He's alright. Young guy."

"Oh." She would miss the couple.

"Don't worry, honey. You'll be back on the *Elendil* yourself in no time at all, you'll see," Patty said, misunderstanding the disappointment she read in Caryl's face.

Caryl grimaced. "I'm not so sure." She remembered the promise she'd made to her father. "In fact, I doubt it. Daddy's contacting his friends at Janus to let them know I won't be returning."

"Caryl! Are you serious, child?" Patty's eyes opened wide.

"Yes." Caryl sighed. "My father wants me to come back and work at the family business."

"Is that what you want?"

"It wasn't something I was planning for anytime soon." Caryl thought hard, searching for what she really felt. "I always knew it was coming. From the time I was a child Daddy would point out exactly where my portrait would go up next to his in the boardroom, right opposite that of my grandfather and great-grandfather. It's something I have to do. It's in the blood, you know?"

"I think I do. Noel's family has been on the sea for ages. They used to build their own boats, sloops they called them then, and sail as far north as the Dominican Republic and as far south as St. Marten. He says the sea is in their blood." Patty winked at Caryl. "Of course, it's not quite the same as having a multi-million dollar business in the family for generations."

"Patty, it's the same, the exact same." Caryl leaned over to give the woman an impulsive hug and was rewarded with a big smile.

"You know, Richardson and I, we felt like there was a little coldness between us and you when you came to," Patty said, and then looked as if she regretted opening her mouth.

"Go on."

"We wondered if you were blaming us for the accident. Like how Richardson was sick and all and you had to take the people down by yourself. It's the most difficult dive we offer and we shouldn't have let you go down alone. You did look a bit under the weather that morning. I'm so sorry. We…"

"Whoa." Caryl held up her hand to stem the flood. "Slow down, Patty. In the first place," she grabbed the woman's hands and looked straight into her face, "I never blamed you for the accident and in the second place, you shouldn't blame yourselves."

Patty's eyes got misty.

"We thought maybe that was why you were being a bit standoffish."

So they had sensed it then.

"Patty, it wasn't that at all, believe me. I was just coming out of being unconscious, trying to get my bearings with everyone around me. I'm sorry you felt that way."

At that minute there was a knock on the door and Alexander pushed his head in.

"Oh, should I come back?" he asked, seeing Patty.

"Yes, don't go far." Good, now he was here she would finally get some answers.

"Okay, Patty? I don't blame you or Richardson for anything. Get that straight."

"Do you blame Joshua?"

"What?"

"That little coldness with him when he found out who you were, it might have distracted you. You might be thinking if he'd been acting right, maybe things would have been fine on the dive. I don't know…it's what me and Noel been thinking."

"No, no, Patty. I don't know what happened so I can't point the finger at anybody other than myself."

Patty continued as if Caryl hadn't spoken. "You're a great diver but maybe the problem with Joshua affected your judgment and you're blaming Joshua for that." Patty shrugged. "Joshua loves you and you love him, so why else would you ask him to leave?"

Caryl struggled to keep her face expressionless, but internally she was reeling. In love? With Joshua Tain? And he felt the same way? Patty was more right than she knew; nothing made sense. These latest revelations and the confirmation by Janus that she had definitely been working on the *Elendil* persuaded her. It was definitely time to confess.

"Patty, I haven't been quite honest with you or anybody else for that matter." She shifted on the bed. "I don't remember anything about the last, I don't know, several months or so, I guess. I don't remember a thing about the *Elendil*, about being her captain, you, Joshua or even the accident itself."

"Caryl! What are you saying?"

"It must be an effect of the decompression illness. I've got some kind of amnesia. When I look at you, I see a stranger."

"Why didn't you say something, child?" Patty's voice was shocked and concerned.

Caryl hunched her shoulders and let them drop. "I don't know," she said, miserable. "I thought it would go away but it hasn't. Every now and then I remember something I didn't know I knew, but for the most part all that time is gone. Joshua Tain is a stranger to me. So are you."

"Oh, child." Patty sighed heavily. "Don't you think you should tell the doctor?"

"No, I really don't want to. He'll want to poke around in my brain or do more tests. I just hate thinking about what it could mean."

"It's the squeaky wheel that gets the grease. He won't be able to help you unless you tell him."

"Yeah, but then if I tell him, I don't know, then it's like it'll become more real. He'll write it down on his chart and it'll be like this big problem. 'Caryl's an amnesiac,' people will say. It's a label I can do without."

Patty stared at her doubtfully.

"It's okay. I'll be okay. I just need some help." Caryl squeezed her friend's arm reassuringly. "Tell me about my life. Who have I been since I've been in the islands? Who is the Caryl you know? What am I like as Captain Cassavettes, I mean, Walker?"

"Hmm, that's the first thing. You changed your name when you came down here. Your father's really well-known in the Virgin Islands and you said you wanted to be anonymous, not get any special favors from Janus or anybody else, so you took your mother's surname."

"So that's why some people have been calling me Miss Walker."

"Yes." Continuing, Patty filled her in on her responsibilities aboard the *Elendil*, how they'd become friends, her history with

JUST AN AFFAIR

Alexander, and finally her romance with Joshua.

"A love affair? That's unbelievable. So quick?" But, instinctively, she believed what the older woman told her. It had the ring of truth.

"Child, he just swept you off your feet. He woke something in you that had been sleeping, sealed away, I guess ever since Alexander."

"I can't believe it. And I was so terrible to him."

"He thinks it's because he didn't come when he'd said he would and maybe, too, because David Cassavettes turned you against him."

"Daddy? Daddy can't stand the thought of him, but he'd never try to influence me one way or another. Patty, I must speak to him."

"Yes." Patty beamed as if she'd been waiting to hear that all morning.

"Is he still here?"

"Of course, child. He isn't going to go anywhere without at least trying to talk to you again. He's waiting for you to get out of the hospital before he tries to see you again. Wants to make sure you're strong enough."

"I've got to see him." Caryl's heart pounded with excitement. She was suddenly very sure that if she just saw and spoke to Joshua Tain again, all the pieces of the puzzle would fall into place. Everything Patty had said made sense. It explained why he'd come, the roses, his pain when she asked him to leave her room, everything.

"When?"

"Not today. Tomorrow. I'll be up to it tomorrow. Right now, I feel like somebody's driven a Mack truck into me. And first, of course, I must speak to Alexander, the lying…" She didn't finish the thought but her meaning was clear.

"So that's why you've been so cozy with him. You thought you all were still in a relationship. I couldn't figure it out."

"And he said nothing to enlighten me. Not one word. Can you

believe it? I'm beginning to think he's pathological!"

Caryl jumped off the bed and threw open the door.

"Alexander!" she yelled. "Oh, sorry, nurse. Alexander, come in please. Patty, please wait for me outside."

"Sure." Patty's eyes begged Caryl not to stress out.

"Alexander, please, have a seat." Caryl waved to one of the three chairs in the room.

For a minute she couldn't speak she was that full of fury. He gave her a tentative smile and was just about to say something when, finally, her anger exploded.

"Alexander Thorne," she hissed. "You are lower than a tick on a street dog's belly, lower than a crack addict's pimp. You are so full of shit, you sicken me." She thumped her fist on the wall behind her.

"Caryl." Alexander's face turned gray and his eyes seemed to contract.

"What?" Caryl paced in front of him. "Did you think I'd never find out about your lies? Was that what the rush to get married was all about? Was that why you didn't give me my friends' messages?"

"Caryl, please." He held up his hands as if to fend off her fury.

"Patty's just told me everything. Everything she knows, anyway. I can't believe what a deceitful, lying, excuse for a man you are. 'Making love by the light of the moon.' Ha! You knew! You knew I had amnesia and you deliberately tricked me."

"I love you."

"That's not love, Alexander. You don't trick people and lie to them. There can't be love without trust."

"I can make everything I said come true if you give me the chance, Caryl. Everything."

Caryl snapped her fingers. "Wake up! Don't you understand what I'm saying to you? You lied to me. You've been lying to me. In fact,

JUST AN AFFAIR

that's been the whole history of my relationship with you, hasn't it?" Damn, if only she could remember seeing Barbara pregnant, herself, but, for now, she had to rely on Patty's word.

"I thought your amnesia was a sign, another chance for us. Caryl, I never meant to cause you pain." Shame and self-disgust were etched into the lines of his face.

"No? What *did* you hope to gain by all these lies?"

"You."

The answer was so simple and so full of truth it took Caryl's breath away and she sat down on the bed.

"Caryl, I know what I did was wrong but, baby, you don't know how good it felt having you watch me again with love in your eyes. When you kissed me, it was like music in my soul. I didn't want that to stop."

"Alexander, you had to know I would find out sooner or later. I mean…Jesus!"

"I was planning to tell you. I was trying to do it yesterday. Don't you remember when I said I had something to tell you? But then your parents came in and…" His voice trailed off.

"You've been lying to me from the get go and it stops here, Alexander. Patty told me I wasn't interested in another go-round, that I was only being nice when you came because I thought you had reformed. You haven't. My God, suppose I'd said yes and actually married you?"

"I thought if we could just recapture what we had for a little while, you would forgive me. Caryl, I love you." Alexander threw himself down on his knees and buried his face in her lap before she could stop him.

For a minute Caryl didn't move. Through the window in front of her she watched a navy-blue ferry head out of the harbor, saw a small speedboat cross its frothy wake and another smaller boat match its speed.

"Do you hate me, Caryl?" Alexander asked, his voice muffled by her dress.

Caryl thought about it. "Alexander," she said, still watching the ferry. "I don't know what I feel about you. I do know what I *don't* feel. I don't trust you and I certainly don't love you."

Alexander rocked back on his heels to look at her but Caryl kept her eyes on the boats in the harbor. He rose to his feet.

"I guess I don't deserve more. I'm so sorry, Caryl. I messed up again big time." He took a deep, shuddering breath. "Damn, this is not how I saw it going down."

Caryl didn't say anything.

He reached for the doorknob, turned back. "Caryl, if ever anytime there is anything you need, anything, you only have to call."

Caryl didn't move, didn't speak. The door closed behind him and Caryl folded her arms around herself. How could he have tried to trick her like that? How? But then, she hadn't been completely honest herself. If she'd confessed her amnesia about the past year from the start, Alexander would never have had the chance to lie to her yet again. She should have spoken up, said something earlier, asked for help but she'd held back for no good reason. Or maybe it was out of some kind of misplaced pride. Again, the image of the confused old woman in her nightgown flashed to mind but Caryl didn't have time to deal with that. She would figure out that mystery later, after she'd sorted out things with Joshua, the man Patty said was the real love of her life.

CHAPTER TWENTY

"Are you sure he's not still angry with me, Patty?" Caryl asked.

She and Patty were in Patty's car on their way to Long Bay Resort, where Joshua was staying. It was about eleven o'clock and Caryl had spent most of the morning hurrying through the hospital's release process so she could leave before her parents came and found out about her plan to see Joshua Tain. They still didn't know about her amnesia because when they'd come to see her the evening before her room had been full of visitors and she hadn't wanted to say anything.

"I'm sure, Caryl. This guy loves you."

Caryl looked out the window at the passing scenery. They were almost at the resort. One more hill and then they would coast down into the breathtaking beach town featured on so many postcards and tourist promotions. But the closer they got, the more doubts Caryl began to have. She had no recollection whatsoever of Joshua Tain and nothing that Patty had said, neither yesterday nor today, had sparked any memory in her. Her physical reaction to him when he'd visited her at the hospital was undeniable, however. She could still remember the curling sensation in her stomach and the way her mouth had dried, as if she fully expected him to pick her up and walk out the door with her in his arms. In some primal way then, her body knew and responded to him, but in her heart and mind she drew a blank.

"Here we are," Patty said as she parked under the huge Royal Poinciana tree whose red petals carpeted the little roundabout in front of the resort's main entrance.

"Yes," Caryl said. When she made no move to get out, Patty turned in her seat to face her.

"A cat that has been scalded once will think cold water, hot."

"What?"

"Child, what you've gone through with Alexander would make any woman want to go running to a convent. I know what you're feeling, but you've got to reach out and grab the things you want. You know that. From the time I met you, that's the kind of woman I've known you to be."

"Yes, Patty, but I don't know if I want him. I mean, I know everything you've said about our love affair and how passionate we were and how kind and loving and everything he is, but you don't understand. When I see him, I see a stranger. A stranger I've seen in my dreams, yes, but still a stranger."

"You've dreamt about him?"

"Yes." Caryl recounted the dream.

"But, in the dream, when you were sitting with him, were you frightened of him?"

Caryl thought hard. "No, I don't think so. Actually, now I think of it, I knew the shark was something separate and apart from him. He wasn't the shark, I'm quite sure of it." Whatever feelings she might get around Joshua Tain, asleep or awake, danger wasn't one of them. Then again, she hadn't gotten those feelings around Alexander either, and that lying man was as dangerous as a boa constrictor.

"That says something."

"Maybe. I don't know." A few seconds passed in silence while Caryl gathered her courage. "Alright, I guess I'm going in then." Taking a deep breath, she exited the Tercel.

"Want me to come in with you?" Patty poked her head out her window.

"No, but I'll phone if I need you. In any case, I'll talk to you later, huh?"

Patty blew her a kiss and drove off. Caryl watched her go, then slowly pushed open the doors to the lobby.

"Mr. Tain is in the Green Restaurant, miss. Right over there," the man behind the reception counter replied to her question, pointing the way.

Joshua's erect figure at a table by a window overlooking the beach was the first thing Caryl saw when she entered the restaurant. Pots of lush palms placed all around and among the tables ensured privacy and had probably inspired the restaurant's name.

"Er, hello, Mr. Umm, Tain, uh, Joshua," she said, coming around from behind Joshua's back to smile diffidently, unsure of her reception.

"Caryl! Hello." Joshua jumped up to grasp her hand. A delighted smile spread across his handsome face. "Are you okay? Should you be out of the hospital?"

"Yes, I'm fine." His nearness and his touch on her arm were doing unhealthy things to her blood pressure, but that information she could keep to herself.

He pulled out a chair for her.

"How did you get here? Are you alone?" He looked around, vague apprehension in his eyes, as if he expected David Cassavettes to leap out at him from behind one of the palms.

"Patty brought me and, yes, I'm alone."

An awkward silence descended on the table.

They both broke it at the same time.

"Would you…"

"I have something…"

They grinned at each other. Joshua held up his hand. "You first."

So Caryl told him everything, confessing how she'd been hiding her amnesia, winding up with Patty's description of the last year of her life.

"Caryl, you don't remember any of that?" Joshua's forehead was in creases.

"Only a little here and there. Somebody might ask me something and, as they're asking, I'm thinking I don't know but then the answer pops out of me and I know it's right."

"Yes, but nothing about us?"

"Sorry." And then she told him her dream.

"I used to call you my wine maiden…"

"Of the jazz-tuned night," she finished the phrase for him.

"Yes, that's it. Do you remember anything now?" Joshua leaned forward eagerly, almost spilling the water the waiter had placed before her as she talked.

"No, sorry." Caryl's mouth twisted in disappointment. "I think I'm just remembering the poem itself."

"Oh." Joshua's face dropped.

"Patty mentioned a picture in a newspaper she thought I might have seen."

"Those paparazzi! Kenya is one of my stars, potentially one of my biggest. Another company had been wooing her and she knew about the trouble I was having with Henry Enterprises, so she was thinking of jumping ship. I took her out, basically to show her I hadn't a care in the world, that she would be making a mistake if she left my label. She's a nice girl but she's eighteen years old and she's business to me, just business. You haven't known me long, but little girls are not what I'm about." He gave her a meaningful look and Caryl grinned.

"You're right, I haven't known you long," she said. *But I'd like to.*

A waiter approached to take their order and Joshua waved him

JUST AN AFFAIR

away.

"So where does your amnesia leave us?"

Caryl shrugged. She had no idea.

"What about starting over?"

"Starting over?"

"Yes, Caryl." Joshua grabbed her hands in his. "I won your heart once and I know I can do it again. Please, let me try. I can't just stand by and do nothing while your amnesia continues."

The way her insides felt like chocolate melting in the sun at his touch, she didn't think she wanted him to do nothing either.

"Start slowly? With lunch?"

"Yes, alright."

"Good! Waiter!" Joshua raised his hand to summon the waiter back. "You know, for someone who was so sick just a short while ago, you're looking real good," he said, after they'd placed their orders.

Caryl's face warmed.

"Thanks," she said and silently thanked Patty who had made her wear the white halter dress she had on. "You look pretty fine yourself," she said, thinking that linen must surely be his favorite material. Her eyes widened. What was that about linen?

"You wear a lot of linen," she said, almost accusingly.

"Yes, yes, I do. Caryl, what?"

But Caryl held a finger to her lips, hushing him, hoping the floodgates of her memory would open. When nothing else surfaced and the silence between them had stretched uncomfortably, she grimaced.

"I thought more would come back to me but that's all." Caryl shook her head wryly. "Very important that I know you wear linen," she said, trying to make a joke out of it but not succeeding too well.

"It's got to be difficult, feeling like you're always on the verge of some major discovery about your past."

"It is." She developed a sudden interest in a huge batik painting hanging on the wall opposite so he would drop the subject. Whatever he had been in the past, Joshua Tain was at the moment a stranger to her, and she refused to discuss her fears and worries with him. Her strong physical response to him back in the hospital was just that, a physical response. It meant that she recognized him on a cellular level but until her heart and her head remembered him, she had to keep him at a distance.

After the food arrived, stuffed eggplant for her and filet mignon for him, Caryl allowed herself to relax. She looked out the window at the distant houses scattered on the hillsides.

"Do your parents know you're here?"

"I left a note at the hospital and a message with their hotel receptionist. I said that I was going to find you but I didn't tell them where I was going to look. Do they know where you're staying?"

"No, I shouldn't think so. Caryl, your father's a warrior, one of the old school. I don't hold anything against him for trying to buy me out. It happens all the time."

Caryl could tell there was more on his mind by the way he tapped his fork against his plate.

"I don't want to hide from him. He's got good reason to be suspicious of my motives, and I don't want him to think I'm fooling around you in some kind of sick power play. We need to be up front with him." He jabbed the air with the fork and Caryl's lips twitched.

"Yes, we do, but there's nothing to be up front about right now. Look, Joshua, I don't remember you here." Caryl pointed to her chest. "I don't know exactly what you want of me, and I don't want you to think I'm promising anything either." She took a mouthful of eggplant.

JUST AN AFFAIR

"Ah, captain of my heart. Even if you can't remember it, you can't deny me the promise you made. Any court would agree you belong with me," Joshua said, leaning towards her.

"Patty didn't tell me I'd made you any promise."

"You told me you were mine. That I was your man and you were my woman."

"But I didn't say I would be yours forever, did I?" Caryl leaned forward herself so she and Joshua were almost nose-to-nose.

"Not exactly, but come on. That was understood."

"Ha! A court would *not* necessarily agree with you. You seem to be talking about an implied contract, they don't always hold up in court, and, in any case, I can always plead diminished mental capacity. Patty said I wasn't acting my usual self."

"That's because you were in love."

"Whatever. The point is, I wasn't myself."

"You can't have it both ways, my captain. If you were in love, then you were most definitely in your right mind. Who could know me and not love me?" He laughed.

Caryl rolled her eyes. Patty had also clearly forgot to tell her the man was full of himself.

"Love or not, I'm not some mango you'll pick off the nearest tree when you are good and ready, Mr. Tain."

"You're quite right," Joshua said soberly, leaning back with his eyes half-closed but still fixed on her face.

"I am?"

"You are more than a fruit. You are my heart, my promise of love, my wine maiden," Joshua said, his tone perfectly matter-of-fact. Caryl felt her temper rise. Ignoring other people's wishes might be a handy talent in the music business but she was having none of it. She was about to tell him so but when she looked into his eyes she found herself dissolving in their dark warmth. Struggling to regain her composure, she looked away, focusing on the waves breaking on some rocks where the hills met the sea in the distance.

"I thought we were going to take it slow," she said.

"We are, aren't we?"

And again something stirred in the depths of Caryl's soul. Taking it slow with this man would be like taking it slow with the bullet train.

They finished the rest of their meal in silence. Caryl refused dessert but Joshua ordered the key lime pie. It was a favorite of his, he told Caryl. She smiled tightly. All she wanted to do was leave. Joshua Tain worried her with every word, every glance. Caryl longed for the refuge of a quiet hotel room and a long, hot bubble bath while she thought things over.

"Would you like to go to the beach?" he asked as he paid the bill.

"No, thanks. I think I'm going to go to Hill House. That's where my parents are staying."

Joshua quirked an eyebrow at her.

"Are you sure?"

"They always stay there," she said, deliberately misunderstanding him. He knew the effect he was having on her and he was enjoying it. Caryl glared at him. "Please ask the maitre d' to call a taxi for me."

"I can do better than that. I can take you there myself."

Caryl wondered if there was any graceful way to refuse his offer without sounding churlish but, unable to come up with any, she found herself minutes later being helped into his rented Land Cruiser.

"You certainly don't stint yourself, do you?" She inhaled the scent of new leather and noted the wood dash and carpeted floor as they strapped on their seatbelts.

"I like the best, Caryl. Class and quality mean a lot to me." He glanced at her, his voice suddenly somber. "You've got both, which is

JUST AN AFFAIR

why I'm going to ride this out. For as long as it takes." Something about the way he said it told her he meant every word, and Caryl looked out the window so he couldn't see how pleased she was.

She was beginning to see what beyond his good looks must have first attracted her to him. Joshua Tain was very much like her father, driven, deeply charming and highly intelligent. These qualities had made her father the successful businessman he was. But she didn't have out a help wanted sign for a CEO; she was looking for a husband, a life-partner who would share her joys and disappointments and be a good father to their children. The kind of man she thought she had found in Alexander. She couldn't afford to make the same mistake twice.

Joshua drove quickly but expertly, taking the island's steep hills and hairpin curves like a NASCAR professional, his eyes focused on the road and his hands firmly on the wheel. Watching him shift easily from gear to gear, Caryl thought how confident and purposeful he looked, a man who knew what he wanted and how to get it. Feeling her eyes on him, Joshua flicked her a glance. The next thing she knew, they were skidding across the road and Joshua was struggling for control of the SUV. Caryl squeezed her eyes shut, heard the screeching of tires struggling for purchase on the dusty road, then the dull thwank as they came to a stop.

"Caryl, are you alright?"

She opened her eyes. The Land Cruiser had come to rest perpendicular to the road and Joshua's distraught face was inches away as he peered at her.

"Yes, I'm fine."

The worry in his eyes receded.

"What about you?" Caryl looked him over.

"I'm okay." He unfastened his seatbelt and leaped out.

"What happened?" She had not seen a thing, it had all happened so fast and there was no other car in sight. Feeling a slight pain in her chest where the drain had been, she got out and walked around to Joshua's side of the car. He was hunched down, talking to a small boy. As Caryl came closer, she saw that the boy could not have been more than four or five and he was crying his little heart out. Just standing there, giving himself up to the huge sobs that seemed as if they would shatter his ribs and fountain up into the mountain air.

"He just ran right out in front of me. I almost didn't see him." Joshua wiped the boy's cheeks with his handkerchief but the flow of tears continued. "He must be terrified."

"Oh, goodness." Caryl joined Joshua in front of the boy and pulled his small body into her arms and rocked him. Slowly, his heaving chest subsided and the sobs quieted.

"Are you okay, dear?" Caryl asked, when she judged the child was calm enough to speak.

"My goat," he wailed and a fresh bout of sobs shook him. Joshua got up and walked around the Land Cruiser, then got into it, put it in reverse and parked it so it wouldn't block traffic. When he came back, he turned his hands palm side up. He had seen nothing.

"Sweetie, don't cry, don't cry. Tell us what's the matter," Caryl urged, gently.

"My goat run off. He run off." The child pointed down the ravine at the side of the road. "I was…I was taking him to Grandma and he run off."

"Hold up! What's his name, little man?" Joshua asked.

The child stopped sobbing and stared at him.

"I call him Oxo but Mama say he don't know his name." The little boy wiped his eyes.

"And what's your name?"

JUST AN AFFAIR

The little boy stood a little straighter.

"Michael Chase. I'm…four, no, five years old."

"Okay, Michael Chase, my name is Joshua Tain and this is Caryl Walker, er, Caryl Cassavettes. She's going to stay with you while I go look for your goat, okay?"

The little boy nodded, sniffling. Taking his hand in hers, Caryl led him away to sit in the SUV, both of them casting anxious glances back at Joshua's disappearing figure.

"You live around here?"

"Uh-huh." He stared at her, his eyes still teary.

"Got brothers and sisters?"

"No, is just me and my mama and granny. But she don't live with us." He sat up to look in the direction Joshua had taken.

Caryl nodded sagely as she searched for something to say that would hold his interest and distract him from worrying about his goat.

"So do you know 'Baa Baa Black Sheep'?" Caryl sang the phrase. She sang a couple more lines, humming where she couldn't remember the words but Michael Chase stared at her as if she were asking him to sing Handel's "Hallelujah Chorus." He turned to look out the window in the direction Joshua had gone. Caryl sighed. So far she was striking out. Stealing a look at the little boy, she began to sing a Bob Marley song and was rewarded when, well into the second verse, he turned to her and began to sing along in a low, hesitant voice. After she segued into a calypso she'd often heard on the radio, Michael's voice lifted. But as the minutes ticked by, Caryl had to rack her brain for more songs he might know. By the time Joshua emerged from the bush at the side of the road, his shirt hanging out of his pants, his face shiny with sweat, a squirming black and white goat clutched to his chest, she was well into "Frosty, the Snowman."

"Oxo," Michael shouted when he caught sight of Joshua. He slid down from the Land Cruiser and ran across the road to reach up and stroke the animal's head. A rope tied about the goat's neck trailed on the ground behind Joshua.

"Thank you," Michael whispered, suddenly bashful. "You got to be real fast. I couldn't catch him at all." His eyes shone with hero worship and he looked quite ready to open the local chapter of the Joshua Tain Fan Club.

"No problem, my man. Now where were you on your way to?"

The little boy pointed down the road in the direction they had come.

"Alright. Let's just put Oxo in car and get you both to your grandma's." Winking at Caryl, Joshua put Oxo down. Keeping a tight grip on the rope, he opened the rear door to the Cruiser, then picked the goat up again and deposited it unceremoniously inside.

Michael sat on Caryl's lap as Joshua made a three-point turn in the road and headed back the way they had come.

"There! Grandma!" The boy pointed to a gray-haired woman sitting on the porch of a small blue and white cottage set a little way back from the road.

Joshua turned down the short, dirt driveway and drove into the yard, alarming a small group of chickens who squawked in protest and retreated under the wooden house.

"Hello, ma'am." Joshua smiled and waved at the woman who stood up to greet them. Her hair lay in thin plaits on her shoulders and her dress was a vivid kaleidoscope of variously colored, giant hibiscuses on a bright blue background. A salmon-pink scarf was tied around her waist.

"Grandma, Grandma, OXO run 'way and I couldn't catch him and this man catch him. Tell her, mister." Michael grabbed Joshua's

JUST AN AFFAIR

hand and tugged him to the porch.

"Good afternoon, sir." The woman smiled through a gap in her front teeth at Joshua. "That goat is a runaway. Always running." She and Joshua shook hands.

"Yes, and the man catch him."

"The gentleman, Michael, the gentleman," his grandma said.

"Yes, the gennelman," Michael said, looking abashed at the correction. He stole a glance at Joshua to see how his hero felt about it. Joshua gave the child a broad wink and Michael beamed, recovering his good spirits instantly.

"Thanks be to you for that, sir. That goat is a trouble but she's a good milker, alright. I wouldn't like to lose her, oh no." The woman nodded to Caryl who was hovering by the Cruiser. "Thanks be to you."

"Ma'am, I'm glad to have helped out, really," Joshua said.

"So where he is now?"

"In the back of the Cruiser." Joshua jabbed his finger in the direction of the SUV.

"Mister, no. You don't mean to tell me you put the goat in your nice new car. Oh, my soul!" She pressed a hand to her cheek, her eyes widening in disbelief, a horrified smile playing on her mouth.

"It was no problem, ma'am. The car will survive. I'll go get him now." Joshua excused himself and went around to the back of the Cruiser to take Oxo out.

"The pen is at back, mister. I'll take you there." Michael led the way.

"Miss, would you like some sorrel? Some mauby? It's a real hot day, today. Sit. Sit." The old woman waved at the chairs on the porch. "It was so nice of you all to bring him in your car. Who will believe Oxo get a ride in a nice car like that?" She chuckled to herself as if imagining her friends' reaction to Oxo's adventure.

"It was no problem at all. Our pleasure, really, and thank you, yes, I'd love some sorrel." Charmed by the woman's graciousness and her age, Caryl chose one of the caned rocking chairs.

"Make yourself comfortable, miss, and I'll be right back. Oxo, boy, uh-uh." Caryl could still hear her chuckling as she disappeared into the sunlit interior of the small house.

Caryl looked around her with interest. The house sat in a little dip between the mountains and was cooled by the two huge mango trees to the left. There was no view of the sea from the house, only of the surrounding countryside. In the near distance, cane stalks rustled in the breeze and, farther away, cows grazed in an open pasture.

"And good-bye to Mr. Oxo." Joshua came around the corner, wiping his hands against his pants.

"Oh, and I thought you two were getting quite attached. Where's Michael?"

"Left him giving Oxo a good talking to."

"Umm, you smell a bit, er, goaty." Caryl sniffed the air.

"Do I?" Joshua held his arms up to his nose. "I do." He looked at her as if to ask what he should do. "Damn goat. I had to throw myself at it to catch it."

"And me without my camera," Caryl lamented, her eyes dancing.

"Thank you, thank you. I risk my life catching a goat and all you can do is joke."

"Tain Music CEO Nabs Rampaging Livestock. Tain Executive Executes Goat Tackle." Caryl chuckled, trying to think up more headlines.

"This is really your fault, you know."

"Mine?" Caryl howled, indignant. "How?"

"If you had decided to spend more time with me, we would have missed Michael and his goat altogether."

"Yes." Caryl sobered. "But I'm glad we didn't."

Joshua nodded. "He's a great little boy, isn't he?"

"Here's the sorrel, ma'am, and some for your husband too." Michael's grandma emerged from the house and deposited an enamel tray with three tall glasses of iced sorrel on a little side table.

"Umm, we're not…" Caryl was going to correct her but Joshua's broad smile told her the misunderstanding pleased him. It *had* sounded nice. *"Your husband."*

"May I use your bathroom? I need to clean up a little," Joshua asked.

"Certainly, mister, certainly. This way." And Joshua was led into the house.

An hour later they were on their way again having made fast friends with Michael and his grandma, Miss Beverly, who had extracted the promise of a longer visit from them soon.

"Those were really nice people," Joshua said as they pulled back onto the main road.

"Yes." Caryl gave him a long look. "And so are you."

"Any man would have gone after that goat."

"You think so?"

"Of course. Got to look like a hero in front your woman, you know. Represent!"

"Oh, yeah?" Caryl snorted. "No hero I know smells like a goat pen except…," she rubbed her chin, pretending to think hard "well, there *is* Billy Goat Gruff," she conceded. "Now there's a hero, kicking that troll's butt. I'm not sure if you're on the same level as Billy, though. Weren't no trolls in that ravine," she explained, fighting to keep a straight face.

"Woman, please, you know your heart went all soft and you heard the sound of violins when I came out of that damn bush."

"Ha!" Caryl sucked her teeth and rolled her eyes, but he was right. Her heart had jumped when she saw him and one thing more, she knew as surely as she knew her father's middle name that Alexander would never have leapt down that ravine like Joshua had. The most he would have done, she sighed to herself, was whip out his cell and call the Fire Department to do it. She suppressed a yawn.

"Sleepy?" Joshua asked.

"Yes." She hadn't noticed it before but she was ready to nod off.

"Don't worry. I think we're soon there. One more hill and then Hill House, okay."

But Caryl had drifted off, her chin on her chest. Joshua leaned over and gently adjusted the recline button on her seat so she could be more comfortable. Caryl stirred but didn't waken.

CHAPTER TWENTY-ONE

"Where have you been?" David Cassavettes flung open the door to the Land Cruiser, startling Caryl out of her slumber. She looked around sleepily. They had reached the hotel and were parked at its entrance.

"Daddy?" Caryl was too sleepy to make sense of the shouting. She waved her hand for quiet. "What's going on?"

"Caryl, darling, we've been worried sick." Marcianne flew to her side. "Are you alright? We got your note at the hospital. Long Bay said you left there hours ago." She nodded a cool greeting at Joshua.

"Mumsie, I'm fine, I'm fine." Caryl gave her mother a reassuring hug, then hugged her father. "What's all the fuss about, Daddy?"

"You said you wanted to stay at the hospital, then you leave, then we find out you have amnesia." Her father shook his head, glaring at Joshua as if it was all his fault.

"Who told you?"

"Patty. We called her about an hour ago," her father answered.

"More to the point, darling, why didn't you tell us?" her mother asked.

Caryl shot a rueful glance at Joshua.

"I don't know," she answered as they began to walk up the hotel's steps, her father and mother on either side of her with Joshua bringing up the rear. No, that wasn't true, suddenly, like a light being switched on, she did know.

"Mumsie," she said, excitedly. "Auntie May, do you remember

...er? Pilar's sister."

"Of course I remember her, darling. I'm surprised you do. You were only five when she died."

"Do you remember the time you took me to visit her? I must have been, I guess, four. She was in a home. I remember light green walls like shallow water. Auntie May was standing talking to herself in front of her mirror, a big standing mirror, in her room and you said, "Hello, Aunt. It's me, Marcianne." She looked right through you as if you weren't there."

David Cassavettes steered his daughter to one of the plush chairs in the hotel lobby.

"I remember, Caryl. I remember."

"You said her memory's gone, she's nobody now. Mumsie, for weeks after, I dreamed you and Daddy would disappear, become nobodies, leaving me all alone."

"Caryl!" Marcianne reached over and drew her daughter into a long hug. "That must have been when you started acting so strangely. Don't you remember, David? You would get out of your bed and come into ours in the middle of the night. We couldn't figure out what was wrong, but then after a while you stopped. We never knew what was wrong. We just chalked it up to some childish insecurity."

David stared at his daughter in consternation. "You mean you've remembered that all this time?"

"Yes. I must have, somewhere in my subconscious. I've only just remembered it consciously. When I realized I had amnesia, I just felt like huge bits of me had disappeared. It was irrational, I know, but something kept me from telling anyone as if I'd be sealing my fate somehow." Caryl shrugged. "I'm sorry. I know now I was silly. I should have said something."

"That's alright, now. We're just glad to have you in one piece and

JUST AN AFFAIR

to know why you've been acting so strangely." Marcianne looked relieved.

"And I thought I was covering so well."

"She means with that Thorne man. We couldn't understand why you were letting him back into your life after all he'd put you through." David cast a baleful glance at Joshua as if to say he had the same question about him.

Joshua rose from his chair.

"You don't have to go," Caryl said. She frowned sternly at her father. "Daddy is going to behave." The incident with little Michael Chase and his grandmother had made her realize there was a whole lot more to Joshua Tain than determined arrogance.

Joshua grinned, carefully avoiding David's eyes. "No, this is your first day out of the hospital. I don't want to monopolize your time and I know you're tired."

"Kind of you," David Cassavettes said dryly.

"But I'll call you tonight," Joshua continued as if David hadn't spoken. "I'd like to take you to lunch tomorrow, if you feel up to it."

"I'd like that," Caryl said and then felt a small electrical shock run through her as he mouthed "*I love you*" before bidding her parents good afternoon and striding out of the lobby.

"Darling, for somebody who tucked herself away in the back of beyond you've certainly managed to find yourself in the thick of things." Her mother cocked an eyebrow at her.

"I wish I could remember this love affair but I can't." Caryl grimaced in frustration.

"That may be so but the two of you can't tear your eyes off each other, right, sweetness?" Marcianne looked at David. "Kind of reminds me of us."

"I don't know what you're talking about, Marcianne. That man is nothing like me, the shark."

"Daddy, you were the one who tried to take his business from him," Caryl cried in protest.

"Man's a shark," David Cassavettes reiterated, jutting his chin.

An image flashed through Caryl's mind. A tiger shark bumping her, then closing in for the kill, the punch, the knife in her hand sweeping down. "A shark attacked me," Caryl said, knowing it for the truth this time and not a dream.

"Both of us, precious, both of us."

Caryl stared at her father's grim face in confusion.

"No, David, I think she means in the water." Marcianne grasped Caryl's shoulders. "Go on, darling."

"It came around us before when we were on our way down but it was when we were going up that it came back. Matthew Silvers was above me." Caryl spoke slowly, sure of what she was saying. "I was the last one on the line. I waved at it and it went away but then it came from behind me and I knew it was going to attack." Caryl's eyes widened. The images were unfolding before her like scenes watched from inside a fast moving train. "I took out my knife. When it came I punched it on the nose and ducked to the side. As it was passing me, I brought my arm down on its back, cutting it with the knife. I hurt it pretty bad. The blood came up and I just knew I had to get out of there." Caryl gave a little shiver. "Either it would come back or other sharks would come to investigate." Caryl lowered her head to her mother's shoulder. "I must have panicked. Come up too fast." She was exhausted now as if the mere act of remembering and recounting had drained her of energy.

"Are you sure that wasn't a dream, Caryl? You've done a lot of sleeping these past couple of weeks, you know." Her father's voice was kind but she felt hurt by his disbelief.

JUST AN AFFAIR

"No, it wasn't a dream. I remember it clearly. That was why I had the knife in my hand when they got me back on the boat. I never sheathed it. It wasn't a dream."

"Darling, you're so lucky you survived, *we're* so lucky." Marcianne gave her another hug.

"It's a story for Ripley's, all right." Her father shuddered at what could have happened. Looking lovingly at her, he noticed her exhaustion. "We have to get her to bed. She's tuckered out." David stood up and reached over to help Caryl to her feet.

"Can you walk, precious?"

"Daddy, I'm fine. Just a little tired, that's all." But she didn't refuse his arm, leaning on him all the way out of the lobby and down the front steps to one of the golf carts used to transport guests around the resort.

Caryl fell asleep on the luxurious, queen-sized bed in the two-bedroom villa her parents took her to as soon as her head hit the pillow. When she woke hours later, night had descended on the island. For a little while, Caryl lay unmoving, her eyes open in the darkness. She relived the harrowing last few minutes of her dive with the shark coming at her, intent on making her its meal. Shivering, she knew she was more than lucky; she was blessed. She wordlessly thanked the ancestors and the Higher Power. Now, if only she could remember everything else she had done since coming to the islands. But she would not push herself. Every day the fog lifted a little more. Soon, she would be able to see her past as clearly as she could see the view on a cloudless day. She was sure of it. Feeling better than she had felt in a long time, Caryl stretched and jumped out of bed.

"I'm so hungry I could eat a buffet table and everything on it," Caryl said through a yawn as she entered the villa's living area. Her father was reading what looked like a project proposal, and her mother was engrossed in a novel.

"Darling, what should we order for you?" Marcianne uncurled herself from the couch, making room on it for Caryl.

"No, Mumsie, I want to take a long bath first," Caryl said, refusing the offer of a seat. "But order their pumpkin soup and barbecue ribs for me. I'll have apple pie à la mode for dessert, if they've got it. If not, anything chocolate will do. By the time they bring all that, I should be out."

"Anything you want, darling." Marcianne reached for the phone as Caryl went back to her room and its adjoining bathroom.

It was big even by luxury hotel standards, its white marble tub almost as big as her Jeep Cherokee. The thought startled her. She'd forgotten all about her car and so apparently had everybody else since nobody had mentioned it to her. Caryl realized it must still be at the Nanny Cay parking lot, but it was probably as safe there as anywhere else since the marina had its own security guards. She sank into the cloud of aromatic bubbles she'd created and closed her eyes as the scent of the bath beads the resort provided enveloped her.

Her memory was returning, sometimes in a flash flood, other times in a gentle, insubstantial trickle welling up from her subconscious. It was all coming back to her from the dark recesses her mind had created in the aftermath of the shark attack. The most important thing was that she had survived intact. It was a wake-up call to make the most of life and never take it for granted. Caryl leaned back and closed her eyes, letting her thoughts float to the surface as easily as the iridescent bubbles around her.

JUST AN AFFAIR

Inevitably, her mind turned to Joshua Tain. Whatever her father thought of the man, Caryl knew she did not share his feelings. So far she had remembered nothing about Joshua and their affair, but she could already feel the pull of his magnetism. If she had fallen in love with him in the space of one week, he certainly must not be a slouch in the romance department. It had taken Alexander months of wooing before she'd accepted a date with him. Caryl shook her head in annoyance. She must stop comparing Joshua to Alexander. She might not know Joshua very well, but what she did know so far indicated that the two men were as different from each other as a dinghy from a yacht.

Marcianne knocked on the door to tell her that her dinner had arrived.

"Have you all eaten?" Caryl asked when she emerged a few minutes later, wrapped in a thick terry cloth robe against the cold of the air conditioner.

"Yes, we ordered in." David looked at his watch. "About six o'clock, wasn't it, Marcianne?"

His wife nodded. She was reclining on the couch while her husband gave her a foot massage.

"They've got a spa here, you know, Mumsie," Caryl said as she sat down at the table. She lifted off the lid covering the soup bowl and took an appreciative sniff of the thick pumpkin soup. They had included ginger, just the way she liked it.

"You mother says I'm better than the reflexologist there," her father answered, more than a note of pride in his voice as he lifted Marcianne's foot higher and kneaded her toes.

"Darling, he is. That so-called reflexologist didn't even crack my joints." Marcianne leaned further back, closing her eyes. There was a look of such deep pleasure on her face that Caryl wouldn't have been surprised to hear her purr.

"Caryl, we talked to the doctor while you were sleeping," her father began.

His daughter quirked an eyebrow at him, her back stiffening. Under no circumstances would she consider returning to the hospital. She was perfectly fine.

"We told him about the amnesia. He said the trauma you suffered could easily have caused that and he wasn't surprised. We told him you're remembering bits and pieces." David squeezed more massage oil into his hand and began working on Marcianne's other foot. "He wants you to come in for a check-up next Monday."

"Okay. No problem." Caryl relaxed.

"He also said he didn't want you traveling anywhere by air for the next couple weeks, precious."

Caryl nodded, swallowing the last of her soup. That figured. People with decompression illness risked further complications by traveling in airplanes at high altitude.

"Fine," she said matter-of-factly, reaching for the plate of ribs. "And you guys need to get back to work long before then."

Her parents glanced at each other.

"Well, darling, your father does at any rate. He's leaving on Sunday. I'm staying on."

Caryl nodded, pleased to have more time with her mother. Her father looked at her anxiously as if worried she might think he was abandoning her.

"I'm fine, Daddy. There's no need to worry about me."

"You just slept for a whole afternoon," David pointed out.

"Daddy, in your world I know that's right up there with a fraud conviction, but I've been known to sleep away afternoons even on days when I haven't been released from a hospital. Anyway, I didn't get into bed until after two so it was only a few hours, not a whole afternoon." Caryl grinned at her father and brought a rib to her mouth. It was good. Spicy.

Marcianne grinned. "Point, set and match," she said.

"I just don't like leaving you right now." David gently put his wife's foot down.

"It's not right now. You won't be leaving for days. And I wonder if the reason you don't like it is really because I'm just out of the hospital or because Joshua Tain will still be here." Caryl crossed her fingers under the table. She *hoped* he would still be here; he hadn't mentioned when he was leaving.

"Darling, that's uncalled for. Your dad's been very worried about you," Marcianne remonstrated.

"I know, Mumsie, and I'm not saying he's not, but Daddy doesn't like the man nor the idea of leaving me here with him. I know Daddy."

"Your father would never interfere with your love life, Caryl."

"Marcianne, it's true though. I don't believe the man's right for her." David scowled.

"On the basis of a business deal that didn't go your way? I remember you once saying you respected him. If you didn't think he'd built a great business, you would never have tried to buy it from him." Marcianne was indignant. "Caryl must follow her heart."

"It's led her wrong sometimes."

"Yes, but they're her mistakes to make."

"I'm trying to protect my daughter." David jumped to his feet and paced the floor.

"Daddy," Caryl interjected, reminding them of her presence. Her father spun around to face her. "I'm not a child anymore. I don't know if Joshua is Mr. Right, but then Mr. Right doesn't come tagged and trussed. I have a good time around him, he makes me laugh, he's kind, and Patty said I was like a new person around him." She got up from the table and came over to stand by him.

"I want what you and Mumsie have," she said, looking him in the eyes. "That's what I'm looking for and if I make mistakes, I'll make them honestly and they'll teach me lessons I need to learn. I enjoy Joshua. Please don't spoil this for me." She grabbed his hand and kissed it, only to be pulled into a tight bear hug.

"Honey, I just want the best for you." Her father's voice was gruff in her ear.

"I know, Daddy, I know and maybe he's it and maybe he's not. But I've got to find that out for myself."

"Alright, you win." Her father pulled out of the embrace, holding up his hands in the international signal of surrender. "I've got nothing more to say on the subject. It is *sub judice* as you lawyers say."

Marcianne clapped her hands. "Great, that's settled. I'm the witness. No more snide remarks and disapproving eyebrow semaphores."

"I'm outnumbered." David sank back down on the couch, a rueful expression on his face.

Not for the first time in her life, Caryl thought that in his few moments of downtime her father must puzzle over the difference in his business and domestic lives. In the former his word held sway over thousands of people while in the latter, everything he said was up for debate. Well, she reflected, that's what you get for marrying a strong-willed woman and teaching your daughter how to be the same.

A knock startled them. Caryl crossed the room and opened the door. A small cloud of mug-sized red roses hovered in the doorway almost at eye level. The cloud lowered to reveal a woman's broad, smiling face.

"You Caryl Walker Cassavettes?"

"Yes."

JUST AN AFFAIR

"These are for you." The woman thrust the bouquet at Caryl.

"Thanks."

Caryl turned to ask her father for a tip to give the woman, but she said, "No problem, I got it already," and left.

Caryl set the bouquet down on a small side table and detached the card.

"Who's it from, Caryl?"

"With all the love in the world," the card read. "Joshua Tain," Caryl answered. She wondered if Patty had told him she'd given the other roses away to the children's ward of the hospital.

"Hummph, doesn't that man ever rest?"

"David," her mother said warningly.

"Alright, alright."

Caryl looked around for something to put the flowers in. In the bathroom she found a tall glass vase full of silk flowers. It was perfect. She dumped the silk flowers, half-filled the vase with water and inserted the roses.

"The table over there would be nice," her mother suggested when she went back into the living area.

Caryl nodded, agreeing. She stepped back to admire the display the roses made, then buried her face in them one more time before joining her mother on the couch.

"Now what should we do tomorrow? Caryl, do you want to just laze around?" Marcianne asked.

"I think so. That pool outside looks real inviting." The resort had thoughtfully provided each villa with a small, pea-shaped pool. Privacy was ensured by a screen of lush plantings that included palms, hibiscus and ixora, whose huge pink blooms reminded Caryl of cheerleaders' pom-poms.

"Nothing better on a hot day," her mother agreed, smiling.

CHAPTER TWENTY-TWO

At nine o'clock the next morning, just as a swim-suited Caryl was getting ready to join her parents outside in the pool, the phone rang.

"Caryl, it's me. I'm at the airport. I just wanted to hear your voice before I left."

"Hello, Alexander." She wished she hadn't picked up the phone.

"I wanted to say again how sorry I am. My biggest mistakes in life have been the lies I've told you, lies of omission and commission. But Caryl, you've got to believe I never meant to hurt you or cause you pain." His voice was choked with emotion.

"We can't undo the past, Alexander." She still didn't remember the incident all the details, but in time she probably would. Then, again, maybe it would be better if some things remained lost to her memory.

"I know, Caryl, but I hate leaving like this. I hate leaving at all." His voice was low.

"This is your fault, Alexander. You...I don't know what to say to you." She was beginning to get angry. "Why couldn't you just be who I thought you were? Why?"

"Caryl...I...I don't have any good answer for that. I was a fool. I know that. I don't blame you for anything."

"Blame me!" Caryl couldn't believe her ears. "You're damn straight you don't blame me. What the hell could you possibly blame me for?"

"Caryl, Caryl, please, I didn't call to quarrel with you."

"You shouldn't have called at all!" And she slammed down the receiver.

That damn man! Who did he think he was? He didn't blame her! She hadn't done anything to be blamed for! He was the one who should be accepting blame, not her. But as she began to calm down, a small voice inside murmured that maybe she *should* accept some responsibility for allowing a married man's lies to sweep her off her feet. She was twenty-six when they met, not some dreamy-eyed, adolescent ingénue. Caryl squirmed uncomfortably. Maybe what had happened wasn't all his fault.

Caryl stared at the phone then came to a sudden decision. Shrugging on shorts and a tee shirt, she strode out to the pool where her mother and father were relaxing.

"I'll be right back. I'm just going out for a little while."

David and Marcianne exchanged puzzled glances.

"Darling, where are you going?"

"The airport. To tell Alexander goodbye." Caryl blew her parents a kiss, picked up the keys to their rental car and headed out. A glance at her watch told her she had forty-five minutes before the next Air BVI flight left the island. Caryl stepped on the accelerator and ignored the island's thirty-miles-per-hour speed limit. Going to see Alexander off was the right thing to do. He had lied and cheated but she should have known better too. It took two adults to tango the way they had, and it had to take two to admit responsibility. If she didn't, then she would always see herself as his victim, weak and wronged. She couldn't allow her bad experiences with Alexander to affect the rest of her life. She had to find some kind of resolution. It was important for herself, and she knew it was important to whatever was going to develop between her and Joshua.

At the airport, she threaded her way around people and luggage, searching for Alexander. When she found him he was standing by an exit door, his back to her. She squared her shoulders and walked up to him.

"You came," he breathed, opening his arms to her.

"No, I mean, yes but…" Her voice faltered and Alexander's arms dropped to his side. Hurt aged his face.

"You haven't had a change of heart," he said, finishing her sentence.

"I came to say," Caryl cast around for the exact words, "that I'm sorry, too, about everything." But, she thought, most of all that he had never been the man she'd believed he was and that she hadn't realized that from the beginning. As if seeing something of what she was thinking in her face, Alexander's shoulder drooped and he looked sadder than ever.

"I don't blame you for everything," Caryl continued. "I was in it too. I should have asked to see your divorce papers before we got into the hot and heavy."

"You came to say that?"

"Yes. I don't want you to feel like it was all your fault. I don't want you to shoulder all the guilt."

He rocked back on his heels, his expression wry. "I feel like I should, though. I was older. You were so young. Still are." He smiled. "I was so attracted to that. You had this fresh vitality and you were everything I admired in a woman. Smart as a whip. Beautiful. Sexy."

"You've got many admirable qualities, too, Alexander," Caryl interrupted before he could go on. "But the lies…"

He held up a hand palm up, as if to ward off her recriminations. "I know, I know. Thanks, Caryl. For coming and for being kind. I guess, well, maybe this has been a learning experience for both of us, eh?"

"Yes." She was uncomfortable now that she had said what she

came to say. She looked around at the crowded airport.

"We talked, you know."

"Who?" Caryl's head swiveled back in his direction.

"Tain and me." He led her to the departure lounge entrance as a brisk voice announced the boarding of his flight.

"What about?"

"You."

"Oh, for crying out loud, Alexander." Caryl almost stamped her foot in annoyance. If he had said anything to turn Joshua from her… But the thought didn't bear thinking. "What did you say to him?"

"That I loved you but you had sent me away."

Caryl glared at him. "You had no right to say anything!"

"Two African-American men at a hotel bar in a strange country. We'd seen each other at the hospital, why wouldn't we talk? Anyway, I remembered him from the photo in the newspaper. The one that got you so upset. I could see he was bursting to know what we'd discussed when you cleared the room and it was just you and me." Alexander shouldered his worn leather garment bag. "He loves you a lot, Caryl, I could see that." His eyes narrowed as if the words pained him. "I didn't tell him much, just that we'd been involved a long time ago and I still had feelings for you but you didn't return them. The rest is yours to disclose or not as you wish."

"I owe him the truth about me."

"Good luck, Caryl."

On impulse, Caryl stepped forward and gave him a quick hug. He had acted nobly at last. His back stiffened.

"Thank you, Alexander. Take care of yourself," she said into his ear.

"You too. Don't forget me." He pressed a hurried, self-conscious kiss on her cheek, put his things through the scanner and stepped through security. With a last wave to her, he walked over to where an airline official was checking boarding passes and disappeared through the door to the tarmac.

Feeling that she had closed a chapter in her life, Caryl walked slowly through the terminal and back to the car. Her spirits lifted as she drove. They hadn't said that much to each other really, not all that *could* have been said, but she felt she had cleared the air, seen him off with no regrets and no ill feelings. Now she could move on with her life without guilt or shame, free to give herself fully to any man without her history with Alexander interfering. With her hands on the wheel of her car, Caryl crossed her fingers. She hoped that man would be Joshua.

Back at the hotel, Caryl donned her swimsuit, ran out to the suite's patio and jumped in the pool, splashing her parents who were sunning themselves on the lounge chairs. Laughing, they joined her in the water, and when Joshua arrived to pick Caryl up for their lunch date they were still there.

"Good morning all," he said, his eyes lingering on Caryl bobbing in the pool.

"Morning," David Cassavettes grunted as his wife and daughter greeted Joshua with smiles.

"Now that's a fine way to enjoy the day," Joshua said, appropriating one of the lounge chairs at the side.

"Would you like to join us, Mr. Tain?" Marcianne asked.

"Thank you, but I have other plans for your daughter. I hope you've worked up an appetite," he said to Caryl.

"I have. I'll be right there." Caryl clambered out of the pool. As she was about to invite him inside to remove him from her parents' scrutiny, she thought better of it. Her father was a fair man. He would get over his opposition to Joshua if he had to. Caryl hummed happi-

JUST AN AFFAIR

ly as she quickly showered and dressed.

When she went back outside she found Joshua in an amiable conversation with her mother about the Grammy awards and his picks for best song and best new artist. Marcianne apparently agreed with his choices. Her father sat in a nearby lounge chair determinedly reading a book. Caryl glanced at the glittery cover and her lips twitched. The book belonged to her mother. David had absolutely no interest in fiction and had clearly just picked it up to have a good reason to ignore Joshua.

"Ready?" Joshua asked.

"Yes."

David lowered the book to look at her. Caryl blew him a kiss and bent down to give her mother a hug.

"See you later," she said.

"Have a good time," Marcianne said, smiling, but David only nodded soberly.

"You look great. Being a hospital escapee suits you," Joshua said as they walked to where he'd parked.

"Thank you." She wore a yellow sundress that had once fit her tightly but now, after her hospital stay, fell loosely over her curves.

"I want to show you something." They got into the Land Cruiser and he handed her a manila envelope. "Look inside," he directed as he started the engine and began to draw out of the resort's parking lot.

Caryl undid the flap and drew out the photos inside. They were eight by ten black and white glossies of her. The one on top was taken on a moonlit night. She was leaning against the rail of a boat she knew without a doubt was the *Elendil*. Somehow she looked glamorous, mysterious and innocent all at once, the moonlight giving her a fey quality.

"You took these?" Caryl was impressed.

"Yes."

"Wow," Caryl muttered as she looked at one picture after the other. There were twenty-six in all. She could see by her dress that all of the nighttime ones were taken on the same occasion, but a few others were taken at The Baths and at a beach on Jost Van Dyke that she instantly recognized. All were sharp, vivid, good enough to be in *Vogue* or *American Photo*. "They're beautiful."

"You're beautiful." His hand reached out to grasp and squeeze hers.

"Are they for me?"

"Yes. I have copies and the negatives."

"Thank you." Caryl hugged the pictures to her. If she had wanted evidence of their relationship, these pictures were it. Joshua had drawn forth something from inside her that shone in the glossies.

"Were we lovers when you took these?"

"No, not the ones on the boat or on Virgin Gorda, but I knew from the moment I saw you that we would be and far more." He kissed her hand and flicked his tongue over her knuckles.

"Watch the road." Joshua's caresses made her insides feel as if a juggler were in residence in her stomach. Every cell, every nerve in her body strained to throw itself into his arms, road safety and "taking it slow" be damned. Caryl steeled herself against any loss of self-control and primly returned Joshua's hand to the steering wheel.

Joshua grinned.

"You may not remember loving me, Caryl, but you feel it. I know you do."

"You know no such thing."

"There is such a thing as men's intuition, you know. I've got it in spades and it's telling me we definitely have a future together."

"Ha! Men's intuition, my foot. We'll see about that." He was probably right, but she would still make him work for it.

"You know, you were just like this at the beginning."

"Like what?"

"Umm, what do they call that fruit they have here? I had it this morning. It's bigger than my hand, green, and has prickles all over. What is it?"

Caryl remained silent, determined not to help him tease her.

"Soursop. That's it. That's what you were like at the beginning."

"And at the end?"

"Oh." He stole a glance at her. "By the end, I had reached the sweetness inside and forgotten all about the prickles." His lips twitched, and in Caryl's stomach, the juggler picked up flaming torches.

"I don't think we should talk about such things right now," she said firmly. She ignored Joshua's smirk.

"What would you like to talk about, then?"

She wondered if she should bring up his discussion with Alexander and decided against it. She wasn't ready for that yet. "How do you like the island?"

Joshua considered the question. "It's very pretty and the people seem friendly, but I've been reading the newspapers. They seem to have some problems with theft. Is that connected to the drug problem we talked about before? Sorry," he caught himself, "you don't remember that, do you?"

Caryl shook her head.

"When we were on Jost Van Dyke you told me that cocaine and crack were a growing problem."

"Yes," Caryl nodded. "I think the thefts are related, but I don't know to what extent. Sometimes it's just poor kids who want brand name sneakers or some other thing that will give them standing with their friends. Not necessarily about buying drugs."

"Same problem as the inner cities."

Caryl sighed, "Yes, but the islands don't have the same resources. There are no residential facilities for drug users and, until just about a year ago, no treatment facility at all."

"*He* looks like he's on something." They were on the outskirts of Road Town and Joshua nodded at a thin boy they passed on the road, his eyes fixed vacantly on the far distance, the pants he wore barely reaching his ankles, his hair ragged and gray with dirt.

"Crack, Richardson says. He lives in an abandoned car in a ravine."

"Do you realize you're remembering more and more?"

It was true. A couple days ago she couldn't even remember who Richardson was.

"You know, the Genevra Hope Foundation helps kids like that."

"Yes, but isn't it strictly US-based?" Caryl was familiar with the organization, what New Yorker wasn't? It was responsible for keeping hundreds of at-risk kids off the city's streets and in its schools.

"It has been but it could change its mind, become broader in outlook." He drew up in front of a charming West Indian style house with curly fretwork and a yellow and green motif. It had been converted from a private residence into a restaurant just a few months earlier. Caryl inhaled deeply, loving the smell of the flowering jasmine lining the walk to the entrance.

"And who would change the Foundation's mind?" she asked after they were seated.

"I would. It *is* my foundation, after all."

"Yours?" Caryl stared goggle-eyed at him.

"Genevra Hope is my grandmother. I created the foundation and named it after her."

JUST AN AFFAIR

"You're kidding me." She remembered that he'd called his gran often while he was on the *Elendil*, but she'd never heard him use her name.

"Do you think it would work here?"

The foundation's after-school regime required strict discipline, but kids who bore the rules had access to programs that ranged from piano lessons to investment basics to chess. Thinking about this, Caryl suddenly remembered attending a dinner at which Mayor Giuliani had presented the director with an award for the Foundation's service to the city.

"Were you at the mayoral awards two years ago?"

"Yes," he said, surprised. "Were you?"

"Yes." They smiled at each other, each clearly regretting that they hadn't met then. But that would have done no good, Caryl reflected. Her affair with Alexander was in full swing at the time.

"It could work here if you linked up with one of the local service organizations, like Rotary, to co-sponsor it," she said, returning to the subject.

"That wouldn't be a problem." Joshua leaned back in his chair after a waitress took their order. "Do you know the names of people I could get in touch with?"

"No, but Richardson might be able to help. You're serious about this, aren't you?"

Joshua nodded soberly. "I was thinking about Michael. There's still so much innocence here, I'd like to help preserve that."

"I'll help." Caryl came to a quick decision. "Henry Enterprises donates hundreds of thousands to charities every year. I'll make sure they put the Foundation on the list."

"Lobby your dad?"

"He wants me to take over, so that can be one of my first initiatives. Living here has taught me how connected we all are as human beings. If you're going to go into this thing here, I'd like to help."

Joshua's eyes softened. "Thank you. I'd like that very much. Partners, then?"

"Yes."

He extended his hand to shake hers, but then held on to it.

"Henry Enterprises is Virginia-based," he said.

"Yes." Caryl frowned. What was he getting at? "Distance shouldn't block our collaboration."

"But will it block our relationship?"

Caryl's cheeks warmed. She tried to snatch her hand back but he held it fast.

"We don't have one yet," she reminded him.

"But we will."

"You don't know that."

"I know it like I know the back of your hand," he answered, slowly stroking it with the palm of his other hand. "Caryl, tell me. How do you feel about me? Do you think you could love me? In time?" Joshua shifted in his chair as if, despite his cockiness, he feared her answer.

Caryl didn't reply immediately. She looked at him, her eyes intent, greedy almost as they drank in the contours of his face, the smooth mahogany of his cheeks, his wide, now furrowed, forehead. A muscle jumped in his cheek and she realized the strain he was under, waiting for her reply.

"Yes, I think so." She more than thought so but she wasn't quite ready to tell him that yet.

"Now there's something I have to tell you," she said, her voice soft. She stared outside at a windblown divi-divi tree in the neighboring yard, gathering her resolve.

JUST AN AFFAIR

"Captain, I already know what I need to know."

Caryl took a deep breath and shook her head.

"When I was in New York, I had an affair with a married man, a lawyer at the firm where I worked." She allowed herself a peek at Joshua.

He frowned, pursed his lips and now it was her turn to wait in suspense. She did not have long.

"Caryl, I don't expect you to be perfect. Nobody is."

The answer was all she could have hoped but she had to go on, tell him all of it.

"That's not all." How she wished it were! Squaring her shoulders, she told him everything about Alexander, Barbara, the firm, her leaving.

At the end of her recital, Joshua leaned back in his chair.

"The man you met at your hotel last night, Alexander, was the married man. He got a divorce and wanted to marry me."

"What did you tell him?"

"What do you think? I told him I no longer loved him, that there was another man I wasn't giving up on in my life."

"It was funny," Joshua mused. "We stayed at the same hotel but I'd never seen him around there before last night. He looked so down in the dumps, I felt kinda sorry for him. Why didn't you tell me all this before, when I was on the *Elendil*?" He had forgotten she had no memory of their time together on the boat but she thought she knew the answer.

"I guess because we had just gotten to know each other. It's not something I would talk about. Patty says I planned to tell you if you came back to me."

"Caryl." Joshua grabbed her hands. His voice was gentle but his face was like granite. He fell silent as the waitress approached and deposited their plates in front of them.

Caryl's heart cringed. He thought less of her; she knew it. She had lost him. For a wild minute she hoped the waitress would never leave so she wouldn't have to hear what he had to say, but the woman quickly disappeared back to the kitchen.

Joshua took her hands in his again. "Your past doesn't matter to me, Caryl. We've all done things we regret. It's the here and now that matters. You are never to feel ashamed or guilty of anything around me. Our mistakes shouldn't stunt our growth or ruin our chance for happiness," he said, his voice stern. He raised her hands to his lips and kissed them. "Now, can we put that out of the way and eat? I'm hungry."

Hours later when they left the restaurant, Caryl felt completely sated, in body and soul. Joshua didn't mind her past, he loved her, flaws and all. Maybe, finally, she had found her Mr. Right.

"So what are you doing tomorrow?" he asked as they entered the driveway to Hill House.

"Don't know yet. Dad is leaving Sunday so I'd like to spend some more time with him and Mumsie. You don't mind, do you?"

"Of course not. After all, I'll soon have you all to myself."

"Maybe and maybe not," she teased.

"Oh, yeah? The only answer I want to hear from you, missy, is 'definitely' or something along those lines. Nothing else."

"Or what?"

"You don't want to know." He looked sideways at her and raised an eyebrow. "Or do you?" He lightly squeezed her thigh.

"Maybe some other time," she said primly. They had arrived at the resort and Caryl opened her car door.

"Caryl." Joshua's hand moved to her arm, his face suddenly serious. "I'll call you tomorrow, right?"

"Yes." And then, because she wanted to, she leaned over and kissed him quickly on the cheek.

CHAPTER TWENTY-THREE

The next morning, Caryl dropped her parents at the botanic gardens and swung into town to mail some letters at the post office. Remembering her mother's love for Yardley soap products, she went into the adjacent drugstore after posting her letters. There was a whole shelf dedicated to the line, but it didn't take her long to decide. She had just paid for a gift set that included four lavender soaps and a body lotion when she looked out the window behind the cashier and saw Joshua exiting a record store on the other side of the street. Caryl grabbed up her change and hurried out the store.

"Hey, good looking." She brought her teeth together, pursed her lips and made that penetrating sound Tortolian people made when they wanted to attract the attention of the opposite sex, a cross between a whistle and a loud hiss.

Joshua's head turned, his face hard. When he saw it was she, a smile broke through and he waved eagerly, immediately changing course to come to her.

"Caryl, I thought you said you were going to spend time with your parents," he asked.

"I am. I just dropped them at the botanic gardens but I had some letters to mail so I thought I'd do that first before losing myself in the pleasures of green things."

"Hmm." His eyes drank her in. "I could sure lose myself in some pleasures today, but I can tell you they wouldn't be green."

"Oh no?" She played along. "And what color would they be?"

"Chocolate. Like a river of sweetness melting on my tongue." He stepped closer to her so she had to tip her head back to look at him.

"Sounds decadent. And tooth-decaying." She grinned, stepping back to create more space between them. She wouldn't be surprised if the heat they were suddenly generating sparked a three-alarm fire in the island's historic capital. "So, have you been thinking about me?"

"I can hardly do anything else, woman."

For one wordless second they stared into each other's eyes.

"And you?" Joshua asked, his voice suddenly hoarse. "Do you think about me?"

"Yes." And it was the truth. She could hardly get him out of her mind. Even when talking with her parents, somewhere in the back of her mind her thoughts were on Joshua. Caryl took a deep breath and pushed away an impulse to jump this familiar stranger's bones right there on the street.

"Noel and Patty said to say 'hi' to you. They called last night."

"They're good people. I told them I'd like to take them out for dinner when they get back."

"That's a nice idea. Am I invited?"

"Wouldn't think of going without you."

They smiled at each other.

"Will I see you later?"

"Come to the hotel. Maybe we can have a drink at the bar. Call first to make sure I'm there, though, because we're supposed to have dinner with some family friends who have a vacation house in Belmont."

"No problem. Let me walk you back to your car."

As they walked, Joshua grabbed her hand and held it in his. Caryl didn't protest. When they said goodbye, she gave him a firm kiss on his mouth, allowing her lips to linger on his before pulling away. She caught a last glimpse of him in the rearview mirror as she pulled into traffic and left him behind. His saffron-colored shirt, thick gold chain and regal bearing made him look like a Maasai prince standing there on Main Street.

Minutes later, she turned into the botanic gardens' parking lot and paid the entry fee to go in. It took her about ten minutes of brisk walking to find her parents.

"Caryl, this banyan tree is amazing! I've never seen one up close," her father said as she walked up to them.

"Darling, did you just see Joshua Tain?"

"Yes, Mumsie." Caryl was surprised. "How did you know?"

"Your skin, darling, you're positively glowing."

"Oh." Caryl looked sheepish. She glanced at her father's suddenly grim face but he continued to scrutinize the banyan as if, with enough attention, it would yield the secret of bringing a recalcitrant daughter back in line. Marcianne winked at her.

There was no further mention of Joshua for the rest of the day which was spent touring and shopping.

"What do you want to eat, people? Italian, French or local food?" Caryl asked when she thought that she would drop from hunger. It was after two and her parents had stopped only once, around eleven, for mango ices at the Lennard's fruit stand in Diamond where they could see the Atlantic on one side and the Caribbean Sea on the other.

"Local." Her parents chorused.

Caryl took them to Quito's in Cane Garden Bay, where they could relax on the beach as they waited for their meals to be served.

"Darling, you look so happy," her mother said when they were all lying on beach chairs.

"I am, Mumsie. I feel really good, clean, like how the island smells after heavy rain."

JUST AN AFFAIR

"Does this have anything to do with your talk with Alexander yesterday?" David asked.

"Yes. We resolved things. I mean, I know I haven't recovered my memory completely and I don't remember the scene with Barbara, but I can't blame him totally for it. He should never have lied and cheated and done the things he did, here and back in New York, but I was in it too. I can't move on with my life if I keep seeing myself only as the done unto and not the doer. Do you know what I mean?" Caryl looked from David to Marcianne.

Her parents glanced at each other over her head.

"Yes, darling, we do. Good for you." Marcianne reached her hand out and grabbed Caryl's as David did the same on her other side. Caryl beamed. She was blessed.

A couple of hours later, after hours at the beach, they returned to the hotel. There was a message waiting for Caryl to call Joshua when she got in. She did and they agreed to meet in half an hour at her hotel's bar.

"I don't have long. I've got to get ready for the dinner," Caryl apologized as she took the stool next to him at the bar. She would have much preferred to spend the time with him rather than with the Olsons whom she hadn't seen since she was a teenager.

"That's okay. I was forewarned. How did your day go?"

"Good. I feel a bit tired. We went to the beach after all the shopping and touring. What about you?"

"After you left me I went to a couple of other music shops. I found an old Jacob Miller album that I just couldn't find anywhere else. Not even in Jamaica. I'd like to get it digitally remastered."

"Who manages his estate?"

"To tell you the truth, I'm not quite sure. The Jamaican music scene can be murky at best. I'm gonna have to find out."

"He had a unique sound," she said and hummed a couple bars from one of her favorite songs.

"Yes, he was one of the greats. Right up there with Marley in my book. You know, growing up, I just loved to go to this West Indian record store in East Orange. The man who owned it had locks down to here," Joshua indicated his bum, "and he was a big Miller fan. He always had the reggae blasting. The ganga was also always smoking." He grinned wryly

"Did you ever smoke any?"

"Nah. Grannie put the fear of drugs in me early. She took me to a methadone clinic one morning after the teacher had spoken to her about the company I was keeping at school. We stood there for maybe an hour watching the people line up. I saw a guy reach inside his sleeve to scratch. His arm was covered with sores. Grannie said it was from shooting up."

"Cured you from wanting to experiment, eh?" Caryl had to hand it to Grannie. Her method had been simple but effective.

"I didn't know of any West Indian shops in Virginia when I was a child, but at school I used to hang out with a girl from Trinidad and one from Jamaica. Pure calypso at the Trini's house and pure reggae at the Jamaican's, but they were best friends." She sipped the cranberry juice she'd ordered.

"Whenever I travel, I like ferreting music out, and I travel a lot. I'd want my wife to travel with me, too. Would you like that?" He shot her a sideways glance.

"Why should it matter to me if your wife travels with you?" she asked, her tone deliberately innocent.

"Because, my captain, you'd be one and the same." He raised his glass to her in a silent toast.

Caryl's skin tingled. Marriage. He was thinking of marriage.

"Don't look so surprised, Caryl. I told you, you're the one."

"Yes, but…I thought we were going to hold off on that kind of talk."

"We are. I'm just letting you know what I'm thinking. Are we on the same page?"

"Joshua, I still don't remember you. You're almost like a stranger to me."

"I know, but that won't last forever."

She wished she were as confident.

"And then you'll be mine."

"We'll be each other's," she corrected. She wasn't having any of that macho possessiveness.

"Exactly." He grinned and she realized he'd outmaneuvered her.

Giving him a quelling glance, she slid off the barstool. "I've got to go get ready," she informed him blandly.

"A kiss good-night then?"

Caryl's insides melted as liquid heat flared up from between her thighs to swell her breasts and lick at her cheeks. Joshua leaned forward and, before she could stop him if she had even had the strength to try, he brought her face to his. Caryl's mouth opened to his and for one sweet minute their tongues entwined. Joshua was the first to disentangle himself.

"I don't want you to be late," he said.

"Umm."

"See you tomorrow?"

"Yes, oh, yes. Sweet dreams." As she walked away, Caryl wished with all her heart that tomorrow was already there.

"Was that Joshua you went to see?" her mother asked when she got back to the villa.

"Yes."

"You could have invited him to come with us, you know."

David's mouth dropped open. "Marcianne. Now, really!"

"David, don't be tiresome. You should get to know him. Your daughter is clearly smitten. Just deal with it."

Her husband yanked on his tie and strode into the bedroom.

"Mumsie, you do think he'll come around, don't you?"

"Of course, he just has to get it out of his system. It might take a little while but your father's basically a reasonable man. Don't worry, darling." Marcianne gave her daughter a hug and picked up the car keys.

"David, we're ready," she yelled.

David strode back out in a changed tie and the family walked out to their rental.

The next day, despite her tiredness from her exertions of the day before, Caryl woke early.

"Darling, how are you?" her mother greeted her as she entered the living room.

"Ready to go again, and you?" Caryl bent down and gave each parent a kiss on the forehead.

"We thought we might take the plane to Anegada. See what's over there. Are you game?" her father asked.

"Sure, Daddy." Anegada was completely flat. On a sunny day, its limestone soil reflected back the heat of the sun to make it the hottest island in the chain but it did have the best lobster.

Before they left, she called Joshua to let him know where they were headed.

JUST AN AFFAIR

"Hurry back," he said.

"I'll try."

As she hung up the phone, she caught the curious glance her father sent her.

"Yes, Daddy?" she prompted.

"Do you love him, precious?"

Caryl sighed. "Daddy, I think I knew I loved him from the time he walked into my hospital room. I just wish I could remember the time I spent with him before, on the *Elendil*."

"It will come. For right now, trust your heart." Her mother gave her a quick hug from behind as she passed with their beach bags.

"Mumsie, *you* like him, don't you?" Caryl was pleased by her mother's support.

"I do and your father will too. Or else." With a mock fierce glance at her husband, Marcianne disappeared into their room to dress for the trip.

The flight to Anegada took ten minutes, during which Caryl pointed out and named the smaller islands lying like huge, somnolent sea cows below them. Great Camanoes was fast turning into an exclusive haven for rich American retirees while Little Camanoe was uninhabited. Necker Island, north of Virgin Gorda, was owned by the British millionaire Richard Bransom of Virgin Air, and was a favorite retreat for privacy-seeking celebrities.

"He's got quite a spread there, I hear," her father said. "But isn't he selling? I thought it was on the market."

Caryl was about to answer when the pilot interrupted to say they would land in about three minutes. Because Anegada was so flat, it could hardly be seen either by air or by sea, until you were almost there. Marcianne and David looked out the window, eager for their first glimpse of the island.

About ten or twelve goats ran across the runway in front of them as the small twin-engine plane landed with a couple of slight bumps. Caryl laughed at her mother's horrified expression.

"It's okay, Mumsie," she said as the pilot deftly maneuvered the plane around the goats. "That's why the runway is so big. That's their pasture over there." She pointed to open grassland on their right.

"It's dangerous, Caryl. For heaven's sake." A nerve continued to twitch at her mother's throat.

"Caryl's trying to say it's island life. They're accustomed to it. Nothing to worry about, right, Caryl?"

"Right, Daddy." Caryl slipped her arm around her mother as they walked to the small shed that doubled as the waiting lounge and airline office. Since Anegada was just another British Virgin Island there was no immigration or customs to go through.

"Looking for a tour, miss?" a short, pot-bellied man wearing a wide straw hat asked.

"Yes. Are you a taxi driver?"

He was, and for the rest of the morning he drove them around the twenty-five square mile island. They saw the flamingos that made the Anegada ponds their home, had lobster at the Big Bamboo, and finished the day at the beach.

When they finally got back to Tortola and their hotel room at three o'clock that afternoon, the phone was ringing. Caryl picked it up.

"Hello."

"Hello, my wine maiden."

"Joshua." She was so happy to hear his warm voice.

"Are you just getting in?"

"Yes."

"Oh, should I call back then? I just wanted to ask when I could pick you up for dinner."

"Seven's good for me. I can take a nap now and be ready by then."

"It's a date. I'll see you then."

She must have been more tired than she knew because as soon as she stripped down to her undies and slipped between the sheets, she was out cold. Marcianne woke her at six, which was good since Joshua arrived exactly on the dot of seven.

"Did you have a good rest?" he asked as they walked to his Land Cruiser.

"I did."

"You look gorgeous, woman. If I hadn't seen you in the hospital myself, I might have thought that was all a nightmare."

"It was, but a real one," Caryl said, soberly. The strapless, purple dress she wore was new, a gift from her mother the day before. Caryl had dusted luminescent powder on her shoulders and tried out some of her new makeup.

"Right now, you look like a dream, a beautiful dream."

"Your dream, Joshua?"

"Yes." He swung her around to brush her lips with his before helping her into the SUV.

"So where are we going?" she asked when he got in beside her.

"It's a surprise."

"Alright, surprise me." She flicked his ear with her finger and laughed as he caught her hand and kissed it before resting it on his thigh. When he moved his hand to change gears she left her hand there, surprised at how easy and natural it felt.

"You've gone quiet," he said as they drove out of the resort's driveway. "You think we're not going slow enough?" There was a worried note in his voice.

"No, that's not it." She squeezed his thigh so he could know she meant it. "I'm just trying to force some memory of you to mind. It's not working."

"Don't worry about it, sweet. It will come when it's ready." And he turned the car into a dark road lit only by the light of the half moon.

"This is the road to Sage Mountain, Joshua. You do know the restaurant there is closed for the season, don't you?"

"Trust me."

A few minutes later they drove up to the park's dark entrance. Squinting skeptically into the darkness of the trees, Caryl waited as Joshua went around to the back of the SUV. A light pierced the darkness.

"Okay, Caryl, I'm ready."

"For what? Spelunking?"

Caryl jumped down from the Land Cruiser. Joshua held a hefty flashlight in one hand and a basket in the other.

"Follow me," he said, and headed for the narrow path among the silent trees. At the edge of the forest he waited for her, training the flashlight on the ground so she could see where she was going.

"I've never been here at night. It's eerie." Caryl could barely see the moon now, its light unable to penetrate the forest canopy. As they plunged forward they could hear the call of coquis, small tree frogs that made a particularly piercing, almost questioning, high-pitched staccato sound. When it seemed that they had reached the heart of the forest and total darkness surrounded them, Joshua stopped.

"Okay, wait here. I'll be right back. Face that way." He spun her around so she was looking in the direction they had come.

"Joshua, what?" But he was gone. She could hear him pushing his way past bushes, his footsteps sounding overloud in the silence of the park. Caryl's heart fluttered uneasily. The Virgin Islands had no wild animal predators, not on land anyway, but she still counted the minutes until Joshua returned.

"Ready?" she asked, hearing him behind her. She *hoped* it was him.

"Yes. Good girl." He turned her around and pressed a light kiss on her lips. "Now close your eyes."

"All these commands," she complained but did as she was told.

He held her hand and guided her along the path, helping her to step over the mossy rocks and fallen logs in their way. Finally, just when Caryl thought she couldn't bear to keep her eyes closed any longer, he told her to open them.

"Joshua! Oh, my goodness, this is magnificent." He had set up a blanket on the ground and several candles illuminated covered containers of food, a bouquet of roses and, on the side, an ice bucket in which a bottle of Moet rested. Looking as if they were only feet away, the lights of Road Town shone cheerfully below them like tiny crystal pieces while the moon hung in the sky like a glowing gold pendant.

"It's a gorgeous view. I've never seen Town from here at night."

"I scouted it out a couple of nights ago." Joshua looked pleased with himself.

"And you had all that in the basket just now?"

"No, I came here before I went to get you and deposited the candles, the wine bucket, and some of the other things. It was already evening so I figured nobody would come up here to discover my plans."

"You put a lot of thought into this." She was deeply touched.

"Are you pleased?"

"Yes. This is the best surprise of my life."

"I have one more."

He took her in his arms. "I love you, woman, oh, how I love you," he groaned in her ear.

"And I love you," she whispered back. Amazed at what she'd just said, Caryl pulled back sharply. Images of them together flooded her consciousness. Like a troupe of carnival tumblers, the memories of her time with Joshua on the *Elendil* danced through her mind. His face, set hard, as he pulled her to shore on Jost Van Dyke, his groans of lust in the pilothouse, her posing before him and his camera, his tenderness the night before he left for New York. Joy flooded Caryl's soul, surging through every vein and artery. She trembled.

"Caryl, darling, what is it? What's wrong?" Joshua held her by the arms, his face creased with worry, his eyes running anxiously over her face.

She looked at his kind, beloved face and suddenly heard her father's voice. "You'll be making the same mistake again," he'd said and an image of his disapproving face flashed before her eyes. Could he be right? When she added up all the time she and Joshua had spent together it was less than a month, less even than two weeks. Was that time enough to really know you loved someone? She could be walking headlong into catastrophe. Or she could, at last, be coming to rest in the arms of the man she had been looking for all her adult life. Joshua was nothing like the deceptive and self-absorbed Alexander, she reminded herself. Her father's view was tainted. Taking a deep breath and holding his hands tight in hers, she looked straight into his anxious eyes.

"Nothing's wrong," she said and smiled. "Everything's right. My amnesia's gone."

"Caryl, what are you saying?" Joshua's voice shook.

"I remember us."

"Caryl, Caryl." Joshua gathered her into his arms and planted kisses all over her face.

"I love you," he said, his voice low.

"And I love you. I've probably loved you from the moment I saw you." Caryl grinned. "I know I wanted you."

"Caryl, I've something to tell you."

"Yes," she encouraged, knowing that if there was a problem they would work it out. If they could overcome her amnesia and his feud with her father, they could overcome anything.

"For a long time now I've been searching for a woman, a woman I could make my wife. I haven't been a monk or a saint. I've gone out with a lot of women but not one that I knew would be able to keep my interest and love into old age. Until you. With you it was different from the start." He brought her hand to his lips, kissed it, closed his eyes and took a deep breath. "I knew I could love you forever and suddenly I was frightened, frightened of what I was feeling for the first time in my life, frightened that you didn't feel it too. And I hesitated."

Caryl frowned. "I didn't notice any hesitation."

Joshua looked away, evading her eyes, then, coming to some inner resolve, he faced her again.

"I could have stayed instead of going back to New York when I did. The thing with your father could have waited but I was testing you. I wanted to see if your feelings would last or if our romance was just a vacation fling for you."

"I don't have vacation flings!" Caryl protested. "I haven't been involved with anyone since I left New York except for you."

"Yes, I know you told me that but I wanted to give you time. I thought if I stayed away then I'd be able to see what kind of staying power your love had, see if you really meant it about waiting for me."

"How long would you have waited?" Caryl was curious.

"I don't know. I was in hell. The sound of your voice when we spoke on the phone, the memory of our lovemaking, made me want to catch the next plane out, but I resisted. Caryl, every day around me I see marriages shattering, relationships dissolving because one partner or both believe in instant gratification. They mistake lust for love and rush down the aisle but it doesn't last." He looked down at his feet. "Then I discovered you were David Cassavettes' daughter and that threw me for a loop. I was wondering what the hell was going on. If you'd been playing me…"

"Never."

"It was a crazy idea but it didn't make sense that you were in the Caribbean working on a boat. I'd heard David's daughter was a lawyer at some powerful law firm. I just had a moment of paranoia."

"Just a moment?"

"I'm sorry, Caryl. It was stupid."

"Well, I don't blame you for being worried about us. I was too." Caryl recounted her fears and told him about her nightly arguments with herself about the wisdom of their involvement. "We had the same anxieties about each other," she pointed out.

"Yes, but I should've come back when I said I was going to. When I found out you'd been in that accident, I was really like a madman." Joshua smiled ruefully. "I swear my secretary was ready to call Bellevue."

"The accident wasn't your fault, Joshua." She told him about the tiger shark and how she had fought it off, shivering slightly with dread at the memory.

"A shark? Honey, are you sure?"

"Yes." She described the feel of the knife in her hand and her fear.

"Wow! You're a hero, girl. Give Xena a run for her money." He planted another kiss on her mouth. "I guess I should be glad your father didn't have you at his side with that takeover bid." He sobered. "What I'm trying to say is that we almost missed out on us, on our love. I don't want to risk that happening again. Love doesn't come around so often we can turn our backs on it even once."

Caryl had never seen him look so serious.

"I agree with all my heart, my love." She let her eyes convey what she was feeling and saw it returned to her tenfold in his.

Joshua reached into his pants pocket and pulled out a small, gift-wrapped package. He held it out to her.

"Open it."

Caryl tore at the wrapping, uncovering a red velvet box. Inside, a fingernail-sized diamond solitaire flashed in the moonlight.

"Joshua."

He dropped down on the ground before her.

"Caryl Walker Cassavettes, captain of my heart, will you marry me?"

"Yes, oh yes, Joshua Tain. I will," she said. Sinking to the ground herself, she flung her arms around his neck.

"I love you," she whispered, salting his lips with tear-dampened kisses. "Was this the other surprise?"

"Yes and no. It's part of it. Your parents gave me their permission to ask you to marry me. I know how close you all are so I wanted them to know what was up."

That *was* a surprise. It was such an old-fashioned thing to do. "When did you speak to them?"

"Yesterday evening before you met me at the bar. While you were sleeping."

"And my father said yes?" She could hardly believe it. No wonder he was pulling on his tie. He'd probably considered strangling Joshua with it.

"Your mother said it for him. She said water is like love, that it always finds its way back to itself and she wasn't prepared to stand in its way. Nor would David."

Caryl hugged her man to her.

"You know, Caryl, I feel truly blessed. You've made me the happiest man on earth."

"Then I guess we really have to stay together because I'm the happiest woman." Caryl reached up and drew his head down. "I love you, Joshua Tain, and I promise I'll never forget that again as long as I live."

Her last year had started with the pain and disappointment of her break-up with a man who had been wrong for her but, as Caryl's lips met Joshua's, she knew that she had at last found her Mr. Right. Joshua Tain had captured her heart and held it tight even when she'd had no conscious recollection of him and now, with her memory returned, she could love him back with the same depth and passion she saw brimming in his eyes. Everything, even the pain, had been worth it now that she had found true love.

AUTHOR BIOGRAPHY

Eugenia O'Neal was born on the beautiful island of Tortola in the British Virgin Islands. She obtained her BA in Communications from Temple University in 1987 and returned to the BVI where she has worked for the government ever since. In 1996, she obtained an M.Phil degree in Political Science from the University of the West Indies and subsequently published From the Field to the Legislature: A History of Women in the Virgin Islands (Greenwood Press) which is based on her thesis.

Ms. O'Neal currently works with the Ministry of Health and Welfare. She is a member of Romance Writers of America and belongs to Outreach International, an online branch of RWA. She has won several awards for her short fiction and poetry some of which has appeared in The Caribbean Writer. Ms. O'Neal lives with her daughter and Champ, the cat, on Tortola.

EXCERPT FROM
SHADES OF BROWN
BY DENISE BECKER

CHAPTER FOUR

After dinner, the family fell back into the routine of drinking coffee while cleaning up. Pop said he was tired, and went to shower and watch TV in his room.

Throughout dinner, Meg had found it difficult to keep her eyes off Michael. Had her feelings for him intensified? Had the time away made him feel like less of a brother and more like a possible suitor?

Tory's husband, Travis, stopped by after having dinner with friends. It was easy to see why these two were together--their affection was so great and their teasing endless. He wasn't a big man and was ordinary looking, but he was hilarious and sparkled next to Tory. Since he was a guidance counselor at the same high school where Meg was interviewing, she had a hundred questions for him, but thought it best to wait.

Luther and Michael seemed to like Travis a lot and Meg knew how important that was to Tory. Many a boyfriend of Tory's had been chewed up and spit out by one or both of her brothers. They had been remarkably accurate in their character appraisals too. This family was fiercely protective of one another. It wasn't a matter of sticking their noses where they didn't belong, although sometimes it could appear that way. It was love, pure and simple.

Meg also remembered Michael and Tory giving her similar treatment when she was dating Bill. Tory never hid the fact that she didn't like him and Michael's disapproval mostly consisted of eye rolls. But Meg couldn't see past the fact that Bill was a popular, blond hunk who went to Princeton on a football scholarship. She thought about how easily dazzled she had been. So young and ignorant.

If only they had stopped me from marrying Bill.

Not long after Travis arrived, Luther left the festivities, claiming to be needed at home.

"I'll bet," Michael teased.

With Tory and Travis in the kitchen getting cozy with one another, making Meg feel like a third wheel, she decided to move to the family room where Michael was. She had been waiting for the opportunity to be alone with him anyway. He was engrossed in an article from an architecture magazine. She grabbed their high school yearbook from the bookshelf and cozied up next to him on the couch. He smiled at her until he saw what she had in her hand. Then his expression went to mild despair.

"Oh, Meg, not the yearbook!" he groaned. It was from Meg's junior year, Michael's senior one.

"Oh, come on, chicken," Meg prodded.

First they flipped through the pages making the usual gossipy comments about people:

"Did you hear about her?"

"He's dead."

"He's gay."

"She's on her fourth husband."

And then a picture of Meg.

"She killed her husband," Meg imagined someone saying.

Their bare legs were pressed against each other. Each of them had on shorts and on this hot summer night, it didn't take long for their skin to start getting sticky. But neither one was about to move.

When Tory and Travis entered the dining room, which was open to the family room, they stopped dead in their tracks. Michael's arm was around Meg, and they were still looking at silly yearbook pictures. In reality, neither of them was actually looking at the pictures any longer. They were pretending. Each was totally distracted by the other.

Travis smiled as he cast a knowing glance at the couple on the sofa. Tory studied the situation and was instantly delighted. They had been trying to fix up Michael for a long time now.

"I assume this woman meets with your stamp of approval," Travis whispered.

She didn't need to answer. She had always thought that Meg and Michael would make a great couple, but Bill had always been in the way. Now he wasn't. As they continued to stand there unobserved, she felt strangely like a voyeur.

JUST AN AFFAIR

2003 Publication Schedule

January	Twist of Fate Beverly Clark 1-58571-084-9	Ebony Butterfly II Delilah Dawson 1-58571-086-5
February	Fragment in the Sand Annetta P. Lee 1-58571-097-0	Fate Pamela Leigh Starr 1-58571-115-2
March	One Day at a Time Bella McFarland 1-58571-099-7	Unbreak My Heart Dar Tomlinson 1-58571-101-2

April	At Last
	
	Lisa G. Riley
	
	1-58571-093-8
		Brown Sugar Diaries
		  & Other Sexy Tales
		Delores Bundy &
		  Cole Riley
		1-58571-091-1

May	Three Wishes Seressia Glass 1-58571-092-X	Acquisitions Kimberley White 1-58571-095-4
June	When Dreams A Float Dorothy Elizabeth Love 1-58571-104-7	Revelations Cheris F. Hodges 1-58571-085-7
July	The Color of Trouble Dyanne Davis 1-58571-096-2	Someone to Love Alicia Wiggins 1-58571-098-9
August	Object of His Desire A. C. Arthur 1-58571-094-6	Hart & Soul Angie Daniels 1-58571-087-3
September	Erotic Anthology Assorted 1-58571-113-6	A Lark on the Wing Phyliss Hamilton 1-58571-105-5

334

October	Angel's Paradise	I'll Be Your Shelter
	Janice Angelique	Giselle Carmichael
	1-58571-107-1	1-58571-108-X
November	A Dangerous Obsession	Just an Affair
	J.M. Jeffries	Eugenia O'Neal
	1-58571-109-8	1-58571-111-X
December	Shades of Brown	By Design
	Denise Becker	Barbara Keaton
	1-58571-110-1	1-58571-088-1

JUST AN AFFAIR

Other Genesis Press, Inc. Titles

A Dangerous Deception	J.M. Jeffries	$8.95
A Dangerous Love	J.M. Jeffries	$8.95
After the Vows	Leslie Esdaile	$10.95
(Summer Anthology)	T.T. Henderson	
	Jacqueline Thomas	
Again My Love	Kayla Perrin	$10.95
Against the Wind	Gwynne Forster	$8.95
A Lighter Shade of Brown	Vicki Andrews	$8.95
All I Ask	Barbara Keaton	$8.95
A Love to Cherish	Beverly Clark	$8.95
Ambrosia	T.T. Henderson	$8.95
And Then Came You	Dorothy Elizabeth Love	$8.95
A Risk of Rain	Dar Tomlinson	$8.95
Best of Friends	Natalie Dunbar	$8.95
Bound by Love	Beverly Clark	$8.95
Breeze	Robin Hampton Allen	$10.95
Cajun Heat	Charlene Berry	$8.95
Careless Whispers	Rochelle Alers	$8.95
Caught in a Trap	Andre Michelle	$8.95
Chances	Pamela Leigh Starr	$8.95
Dark Embrace	Crystal Wilson Harris	$8.95
Dark Storm Rising	Chinelu Moore	$10.95
Designer Passion	Dar Tomlinson	$8.95
Eve's Prescription	Edwina Martin Arnold	$8.95
Everlastin' Love	Gay G. Gunn	$8.95
Fate	Pamela Leigh Starr	$8.95
Forbidden Quest	Dar Tomlinson	$10.95
From the Ashes	Kathleen Suzanne	$8.95
	Jeanne Sumerix	

Gentle Yearning	Rochelle Alers	$10.95
Glory of Love	Sinclair LeBeau	$10.95
Heartbeat	Stephanie Bedwell-Grime	$8.95
Illusions	Pamela Leigh Starr	$8.95
Indiscretions	Donna Hill	$8.95
Interlude	Donna Hill	$8.95
Intimate Intentions	Angie Daniels	$8.95
Kiss or Keep	Debra Phillips	$8.95
Love Always	Mildred E. Riley	$10.95
Love Unveiled	Gloria Greene	$10.95
Love's Deception	Charlene Berry	$10.95
Mae's Promise	Melody Walcott	$8.95
Meant to Be	Jeanne Sumerix	$8.95
Midnight Clear (Anthology)	Leslie Esdaile Gwynne Forster Carmen Green Monica Jackson	$10.95
Midnight Magic	Gwynne Forster	$8.95
Midnight Peril	Vicki Andrews	$10.95
My Buffalo Soldier	Barbara B. K. Reeves	$8.95
Naked Soul	Gwynne Forster	$8.95
No Regrets	Mildred E. Riley	$8.95
Nowhere to Run	Gay G. Gunn	$10.95
Passion	T.T. Henderson	$10.95
Past Promises	Jahmel West	$8.95
Path of Fire	T.T. Henderson	$8.95
Picture Perfect	Reon Carter	$8.95
Pride & Joi	Gay G. Gunn	$8.95
Quiet Storm	Donna Hill	$8.95
Reckless Surrender	Rochelle Alers	$8.95
Rendezvous with Fate	Jeanne Sumerix	$8.95

JUST AN AFFAIR

Rivers of the Soul	Leslie Esdaile	$8.95
Rooms of the Heart	Donna Hill	$8.95
Shades of Desire	Monica White	$8.95
Sin	Crystal Rhodes	$8.95
So Amazing	Sinclair LeBeau	$8.95
Somebody's Someone	Sinclair LeBeau	$8.95
Soul to Soul	Donna Hill	$8.95
Still Waters Run Deep	Leslie Esdaile	$8.95
Subtle Secrets	Wanda Y. Thomas	$8.95
Sweet Tomorrows	Kimberly White	$8.95
The Price of Love	Sinclair LeBeau	$8.95
The Reluctant Captive	Joyce Jackson	$8.95
The Missing Link	Charlyne Dickerson	$8.95
Tomorrow's Promise	Leslie Esdaile	$8.95
Truly Inseperable	Wanda Y. Thomas	$8.95
Unconditional Love	Alicia Wiggins	$8.95
Whispers in the Night	Dorothy Elizabeth Love	$8.95
Whispers in the Sand	LaFlorya Gauthier	$10.95
Yesterday is Gone	Beverly Clark	$8.95
Yesterday's Dreams, Tomorrow's Promises	Reon Laudat	$8.95
Your Precious Love	Sinclair LeBeau	$8.95

ESCAPE WITH INDIGO !!!!

Join Indigo Book Club©
It's simple, easy and secure.

Sign up and receive the new releases
every month + Free shipping and
20% off the cover price.

Go online to www.genesis-press.com and
click on Bookclub or
call 1-888-INDIGO-1

Subscribe Today to Blackboard Times

The African-American Entertainment Magazine

Get the latest in book reviews, author interviews, book ranking, hottest and latest tv shows, theater listing and more . . .

Coming in September

blackboardtimes.com

Order Form

Mail to: Genesis Press, Inc.

1213 Hwy 45 N
Columbus, MS 39705

Name _____
Address _____
City/State _____ Zip _____
Telephone _____

Ship to (if different from above)
Name _____
Address _____
City/State _____ Zip _____
Telephone _____

Credit Card Information
Credit Card # _____ ☐ Visa ☐ Mastercard
Expiration Date (mm/yy) _____ ☐ AmEx ☐ Discover

Qty.	Author	Title	Price	Total

Use this order form, or call 1-888-INDIGO-1

Total for books _____
Shipping and handling:
 $5 first two books,
 $1 each additional book _____
Total S & H _____
Total amount enclosed _____

Mississippi residents add 7% sales tax

Visit www.genesis-press.com for latest releases and excerpts.